Tales From The Conch Republic

Ralph Krugler

For Jennifer. Thanks for the encouragement and not calling me an idiot because I thought I could write a book.

Tales From The Conch Republic © 2008
Editing by Ursula Krugler
(Although I didn't always take her advice.)

Tales From The Conch Republic

Part 1: Just Another Ordinary Day
And A Bottle of Rum... 5
The Whispering Winds   22
Discovery   31
Disappearing Act   33
Helping Hands   35

Part 2: Getting on Board
Dead Men Do Tell Tales   46
Taken Down A Peg   64
The Pirate Way   75

Part 3: Lying, Drinking and Seasick
Luck In Odd Places   80
Tequila At Sunrise Makes A Head Spin   91
Place Yer Bets   100

Part 4: Forming Of The Brethren
New Places, Old Faces   105
Chance Meeting   112
Why Not?   116
Pledging Revenge   118
Keys Crab Shack   126
Conch Republic Sunset   152

Part 5: Elbow Room
Tight Fit   162
Cuban Crime   167

Part 6: Not Always As It Seems
A Sign of Things to Come   182
Midsummer Nightmare   186
Last Rites   196
What's In A Name?   198

Part 7: Sea Legs
Making Way   209
Clem or Clam?   220
Best Laid Plans?   225
Sea Friends   232
Trying To Reason…   234
Another Distraction   242
Now What?   245
No Leg To Stand On   252

Part 8: Missionary Help
Just In Time   261
Ungrateful Freeloaders   265
Making The Best With The Hand You're Dealt   269
One Last Detail   273

Part 9: Falling In Place?
Stakeout   278
Four Offshore   288
Morning Signs   289
The Plan Begins   291
And Now, We Wait   292
Random Thoughts   294
And Wait …   296
You're a Pid   296
And Wait …   297
Who Has The Time?   298

And Wait, 299
LET'S GO! 299
MAKE HASTE!!! 300
Surprise! 301
Redemption in Blood 303
Déjà vu 310
We'll Be Right Back 313
Back To The Battle, Already In Progress 314

Follow the ongoing story; find out more about your favorite characters, submit your artwork at:
www.conchrepublictales.com

Part 1: Just Another Ordinary Day

And A Bottle of Rum...

As the mid morning sun baked the sands of the remote island, a hermit crab slowly made his way to the cooler water of the turquoise sea. A mild breeze began to rustle the long grasses along the shoreline, as they brushed across the face of a well-seasoned pirate, slumbering off the effects of a rum laden night. He is a typical wretch in the pirate way. Unkempt and unshaven, his scarred skin on it's way to leathering from years at sea under the blazing Caribbean sun. His clothing is partially tattered and full of his stench. It could probably carry him to the shade of the palms if it weren't also full of rum. He is a terrifying sight. Though he lay unconscious, his weapons rest in their places, ready to defend the slumbering creature. His blades lay at his sides while his numerous pistols were tied to the ends of silk scarves draped around his neck. The breeze, which intensified in strength, pushed the grasses into the face of the dormant traveler. Burrs stick like glue to his beard while a lone blade of beach grass tickled his nose. The mysterious chap scratched at his nose as the pestering blade continued its nasal attack. With a jolt he awoke and sat upright. Burrs and grass nestled deep in his beard as he mumbled to himself about his whereabouts. Quickly the man turned his half conscious thoughts to how he got into this mess, and incoherently measured his options to get away from this place. Being a veteran of the pirate life he knew too well what could be in store for him if he remained here in this condition for too long. You see, when you awaken in a place and have no memory of the night before; or even your current location for that matter, there is a great chance you did something that you shouldn't have. Therefore remaining in that place could lead to serious repercussions, like the hangman's noose.

Removing his hat and scratching his head, "I need to get out of here." he mumbled. "Course, it'd be better if I knew where I actually was," he paused. "That could help a bit I guess," he sputtered rubbing his scalp as if to push out the pounding sensation. From behind him a young boy's voice spoke, "Why, you're on my father's property." Jumping to his feet suddenly sober, he wheeled around desperately trying to gain his equilibrium, hands clenching the handles of his pistols only to see a small boy. His dress suggested that he was of a well to do blood line. The child stood staring wide eyed at the frightful sight. "Your father's property say you. And who might your father be" he asked inquisitively. "Why he's Governor Blankenslip," the boy replied as if everyone should know of him. The pirate stood erect placing his hat back upon his head then dusting himself off as if to be presented.

Slyly, "Governor eh," he said, placing one hand upon his chin and stroking his mangy beard suddenly finding the burrs. "Interesting. I don't recall putting these here," he said as he began to pull them free. "Of course, I don't *not* remember putting them there either. So it's quite possible that I stored them away for future use," said he. "Then again, why would I want to save burrs and to what use would they serve," he pondered raising a dirty eyebrow.

"Did you put them there," he semi questioned the lad, not looking at him still off in his thoughts.

"Sir," the frightened boy questioned. "Ah yes my lad," jolting back into the present moment. Boldly, "And what pray tell might they call you, young lad?" "My name is Bartholomew sir." The pirate started to mumble, Bartholomew, Barty, Bart, Barry. Hum, yes I like Barry better." Completely puzzled by what he said, "Who is Barry sir," Bartholomew asked.

"You of course my good lad. You said so," he countered. Stumbling and confused, "But, my name is Bartholomew sir. I said so." "Not any more Garry," the pirate replied.

"Barry. I mean Bartholomew," he corrected, the fright beginning to leave him. "What Larry," the pirate returned. "Garry, I mean Barry, I mean Bartholomew! My name is Bartholomew!" "Right," the pirate said boldly. "Now Jerry," he questioned, "how might I acquire a bite to eat?"

"My given name is Bartholomew. Bartholomew James Blankenslip sir," he countered, frightened no longer, his manner more annoyed at the wretch.

"Are you still on that Dairy," he exhaled. "I've moved on to more important matters. Please keep up Harry," he begged. "You are confusing me sir," the boy pleaded, "and you can starve for all I care!" "Now how can you say such things young Terry," he exclaimed. "BARRY! Uh, BARTHOLOMEW! At least get to close to my proper name you unkempt, smelly, vagabond," now angered he shouted. "Vagabond eh," he questioned calmly. "Now where would such a fine young lad learn such a dirty word," he asked leaning in towards his little face. The pirate's foul breath made the boy's eyes begin to water. As quickly as he leaned in, the hung-over man bobbed unsteadily and quickly was back erect continuing in his thoughts. "Then again I guess it's a rather common word. Isn't it then? Hum… How do you suppose some words become more common then others young Kerry? Is it just a matter of happenstance or is it something greater? But who is to say what is greater? Now, wait. I always forget. Is it who or is it whom" the pirate questioned.

The boy stood looking blank faced at the disheveled man. Thoughts bounced around his tiny head as he tried desperately to comprehend what the stranger was talking about. "Whom what," the puzzled boy finally said as blankly as the look on his face. "AH! Whom you say," the pirate questioned. The little boy puzzled him back, "What?" "What," the pirate quickly asked in return.

"Pardon my forwardness sir, but what are you *talking* about? You're making my head hurt vagabond." Snapping back in time, "Vagabond, I like that. Yes, I like that very much. But watch your language Timmy, and now back to my growing desire to acquire a morsel of food young Tad," he said clapping his hands together. A cloud of dust gently formed around his hands and slowly dissipated into the air.

"AAAGH," he screamed. "Bartholomew! Bartholomew! Bartholomew! Bartholomew! Bartholomew! Is it really that hard of a name to remember," incensed he pleaded. "I mean honestly! It's a very popular name you know."

"Now who told you that," the pirate inquired. "What," the boy asked rather stunned. "That your name is a very popular name. Mary? I mean honestly. Mary is a girl's name isn't it then," the pirate said scratching out another burr from his beard. "Certainly it's popular with the ladies… you aren't a girl," he asked suddenly eyeing him inquisitively.

"MY NAME ISN'T MARY YOU FOOL," Bartholomew screamed! He had never before shouted at an adult, but at that moment he wasn't afraid of the repercussions. Seeming more interested in the tangled burr he could not remove, the pirate's focus returned to his facial hair. "Fool? What happened to vagabond," he asked staring at the nested burr. "And what happened to that scrumptious meal you'd promised earlier?"

"Meal," he exclaimed. "I promised you no such thing," he huffed! Still examining the burr from all angles, "Well, let's pretend you'd had," the pirate said. Suddenly looking up and releasing the beard, "Now let's get us something scrumptious, shall we," he exclaimed more than asked, as his face lit up.

"NO," Bartholomew shouted back. The young boy protested in his posture, arms crossed and stamping his foot as he shouted. "Come here young Chad," he said rather calmly taking a knee drawing him in. "Let's put it this way shall we. If you help me I'll help you." "How can you help me," the boy puzzled trying to avoid the invisible cloud left behind the pirate's foul breath. "Well," the pirate started, "I can start by giving you a proper name Perry." Angered, his fists clenched, but speaking in a low voice the boy responded, "I'm quite settled with my own name sir. I will *NOT* change it," he spat through his clenched teeth staring the pirate in his eyes. "Excellent," the pirate replied. "Then we are finished." "How are we finished? You haven't done anything for me to want to get you food," the exacerbated boy shot back. "I haven't," the pirate questioned. "I thought I just talked you out of your foolishness and into keeping your name." Slapping his hand to his cover his face, the boy replied through still clenched teeth, "No you most certainly did not!" "Right," the pirate said. "Then I'll have to do something even better." "Such as," the beleaguered boy asked? "I'll suggest that you stop clenching yer teeth. Tis bad for the molars me boy." "What in heaven or earth are you speaking of! And how is that better?" "Well it'll relieve yer jaw pain for starters. And, everyone loves a child's smile mate," he said with a toothy smile. "That still doesn't help me," the frustrated boy exclaimed." "Certainly it does. You'll keep yer choppers me boy," he said chattering his own teeth. The beleaguered boy pleaded with the stranger, "What else can you offer please?" "I'll leave," the pirate exclaimed, as he stood up! "DONE," the boy shouted as he sprung to life hugging the pirate. Suddenly realizing his arms were around the waist of the pirate, his face pressed against his belly, an awful stench emanated from the man's pores. "Uugh, no offense but, you stink sir," the boy said releasing his grip and recoiling to cleaner air. Smiling, "All the more reason to get me out of here quicker son." The boy agreed and used his best judgment to decide where to procure a meal to get rid of the pirate.

The child cautiously led the man up the sandy trail

through the tall grasses to the young boy's home. He was amazed how the smell of the wretch lingered in his nose making his stomach churn. Reaching one side, they snuck around the outside of the large home of an obviously well to do family. The pirate concealed himself behind a group of broad green and brown leaved ground shrubs. Seeing that his companion was well hidden, Bart crawled in through the open window and slipped behind some chairs. He made his way to the large wooden table bedecked with fine china and expensive silverware with ivory handles. The table was covered with a large breakfast for the family. There he eyed his prize. Bartholomew's father sitting intently reading a book in the adjacent room didn't hear the stealthy lad. Quietly the boy grabbed a handful of food and escaped back out the window whence he came.

"Well done! Well done indeed young Stan," the pirate exclaimed with glee. Grabbing the food he devoured it like a starving animal that suddenly came upon the leftover scraps of another's kill. "However, don't you think you could have gotten a little more," he asked. "I mean you don't quit a rum spree with a few bits of grub." "More," the boy sighed.

"Here, let me see your hands." Bart held out his hands as the pirate took them in his. Examining them as a surgeon would he stated, "No, no I guess not. These are tiny little hands you have. My goodness but they are minute." "I'm only seven," the boy stated dumbfounded. "How big should my hands be," he wondered aloud holding them up visually going over them.

"Well," the pirate stated quite puzzled, "I'm not certain.

It's been quite a while since I was seven me self. However, I'm certain that mine were quite a bit larger than yours," he said now examining his own outstretched hands. "Look," the boy interrupted, "I held up my part of our agreement. Now please, be a gentleman and hold up yours."

"Are you certain that you're only seven," the pirate inquired. "I am," he said. "Why sir?"

"Bartholomew," the voice of his father sent a cold shiver down the young boy's spine. If his father were to find him with this stranger, there was no telling what the stern head of the house might do. His father was an unhappy sort who seemed to only be happy when he was unhappy. In fact he reveled in his misery. This meant that the young boy would have to find his joy with his mother, sister and the servants of the house. "Yes father," the boy called back. "To whom are you speaking?" The boy's father was still in the sitting room as he called to the lad. "I'm just playing father," the young boy returned. "Young children should be seen, NOT HEARD," the grown man bellowed. "And they should only be seen when CALLED FOR!" When his shouts dissipated, silence fell upon them like a blanket.

The pirate's eyes darted about. Quickly he stood up from his concealment and ventured away from the home and out of earshot. "Well my young friend, you kept your part of the accord now I will do mine and take my leave. I thank you very much and wish you well in your adventures. Now I shall go," he whispered and quickly made his way from the house. He looked around and paused, "Um, however, before I depart I must ask you one thing." Exhaling, "What's that," Bart asked still frightened of his father.

"How do I get out of here?" "How did you arrive here sir," Bart inquired. "Well," he paused, "that bit of knowledge is a tricky thing." "How so," Bart queried. "Well," again pausing, "like I made mention to earlier, I was rather intoxicated at the time and now I'm not quite certain of that bit of knowledge," the pirate confessed. "Pity for you sir," Bart proclaimed. "Might I ask you a question sir?" "Certainly Mort. You just did," the pirate responded. "It's Bart. And *pardon*," the boy asked.

"Well think of it chap. If you're asking permission to ask a question, you've already done the thing that you're in the process of asking permission to do. It really isn't fair. Don't cha think," the pirate elucidated. "However, I don't make the rules, I just explain them." "But I was just trying to be polite," the lad retorted. "That's part of your vexing snafu Randal. Either you are polite or you are not. You don't try lad. It's just a matter of being," he exclaimed. Turning away, "Now what was I doing," he said scratching his head. Seeing a rare opportunity, the astute Bart jumped in, "You agreed to answer my question."

"Ah yes," the pirate started twirling around, "What did you want to know?" Even though he had his wits, the full effect of the rum had not completely worn off. This caused him to stagger a bit before regaining his equilibrium. "You're not a very good pirate are you," Bart inquired. "Be fair, that's not really a question Ronald. That's more of a statement to belittle me," he said. "Besides, what makes you think that I'm a pirate?

Let alone a bad one at that? I never said I was a pirate. I don't have an eye patch. As you can plainly see I have two good eyes. Well, good when I'm not intoxicated that is. I do not have a peg leg as both of mine are in fine working order. I have no hook fer me hand. There is no parrot on me shoulder. And I have never once in your presence uttered the phrase 'Arr!' Now have I Donald?"

"It's Bartholomew sir," he proclaimed, "and no you have not," he said rather dejectedly. "I apologize for my insolence." "Well no matter," the pirate said, "those are just bad stereotypes anyway. Honestly, who walks around saying, 'Arr!' No one I know. It just doesn't make any sense." "But you are a pirate. Of that I am certain," Bartholomew declared. "Why think you so," he asked. "Because you are. Look at your dress," Bartholomew excitedly exclaimed.

"Dress," the pirate called out looking down double-checking himself. Seeing that he was in the clothes he last remembered himself in he responded, "These are men's clothes young lad. Perhaps you need to have your vision checked." "I meant state of dress sir," Bartholomew defended. "State it in any way which you wish," the pirate replied, "a dress is a dress is a dress. Where as, a fashionably attired man, such as myself, is the very essence of what stands before you," the pirate stated with mock pride. His fully erect posture gained him a benefit he was not expecting. "Ah-ha," he says spotting the governor's boat peering out from behind a little dune. It's a small vessel, thirty-two feet in length or so. Typically a rig of this size would require two, to crew the boat. However, the pirate discerned it not to be a problem. "Ah-um, I wish you good day young Brad."

"It's Bartholomew sir, and good day," he answered rather puzzled.

Making his way to the boat, the pirate began humming to himself trying to look inconspicuous as the curious boy followed close behind. As the pirate strode onto the dock, the wood creaked under the weight of his boots. Finally getting an unobstructed view of the boat, he stood surveying her. "What in the bloody world *is* this wretched excuse for a sea going vessel," he wondered. Before him lay a type of ship he'd never encountered before. Wind puffs were coming in steady pulling the boat away from the dock. Waves lapped at the hull with a small spray coming off from time to time. The securing lines pulled at the pilings mildly jarring the pirate as he stood gawking at the vessel. For certain she had a mast, a deck, a keel, and all the things that made up a ship; however, she was put together rather uniquely.

"What do you think you're doing at father's boat," the boy demanded. As if knowing he was there the entire time the pirate responded yet still looking in sheer amazement at the ship. "That's what you call this thing? A boat? Looks more like the excreted remains of a sad little boat that a sea dragon snacked upon." Again the dock was jolted by the tug of the ship.

"Yes, it is father's boat and he's rather fond of her sir," Bart spoke rather proudly. The stranger pondered in his head for a moment whether or not to commandeer this thing. "If I take her I can be gone from this barren little spit of land," he started in his head. "Then again, if I'm spotted sailing her by one of me brethren, I'll never hear the end. I mean really, look at this piece of," this thought was cut off.

"Pirate, why do you stare at her so? Surely in all your travels you must have come across something like her in her class before," Bartholomew said. "Where exactly did you say yer father acquired this, this, *thing*," the pirate asked.

"I didn't sir," Bartholomew began, his hair blowing into his eyes. "Father acquired her from a rouge, not unlike yourself. He said that the rogue had built her himself so I could see why he was especially upset at having to part with her. That man comes about quite a bit." The boy paused as a look of fright started to overtake him. "Usually under the moonlight and stays only briefly. He's a scary man with several scars about the face. And his arm is terribly frightening! He had owed father a debt that he could not repay and therefore had to settle by giving her to father."

"What? The arm or the boat," the pirate prodded. "Oh heavens no! The boat. The arm is something else entirely," the boy shuddered. "What kind of debt did he owe," the pirate inquired, balancing himself while the wood underneath him shook again.

"Um, I'm not certain sir," he started, "perhaps a tax or something?" "Tax you say. Pray tell, what line of business was this rogue of yours in," the pirate pressed. "Of that I'm not quite certain sir," Bartholomew confessed. "I'm not allowed to inquire of such things at my age. At least that's what father tells me." "And what of his arm," the stranger pushed more.

Still the puffs blew tugging at the boat and in turn shaking the dock. "It's not like you or I have sir," he started, the fear growing again in his voice. Bartholomew reached out to hold onto a piling for balance. "It's dead! Last time he was here he even had a dagger thrust through it. He showed father how it was to be used as a weapon for his defense."

"How do you know of all this? Does your father allow you around him," the intrigued man asked. "Gracious no. Father doesn't allow me anywhere near him." The young boy began offering more information and delighted in the attention. He pressed on hoping to gain some praise. "As you saw, I can easily sneak into and around the house. I have learned quite well how to sneak about without detection. Father never knows I'm there watching. However, when I saw the arm I let out such a gasp. If it weren't for my cover I'd have certainly been discovered."

"Interesting. Very well done lad," the pirate praised him hoping to gain more information from the giving boy. "Would you happen to know the gentleman's name," the mysterious stranger inquired further, feeling he already knew the answer he was looking for.

Bartholomew thought and thought. The attention he was being given made him yearn for more and more. Clutching one of the dock pilings in one arm he thought until the name ventured into his head. "It's, it's a Mr. Albright sir," he excitedly spoke.

"Samuel Albright," the man asked.

"Yes, yes I believe so," exclaimed Bartholomew. "Why?"

Mr. Samuel Albright was a well-known rumrunner and smuggler. He often traveled from the Jamaican islands all the way to Bone Island. Along the way he had created many trade routes and storage cashes for his stock. The dead arm was from a loss of nervous control. The result of a dagger wound to his shoulder. The fight occurred in Nevis when a bounty hunter tried to take him from the tavern. The hunter slashed him from behind across the shoulder as a warning that he wasn't fooling around. The hunter wanted him alive for a bigger bounty, yet could have easily taken his life. The meaning fell short on Albright though; as the only thing other than excruciating pain on his mind was killing the man who did this to him. Which he did quickly and without the aid of his men. The drunken rumrunner, doused in his own blood, sat back at the bar and poured the nearest bottle upon his gaping wound. Even the alcohol in his bloodstream could not completely dull the sting of the tequila that was being dowsed on his incised flesh, yet he hoped. "There, that'd outta kill the pain," he exclaimed. The wound eventually healed, but the nerve was severed, rendering the arm lifeless. The pirate was curious as to the dagger being thrust through it though. Surely that would make the arm gangrenous and have to be severed, lest he lose his entire life. The entire situation raised the pirate's suspicions of the governor of this island to have dealings with a man like Albright. A governor shouldn't have dealings with a well-known criminal for starters. And then to only take his ship on non-payment while presumably setting him free. That must have been a warning and his freedom came at either the price of paying the difference, or his continued employment. No, Albright was to cunning to be put down. He was much more valuable to a business partner alive.

"Tell me good chap, did your father tell you anything else about this, *Albright* was it," the stranger asked innocently.

Bartholomew showing his age did not pick up at all that the forgetful pirate remembered Albright's name yet could not remember his own. All the dock jostling was making the young boy seasick. His face was becoming flushed and his stomach was tossing its contents to and fro. Bart's level of attention was lowering as he tried to maintain his composure.

"No sir. He just set him off on the next ship that left our port," Bartholomew offered still wanting to please. The words were oozing out of his mouth. "Your port," the pirate asked in shocked amusement. "This is a port," he chuckled. "No sir, on the other side of the island is our entry port," Bartholomew said spitting out the words. He began backing off the dock for more stable ground. "This is just our private dock."

The pirate got excited at the possibility of there being a better vessel to acquire. However, as soon as those thoughts entered his mind Bart quickly spoke much to his chagrin. "She's empty right now though sir. We don't get many visitors and father's other ship is off on business, I suppose." The air let out of the man like a balloon being slowly released. His shrinking posture reflected this as well.

"Another ship, and she's off on *business*," the pirate pondered in his head. "This poor chap's old man is probably in the rum running business himself. Possibly a link in the molasses or slave trade as well. This inhospitable spit is a good place to run that type of operation from, as it's not worth investigating by the enemies of his flag," he thought to himself. "Under these circumstances," he started to think, "commandeering his so-called boat really isn't an act of piracy. Well, at the very least, not to me anyway. More like payback for his transgressions," he thought rather arrogantly.

The pirate swayed with the unsteady dock and again scanned the so-called boat. He breathed a very heavy sigh and shook his head in disbelief. "Well, you kept your word," he paused, lightly tilted his head to the side still surveying the silly little ship, "and so shall I."

"What mean you sir," Bartholomew asked, only a few yards away standing on the stable shore. Taking a step towards the boat, "I'm making my leave of you good Moe," the pirate said. "By stealing father's boat," Bartholomew shrieked as he suddenly ran back on the dock? "I knew ye were a pirate!" He rushed to the pirate as if to stop him from boarding, then quickly grabbed a piling again to stand his ground.

"Young lad," the pirate professed, "I have never stolen anything in me long glorious life! Granted, I may have *borrowed* a few items in my day; however, I have clearly never *stolen* anything," he said boarding the boat. "So young Chad what do you think," he started. "How would you like to join me? It'd be awfully difficult getting this... *thing* going on my own. I could use another set of hands. Even if they are tiny." "Nonsense," Bartholomew protested. "I should most certainly think not! And my hands are not small!" The pirate shrugged it off, "So be it. Now, be a good boy make with that bowline! And stop with all this pirate gibberish," he said as he prepared the boat to sail. "But SIR," Bartholomew declared. "Father would wring my neck if I helped you steal his boat!"

Pausing to exhale, he stops and turns to face towards the boy, "Again young Frederick, I am only *borrowing, borrowing* your father's vessel as to keep my half of our accord," he said. "You can surely see that there's a big difference, plus, don't tell him that you were here," he said with a smile. "Besides, shouldn't you be on shore? You're looking a bit pale. Wait a tick! You didn't happen to get into me rum last night did ya?"

The nauseous boy grabbed him with his free hand to get his balance. "Heavens no!" The boy felt queasiness in his belly. "I'm going to tell father!" The boy feared his father, but he feared the wrath his father may have if he were to discover that Bart actually knew this had been happening. His seven-year-old logic couldn't comprehend how his father could discover the truth, but he didn't dare chance it. "Wait," the pirate shouted. "What is it," the young boy pondered. "What day is it today," the pirate inquired. The boy thought a moment, "It's Friday sir." "Blimey," the pirate paused knowing full well that it was bad luck to set sail on a Friday. Quickly weighing his options he surmised that he'd rather take his chances on the water than on this small island. His facial gestures gave away his thoughts and the boy knew instantly that he wanted that ship. Turning away, he ran rather zigzagged towards the house. "Father! Father," he uttered! "Come quick," he briefly covered his mouth from the nausea! "Father!"

Watching the boy run off the pirate scratched his head. "Pity, I was just starting to like him. Never-the-less, back to work."

Quickly the pirate untied the boat and with haste made her ready and ran up the sails. With that he was off, tipping his hat to the Blankenslip estate. Breathing very heavy, his lungs burned with an intense fire. His fatigued and dehydrated muscles ached from the sudden stress they were placed under. "My sincere thanks my good governor. Here's hoping that old Albright repays you for stealing his ship."

He stood by the gunwale surveying the island he was departing. With a faint chuckle he exclaimed, "Pirate, indeed. And a damn good one I might add."

The Whispering Winds

Not much sand had passed through the hourglass as the boat glided its way across the turquoise waters. Waves lapped at the hull as she cut a path towards an unknown destination. From the bow, all sorts of sea life could be seen going about its daily business. A slight breeze fluffed the main sail while the jib failed to catch the full effect of the puffs. Unsure of where he was heading, the pirate was just happy to be upon the water. He made his way up and sheeted out the halyard allowing the jib to catch the breeze. Quickly she filled and the ship accelerated. The pirate realized suddenly the advantage of this odd vessel. She indeed was a ship for someone with criminal intent. The boat was ugly as anything, but her acceleration rate was unmatched in anything her size. As the winds decreased in strength, she fell back quickly.

Suddenly a sound passed in the distance grabbing the pirate's attention. He looked up and around toward the bright cloudless skies. "Hum, odd," he pondered. "Doesn't look much like rain. Interesting that there should be thunder when not even a cloud be in the sky."

Another thundering boom rambled off in the distance. "Again? Hum? Very odd indeed," he thought aloud. "What kind of magical waters be these?" He looked over the port gunwale into the water as he spoke. "I've never experienced anything like this. Keep yer eyes open me boy. You never know what might occur. Spirits are in the air."

Again a boom was heard echoing off the seas, this time escorted by a splash. This really piqued his interest. As he made his way towards the starboard rail the pirate laid his tanned, well-calloused hands upon it. "Thunder. Spotty rainfall. Bright blaring sunshine." He paused then sang to himself, "Which one of these be different than the others?" The winds quickly returned and jolted the boat to life. She sailed several minutes then the breezes calmed yet again, slowing the boat. As a smuggler, she was built for speed and acceleration and used her talents well.

A bit of time had elapsed when another faint boom and spotty rainfall returned. The difference this time was it was accompanied by faint voices. Indistinguishable voices; yet voices none the less. "Interesting," the rather woozy, still hung-over pirate proclaimed, "I don't recall these waters being haunted. Then again, I'm not certain of what waters I'm sailing in. So it's quite possible that they are haunted. Not like any haunt that I've come upon before though. This is very intriguing."

The disembodied voices he heard were beginning to increase in volume and volatility. "Very odd indeed." He pondered a moment when a memory suddenly jarred loose in his head. "Wait a tick! I do recall me old captain once telling me that spotty water in the open waters..." He shook his head, "No wait. What was it? What the devil was that? Ah yes! I must be treading on someone's hallowed passage. Wonder if I knew the chap. Hopefully I didn't bring about his demise." He pondered that thought a moment. "Um, pardon me sir. Um, Mr. Spirit. If I was the cause of your current status... um sorry 'bout that. Uh, it's nothing personal you know. Just doing business then eh?" He waited for a moment. "Um, hello?" There was no reply. "Well there's no need to be standoffish good chap. It's a tad rude to disturb me then bugger off like that." The pirate was beginning to relax, when suddenly the voices returned. "Back again eh! Hum. Pardon me good spirit, but could you give me a sign if we once knew each other?" Nothing happened. "Ah, yes, terrific! Ok. How about a sign if we didn't know each other in a previous time?" This time a sound like cannon fire rang out. The excited pirate rejoiced at the sound. "Tremendous! So we did not know each other.

Well then good spirit, if you don't mind, I'll just be on me way and out of your haunt. Much obliged, thank you!" He paused a moment while he heard the voices which were intensifying. "Wonder who the chap was... or were by the sounds of it. Perhaps these are Capt. Calhoun's old passages. Tragic, tragic way for old Cal and his crew to pass."

Still the noise kept intensifying.

Puzzled and completely oblivious of the fact that a ship was bearing down on him, he kept on reminiscing, "Surrounded, ambushed, shackled, beaten, starved, overfed and then forced into the deep dark abyss. That's no way for an old pirate to go. Then again, no way for a young pirate to go either I guess."

Finally a voice was discernable, "Ahoy," a faint voice shouted.

Puzzled and quickly looking up then side-to-side, he saw not a man in sight. Therefore the pirate continued to think the person speaking to him was the ghost. "Ahoy ghost... Capt. Calhoun," he inquired.

"Ahoy, you are to lower your sails and halt," the voice said growing louder and clearer. The pirate ignored this and continued in his own fantasy. "Really, good captain. I'll be out of here soon." Silence returned to the ship and the pirate waited for the next move.

"Ahoy pirate," the voice returned. "Greetings mate" the pirate shouted. "I didn't mean to tread your hallowed waters; it just seems that I've temporarily lost my way.

You see, I've had a bit of the rum," he said patting at his flat belly.

"That gives you no right to steal my boat," the voice sternly replied. Extremely puzzled, he stood upright and wondered aloud to himself, "How did he know that I borrowed this boat?" 'No matter,' he thought shaking his head. "Um, pardon," he asked.

"Prepare to be boarded," the deeply angered voice demanded.

The dumbfounded pirate stood with his mouth agape. He continued to think aloud to himself, "How does a ghost prepare to board? Wouldn't he just float on," he mumbled to himself. What the pirate hadn't counted on was Blankenslip's other ship returning just at the right time to chase him down.

As the trailing boat nuzzled up to his, the two met with a dull wooden thud. The sudden jolt finally jarred the pirate into reality. "Your hands held high would be most appreciated you smarmy pirate," an angered man demanded. Whirling around, he finally realized that there actually was no ghost; but rather the bad luck from having left on a Friday caught up with him. "Ah! Good sir! What might I do for you and your, um, rugged good chaps," the pirate asked scrutinizing the scene. Standing before him was one impressively dressed man flanked by two guards dressed in royal navy uniforms, their guns drawn.

"Like I have previously commanded, you can raise your hands up high before we sever them from your filthy body." The pirate rubbed his wrists silently mouthing the word, "Ouch." The well-dressed man eyed him up and down, "Then we shall flog you for stealing my boat," the central figure declared.

"Well now that sounds smashing," the pirate acknowledged trying to hide his sarcasm. "I have a better idea," he retorted clapping his hands together. "How about you let me off at the closest port and we'll call it a day! We'll have a big hug, perhaps an ale. We'll share a couple of laughs. Maybe a smoke? Eh, what say you to that? Hum, sir? Governor?" He paused looking at him with an uncomfortable smile. "Um, no," he asked raising his eyebrows.

"Unfortunately for you sir, you are a pirate and you stole this boat," the governor stated. "In these waters, or any waters that's a high crime you scoundrel!"

Quietly the pirate said to himself, "That's the second time today." "What, pirate," the governor asked. The pirate replied, "Now how do you equate *me* with being a pirate?" "Well... look at you," the governor plainly stated. "Again..." looking down at himself and seeming pleased, he began speaking quietly to himself again, "what's with this family?" The governor continued, "Disheveled, unkempt, smelly." The pirate cut in, in a low mocking voice, "vagabond." The governor continued, "lethargic, disgusting, shall I go on," the governor asked. "Who's lethargic," he asked. "What's your cursed name pirate," the governor inquired.

The pirate completely ignored his question and carried on, "I'm very spry. Rather ingenious. Completely sheveled. Yes, I'm rather fond of my cultured appearance. You know I just might have to take offense with this entire family."

Ignoring the ramblings, "I asked you a question sir," the governor demanded stomping his foot on the wooden deck! "Governor Blankenslip," he replied plainly. "Yes," the governor puzzled. His ego preceded him as to believe that everyone automatically knew his name.

"Yes, what," the pirate asked confused. "You said Governor Blankenslip," the governor stated, "and I want to know what you were going to say." "But that is what I wanted to say," he returned not understanding why he was in this absurd line of questioning.

Scratching his head the governor puzzled, "I'm confused. Look," he said shaking his head, "All I want to know is your name pirate." Not saying anything the pirate stares blankly off into space. "Maybe I could use a bath," the pirate said quietly to himself. "Twas a bit ago when last I bathed. However, that's no reason for all the personal attacks I've endured today. Then again," he paused, sniffed his armpits and finished, "maybe it does."

The governor didn't let his confusion cloud his anger for long and soon he was again demanding his question be answered. "Pirate, I asked you a question," the governor restated. Snapping back into reality, "Governor Blankenslip," the dirty man repeated.

He let out a sigh. "Granted you are a drunkard, of that I am well certain. However, what I'd like to know is, are you drunk right now pirate," the governor inquired.

Acting completely insulted, "Well now you've changed your way then haven't you," the pirate insinuated. "What do you mean," the governor inquired. "Well just a moment ago you clearly stated that all you wanted was a name. Now you go off and try to slide this other question in there like I'm not even supposed to notice. Calling me a drunkard. Why, I never touch the stuff. Leads to foul matters," the pirate replied.

"Do you think you're fooling anyone pirate," the governor queried. "Do you," the pirate shot back. The governor couldn't believe himself, "Do I what?" "Do you honestly believe that you can go about saying one thing and then contradict yourself by saying another. Oh wait. You're in politics. What am I talking about," the pirate stated as a matter of fact.

"I'll give you this much. You are clever as a wordsmith. However, as a pirate you leave a lot to the imagination, vermin," the governor insulted him wanting to regain control of the conversation.

"Why in blazes do you keep referring to me as a pirate," the pirate asked. "Because you are," the governor responded growing more and more exhausted from the conversation. Puzzled, the pirate retorted, "How do you figure," he said tilting his head to one side.

Disgusted the governor answered, "Because of the very fact that you stole this boat!" "How so," the pirate quickly returned. "*How so*," the disgruntled governor shouted. "*How so!* You're on it aren't you?" "Yes, but so are you then," the pirate deflected. The guard to the left of the governor stood by quietly, trying desperately to hold back a smile and a chuckle.

"But it's MY boat," the governor demanded again stomping his foot. Scrunching his eyebrows and retracting his head back the pirate held his ground, "But I was here first." He figured if the governor was going to act like a spoiled child, then he would have his fun too.

"*You were here first*," the governor screeched! His fists tightened, arms pinned to his side. It was clear that Bartholomew was his father's son. They both acted identical when they were angered.

"Yes, then you fellows came aboard. So as I see it, it is *you* who are the pirates," the pirate replied pointing and waving his finger at the governor and his men.

Disgusted, "I've had enough of this. Guards," he shouted! "No need to shout," the guard on the left said. "WHAT," Blankenslip screamed. "I'm standing right here," the guard said, standing one foot from the governor. Blankenslip let out a cry of frustration, "ARG! Clap him in irons; remove his weapons and lock him below," he demanded still shouting.

The pirate began speaking to himself again as he was being lead away in shackles, "This family really needs a sense of humor." "And a lesson in volume control," the guard chimed in quietly. The pirate raised an eyebrow and slightly turned to him with a faint smile of understanding. "Agreed."

Discovery

Below deck locked in the cabin the lowly pirate investigated the situation he suddenly found himself in. For being captured and in shackles he was in rather upbeat spirits. "Interesting room. Lovely bed," he said as he jumped on and stretched himself out. Well as best one can while your hands are shackled together. "Ah. Now that's comfortable."

Looking around he saw the ramshackle remains of Albright's many travels throughout the Caribbean. Blankenslip either hadn't had this ship a long time, or he didn't really explore below deck. Maps and charts scrawled upon in his hand littered the cabin. The sleeping area was not separated from the galley. Lanterns clanked as the ship rocked upon the waves as the wooden keel creaked and cracked. A few cast iron pots clanged as they hit the wall. Payton sat up and quickly perused the charts for anything worthwhile. Finding one that may be of use one day he quickly folded it best he could and tucked it away deep in a coat pocket. Even though he was alone he instinctively looked around to be certain he wasn't being watched as he did so. He sat back upon the bed, hitting his head upon a cooking pot hanging from above. "What the blazes is this doing here? Um yes… the nightmare boat. Well I'm certain that this was never used, at least not for its intended purpose anyway." The pirate briefly rubbed his hurting head and continued to inspect his surroundings.

The cabin was filled with the usual items; a few miscellaneous items of clothing, a single mug, several containers with various ingredients and elixirs, yet nothing worth acquiring. He sat back and focused upon a bench on the far side of the cabin. It was a part of the ship, yet it puzzled the pirate. There was nothing to make it seem anything more than it was; however, his natural curiosity and instincts got the better of him.

"Interesting, very interesting. Very interesting indeed," standing back up he spied a cushion sitting oddly upon the bench. Moving it, there was a wooden panel behind it. Rapping upon it with a knuckle it gave off an odd sound. The pirate continued to investigate until he found a rather small, thin piece of twine. Giving it a tug, nothing happened. He tried yet again. This time he pulled in a different direction, causing the panel to pop off. A smile overcame his face as he peered into the opening. The extremely tight entrance opened to a small passage, which lead to a smuggling compartment. "Yes, excellent," he exclaimed. He started climbing in headfirst then suddenly was overcome with a thought. "What the devil am I doing," he wondered. The compartment was so tight that once in, he couldn't turn around to close off the door. Inching his way out he gasped and gulped in the fresh air. "Good Lord, when was the last time that thing was opened? He knew that he needed to act fast so he fit himself in, feet first this time. Grabbing the panel and cushion as best he could in his fingers, he sucked in the last fresh breath he could. He refitted the piece hoping the cushion was covering the panel; inched his way back and settled in for the rest of the journey in the stale compartment.

"Obviously this is the reason for the oddness of this vessel. She's a smuggler," he mused to himself. "Well, let's just see how good of partners these two chaps actually are."

Disappearing Act

Back at the island they tied the ship up to the governor's private dock as the other ship went to the main port. "Go below and retrieve the prisoner." "Sir," one guard responded and headed below deck! Throwing the door open he quickly found the cabin empty and panic struck. Tearing the room nearly apart he found nothing. Gulping in terror, he headed back up on deck. "Sir," he said with a quake in his voice, sweat pouring down his face. Seeing that the guard was alone Blankenslip exhaled a deep breath, "Where is he? Sleeping? Passed out?" "Gone sir," he said sheepishly. "*Gone?* As in passed away? Well good riddance," Blankenslip declared. "Very well then, dump his remains overboard and let the creatures of the sea feast upon him."

Cautiously the guard interrupted, "Um, no sir. Not deceased. Just," pausing, "gone; as in no longer on board." Shaking his head at the news the governor exhorted, "How can he be gone? Isn't the window fixed?"

"No sir," the guard replied, "but it is shut." Turning around to see the wide-open sea Blankenslip coldly stated, "Well if our friend did go out the window he'll have surely drowned by now. Even *his* rum saturated carcass would be accepted by the deep." The guard felt as if he had failed his position. He stood looking down at the deck. A forlorn look cast upon his face. Governor Blankenslip stood with his back to him eyeing the ocean. "Check the boat again. If he's not aboard then we'll assume that he's at the bottom of the sea where he belongs. However, that doesn't excuse *your* failure though. You two will be dealt with later." With that, he turned not even looking at the guards and disembarked. Ambling his way up the cobble stone path to his mansion, the governor stumbled over an exposed root causing him to topple to the ground. The guards looked on with suppressed laughter; they rushed below deck as not to be spotted by the boss.

"When could he have gotten out Reg," the first guard asked. "Good question Sam," the second replied. They inspected the cabin and again came up with nothing. "I can't believe it Sam. Why would he do that?" "My guess is that he preferred to attempt to gain his freedom as opposed to the gallows," Sam explained. "I know that I would. Let's go Reg. We're just wasting our time." "Still though, how did he do it? The windows are shut tight." They made their way up the narrow stairwell and out of the boat and headed back to the estate.

Back below deck the pirate waited till well beyond the time he could no longer hear any voices, "Well it's got to be night at anytime soon. God knows that I can't stay cramped in this little hole much longer. How do packages handle this cramped lifestyle," he wondered to himself.

The guards had made their way into the home and approached the governor who was deep into a thick text in his study. "I'm sorry sir but we've checked the ship over and the pirate is nowhere to be found," Reg said. Slumping back upon the high back chair the governor pondered, "Inconceivable! How did he make his way out so quietly," Blankenslip spoke. "I am very sorry Sir," Sam responded. Blankenslip adjusted himself in his favorite chair and sighed, "Oh, never mind. We have the boat and no worse for ware. Just keep a weather eye out for the pirate. If somehow he did survive, we're the only island close enough to get to. We'll have him then." Pausing to reflect a moment, "He surely has to be in the belly of a shark by now," he paused. His eyes darted to the pair, "Off with you two rubes," he sneered. "And only a quarter ration of food as your punishment!" "Yes sir," the guards responded as they exited the study. A quarter ration of food was an insult as it wasn't enough to fill the men, but it was just enough for them to yearn for more, increasing their hunger till the morning. Fortunately for the men, the guard often prepared their own meals and so they would receive a full ration that night. When they were significantly far enough away, "I really hope that that ole bloke made it," Reg said under his breath. Sam, engrossed in his own distain for Blankenslip, agreed.

Helping Hands

Sneaking out of the smuggling hold, the pirate made his way out of the hole. He took a moment to stretch out and get feeling and blood flow back into his extremities. Fresh air filled his aching lungs and he enjoyed every moment. Cautiously he rambled back up on deck. Seeing that he was totally left alone he smiled his trademark smile. "Yes, that's more like it. Fresh air! Open seas! A ship beneath my feet!" He looked down and chuckled at that. Shrugging off the ship comment, "What more could one want? Hum? What else? Well, I guess a bottle of rum would hit the spot. I need my weapons back as well; that and a bite to eat." Still smiling the small grin he turned to look up toward the house. Even though he had taken the time to stretch out below deck, it was now that he suddenly realized the shackles were still affixed to his wrists. "Oh yes, and there is a matter of this too. Wonder what my good friend Timmy is doing right now. Only one way to find the answer to that eh?" He headed cautiously back up to the house under the cover of growing darkness. Tried as he could, the pirate concealed the clanking chain on his shackles. Upon reaching the building, the pirate peaked in through several windows only to find nothing. Spying a trellis, he concluded that the bedrooms would likely be upstairs. A rather thin ledge ran the length of the building. Chuckling in disbelief, the pirate began to make his way up the trellis. It creaked and swayed under the weight of the man climbing it. "C'mon ole girl," the pirate thought to himself, "hold tight." Step by cautious step, he slowly made his way up the flimsy device. There he reached the three inch ledge and stepped on. Using his fingers to grasp the blocks between the mortar, he came upon the nearest window. There was no light or sound emanating from it. Unfortunately for him, the window was secured. Further on he pressed. Inch by inch he cautiously went down the line. The next window had candlelight filling it. Peaking in quickly he spied the figure of a young woman. The smile had returned. Again, he looked in only to see her exit the room. This window was secured as well. "Drat," he thought to himself feeling his finger grips starting to slip. The sweat from his labor was making his task more difficult. He continued to press on. Finally, he came upon an open window. "Good lord," he thought to himself. Peaking through the window, young Bart sat reading by candlelight. "Bout bloody time," the thought continued.

"Psst! Psst," the pirate whispered. Looking up and around the boy looked puzzled. "Psst! Young Freddy," the pirate said in hushed tones. Instantaneously knowing, Bart lowered his head and sighed, "Pirate," he said between clenched teeth. He sat looking out the black window, "But how?" "How what," the pirate asked from the shadows? "How could it be you," Bart inquired. He stepped inside the window into the light. Touching his chest and looking at himself the pirate replied, "Um, because that's who I was a moment ago." "That's not what I mean," Bart said.

"Don't you know that that's bad for your eyesight lad," the pirate offered. "Don't you recall you thinking I was in a dress?" Shaking his head at the reflection Bart exclaimed, "But I have enough light sir." "No I mean reading such drivel," the pirate stated as he picked up the tome and eyed it over. Stunned Bart stated, "It's Shakespeare sir." "Right! Bloody plagiarist," the pirate expounded. "But he's my favorite," Bartholomew cried in defense! "Nevertheless, drivel. Besides how does a seven year old read Shakespeare," the pirate inquired. "I read from the left to right," Bart joked. Nodding his approval, "Not bad Chad. Not bad," the impressed pirate replied. "Now, how about a bite to eat?" "AGAIN," Bart yelled. "Sssh," the pirate demanded as he instinctively ducked behind the boy's clothes chest. Peering out he saw no one coming to the boy's aid and gathered himself up. "Well it's been several hours since you last did your thing. Oh, and can you get me the key to these Jimmy," he asked showing off his shackles smiling. "Bartholomew! Bartholomew! Bartholomew! Bartholomew! I mean it's not that difficult to remember even for a drunkard like you," he professed.

"Vagabond drunkard... it keeps getting better. Now how about a few scrumptious morsels and a key? Eh swab?" "Absolutely not," Bart said folding his arms and sitting back in his chair, legs kicking back and forth in the air. Thinking a moment the pirate brightened up. "We might make another accord!" "But you didn't hold true to your last one," Bart countered. "I did," he opined. "However, your father didn't know about our deal and returned me to you. Perhaps he wishes my presence in your lovely homestead," the pirate prodded. "I could see myself living out my days in this lovely abode," he said as his shackled hands stroked the wall. "Absolutely not," Bart countered. "Father wishes you strung by your neck for your transgression." "Well my good swab if that were true, then don't you think that I'd be in the stocks waiting the morning light? Only to be brought to the gallows come daybreak? I mean your father *did* return me to this place and here I am; safe, sound and small necked," the pirate wily carried on.

"True, but then why do you make your way in from the window? And in shackles," Bart queried. "Wait! How did you come in through the window? We're on the second floor," the boy stated. "I've always been a fan of extravagant and interesting entrances and exits. Besides there's fresh air, a starry sky, soft breeze. What's not to enjoy," he answered. "And the shackles," Bart stated dryly. "I was just showing your father a trick I've been working on. Sadly I haven't perfected it just yet," the pirate quipped. "I do not believe you sir." "Fine," the pirate replied, "We'll just go down and speak with your father and we'll tell him all about how you assisted me in our previous accord. How does that sound eh?" Bart suddenly realized that the pirate had him in a bad spot. He mulled the consequences then spoke. "Well, I guess I could get you something to eat. *IF* you then take your final leave," Bart insisted.

"Why Billy I'm beginning to feel like you disapprove of my presence," the pirate quizzed. The breeze was steady and blowing in from behind the pirate, blowing directly into young Bartholomew's room. "Well Pirate," he started, "it's like I told you previously. It's just that you smell. I mean you smell bad! And father isn't a kind man. He'll punish me right awful if he ever finds out that I know you were here!" "All the more reason to get me some food. Oh! And that key you were speaking of. Oh! And my weapons," he countered. "Will that make you smell better," Bart wondered. "In a sense. See, once I get a bite and get free of these toys, grab my weapons and I'll be off. Smells gone then eh," he said. "I like to take it with me." Holding his nose young Bart exclaimed, "AGREED!"

Sneaking down to the kitchen Bart again smuggled out some food. He quickly stopped and snuck out the spare keys his father maintained. He was free and clear when a voice suddenly stopped him in his tracks. "What have you got there Bartholomew?" He didn't turn to face the voice. "Um, nothing," he replied trying to maintain innocence. "Right," the voice said sarcastically. "Come, let me see what's in your hands little brother." Obediently the boy did as he was told. He turned to face his older sister, food in his hands. She smiled a big smile, "Why you must be growing. All the food you ate for supper and now this?" The boy could not look her in the eye, but rather cast his gaze toward the floor. She took her index finger, placed it under his chin and calmly raised his gaze to meet hers. Her pleasant smile reassured him. "Don't worry my brother. I won't tell father. I'll protect you." He smiled back, "Thank you Virginia." A wave of relief came upon him and he turned to scurry back to his room.

Entering, he quickly put the items in his hands down. He hurried back to the door and slowly closed it with a lifting and pushing motion towards the hinges. It was almost as if he were placing the door as opposed to just closing it. The pirate watched with interest as the boy went about his task. "Must have done this before," he thought to himself. "You know you're getting quite good at this," the pirate stated. "I feel awful deceiving father like this, for if I get caught," Bart squirmed stopping his train of thought. "Plus now my sister thinks I have an insatiable appetite." "And that's a problem because…" the pirate trailed off. "Because she delights in making me feel like a child," he protested. "You are," the pirate said flatly. "I'm old enough," the boy countered. Quickly changing the direction of the conversation, "Um, you have the key?" "Ah, yes. Sorry," he said tossing the key to the man. Catching it in one hand he stated, "You know that I could use a good *man* like you." He slyly slid 'man' in to delight the child. The pirate removed the shackles handing them over to Bart in exchange for the food. "What for," the boy asked. "Um, gathering food. That is if you could do something about those small hands," he said. "I'm going to grow you know. And stealing is wrong!" "But you've gotten quite a gift today," the pirate exclaimed. "How do you figure," the boy asked. "Well you've discovered that you have quite a talent then. And at such a young age! Some people go their whole lives never knowing their passion and today you've discovered yours," he professed. "What's that," Bart inquired. "You're good at wrangling things for my consumption," the pirate stated plainly. "Stealing? I'm good at stealing?" Bart declared with shock in his high voice.

A knock at the door froze both man and boy in their tracks. Simultaneously they turned their eyes slowly towards the door. "Bartholomew, are you alright?" It was Virginia. "I'm fine." "Whom are you speaking to," she inquired as she tried to push the door open. An overwhelming sensation to correct her grammar was overtaking the pirate, causing him to almost give himself away. The humidity had swollen the door making it difficult to open and discouraged her. What Bart had done earlier was that he learned recently how to lever the door to be able to open and close it silently. "I'm just reading Shakespeare aloud. All's well," he nervously replied. The pirate just nodded his approval. "Alright, don't stay up much longer. You need to get some sleep." "Yes Virginia. Thank you and good night," he said. They waited a moment then the pirate picked up the conversation exactly when they had left it off. "Nay young Thad! I keep on telling you. It's not stealing. It's borrowing, borrowing! Perhaps it can even be viewed as simply acquiring. Remember, it's inconsequential if the rightful owner ever gets the property back. But if they do, bully for them," the pirate explained.

"How so," the boy asked. "Well, after I'm finished with it, they can have it back if they so choose," he said. "Food? How can they get food back," Bart wondered aloud? "Let's not discuss the semantics of it young Frederick, just go along with me on this, righty then," he pleaded. "Done," the disgusted boy said.

"Yes young Samuel. You'd make a fine pirate," the visitor stated. "PIRATE? I'm no pirate! I'm going to be governor of this island like my father before me! He tells me so," Bart proclaimed. "Pity, you'd make a wonderful swab right now," the pirate said. "Just take your leave as promised sir," the boy begged. "Certain?" The man quizzed.

"Be gone pirate," Bart demanded. "Alright my young apprentice. If you change your mind though, just look me up," the pirate stated. "Now how am I supposed to do that you smelly pirate," he inquired. Stepping out the window and tipping his hat with a smile, "Follow yer nose. Farwell," he said. Apparently he had forgotten just how small the ledge was. He backed right out the window and didn't stop until his fall concluded with a dull *thud* in the sandy surface below. Bart ran to the window, but it was too dark to see, "you ok sir?" "Uugh," he muttered to himself. "Splendid. Now go to bed," he said in a hushed, winded voice. Bart left the window just happy to be rid of him. Rolling to his side, he took a knee then grunted as he made his way to his feet. Holding his aching hip, the pirate ambled his way through the tall grasses and sand to the hideous ship. "Blimey," he thought, "My weapons!" He limped his way back up to the house, looked around and found a small rock. He threw it up at the open window and it went right in. "Ouch! What the… oh come on," the boy stated and made his way back to the window. He peered out and whispered, "What is it?" "Um, you forgot my weapons," the pirate replied. "I forgot," the boy questioned. "Ok, ok, *we* forgot," he corrected. "Where might they be?" The boy thought a moment, "Probably in the guard house." "Wonderful," the pirate said sarcastically. He looked up, "Well c'mon, get down here. I can't do this alone. You are a master of this." The boy was experiencing mixed emotions. He was unused to praise from an adult, yet knew that his father's wrath would be uncontrolled if caught. Bart sighed and made his way out the window, thinking he was as clever as the pirate. Sadly he was too inexperienced and tumbled down free falling and into the open hands of the pirate. "There we go then, that's more like it," the pirate spoke. "Thank you sir," the boy was truly grateful for catching him. He was placed on the ground and led him under cover of darkness to the guardhouse. The house was empty except for one sleeping guard. The guards had learned a long time ago that once the governor had his dinner he'd never call for them. This freed them up to go to the ship when she was in and raucously enjoy themselves for the night.

The pirate lifted the boy to the window and he slipped inside. From only a few feet away the slumbering man snored deeply and loudly. The small boy searched the room and discovered the weapons on a table in the corner. He tried at first to gather them all at once, but he was not able to pick them all up. The sword and various daggers were falling between his arms crashing to the floor. He peered over his shoulder at the beds, but the man snored on. Bart left the guns but grabbed the blades and made his way to the window. The pirate looked in and took them eagerly from the tiny hands. Quickly, they found their respective places and he waited for the pistols to be delivered. Bart made his way back to the table accidentally kicking the table leg with his little toe. He let out a yelp and slapped his hand over his mouth. The sleeping guard awoke. Dazed and sleepy eyed, "Wha," was all he mumbled as his eyes scanned the room. Bart dove under the table clutching his aching toe as a tear cascaded down his cheek. The guard didn't see him and rolled back over. Bart was terrified, but gathered the courage he needed and came out from under the table. He grabbed the scarves where they were tied to the pistol handles and hurried his way to the window. The pirate eagerly accepted them, slung them around his neck; reached in and pulled the boy out. "Excellent work lad! Excellent work," he whispered. The boy smiled back up at him and they made their way to the main house.

The pirate whispered, "Will you be able to get back in alright?" Bart nodded, "Remember, I have a secret way in and out." He suddenly recalled the story of him spying on his father and the smuggler. Nodding he smiled, "Aye. Good luck to you boy," and limped away.

Bart was feeling the adrenalin rush still having done something he knew to be so wrong. Carefully he made his way into the house and into his room without being noticed. Quickly he changed his clothes and crawled into his bed. His heart was still beating fast and he could not fall asleep. For the first time he fantasized that he was a pirate and not a royal navy man. He would remain awake for another hour before sleep finally found him.

The pirate made his way to the dock yet again. Having prepared the ship already once this day; he made slightly faster work of prepping her, but the hip slowed the process a bit. As rapidly as possible, he sailed out under a clear starry, moonless sky.

After regaining his breath, he noticed a bottle of rum of unknown origin nestled in a corner on the deck. "'Ello there then! Where the devil did you come from," he mumbled to himself. "No matter. Seems me luck has turned. Obviously not a Friday," he muttered as he took a swig, then began softly singing a whaler's tune.

Part 2: Getting On Board
Dead Men Do Tell Tales

The ship lay dead in the water. The seas were perfectly calm with no change in sight. The lone pirate wandered the small deck of the ship, grasping the rigging and bemusing himself at the vessel's appearance. "Well this is truly an exciting experience… wonder how long these doldrums will last," he wondered aloud. Climbing the mast like a monkey, he scanned the vast open sea for any signs of life. "No ships are in sight." He continued to scan the horizon holding the rickety mast, "Then again not much else is either. Well, we're not going anywhere any foreseeable time soon, eh old girl," he said hugging the mast with one arm, telescope in the other. He thought to himself a moment. If he whistled, as the superstition went, it might cause a storm. This could be good as the winds could carry him on his way. However, it might be bad as he was alone on this ship. Good as he was, he was still just one man to work this ship. His eyes darted side to side as he contemplated his idea. The pirate decided to try it, even if just for a moment. He shut his eyes tightly grabbed the mast with even more strength, pursed his lips and began to whistle. Quickly he stopped, eyes still shut. Slowly his courage grew and he opened an eye. Looking around he saw that nothing had changed. "Huh, guess it doesn't work eh," he said exhaling a nervous breath. "Might as well get comfortable and just enjoy the time." Climbing down, he jumped to the wooden deck below with a loud thud! It took him a moment before slowly straightening himself up, hand on his still aching hip,

"Ugh, I may be getting too old for this jumping nonsense. Well now, I uh, what was I doing again? Ah yes, a little shuteye ought to do the trick." He patted his hip, "Hopefully get you to calm down too eh." Eyeing the ship, he found himself a good place on the gunwale. Even though the comfortable bunk was below he preferred the fresh air of being outdoors. The pirate lay down on the rail, leaning against a halyard his hat was tipped over his eyes. Time slowly passed as the pirate attempted to slumber under the summer sun.

A few hours had passed when finally a gentle breeze blew past his nose. Unfazed, the pirate continued to slumber. The breeze blew again a bit harder and quickly stopped. This particular time the slumbering man twitched his nose, but still took no interest. As if irritated by the pirate's non-action, a sudden wind gust blew him off his perch and slammed him down to the deck. "Ugh. Bloody hell."

"What the," he took a knee, guns drawn as he peered over the rail. Nothing happened, nor was anyone in sight. He continued to scan the boat and the surrounding waters. Still nothing happened. There was nothing around but the blue of the waters and the bright sun in the cloudless sky. The pirate simply shrugged his shoulders, "I must have rolled over," he thought. Climbing back on the rail, he reassumed his position complete with the tilting of his hat over his face. It took only a matter of moments when another wind gust returned and knocked him off again.

"Who goes there?" he asked as he again took to his knee, guns drawn. The wind howled now, knocking his hat off continuing to blow. It blew so hard that he had to lean into it to prevent himself from toppling over. The pirate looked around and noticed that even though the winds blew, the seas remained dead calm, the sails limp, and the ship unmoved. Holstering his pistols, "Look, I asked you a question. Now, who goes there?" "How did you know that there was someone here," the voice asked accompanied with a hearty laugh. "Any good salt knows that when the wind blows and yet the sails don't sing that there is a spirit in the air," the pirate returned.

"Very good pirate," the spirit congratulated. "Now why do you disturb my sleep? And why can't I see you good spirit," he inquired. "You whistled mate, not me," the spirit countered. The pirate's mind raced in wonderment. "Actually, I come to you to request a favor," the spirit stated. Laughing at this odd request, "And what's in it for me," the pirate returned. "A good story," the spirit offered. "I've got plenty of good stories chap," the pirate countered. "Of course you do. Of course you do," the spirit said. However, you didn't let me finish. My name is Captain Jonathon Melbourne," he paused, "of His Majesty's Royal Navy," he continued.

Interrupting, "His Majesty's Royal Navy," he said laughing. "What in blazes is a stout fellow of HMS doing beckoning a lowly pirate," he pondered. Melbourne paused, "My ship was commandeered by scoundrel pirates as I and most of my crew were slaughtered," the disembodied voice replied. "Odd," the pirate returned. "How so," Melbourne questioned. "Well, you come to a pirate for help when it was a pirate that took your very life," the pirate said pondering the thought.

"Again, you didn't let me finish," Melbourne returned. The pirate bowed his head in mock sorrow, "Beggin' you pardon kind sir!" "Well it wasn't so much the pirates that I have issue with as they are an occupational hazard" Melbourne started, "rather, my old school chum, Captain Brightside watched the entire proceedings without even so much as lending a hand. In fact he reveled in the sight!" Puzzled by what he just heard, the pirate asked, "How do you know this?" "Once you pass on as a spirit, you become quite knowledgeable of the events that lead to your demise. You get to see the events unfold before your very eyes from any vantage point that you wish to see. It's really quite fascinating," the spirit stated.

"Remarkable," the pirate gushed. "Can you get me the winning lottery numbers?" "The what? Wait. Stop it," Melbourne commanded. Apologetically, "Sorry good spirit, so say you were slain by a pirate, a friend let it happen and now you beckon a, what was the word… ah, vagabond pirate for assistance. Am I correct," the pirate asked. "Yes, except for the *friend* part," said the spirit. "Um, yes. However, that doesn't explain why you haven't shown me your true form," the pirate inquired. "You see sir pirate if I can tell you my tale it will all become apparent," the spirit said. "Beggin' yer pardon again good spirit, carry on. Do go on. Tell me your tale," the pirate returned.

The disembodied spirit began his tale; "The events that led me to this current state are as follows. Captain Brightside had been trailing the Pirate Williams and had come up behind him. Brightside lay in anchorage and had been waiting for the tides and winds to change as he had been in want of a retreat route, in case his men had not been up to the challenge. You see, whereas Brightside's strength lay in the art of seamanship, his weakness lies in his cowardice. So even though the tides were low, he was freely able to happen upon them if he so chose. However, he was trapped by the shallows that sat behind him."

"'Captain,' Mr. Goodwind approached Brightside. 'Aye, Mr. Goodwind,' Brightside said. 'Captain, shouldn't we engage the enemy soon? As the tides come back in he'll be able to slip away,' Goodwind offered. 'I'd rather see what he's up to first Mr. Goodwind,' Brightside responded. Puzzled, 'I'm not certain I follow you Sir.' Stoutly Brightside responded, 'Well my good man, this Williams fellow, he's been known to have sacked several ships recently. He also hasn't had much time to have pilfered his booty, so I'm under the impression that he's squirreled it away somewhere for the time being. Most of these scoundrels don't hold their cargo long, wanting to lead a decadent lifestyle. However, from time to time circumstances dictate that they store it in a cache for later retrieval. If he hasn't offloaded yet his holds must be bursting. That extra weight will bog him down and he'll require more time for the tides to raise him up. More importantly, some of the treasure was bound to the King himself, and I intend to return it to him.'"

The spirit interrupted the story, "Which is a bold-faced lie! The man's a well known coward and Williams', though not a superiorly skilled fighter is still a pirate nonetheless. That being the cause of his trepidation, not booty. And even if he had found it, returning it to the king would be the last thing he would do."

Interrupting the disembodied voice, the pirate quizzed, "Are you telling me a story or commentating? "Oh, sorry, it's just that he's so unnerving," the spirit returned. "Carry on," the pirate said.

"Goodwind inquired, 'So when do we make our move then? The crew is ready for orders sir.' 'Tell them to stand down and be ready for further orders' Brightside commanded. 'We'll follow her as she rounds between those islands. The corals will be too shallow for her to pass through the channel and she'll have to sit and wait. We'll come up on the leeward side of the island and drop anchor.' 'Drop anchor sir,' Goodwind asked as if he hadn't heard correctly. 'Aye,' Brightside said. 'Then we'll, no check that, I'll make a boarding ready and head to the island by myself. I'll do some reconnaissance up on the hill and see if they've come to reclaim their prize. If they have, we'll have it! If they are just waiting for the tides, we'll have her!'

Stunned by this unprecedented decision, 'I'm begging your pardon sir. You'll be going ashore *alone?* And what makes you think that they're there for anything other than shelter from the low tide?' Goodwind, though loyal to his captain knew he was no brave hero. 'It's a rather odd place to be sure. That's exactly what makes it so inviting a place to drop cargo for future retrieval. So yes, I'll be going alone,' the captain continued. Interrupting, Goodwind protested, 'It's unheard of sir! I must issue a formal protest. What if they have you then?' Posturing himself, 'My good man, you think any mangy pirate can best me?' Apologetically Goodwind retreated, 'I'm sorry sir, that's not what I meant to infer.' Even more boisterous now, the captain exclaimed, 'I'll tell you good sir! I am renown for my seamanship as well as my cunning, resolve and bravery!'"

"And don't forget his modesty," the pirate interrupted. "Now who's commentating," Melbourne said. "Sorry, I can see how easily it is to do that. But be fair he is spinning a plate of filth. Any fool can see that," the pirate continued. "Ah, yes his ability to spin a plethora of falsehoods is well known! Listen to the next one. It's a doozy," the voice returned.

"Brightside continued his plan, 'Then you'll watch for my signal. I'll use my mirror and catch the sun's rays. If you see me flash once, it will mean they are seeking their treasure. If I flash several times in succession it means that they are awaiting the tides. Either way that's when you'll make your move and surprise them from the rear. I'll charge them from the front and we'll have them for certain!' Goodwind still stunned returned, 'Captain, the men ...' Cutting him off, 'The men will be under your command and will do as they are told. Is that understood?' The man still objected, 'But sir.' Again the captain reiterated, *'IS THAT UNDERSTOOD?'* Obediently, 'Aye-aye Captain.' The captain continued, 'As for your formal protest I would seriously consider your future in the royal navy before doing so!' Goodwind just nodded his understanding.

Melbourne continued, 'With that Goodwind was off. Brightside was indeed interested in treasure. He actually talked himself into believing that there was treasure to be had there. He then started planning on keeping most of it for himself and how to get away with it. You see he is also very delusional when it comes to life. Brightside thought to himself, 'Imagine what may be there if they actually are retrieving stolen treasure. We'll have to inspect the booty and decipher what was to be her true destination. If she were to go to an enemy of the King's then we shall, nay, I shall keep a fair share, turn the rest over to His Royal Majesty and surely receive another reward and promotion! If she were meant to go to the King or his constituents, imagine the possible reward!' He briefly paused, 'Commodore Brightside. Now that sounds wonderful!'"

Interrupting, "Now wait, wait, wait, wait, wait, wait just a moment then,' the pirate started. "Yes," replied the voice with an almost audible smile. "This man is more a pirate than any pirate I've ever known. Including the time I happened upon me self. There was a lot of rum that night," the pirate ventured. Agreeing, "Aye! And that's just one reason why he shouldn't be in the Royal Navy. Here's another," Melbourne started, "Brightside carried on, 'Then again, if there is no treasure they're in for one hell of a fight. Today may be a good day for my crew to die, however, it's a dreadful day for me to go. So, I think that I'll just observe from the comfort of my hideout.'"

Again interrupting the story the pirate bellowed out, "Bloody hell! And they call *me* a scoundrel!" "Aye, and that's the other reason that he shouldn't be in the Royal Navy! Nor should he be allowed to live freely! He's a liar, a coward and more than willing to let his men perish," the angered spirit spouted. Once again interrupting the story, "Wait a moment!" "Yes pirate," the voice said. "You can also know someone's thoughts after your dead," questioned the pirate, "Or are you just making it up?" "No chap, not making it up," the voice said, "it's complicated like I said earlier, you are privy to special things. I'll explain more later." Taking a seat on the rail and scratching his beard the pirate desired to hear more, "I'll hold you to that. Your tale intrigues me, good spirit, carry on!"

Happily the spirit agreed, "They stayed a good distance behind her and watched as she slipped beyond sight around the island. Quickly the call went out. 'All hands! Raise the sails,' Brightside commanded! 'Set your marks! Make haste! I must get on that island immediately!' Melbourne continued, 'There was massive action set into play. Sails went high and taught. The helmsman cleverly guided her to her destination and as quickly as the sails went up they unfurled and weighed anchor! Oh what a sight to see!

'Drop the jolly boat! I'm going ashore men. Everyone listen to Mr. Goodwind in my absence, he's in charge. Watch for my signal,' the weasel commanded. 'Captain, begging your pardon sir, but should I or Hodges here go? We're not as important to the ship,' a brave crewmember volunteered. 'Hey? Not important,' Hodges asked. 'Let it go man. It's true. You're pretty useless to us,' crewmember Watts joked. 'Oh very whimsical Watts. Very whimsical indeed,' Hodges said sarcastically. 'No really, we've all placed bets on when we'd get sick of you and feed you to the sharks,' Watts again joked."

"Nice lot indeed," the pirate broke in with a smile.

"Brightside continued, 'No my faithful chap. I must go it alone. I am very aware of your courage and bravery that you display and I assure you that it will not go unforgotten. Now, lower me.' They lowered the boat and he quickly made his way," said the spirit. "Yes, I'm very aware of your bravery. And I'm aware that you almost ruined my chances to go it alone. If I'm on that ship when they go into battle there's a good chance that pirate will have my head! Yes, I'll remember you! Good luck you brave fool! You're going to need it. Fortunately for me I'll be watching you either win or lose through my spyglass,' spat the captain. As Brightside made his way towards shore he plotted out several places he thought would make good shelters to view the ensuing battle. Being a member of the rodent family, he quickly scurried about the hill on the island till he found a thicket where he could cower like the vermin that he is," the angered spirit hissed. "Marvelous', exclaimed Brightside. 'This will be a wonderful place...' He was cut off by something unpredicted," said the voice.

"A snake that could speak Latin," the pirate said, himself interrupting. "What," questioned the voice suddenly stopped cold. "No, no! A wild boar that could sing and dance," guessed the pirate. "Are you completely mad or do you just enjoy driving others daft," retorted the spirit! "Sorry, I was just trying to guess what he saw," the pirate offered. "Then quiet down and listen," commanded the spirit. "As he peered through the thicket... 'Well I'll be! That's old Melbourne they've stumbled upon!'" The spirit breathed a heavy breath, "Indeed it was us. We had been at anchor and in the midst of cleaning the hull of our ship. We had been besieged with barnacles and since we had the time, we seized the opportunity. The men were scattered and completely unprepared for an ambush. Seems our scout party was on the hunt for deer they saw and left us unprotected. The bastard Brightside could have sounded an alarm but chose not to.

'By the heavens,' Brightside screamed in his head. 'I have always wanted that ship! *The Scavenger*, that's no name for a Navy ship! Nor is that any commission for a man like Melly! I deserve that ship! What a prize indeed! I thought there may be booty to be had today. I just never dreamed that my prize would be *that* ship!" "Um, begging yer pardon good spirit," the pirate politely offered. "Yes pirate," the spirit said. "I hate to agree with your sworn enemy, however, he does make a good point," said the pirate. "And that would be," wondered the spirit. "Well, he said that the name of your ship was *The Scavenger*. Is that correct," questioned the pirate. "Aye," replied the voice. "That's not very militaristic now is it," asked the pirate. "It's more of a pirate ship name. In fact, I do hesitate to say that it was the dread pirate Jones' storied ship. Is that not a fact good spirit?"

"Once again you are correct pirate. After the dread pirate Jones fell in battle, my commander, Admiral Walters took command of her. He tried to change her name, as he was not a man of superstition. He ordered her name changed to *The Protector*; however, that was not meant to be. As the men descended to rename her, the lines snapped without cause and they plunged into the ocean where they were immediately devoured by sharks. The next attempt also proved fatal and thus it continued until the crew prevailed upon him to maintain the name." "Fascinating," the intrigued pirate mumbled. Righting himself the pirate asked him to continue his story.

"Back to Brightside. He sat back and watched as the pirates quickly descended upon us," the voice offered. "Man after good man fell that day to the joy of Brightside. He watched with glee as he saw my final demise. My sword had broken and all that I had left was a dagger. Quickly I grabbed it, but to my surprise a pirate to my left had turned and slashed me across my chest. I fell to my knees in pain and horror. Promptly I fell dead. 'Oh Mel! You poor, poor fool,' said the bastard with glee! 'To think that you graduated ahead of me and here it is I that is the smarter of us two." The voice continued, "With that he suddenly remembered to flash his mirror. 'Heavens! I nearly forgot to signal my men. They'll be wondering what happened to me. I'm going to be a hero for helping save the pride of our navy! The gods have indeed smiled down upon me today.' He signaled several erratic and seemingly frantic flashes to his ship.

"Goodwind saw the flash, 'There's the signal men! All hands prepare for battle!" The voice continued, "The drums sounded and again there was massive action on board. The sails again were taught and the men made their stations. They rounded the bend and came upon the fight already in progress. The pirates were stunned as cannon fire ripped across their deck and masts. Though most of my men were already dead the survivors fought back with much bravado! I am very proud of their efforts. With the help of Brightside's men not a pirate survived that day and my men were indeed grateful."

"Aye, but what of Brightside," questioned the pirate. "He made his way down in haste to await his ship," said the spirit. "He then waited till his ship had opened fire on the pirates then came out to where several men lay dead.

Quickly he took off his coat and shirt and rolled them in the fresh blood and dirt to make it appear that he was indeed a battling hero. He splashed dirt upon his face along with some of the blood, then panting as if to seem exhausted from the skirmish; 'We have them! Huzza,' shouted the coward! The men responded with arms held high. Huzza!'

"Goodwind was the first to offer his misguided praise, 'Captain, you are truly a hero!'" The spirit continued, "The surviving men of my crew never truly believed that he had fought on their behalf. Never a one could remember seeing him until the fracas was at its end. That has never sat well with the survivors. They quickly gutted the pirate ship and sank her. All the booty, food, fresh water, grog, it was all taken aboard their ship. Only a few hands were sparred to help sail *The Scavenger* home. Brightside deliberately made it seem like *The Scavenger* wasn't part of the prize, when in actuality she was his biggest desire."

"So what happened next," asked the pirate. The voice started, "Well upon arriving home the King was so pleased with Brightside's accomplishments that he was promoted to Admiral. The filthy liar! He was placed on Port Elizabeth; an easy position, to protect her and given *The Scavenger* as a reward for service to the king. As for the scout crew that was deer hunting, they were court-martialed for *leaving* their post and are currently serving time under Brightside's watchful eye. He was always worried that one of them would come forth and expose his treachery. Since they were not sentenced to the gallows, he begged for the custody to be placed under his supervision stating his grief over what had happened. He said that he'd be able to have them serve their time and then possibly help them see the error of their ways, helping them return to naval service. The scant few left of my crew have been either discharged or relegated to shore duty at Port Elizabeth, no doubt for their allegiance to myself. As for the rest of us who met our demise, we wander this plain hoping to find our rest. The reason that my crew and I have been stripped of our earthly forms is that we were done in by a traitor. When Admiral Brightside took his commission for captain, he and I did so together. The king himself oversaw the ceremony as we had fought so valiantly side by side in the battle of *'The Main.'* It was our combined efforts that turned the battle for Mother England and helped our limp ships return home. If it weren't for him, I would not have survived. And if it weren't for I, neither would he. So the king commanded that we always be linked in this world and the next. By his treachery my crew and I were nearly stripped of our very souls. To undue the treachery he must fall the exact same way I did. And so my good pirate, it is for *this* reason that I come to you. I need a pirate to undue what a pirate and a traitor did to my crew and me."

There was a pause as he took it all in. "Fascinating tale good spirit. Simply fascinating. So what is it that you propose," pondered the pirate. "Revenge," the disembodied voice coldly said. "Obviously," the pirate said dryly. "I can guide your, ahem, *boat*, to where my old sailing master is and he can lead you to the rest of my remaining crew. Together you can take my old ship and seek my revenge on Admiral Brightside," offered the spirit.

"And," the pirate said slyly. Coyly the spirit replied, "And it would give me my dignity back. My crew and I would get our spiritual forms back. And…" Interrupting, "And that's all terribly exciting. However, I see no reason to try to help you get your ethereal body back. What's in it for me then," questioned the pirate. "Well, if you don't help me, I won't help you," said the spirit more confidently. "Help how," wondered the pirate. Ever the more confident in his position, "Out of your predicament," the spirit said. "Which is," the pirate asked cautiously.

"Beyond your vision is a naval frigate bearing down on you. Whereas you rely on the wind for power, they have a fully staffed crew and sweeps, for just such incidences. The gracious Governor Blankenslip gave up on you once; I doubt that he'll be so forgiving a second time," the bold spirit offered. "Interesting," said the pirate again scratching his face. "And if I assist you in your plight?"

"You get your life, your freedom and when it's all over, your own ship. A real ship. A real *pirate* ship, *The Scavenger*; complete with crew and sailing master with his own sextant, charts and sailing equipment," the spirit offered. "My crew and I get our form back and get to rest in peace. I beg of you good pirate, please. These were good men. Honest men. Men of the sea, not totally unlike yourself. Men who were done in by one of their own and do not deserve such a fate."

He took a few moments to weigh out his options, the pirate did. Strolling the deck, he milled over the story he just heard and pondered the possibilities of commandeering the fabled ship *The Scavenger*. That ship was legendary for her speed and maneuverability. Yes it was true; she was well past her prime and severely outclassed by modern ship design. The pirate knew in his very soul that there was something special about her. She's a ship made of wood just like any other. Her sails made of the best cloth available at the time. Her hold was small and not heavily gunned. However, she had something that no other ship that he had ever commanded had. She seemed to have a soul. A soul of a true pirate and privateer. The soul for adventure, much like his very own. "Very interesting," he finally stated. "Now why do you call on me? There are several good pirates out there who are available. Plus, the entire Royal Navy would be interested in your story. So why is it that you call on me, good spirit?"

Boldly the spirit countered, "You are Captain Daniel Payton, are you not?" "I am," the pirate said plainly. "You are the pirate who sacked St. William with a skeleton crew," Melbourne continued as to bolster the pirate's spirit. Smiling while recalling the moment, "I am," said the pirate. "You are the pirate who defeated the three Royal Navy ships in a single day as they escorted the incoming governor of Port Royal and her payroll," the spirit continued, concealing his true feeling for that action. Smiling and looking towards his feet as if embarrassed by the 'compliment,' "I am," stated the pirate. "You are the only man to ever navigate the Temple Ridge reef outside of the Isle of Nova," the truly impressed spirit stated. Now more proudly, "I am," still smiling from ear to ear, Payton said. "Need I go on?" questioned the spirit. "Please do," the pirate answered. "You are the best at your craft, and therefore the best one on whom to call upon to take my revenge! Besides, the Royal Navy is too grounded, to steeped in tradition to be listening to the plight of a spirit. Any Royal Navy man who'd take up my cause would be placed under observation, locked in the Tower of London and humiliated beyond reproach. So it is for that, that I, a humble spirit come to ask your assistance. Do we have an accord, my dear Captain Payton?"

Pausing a brief moment, "We are agreed," said Payton sticking out this hand to shake upon their agreement. Then suddenly realizing that there was no hand to be shook he coyly replaced it at his side. "Splendid," the voice returned, choosing to ignore the failed handshake! The spirit feared that embarrassing the pirate might change his mind.

"Oh, wait," stopped the pirate. "What," the cautious spirit countered? "You said that your old sailing master had his own sextant, charts, etc. Correct?" "Correct," answered the spirit. "Would he happen to have a working compass among his effects? I haven't had one in years," said Payton. Sighing aloud, "Yes his compass works properly," said the spirit. "Accurate maps too," questioned the pirate. The once cautious spirit began growing perturbed, "Yes, I think so," replied Melbourne. "We are agreed then," said the pirate. Then pausing a moment, "Oh, one more thing?" Getting continuously more perturbed, "What," said the voice. Shyly Payton inquired, "Would he happen to have some food with him?" Stunned by this question the agitated spirit spat back, "There's food in the galley below. Just open your eyes man!" "Ah, yes! Thank you! Blow on! No Wait," pleaded the pirate! "Goodness sakes man! What can you possibly want now," the second guessing spirit shouted. "How did you know all that about Gov. Blankenslip? I told you I'd hold you to that," queried the pirate

Knowing that he had promised him that knowledge the spirit relented. "I told you, spirits are privy to incredible knowledge. We can see the places we were; hear the words that were spoken, hear the very thoughts that were thought by other men. The only problem is, that you are only made aware of things that may benefit you at achieving your peace. This even goes for things that are happening as we speak right here and now. So if a man thinks about anything that pertains to your situation you can gain knowledge of said thought. However, if his very next thought does not pertain to you, then that thought is kept hidden in secret. For example Blankenslip just ordered his sweeps to double their efforts, then all went silent. This is to help us gain the rest we so deserve without taking advantage of others."

Stroking his full beard, Payton pondered this new knowledge. "Interesting, very interesting indeed." Sensing that Payton was pondering something that may benefit him, Melbourne cut him off mid-thought. "Typically access to that type of knowledge only happens to those who were either pure of heart and/ or severely wronged at the time of their demise," stated the spirit. Realizing he was just outed by the spirit Payton quickly recovered, "Ah, always a loophole. Very well good spirit, blow on," he requested. Exhaling, the exhausted spirit conceded a heart felt, "Thank you."

With that, the ghost summoned a mighty wind that filled the sails and Captain Daniel Payton was on his way.

Where, he did not know.

Taken Down A Peg

"Well now, doesn't this look a tad treacherous," Payton offered as the ship sailed around a mountainous peninsula. The winds from the now gone spirit, continued to guide his ship. Lush thick vegetation overgrew the land down into a semi-hidden cove with a single rickety long dock. No ships were moored, nor did it appear that any had been in quite some time. The dock extended out from the jungle with only a narrow path cut into it, which gave the impression of being completely uninviting. The sun bleached dock sat decaying in the salt water. Several planks had rotted away leaving gaping holes in their place. A pelican sat perched upon a piling and watched with interest as the odd ship came towards it. Gracefully, Daniel docked the boat to the dock, keeping his wits and eyes open to any "unwelcoming committees.'" He nodded toward the pelican that continued to watch him unfazed.

"Well then, that's secure," he reassured himself after tying her off. "Let's have a look around shall we," he paused for a brief moment, "Whom exactly am I speaking to," he pondered aloud. Turning to the pelican he shrugged his shoulders he carried on. "Never mind then."

The well-seasoned pirate cautiously walked the dock and maneuvered up the path cut into the jungle; machete in hand and ready for friend or foe. "That good feller, Phil, Johnny, Reginald… what's his name, said that he'd guide me to my sailing master then? Unfortunately, he didn't give me a name. I can't believe that. I'm great with names. Let alone he could have given a description, or even the location of a single bottle of rum. I…"

"Rum, rum, who wants a bottle of rum?" a disembodied voice projected. Stopping dead in his tracks and standing upright, pistol in one hand and machete in the other, "Who offered that," Payton inquired. The overgrown path obscured his view.

"Rum, rum, who wants a bottle of rum," the high-pitched voice repeated? "Why I do!" Daniel returned, weapons still in hand now more interested. "Name, name what's your name," the voice commanded. "Captain Daniel Payton. To whom am I speaking?" He moved the palm fronds aside from his vision with the machete.

"Squawk," the voice returned. Tilting his head to one side, curling his upper lip causing the same side eye to squint the befuddled pirate could only say, "Pardon?" "Deaf, deaf, I said squawk," the voice continued. Looking around and not seeing anyone he stood scratching his face, gun in hand, in wonderment. "I'm begging your pardon, but I'm not familiar with that name." "Name, name, tis not a name," the voice countered. "Ok then," the perplexed pirate stated. "Never, never, never heard a parrot say squawk before," he said. Putting his weapons by his side, "Why certainly, but how does that help now," he inquired still peering around the broad green leaves of the brush. "Up, up, look ye up," the voice demanded. Daniel leaned back. Peering up he saw perched on a branch a Macaw parrot, brightly colored with red, black and white feathers.

"Nice, nice, be nice or it's time to dump my cargo," the parrot instructed. Still looking up, "Well you're a clever fellow now aren't you," Daniel praised. "Thank you, thank you, it's the rum you want," the parrot said. "Ah yes," he started, sinking back into his previous state. "Might you know, good Mr. Parrot, where I might procure just such a bottle?" "Master, master, he has the answer," the parrot revealed. "Might you take me to him," the pirate asked completely forgetting about his mission and instead thinking only of his desires. "Yes, yes, only requirement is you share," stipulated the parrot. "Well of course. I'll gladly share with your master," Daniel offered politely. "Master, master, master has his own." "Well then, share with whom," Daniel wondered. "Me, me, you dolt. You must share with me," the parrot replied. "Do parrots even drink rum," Daniel asked. "Might make you sick good friend parrot." "Share, share or I'll drop my cargo on your head," he demanded. This took Daniel by surprise. "Cargo. What cargo friend?" "Food, food, my breakfast sits waiting to unload," said the parrot. "Ah! Fair enough good Mr. Parrot. Since you gave me fair warning I'll gladly share my drink," the pirate said. Singing, "Rum, rum, I love the rum," the parrot professed. Speaking to himself, "A bird after me own heart," Payton said. "Now, show me the way good Mr. Parrot."

The parrot hopped off the branch to the ground ahead of Payton. Cautiously he led the way with mixes of short distance hops and flight. His wings brushed and slapped against the wide leaves hindering his efforts. However, the determined bird pressed on. Daniel followed the parrot deeper into the jungle slicing through the thicket. "You sure you don't want me to lead the way friend," Payton offered. "No, no, this way we must go," he replied leading them to the mouth of a cave. "Well good parrot," Daniel started. Quickly cutting him off, "Sarika, Sarika, my name is Sarika." "Ah good. Mr. Parrot has a name! Well Sarika, what have we here then," Payton said. "Home, home, not much master says, but home," Sarika cawed. "Might I have a look inside feathered friend," Payton inquired. "Master, master is gone to look for the channa," he returned. "Well with master gone someone should take watch over the place," Daniel pushed. "I do, I do, no one is allowed to pass," Sarika bellowed. "Arr, but it's me. What say we let me have a sit inside and maybe a bit of that rum you promised," Daniel pushed! "Eye out, eye out master tells me to take your eye out," Sarika defended.

"Uhm," Daniel paused to ponder his statement, "well I'm rather quite fond of my eyes. They're a matching set you know. I think I'll just look around." He stopped cold as he heard the click of a trigger being cocked and the barrel of a pistol stuck into his cheek from the side. "Around what," the mysterious voice inquired. "I don't know! A round what," Daniel returned, not in a sarcastic way, but a truthful inquiry. The voice tried to sound demanding but barely concealed the tremor, "You said around, and I'm just wondering what?" Still indifferent to the situation and answering as truthfully as he thought possible, "Well many things are round. Some cheeses, sausages, a ships wheel...," Daniel said. "All right enough with the smart talk," the angered voice now more confident demanded. "Who being ye?" "I am but a mere sailor looking for a sailing master," Daniel relayed, feeling confident that he found his man. He just didn't want to tip his hand too soon. "Who sent ye," he demanded backing away yet still pointing the gun at him. "Well good sir an old friend sent me," Payton eased. Curiously the voice beckoned, "And who is this old friend of yours?" "No. Not my friend," he said in a deeper tone. "Yours," he said turning to see his companions face. "Who," the startled man questioned. He fumbled with his gun, as it had been quite some time since he had been forced to use one.

"Uh, um, what was his name," Daniel said feverishly racking his memory? "You see I'm really not that good with names," he said rather embarrassed. "Well then, what did he look like," the man demanded. Payton let out a small laugh. "Ok, well that's a peculiar thing." "How so, he has a face," the man said. "Well yes, he did... once," Payton quipped. This statement completely took the man by surprise, "Did? Once? You spoke to a man with no face," he said laughing. "Quite," was all he responded with. "Now that's a story if I'dn ever heard it! How speaks one to a man with no face," he asked still laughing. "Can't be done," he added.

Speaking plainly, Daniel returned, "You can when he's a ghost." "Ghost you say," his laugh dyeing down. "Ghost of whom," he asked sternly. "Drat," Daniel spat. "I was hoping that ye'd not ask that." Taking a moment to try to recall the spirits name he pondered, "Jimmy, Steve, Patrick, Michael, Matthew. No those aren't right. Captain, Captain," "Quit yer stalling and give me a name or the last sound ye'll hear is the sound of the hammer hitting her mark," the man demanded raising the pistol to his head again. "Ah yes," Payton said recalling the spirits name. "Captain Melbourne. Captain Jonathon Melbourne. No wait," he stopped suddenly thinking he had the incorrect name. "That's not right." Stumbling back at the sound of the name, "*Captain **Melbourne!*** How is that so," he cried. Payton still in his own world trying to recall the name he already got correct; "Captain Walter Waddell? No, Captain Lawton Leonard? No." Interrupting him, "Pirate! I asked you how you know of Captain Melbourne," demanded the man.

Snapping back to the present moment, "Right! That's the chap. Tell you what. You lower that pistol so I don't have to hurt you and we'll have us a right good chat. What say you to that," Payton offered. Still stunned the man agreed and slowly he lowered the pistol. "Yes, but don't make me use this." He shook the pistol as he spoke. "Aye. I wouldn't be wanting you to have to clean any messes. Be they mine or the one in yer britches," Payton said.

The pirate told him his incredible tale of his trip; his meeting with the ghost; the mission and ultimately to commandeer his new ship. Sitting back in complete amazement the man pondered what he has just heard. "Brightside! That bastard saw it all." His eyes darted around as if he were visualizing the scenario in front of him. "He could have helped us… but he just sat and watched. Then… then… this" the angered man spewed. The pirate offered his condolences, "Sorry there chap. But that's the tale." "Well that's all very well and good for you pirate, however; why should I help you," the defeated, dejected man spat. Sarika offered his own input, "Yes, yes, why shouldn' the master be helpin' you?"

The pirate thought a moment before speaking. "Because you're a mixed bag, aren't you" he started cautiously. "You feel bonded by honor to your former captain and crew; yet," leaning in, "you've always had a burning desire to see the pirate life for yerself." Payton stared him in the eyes. Though he had blue eyes by birth, they burned red as he spoke. The man sat puzzled and taken aback. "Never," he shouted, then slumped a bit, "well perhaps. But just to understand them better," he stated with extreme caution still not thoroughly believing his ears. "But how do I know that I can trust you?"

Immediately the expression on Payton's face changed. Sitting back smiling, "You can't." The smile vanished, "But I can't trust you either mate, so we'll have to trust our distrust!" The smile returned, "It'll help keep us more honest with one another. Besides, what else does a sea dog want to do other than sail?" "True," the man said staring off into space. Quickly the moment passed and the man focused on his new enemy. "And it'd feel great to wring the neck of that devil Brightside. And repayment of my time on this desolate spit!" Still Payton continued his efforts to convince the man to join him. "That parrot of yours is a good lookout for yer safety as well," Payton said. "That he is," returned the man.

Payton stood and looked around to illustrate his point. "Now you do have a wonderful home" he began in a sarcastic tone, arms outstretched. Immediately he turned, got directly into the face of the man and deviously spoke these words; "but you crave the blue waves; the twinkle of the stars high in the night sky, the song of the whale; the feel of a deck under your feet and the adventure of the open seas! It's not a hermit's life fer the likes of ye. Holed up in a dark, dirty cave like a slumbering beast. Nay, tis the life at sea. The salt air, the wind as she makes the sails sing… and being a hero. Knowing that ye lifted the curse off yer ole mates can save yer very soul." Smiling a convinced smile, "When do we leave," the man asked eagerly. Payton resumed his normal cheerfully bliss self, "Just as soon as we finish our dinner mate!" "*Our dinner*, the stunned man asked "Well you can't have your captain going hungry now can you," Payton asked.

Defiantly the man stood up, "My captain will always be Captain Melbourne," he proudly defended. Payton could only sigh, "Yes, yes and Sally's yer aunt. Can you at least agree that on my ship that I'm the captain?" "Alrighty mate," he conceded. "First we dine then we sail!" Interrupting, Daniel returned, "And as per our agreement, a bit of the rum!" Unsure of this turn of events the man asked, "How does that fit in our agreement?" "Aye! Not our agreement mate," Daniel spoke. "The agreement between me and your bird," he said turning to look at Sarika! "Sarika," the man huffed. Sarika cowered back saying, "Sorry, sorry, sorry master, I'm a sorry." The man turned back to Payton, "Bloody bird, 'e drank my last bottle yesterday!" Knowing when to push and when to hold back the captain professed, "So food it is and then we sail." "Aye," agreed the man. Sarika rejuvenated suddenly, "Three for food, three for food all I can say is three for food!"

The sailing master felt a bolt of electricity charge through him. The thought of leaving this horrible place excited him immensely. Although, he thought, he had been here for quite some time and it was safe haven. He knew that no one would bother him here and he could live out his life in safety. But he quickly ushered that thought out of his brain. He wanted to be back on the sea and to avenge his old captain.

The two men sat on the earth floor for a light meal with the parrot perched on the man's shoulder. "You know I typically know a man's name when he joins my crew," Daniel said not looking up from his tin of peas. "And I typically know the man's name under whom I intend to sail," retorted the man, also not looking up. Payton stood up as if being given a huge ovation, taking off his hat and taking a bow, "I, good sir, am Captain Daniel Payton; pirate extraordinaire, vagabond, scoundrel, friend of fine women, connoisseur of fine rum, storyteller par excellence, fisherman amongst fisherman, seaman amongst seamen, navigator of dangerous reefs, communicator with the winds, seducer of mermaids, passer of gas, and in my free time I like to read!" "Very impressive," the man said in half-truth. "You should see my business card," Payton said dryly. "Your what," the befuddled man asked. "Never mind," Payton passed off. "So what pray tell is your name matie?" "I am Martin Finny, one time Sailing Master of *The Scavenger*. After the battle Brightside had fabricated some charges against me that I had ordered the scout team to leave rendering us out-manned. He knew my allegiance to my captain and knew that I'd eventually discover the truth. I suppose he was correct. Anyway, I was taken by ship with a few others headed for Mother England when I knew that if I stepped foot on shore that would be the last time I saw my freedom. Betrayed by one of our own… a second time it seems. So one night I was wide-awake and went to the cannons, opened the hatch and lady fortune smiled upon me that night. I spied this island and decided that I'd rather take my chances here in my own way than in someone else's. I crawled out, lowered the hatch and sprung from the ship. Nearly drown I did as I swam for freedom. Luckily for me, there was this cave all ready for a new tenant. It was shortly after, that I met my feathered friend here. He keeps me good company."

"My pleasure Marty," Daniel said reaching out to shake his hand. "Martin," he retorted trying to maintain the formality of the Royal Navy. It was so engrained in him that it was a reflexive action. "No, Daniel," he replied confused. "No I'm Martin," Finny returned. "Yes, I know Marty," Payton said. "Martin," Finny protested wanting formality. "Daniel," Payton returned confused at the conversation. "What," an equally confused Finny replied. "What what," Payton asked not knowing where the conversation went. "Why do you keep doing that," Martin begged. "What," Daniel asked? "Daniel," Martin said. "Yes," Payton replied dryly. "I'm Martin," he shouted! "I know that. You're Marty, Sally's still yer Aunt, Phyllis is yer parrot and I'm Daniel. Hey I'm getting better at this," Payton said with glee. "*Martin*," he demanded wanting naval formality! "No it's *Daniel*. Where did I lose you? Please keep up. If you're going to sail under me you're going to have to know my name," Payton said rather exhausted.

"STOP IT," Martin begged. "PLEASE!" "What," asked the pirate quite plainly? "AAARGH," screamed the battered man! "When I say Martin I'm saying my own name." Payton sat completely oblivious to the fact that it's been his misunderstanding that has created the mentally exhausting confusion. He spoke in a plain voice. "I'm quite aware that you are saying your name when you say Martin. However, you keep calling me Martin when my name is in fact Daniel. And that is rather confusing." "No," he interrupted, "you keep calling me Marty!" Interrupting in return, "That's your name" the pirate said. "Martin," he postured begging for the formality of his former naval days!

Frustrated in return, "Stop calling me Martin! My name is Daniel," Payton begged. Screaming at the top of his lungs, "I'M MARTIN! YOU'RE DANIEL! LET'S JUST EAT! AND NO MORE TALKING!" With that the two sat in complete silence. Slowly Sarika started to bob his head side to side. Payton was the first to resume eating as the silence sat heavy in the air. Martin resumed eating, not out of hunger, but rather out of necessity. He wondered what the man before him was thinking. He was a captain after all. A *pirate* captain at that! However, he had not yet pledged himself or his loyalty so there might not be full retribution. Or would there? "He could easily kill me and no one would ever know! What have I done! Why doesn't he speak," he thought. "What could he be plotting? He is a pirate! Is he going to slit my throat? Why won't he speak," he screamed in his head! Finally yet quietly, almost as if to himself Daniel spoke, "It's not my fault if you can't seem to remember my name is Daniel."

Suddenly realizing that in fact he was not plotting revenge he blurted out, "You're an idiot!" Saving face, or

at least thinking so, "That's Captain Idiot to you sir."
"Fine. Captain Idiot," Martin huffed. Completely
oblivious to the fact that he was just insulted, by himself,
"Delicious food mate! You can always double as the
ships cook," Daniel cheerfully offered. "All I did was
pick these. There's no preparation involved," a confused
Martin said. "Fabulous," the pirate returned. "It'll give
you extra time as the Sailing Master." Finny sat back.
The day's events swirling around in his head. It was all
he could do to wonder, "Captain Melbourne why do you
hate me so much? Why did you send this buffoon, if it
was you who indeed sent him? Brother, it'll be a miracle
if he doesn't drive me insane!"

The Pirate Way

The three left the island aboard the tiny boat making way towards their next destination. Though their numbers were low, spirits were remarkably high on the small vessel. Martin thought this to be an odd looking vessel, but didn't want to question it. He was merely happy to be back at sea. Payton busied himself and paid no heed to what Martin was doing. Martin couldn't help but watch as the island he called his home for these recent years grew smaller and smaller in the distance. Thoughts crisscrossed through his brain if he was doing the right thing in leaving the safety of his island or not. He had not been among other living humans in quite some time and prayed that there wasn't a bounty on his head for his escape. The island continued to shrink in the distance till it vanished. Even if he wanted to return, there was nothing he could do about it now. He breathed a heavy sigh and decided to focus on the task at hand.

"Captain. As per your request, I've plotted a course for an island where we can rest and supply ourselves before we make our next move," Martin said. "Murray," Daniel spouted. "Martin," said Finny plainly. "Right," he returned rather abruptly. "I was wondering; who in your previous crew made it through the ordeal?"

Martin pondered that thought for a moment. He looked deep within for a moment until finally speaking up. "I'm quite certain that Dr. Fitzgerald made it out alive," Martin said with as much confidence as he could muster. It was as if he were trying to convince himself. He desperately hoped that his old friend was still alive.

"A physician! Quite excellent," Daniel said excitedly, ignoring Martin's unsteadiness. "Yes, he's a brilliant man who has helped many a man at sea," Martin spoke with pride. It was obvious that he was rather fond of his relationship with the physician. This was a good start; however, the pirate was not satisfied with only one person. "Who else," inquired the pirate.

Again Martin seemed rather dejected at the memory of the event. He carefully chose his words before speaking. With a deep breath he spoke, "Many of the crew met their end that day. However, I'm certain that there are enough to crew *the Scavenger*," Martin offered half believing it himself.

"And they'd be willing and able to convert to piracy,"

Payton asked deviously. Martin thought a moment, "Well, um, quite possibly? If, of course, you first point out the revenge factor," Martin offered. "Then they might be more inclined to assist you in your... I mean, our plan." "Marvelous, simply marvelous," Daniel said with a devious smile.

The boat made its way along its plotted course. The tiny island of San Palente, a moderately inhabited island under the flag of Spain, loomed off in the distance. The two men continued in silence towards their destination. A small port began to appear and minor activity was clearly visible on the docks. "Captain we should beware;" warned Martin, "This island is a known haven for pirates." Looking over his shoulder and back at Martin, Daniel stared at him a moment before he returned dryly and very sarcastically, "You don't say." He paused. "We'll have to keep a watchful eye then," Daniel said with a serious tone. "I'm just saying... oh wait," suddenly realizing that he was now on his way to becoming a pirate himself.

"Look friend," Daniel started. "This is an island I've been to many a time. I fancy it rather as a home away from home." He suddenly switched gears to a more puzzled tone, "That is if I knew what a home actually was... then that might mean more than it does." He suddenly snapped back to reality, "Nevertheless, you need to act more like a pirate because that is your new vocation, your new trade, your new calling, eh!"

"Arr! Arr! We now say arr!" Sarika squawked.

"QUIET," Martin and Daniel shouted in unison, causing

the bird to recoil in fright! "You need to watch yourself mate. Any slip ups and they'll know that you've got Royal Navy blood in those veins. Don't worry chap, one good act of piracy should wash that clean out of your system," Daniel prophesied. Suddenly having second thoughts Martin replied, "I'm not too sure about this." "Relax and enjoy the pirate life, friend. It's much easier than your previously tormented days," eased Payton. Still not totally sold on this mission while trying not to give that impression, Martin thought to himself. "Right, just relax and enjoy the process… of losing your dignity, your mind, your very soul."

"Listen up matie," Daniel began. "On a pirate ship there are rules and regulations to follow just like you're used to. The difference is that on *our* ship you get a voice in all matters. You also get a share of all plunders. And you get more freedom than you've ever had before." "So it is true then," Martin mused. "What's true then?" "The storied life of pirates. I've heard that even though they be dirty scallywags, they live the life of freedom." Payton quickly countered his statement, "Aye mate, you are now referring to yerself as a dirty scallywag. And finally it's a fitting moniker. You stink." "Well I never!" Martin was clearly offended, but he took a moment to sniff check himself. "Aye. I guess I could use a bath." "Acid bath," Daniel spoke softly to himself. "But don't go fantasizing yerself into something it isn't. Pirate life is hard. It can be tedious. And worst of all, it could be very short. But, I'll gladly take that any day over yer military way," Daniel spoke. Martin regained his composure hearing this and recalled his train of thought. "Sounds very much like the navy. Now, as far as I was saying, did I once hear that pirates were a democratic society?"

Payton wondered aloud, "How should I know that?" "Well you are a pirate then," Martin returned. "No, not that," Payton stated. "I mean how should I know how many times you heard that? It is completely in the realm of possibilities that you are hard of hearing. Heaven knows that you hardly can follow a word I say."

"However…" Martin stumbled again reconsidering his decision to enter the world of piracy. Payton interrupted quickly, still standing with his back to Marty, "Remember mate, one of your own gave you up." Again his mind was suddenly flooded with the horror of the night. All Martin could do was to reply simply with, "Aye." Again, his focus returned to revenge!

Part 3: Lying, Drinking and Seasick

Luck In Odd Places

As the boat came to rest against the pier, the dock master ventured out to greet them. He was a man trying to look somewhat professional, yet he couldn't hide the fact that he, like most, had a past.

"Hola Amigos and welcome to ta Isle of San Palente. Docking fees be small, our bounty abundant, and we hop' ta heck dat you have a won'erful stay mon," the dock master said. It took just a split second to suddenly recognize whom he was addressing, "Capt'n Payton! 'S been a long time amigo!" "Aye mate! Good to be back again," the captain said gleefully. "I take it that the honest life has been good to ya?" The captain said with a smile.

The little man half-heartedly responded to his former captain's question. "Si senor. Well… tis good fer now, eh." He then looked to the captain's immediate right and was surprised by the man that stood before him. He wondered to himself that he wasn't absolutely certain, he doubted that this was a true pirate next to him. Regardless he treated him like any other member of his former captain's crew. "Hola. Me nama is Pedro Santiago," holding out his hand to Martin, "dock master 'ere in San Palente, an a former Quartermaster under da Captain Payton."

Cautiously Martin returned, "Greetings. I am Martin Finny sail," He was suddenly cut off by Payton. "Sailor extraordinaire," he said with a fake smile. "Interesting," he said nodding. "Wha' make you so extraordinaire Senor Finny," Pedro asked. Martin had a puzzled look on his face. Uncertain of this turn of events he didn't know how to respond, "Um, uh, um." "See what I mean mate?" Placing a hand on Martins shoulder, "Johnny here can hardly string a thought together from time to time, yet he has a natural ability to navigate any reef without any charts." Pedro knew the captain well. Well enough to know when he was being bamboozled. With a look of disbelief he responded, "I'm Spanish. Not ta fool senor."

Payton threw his arm over Pedro's shoulder and strolled him down the dock out of Martin's earshot. Martin tried in vain to look over their shoulder from the distance to see what their discussion entailed. Yet he could not. "Sarika, remain silent. Fly over there and try to ascertain what they speak of. Go now!" The bird took off and found a perch on a stay nearby where they spoke. Without looking at the bird, Payton drew his pistol and pointed it directly at Sarika. Looking over the arm still wrapped around Pedro's shoulders, "Don't trust me yet mate," he spoke loudly to Martin. Martin nudged his head signaling for Sarika to make haste. Terrified, the bird obliged and darted back to his master's shoulder.

Payton smiled at Martin, "You're going to have to be a bit more trusting of yer new captain eh." He lowered the firearm and returned to his conversation with Santiago. "Listen mate, I didn't believe it either so I made him a wager," Payton started his tall tale. "Si," Pedro returned. This chain of events didn't phase Santiago at all as he had seen so much in his previous time with the captain. He was also intrigued as to the tale that was about to be laid before him. "I made him take his old master's third ship; that piece of rubbish we came in on, and prove he could navigate the chapel reef," he continued. Surprised beyond belief, *"Chapel reef!?* Dat's da second most dangerous reef behind da Temple Ridge rocks dat only you did," Pedro exclaimed suddenly forgetting that this may be complete rubbish. The reef in question had taken more than her fair share of victims over time. Few would even dare to attempt lest they wind up at the bottom of the sea.

"Aye," grinned Payton. "How dat be so," pondered the Spaniard. "That's just it. I have no idea, but here we are then," Daniel said with a stunned surprise. "If'n dat be true, dat's incredible. By da way. How did ya do it," Pedro asked. "Once again; I have no idea, but here we are, but that's neither here nor there. He's got what I've got and it'll make things easier on me," Payton said weaving his tale. "So dat still doe'n't tell me ha you got em 'ere senor," Pedro remarked.

"Well I was in the market for some new transportation; albeit shoddy at best, I wanted to get him and the ship away from his old master. So, I hired him to take me to a neighboring island. It was past the bay and across a nasty channel and I praised his ability. He took quickly to the praise, so I challenged him with another dangerous area. Again he rose to the challenge. Every challenge grew more treacherous and he kept proving his prowess, reef by reef, until we were far enough away. Next thing I knew we were close to here and in desperate need of grog," Payton beamed. "I suggested that we stop and he was concerned over his old master becoming irate with him. I told him that there was no need to worry as his old master was about to be arrested for nefarious infractions against the crown. I really just took a shot in the dark on that one, but I guess I struck a mark as he simply smiled and said that it was about time."

"Eh, so'n what ya intend ta do wit him Capt'n" questioned the Spaniard. "Live the life of adventure," the captain slyly grinned. "Si," he returned laughing. "Ole sea dogs, dey never dies! But won' he wan ta be getting a back? I mean e'vn if'n da ole capt'n be gone?" "You might think so ole chap, but his old captain was as you'd say, 'el Diablo,'" Daniel said emphasizing the nickname. "He was in terrible servitude there. Besides, how can ye resist me charm?"

Laughing a deeply knowing laugh, he turned to Marty, "Hola amigo! Don forget ta pray 'ery day. You're gonna ta need da help," Pedro exclaimed still laughing.

They walked up the dock together. Pedro leaned in to Marty and spoke softly, "Nice ta see da capt'n still can't remember da name." "So that's nothing new then eh," quizzed the navy man. "New," laughed Pedro "Da capt'n, He call me ery name in ta mighty Lord's creation during mi time wit him." Pedro turned to Payton, "I'd meet ya at El Durante's later. Outta da earshot of all dese folk," Pedro said slyly. "Aye mate! Thanks again for the dockage," Payton shrugged as they left the pier.

The two walked through the town square where all types of merchants and characters were about. Sarika was perched upon Martin's shoulder taking in the sights unsure of this new world that was unfolding before his eyes. For a jungle bird, this was mass chaos.

Martin had a thought swirling through his head, though he was unsure if he should ask it. "He said that he was your former Quartermaster. Why is he no longer," Martin finally asked. "People come and people go. I hold no man to a job unless we are on a mission. Once all business is complete any man on my crew is free to do what he pleases. Be that stay in service or depart," the captain said in a diplomatic voice. "Honestly," the perplexed Englishman inquired. "How do you maintain control," pried the curious man. "Especially over a Spaniard?"

The captain just smiled a devious smile that scared Martin to the bone. "*The rules*" Payton said devilishly. "I told you," Payton returned to professionalism, "every man has a voice and every voice a vote. Just make sure you *follow* the rules," the smile returned, "and all will be well. Now as fer yer dislike of Spaniards you'll have ta let that go mate. I know it'll be hard as that's so engrained in you since birth, but I'll let you keep yer distrust… till they take the oath." Martin never considered that his new mission might require him to expand his horizons to the point that he'd partner up with life long enemies. Other than pirates that is. He pondered the thought and decided to trust his new captain.

They strolled upon a tavern, the El Durante. It was a typical ramshackle, all wood construction, tavern full of shady characters. Smoke and voices filled the air. A busty Spanish bar maid busied herself pouring and serving beverages to greedy patrons. Several men sang some whaling songs; while a small fight in an opposite corner went on, with no one else concerned. There in yet another opposite corner they found an empty table only a few feet from the bar. Daniel and Martin sat perusing the crowd as an unkempt, overweight barmaid approached them. Her straw-like hair gave her the appearance of a witch that frightened Martin into wondering what manner of people these were. Obviously they were not the God-fearing folk that made up his original life. Nay, these were different people that he had made a life of avoiding. The barmaid placed an ale in front of each man without a word and simply squeezed between them and the bar and walked away. The two men turned to each other and only shrugged in amazement. Payton grabbed the mug, but cautiously. He had perfected, over his career, a way of appearing to take a swig from a glass while waiting for someone else in his party to do so first. Caution had been his salvation on more than one occasion, as a few dispensable men met their poisoned end. These results had made this action become habit. Nonchalantly he waited to drink until well after Martin had his first couple of swigs. Showing no signs of distress Payton assumed that Martin's drink was indeed safe. Waiting for Martin to place his mug on the table, Payton used the fight to distract Martin's attention. "Bloody pirates," he said mockingly as he nodded toward the fight. Martin automatically turned to see what the reference was towards. As his head was turned Daniel quickly switched their mugs. The noise and ambiance of the tavern distracted Finny to the point that he didn't notice the suddenly full mug in his possession.

"I'm curious Captain," Finny spoke up. "Why didn't you

tell Pedro that I'm a Sai..."? Martin was cut off by Payton speaking loudly, "A sarcastic wit!" Surprised, Martin again tried, "A s..." And again he was cut off by Payton who was starting to look perturbed, "A pest!" The captain leaned in to him and spoke quietly, "Now look here you daft fool. I told you to follow my lead didn't I?" "Of course," Martin replied. "Then shut yer bloody trap," Payton said between clenched teeth! Speaking as quietly as possible under the noise of the tavern yet still able for Martin to hear; "If anyone here had knowledge that you were a." He paused to ensure that he was not being overheard, "well, a what you are, they'd either kidnap you, or slit yer throat for yer... 'tools!' Capeash?"

Suddenly Martin realized that his talents and navigational tools were well sought after in certain areas and by certain types of individuals, Martin was quick to comply. "Oh! But he was yer old mate."

"Trust in yourself matie, not your former crew," Daniel warned. "Once a pirate, always a pirate. Only trouble is that once they're not in yer service the pirate in them may feed their imagination," Payton glared. "Their imagination," Finny asked cautiously. "Aye, like they may think they can slice yer throat and take your fortune," Payton answered. "Even old friends," Martin asked with growing concern in his present situation. Darkly, cautiously Payton scanned around then glared into his eyes. "Especially old friends, as they know yer trends! Aye, trust in yerself mate! When they come back under yer command and take the oath, then and only then, can the trust bar again be lowered," Payton said. "Till then treat everyone as a possible threat."

Suddenly they were interrupted by the barmaid. "Aye Capt," she said flirtatiously. "How long has it been?" She was a seductive woman of Spanish descent whose obvious physical charms could be perceived even by a blind man. She was perched in the corner of the bar with her back to the rest of the patrons. Her brown eyes transfixed upon the well-traveled sailor. Puzzled by the question Payton sauntered to the bar, "Well now that's a personal question. Don't cha think?"

"That's not what I meant Senor! When was the last time my eyes have rested upon you?" she said slyly. "Ah, being about three years now I reckon my dear Alexis," Payton said. Martin approached the bar in amazement that he not only knew this woman, but also knew her name. Not to mention the fact that she actually seemed enthralled with him! The two continued to make small talk while over her shoulder many patrons were starting to realize that they were being ignored. Martin saw this and began to indicate that his mug was bare and in need of a refill as well. "Three years. Where have you been," she smiled, completely ignoring Martin.

Payton sat back on a stool, mug in one hand and the other arm outstretched and gesturing, "I've sailed the waters of the world my dear. Sang the songs of the emerald seas. Danced under the stars on the beaches, wishing your beauty were more present than memory," Payton flirted back. Martin continued to attempt to gain her gaze from Daniel to refill his mug, but was met with the same results. "Aye Capt.," she gushed. "You always knew the sweet words that make my heart sing." "Well my sweet senorita I'll be in port for a night," Daniel said boldly. Still Martin persisted vying to gain her attention. "Um, please, I'm really thirsty here." He wanted to break them up for several reasons. The most obvious one being that he didn't want a fight to break out with them in it. But his pride tried to break them up because she was far too beautiful for this scallywag he thought.

As Martin persisted, she continued to ignore him, "Well Senor Payton, I just may have to make your…" Boldly Martin finally interrupted the conversation, "Can I *please* have another drink my good lass." Suddenly she snapped back to reality realizing that half the bar was clamoring for a refresher. "Si, I get you one immediately." Slowly Payton turned angrily to Marty, his eyes wide open and speaking as sarcastically as possible, "*Can I Please Have Another Drink!* Are you kidding me man," waving his hands in front of Martin's eyes. Are these made of glass? Are they fogged?"

Martin pretended to be quite sorrowful replied, "Sorry Captain; however the entire tavern is about to have your neck if you hadn't let her back." Payton eased his eyes around and before him a sea of angry faces sat murmuring at him. "Aye, sometimes I forget myself. Next time perhaps you should do something that gets their attention to you." Annoyed Martin queried, "Such as?" "I don't know sing a song. Juggle a trio of ferrets. Light your hair on fire. I don't care," the perturbed sea captain spat. "Well if I sing or try to juggle they'll definitely light me hair on fire," joked Finny. "Fabulous! Then we have an agreement," mused Payton. "But," the surprised man started, but was cut off.

"Ah Mr. Santangello," Payton garbled rather incoherently at Pedro's entrance! Santiago joined them and they made their way back to the table tucked away in the corner. "I only 'ave da few moment til I 'ave ta get bak. Now ole friend, wha' can I really do fer ya?" "We're in need of supplies, and good fortune," the captain said. "Supplies I kin do. Fortune, she'd supplies by da gods," the Spaniard said. "Aye, but fortune is also where you make it, and take it," the captain said. "Where ya be a headn' sir," Pedro solicited. Payton eyed the room before speaking, "In search of," he paused, "*the Scavenger.*"

Stroking his chin, "Well Lady Fortune, she be a smiling on da good Captain af'er all." Pondering this possible turn of events, "Aye," questioned Payton. "Aye," replied his old mate. Santiago taking a cue from Payton shifted his eyes back and forth to be sure no one was listening in. "She sail out da Port Capulco bout a week past. She was a heading ta da Port of 'Lizbet. Fishers dat be refittin' in port was jus' a talkin' bout dat, 'bout a day past. Dey say dat she'd done bus'ness der and was headin' home wit fresh supply."

"The Port Elizabeth," Martin said stunned! "Ju know it senor," questioned Payton. "Intimately." Martin said with a smile. "Dat be more good fortune for da capt'n," Pedro told Martin. Martin smiled a mischievous smile, "Aye!" "Tell me capt'n wha be ta booty," Pedro questioned. "Revenge," he said coldly then paused, "and a glorious new ship, fer me," he finished with a smile. "Revenge sir? Wha' she do ta ya," Pedro asked surprised. "Well lets just say that there's a helping hand behind all this. The revenge is for them, the ship is for me," Payton answered.

Pedro nodded and pondered this a moment before speaking up. "I be part da yer crew," inquired his former mate. "You're a respectable man now Honcho," Payton said flatly. Quickly he became devilish, "Can ye sail under the Jolly Roger again?" Pedro laughed a hearty laugh. "Ressiptable 's far ta Royal Navy. Wha' ju used ta call dem?" Trying to wave him off, "Nothing ole chap. Nothing," Payton said. Martin raised an eyebrow to this more than probable insult. "How ju say it mon? Um, uh, I kno dat s was somthin' like loofta. No dat's not it," he questioned. He continued to ponder the jab.

Martin now thoroughly insulted sat, arms folded grimacing back at them. Santiago didn't have to say the actual word, but he knew that is was meant in a derogatory fashion. Payton smiled and shrugged his shoulders towards Martin as if to say 'oh well. It is what is.' "We sail at dawn," he commanded. "I be on da ship," again asked Pedro? "You must make up your own mind my friend. However, I could use my best Quartermaster at my side mate," Payton said leaving the decision up to Pedro.

He didn't need time to think about his decision. "Goo ta be back un'er ya capt'n!" Payton sat, eyes shifting side to side. "Uh, ya might want to rephrase that chap," Payton said awkwardly. Suddenly understanding how he could have been misunderstood, "Oh, Si! I mean, it's goo ta be back in yer service!" "Aye," Payton said nodding his head knowingly. "Good to have you back my friend. Jolly good indeed!"

Tequila At Sunrise Makes A Head Spin

Dawn broke as the sun began to peak out above the horizon. Daniel lay passed out in the tall island grasses near the ship. Meanwhile Martin, though conscious, was woozy from the tequila. Pedro came bounding around the corner all ready for his next adventure.

"Ah yes, dat's ta ole capt'n I know," Pedro mused. "Wha' happen wit Alexis," he mused. Groggily, Martin rose off his back to his elbows. His head bobbled while his vision circled like buzzards eyeing their prey. "Bloody hell. How should I know? I lost track of everything and... where is the captain?"

Pedro failed to hold back the laugh, "E's righ' o'er dere." Martin turned his head in the direction towards the captain, bobbed his head then turned it the opposite way. With that extra motion in his cranium, the Englishman could no longer hold it down. He spewed the entire contents of his belly all around him. "Dat's unpleasant senor... but it dos' make ju more of a man fer da crew." When he finished, Finny looked back at the captain. "We'll at least he didn't fare too well last night either." "I woun't be so certain 'bout dat senor. Da capt'n, he be a wily one eh." The Englishman looked back over his shoulder at the passed out pirate and wondered what that meant. As he turned his head back the Spaniard read his mind. "Ju be tinkin' dat he's not dat special eh? Ju gonna hav' ta understand dat he can do unbelievable tings... ev'n when pissed drunk. Ju'll learn eh! Jus ju watch im eh!" Martin looked back at the pirate as his mind began to wander as his eyes circled unable to focus on their target.

The captain lay strewn out snoring away, blissfully unaware of the proceedings. A little monkey sat grabbing his nose playfully squeezing it, like he was honking a horn.

"Ja. Keep squeezing dat little guy. He jus mi' wake up," joked Pedro. Martin regained semi-consciousness holding his head, still feeling woozy and groggy, "Why the blazes did I drink all that?" "Cause ju on da crash course ta be'ng da part ta capt'n Payton's crew. Jus like I said," Santiago warned.

The monkey still sat honking Payton's nose as he dozed merrily. "Honk, honk, squeeze the schnoz," Sarika commented, perched in a tree overlooking the situation. The monkey looked up and let out a frightening screech, swatting up towards the parrot. "Hey! Hey! What'd I say," the parrot questioned.

Martin still lay scratching at his head looking upon the scene unfolding before his eyes. The birds squawking fully awakened Martin. "Good Lord, my head is killing me." "Ja bet'er get use ta it. Dere's gonna be more a-comin'," Pedro prophesied. "Water. I need water," Martin decided. "Parched, parched, master's hung-over," Sarika offered. "Quiet you," Martin scowled at the bird.

The monkey had returned to grabbing Payton's nose. The excitement had agitated the little monkey began jumping up and down on the pirate's chest while maintaining a vise grip on the nose.

"Da capt'n find h'self a lil' friend," Pedro mused to himself. "Seriously, I need water," Martin said flatly. Pedro handed Martin a flask of water with a half smile. "Many thanks," Martin graciously offered as he finished the bottle quickly. He wiped his mouth clean and stumbled to his feet. Getting light headed he bent over in an attempt to gain his equilibrium. He shook out the fogginess and tried to stand tall again. Unfortunately the blood hadn't fully gotten back to full strength in his head causing him to fall backward in the sand.

"Master, master, fall flat on his ass-tor," Sarika mused. "Dat's my kin-a bird," Pedro said to himself with a chuckle. Seeing that Martin needed extra assistance he offered him a hand. "Thanks mate," Martin said reaching for the outstretched hand. Pedro pulled him to his feet trying to help balance him out. "Ju okay mon?" "Yes... I think so," Martin said almost questioning himself. He took a few moments then decided to sit back down a moment. He looked around and wondered to himself if he truly was up to this lifestyle. After collecting himself he looked up towards Pedro, "Now what say we wake the good captain?"

"Aye, ja ev'r awaken ta man," Pedro inquired. "No, why," Martin said standing up brushing himself off. Payton was still laying unconscious. The other men still had their backs to him and the monkey. The monkey had calmed down, but was still honking Payton's nose. In addition, he began pulling on Daniel's facial hair, but that wouldn't be the end.

"Here be yer firs lesson eh. Remember wha I tole ju 'bout da capt'n? How he can be amazing? Dis one time," Pedro started, "we was at sea. Da capt'n, he be a sleepin' on da stern rail when dis crewman, he try ta wake up ta capt'n. Capt. Grabbed da mans own dagger, slit his throat, re-sheathed da blade, push him back, fol'ed his arm ana never ev'n open his eye. Dat's a man who like his sleep."

Martin stood stunned in amazement not knowing whether or not to believe him. "Aye," he said. "Now, you s'ill be a wan'ing ta wake him," Pedro asked coyly.

The monkey had started pulling on Payton's cheeks, inadvertently making funny faces with them. All the while the two continued speaking as this continued on behind them. Chuckling, the monkey was surprised by the fun he was having.

"Um, noooo," Martin offered. "I think we should just let the good man sleep." He paused briefly then offered flatly, "Really, he never even opened his eyes," he said half believing, half asking.

"Aye, senor. Dis o'er time we was on dis i'land an a bat came a flyin' round. Da capt'n rolled o'er wit out a lookin', he shot da bat out de air." Having not yet tired of his fun, the monkey jumped up and down on slumbering pirate's chest.

"He say dat it were makin' too much noise," Pedro continued. "The bat was making excessive noise," Martin asked. "What kind of bat makes excessive noise?" "None," Pedro said matter-of-factly. "Okay... I see your point sir. I vote for us to be very quite then," Martin replied.

Payton opened his eyes and looked around trying to gain his bearings. Suddenly he jumped up staggering and struggled to regain himself similar to Finny, but without the fall. Quickly, he stood tall but within moments he started to stagger again. When he finally stood erect it finally dawned on him that something was different about him. He wasn't quite certain, yet he was sure that there was something amiss. His eyes focused on his nose. His gaze transfixed on a little claw that was holding on for dear life. The little monkey swayed back and forth smiling up at Payton. The captain swatted the little critter off his nose, which hit the ground running until he disappeared up a palm tree. The captain rubbed his nose with his rough fingers as he crossed his eyes trying to assess the situation.

"I'd hate to see the dark side of him," Martin said coldly. "Si, da capt'n ain't one ta mess wit," Santiago returned.

Satisfied that his nose was fine, Payton brushed himself off, suddenly finding an article of Alexis' clothing stuck to him. He removed it, inspected it, sniffed it and with a smile tucked it away in a pocket as a memento.

"So let's agree that we shouldn't disturb him then," Martin vowed. Payton silently walked up behind the two of them listening intently. "Aye," Pedro returned. Payton slapped them both on the back, "Aye!" Shocked, they both screamed like little schoolgirls, "AAAH!" "Ya blokes ready," Payton inquired completely unaware of the conversation that had just transpired. "Tis a exciting day ta be alive!" "Yes sir… quite a day indeed," Martin mumbled still stunned. "How do you feel captain?" "With my hands typically. Except last night I… well never mind. What's to eat around this place Paco," Payton questioned? "Senor, we c'n grab a bite at Martina's casa," Pedro replied.

Of course who Martina was didn't matter to Payton just as long as she was providing sustenance. "Fabulous! Lead the way, lead the way," Payton commanded smiling. The Spaniard lead the trio down a sandy path where the windblown long brown and green grasses would obstruct the sandy clearing. They ventured past several homes where children played and wild chickens roamed free. They finally came up to a bustling shanty. Several men were going in as others passed as they exited. Martin was unsure what to make of this. "Mr. Santiago, what is this place?" "Is wha' I said. Is Martina's casa amigo," he replied. Martin was not satisfied with this basic response. "Granted, however that doesn't explain why all these people are coming and going from this woman's, Martina's, home."

"Si, jes it does honcho. She's a won'erful senora. 'Dey say she's 'bout 120 jears ole. She cook every morning for da fishermen. She always come down ta da dock and bring me food. She give us a good meal for da trip," Pedro exclaimed.

Martin whispered to Sarika, "You probably shouldn't come in with us mate." He looked around a bit and noticed some trees. Why don't you hide out up there and find some food for yourself. I'm afraid that if you come in with us that you might become part of the main

course. These don't seem to be discerning people."
Sarika nodded, "Yes, yes, I'll watch from the trees."
With that he spread his large wings and launched himself
into the air scouting out the terrain. He came to rest in a
tree where he fed upon the vegetation.

Pedro stepped on the wooden stoop, which creaked under
the weight of his footfall. The house was a simple small
open dwelling. Wooden shutters that were only half
attached at this point were retracted revealing glassless
windows. It was a solitary room that contained only a
few items. A makeshift bed butted up in one corner. On it
sat a thick Spanish version of the Bible. Along the
opposite wall was a crude hand crafted table and chair
and various bottles of spices rested on a shelf above it. A
straw broom was leaning in another corner waiting for
the crowd to dissipate before being called upon to do its
daily work. The table was decked out with metallic
platters upon which sat a pile of scrambled eggs, roasted
chicken, bananas and flatbread. The men who had
entered to dine had all brought their own makeshift plates
and most just ate with their fingers. Martin was disgusted
by the sight of the crudeness while it was old hat to
Pedro and Payton. Pedro spoke in a Spanish dialect to
Martina who greeted them with a large toothless smile.
She sat on a chair, rocking in it, though it was not a
rocking chair. She motioned to them to "*eeat, eeat!*"
Pedro nodded, smiled and thanked her in their tongue.
"Ju hold on eh," Pedro said as he turned and hustled out
the door. Payton and Martin just looked at each other and
smiled awkwardly in the silence. Payton turned to the
woman who sat smiling and nodding her head. Again she
motioned, "*eeat, eeat.*" Payton wasn't certain what to do

as his interpreter had left the building. He smiled back, "We eeat, eeat... sssoon... I hhhoope. I'm famished... fammmmishedddd." This didn't faze the elderly woman at all as she continued to rock and repeated, "*eeat, eeat.*" In a few moments Pedro returned with a few large cabbage-like leaves. "We juse dese as plates, eh senor?" Payton smiled taking one in his hand and promptly filled it with food. He dug his bare hands deep into the eggs and cradled them in the leaf, followed by chicken. His eyes darted across the small jars and motioned to Martina if he may try some of the various powders. "She say jess capt'n," Pedro informed him. With that he took a dash of one, several indiscriminate dashes of another and another pinch of yet another. He held the creation close to his face as he eyeballed the toppings. He decided that he needed a touch more of the first powder and with that he rolled up the leaf. Martin stood in disgust watching the proceedings, yet his growing hunger overcame his civility and decided to follow suit. Though he didn't make his as wildly as Payton's, he quickly filed his leaf. Payton showed off his breakfast concoction to Martina who just smiled and nodded her approval. "*Eeat, eeat*," she urged him. With that Payton tore into his food like a wolf that just took down an elk. Pedro eyed the captain, "Senor, ju wern't sapposed ta eat da leaf." Payton suddenly looked concerned, "It's not dangerous is it?" "No. Is jus not done," Santiago returned. Payton looked at the wrap with outstretched arms, then close, then far again. He looked at Pedro then back to the wrap. Shrugging his shoulders he took another bite, rolled the food around in his mouth, smiled and swallowed. "Why not," Payton inquired? "I dunno," Pedro started. "It jus taint." Payton shrugged, "It's just another breakfast burrito Pasquale. And it's delicious." Pedro looked at his, rolled it up and sampled the mix. "Dat's not bad capt'n. Bu' wha's a bressfast burrito?"

Martin didn't follow along and just devoured the bulk of his food off the leaf. Slyly, he stashed some away for a friend. When the men were finished they all thanked Martina who continued to rock in the stable chair, "*Eeat, eeat.*" Pedro leaned in with a half hug and whispered something quietly into her ear. As he spoke he slipped her a coin for all the food she had given him during his time on the island. She didn't understand why he had given her the trinket, nor did she understand what it was. But it was a gift from a friend, so she tucked it away for safekeeping. She smiled and waved as they left. They bade her farewell and made their exit. Martin confessed, "Well that was a lot better than I expected. Thank you Mr. Santiago." Payton agreed, "Wonderful woman. A bit chatty though eh? Couldn't get a word in." "Si," Pedro said in amused agreement. "Bu' I sill wanna know. Wha's a bressfast burrito?" Payton just looked over his shoulder and smiled, "It's going to be all the rage my friend. All the rage."

"Yes, that's all well and good, but why didn't we have to pay for our meal? Or give something in trade," Martin wondered aloud. Pedro smiled as he spoke. "Ju see, her husband, he was once da fisherman. He wen out dis one time. Da big blow came down upon him eh." "The big blow," Martin interrupted. "Hurricane mate," Payton interjected. "Das right. Da cane come an gifted his ship ta da deep blue. Da islanders all look out fer der fellow man and all come ta her and comfort her. Since den dey all bring her some fish ery day. Even when dey havn't enough fer demselves. Dey all make sur dat she taken care of. Since dat day she always make da bressfast fer dem. Never askin' fer anyting back." "That's one amazing tale Pedro. Yes, quite amazing indeed," Martin said softly.

As they strolled back to the ship Sarika swooped down and casually landed on Martin's shoulder. He whispered into Martin's ear, "Good, good was it good?" Martin smiled and produced some food from his pocket and hand fed his friend. "You tell me."

Place Yer Bets

The three person, one bird, crew made their way off the dock and quickly into open waters. They followed a path Martin plotted toward an island where he believed that some more of his former mates had taken up residence. Even though Martin had recently eaten, still the alcohol permeated his blood stream. The rolling seas had returned his level of nausea and poor equilibrium. "Just how much had I ingested," he thought to himself? "I must remain focused. If that man is as evil as the Spaniard has suggested, I shudder to wonder what he may do if I fail my task!" Martin's fear helped to sober his thinking, if not his nausea. "AYE," the captain shouted in his ear while slapping his ill feeling mate on the back. "What did you say was our heading?"

"I didn't sir," Martin shuddered. Payton sensed that Martin truly feared him and his intoxication amused him. He used all that he could to make himself look even more frightening than usual. "Well pretend ye did. Where are we heading?" The wild-eyed captain was right in his face causing Martin to recoil in fright. "Well sir, as long as we remain inconspicuous we should be able to pick up some crew in Cayo Longo. I believe there are a few old mates there," Martin offered as he caught his breath.

"I have no mates there. Well at least that I'm aware of," Payton replied. "No sir, my mates," Martin gave back. "Your dates? No, I don't like dates, thank you," Payton pondered stepping away from the man. "Dates? Oh you mean the fruit," Martin asked, his fright subsided. "You have fruit," Payton questioned inquisitively. Payton forgot about trying to scare him as he was sidetracked onto the trail of food. "No sir," Martin relayed flatly. "Then why did you bring it up," Daniel wondered. "I didn't," Martin said mildly irritated. "You brought up fruit. Then you gadded about saying that you had fruit, and now I'm desiring of some fruit," Payton said looking around the boat. "You do this all the time! Get my hopes up just fer yer jollies eh!" "Senor Payton, dat Cayo Longo shou' ave some fruit," Pedro injected. "Aye! Good thinking ole chap! We'll head then to Cayo Longo," Payton said turning to Martin. "Now why didn't you think of that," Payton said walking to the bow. "Make our heading towards Cayo Longo Zippy." Pedro turned to Martin, "Now dats how it a done senor." "Aye captain… Cayo Longo," Martin repeated the order. "Wish I would have thought of that myself," he said under his breath, not sure if he was toying with him or not.

They continued to sail through the rolling seas causing Martin's nausea to intensify. The contents of his stomach rolled around and sloshed deep within him. Occasionally he would experience a verp. A vomit burp, one of those nasty moments when the gas in his stomach caused him to burp bringing up a touch of vomit along with it. The awful taste in his mouth didn't help his condition at all. He tried to hold out as best he could. Occasionally a larger wave would hit the hull and salty sea spray covered his red, sun-baked face. The first spray that came upon him caused Sarika to leave his perch on Martin's shoulder and go below deck. Martin tried to hold off vomiting and it seemed that he was winning the battle, until a rouge wave hit the ship. His stomach shuddered and he had another verp, buckling him over. The spray covered him and now he felt sticky both inside and out. He tried valiantly to stand erect when another rouge wave slammed into them turning the ship slightly.

"Martoni," yelled the captain. "Right the ship. Hold the course sir!" The captain had intensified the directness of the orders because he knew that Martin was not feeling well. "Dat man. He's not lookin' too good," Pedro noted. The two of them were at the bow looking back at him. "How much longer till he blows," Payton asked. Pedro looked back at Martin who was looking green from the nausea. "I giv' 'em 'bout five minutes." Payton looked at Martin, "I'll take that action. I give him less than five. What say you to five shillings?" "Dat's goo' fer me," Pedro answered.

Martin held the wheel in a half hunched position

desperately trying to hold himself together. "Come on old man, let it fly," the captain urged. "No, no! Hol' on amigo," Pedro countered. "Come on wave. Come on wave!" "Ju can do it senor. Jus 'bout four more minute ta go." Another wave hit the ship and Martin doubled over yet again. "Yes, here it comes," the excited sea captain announced! "NO, NO. Hol' out," Pedro countered! "DAMMIT Melvin! Hold yer bloody course," the captain shouted at him! "Dat's no fair," Pedro whispered to him. "Yer gonna scare him ta blow." Payton coyly smiled as he denied the claim. Martin held himself together and stood tall once again. "Damn," Payton said at seeing this. Pedro laughed, "Dat five shilling, gonna be mine! Jus' hol' on!"

The seas were still rolling with eight-foot waves and their eyes were transfixed upon Martin. "Bloody seas. Give me something I can work with! Come on! Rock this stupid sorry excuse for a ship," the disgruntled captain commanded. "Senor, dis ding can no witstand much more den wha' she's already taken," Pedro advised suddenly concerned. He knew that the captain didn't like to lose a bet even if it meant that the ship capsized in the process. But he felt obliged to agitate the beehive a bit more.

"Time's a runnin' out capt'n!" "Quiet you! It's not over yet. Come on, come on, come on," he urged. The seas obliged his repeated requests and sent a wave crashing over the stern. Martin was drenched and tossed about. Though he held fast to the wheel his feet slipped out. Regaining his footing he wobbled and could no longer hold the contents of his stomach down. He stumbled to the rail and grasped on for dear life. "Come on Milton!

Come on! Let it fly," urged the captain. "NO, NO," shouted Pedro! "Don' do it senor!" "It's ok Mallory! Let it go," Payton also shouted. Martin heard the shouts but didn't let it faze him as he focused on the rolling and swirling seas underneath him. His eyes and nose watered and his head began to spin. A dull headache was forming as sweat began to pour down his skin. The twirling waters unbalanced him and he could no longer hold out. He violently erupted much to the delight of the captain. "YES! YES! YES! Way to go old chap!" He slapped Pedro on the back just as he reached deep into his pocket. "Ere," Pedro said shaking hands with Payton, the coins in his palm. "Nice doing business with you my friend!" Martin looked over at them, "You know someone could offer me a hand here." "Eech, no tanks senor," Pedro replied. "Alrighty mate. Since you won me five shillings, I'll take the wheel for a bit." He eyed him up and down, "Clean yourself up mate. Have a little self respect," Payton said in commanding voice yet full of sarcasm. Martin still leaned on the rail. "Five shillings? You two bet on me?" "Of course," Payton replied. "What else do you suggest we are to do while you're in the condition you're in," the captain questioned. Martin didn't reply still sprawled on the rail. He turned his head back over the edge and let more vomit fly. This made Payton smile. "Just make sure that you're not getting that on the side of the ole girl, eh mate?"

Part 4: Forming Of The Brethren

New Places, Old Faces

They made their way to the island and easily docked. Pedro quickly made the connection with the harbormaster knowing the lingo of the trade. The trio made their way through the big seaport. Martin was feeling better now that he was on stable land and had no food in his stomach. Sarika sat again on his shoulder and looked in wonder at the sights of yet another new destination. The hustle and bustle was a bit unnerving to the bird as he sat wide-eyed in fascination. In the town square a local entertainer had his audience in awe as he juggled knives and told jokes. This was a big time seaport complete with a slew of street vendors that were busily exchanging goods. The trio stopped to watch the show while looking as inconspicuous as possible.

The juggler enraptured his captive audience, "This is quite a difficult trick," he said as his three blades were twirling. "As I attempt to close my eyes and not stick myself with a razor sharp blade." The audience, mostly women and children gasped, "I'm going to close my eyes now." Still juggling and making this a joke, "I'm planning on closing my eyes now." He paused for effect. "No really, I'd appreciate quiet." The marketplace was still buzzing with activity all around them. "Ok, no really, I'd appreciate some quiet," the blades still going. "No? Ok then. If I should die be it on yer heads!" The audience laughed a palpably nervous laugh. He paused his well-rehearsed speech a moment for effect. "I mean it's really difficult to do with all this noise. I'm not joking! This is my job!" There were people still murmuring and the juggler stopped, catching all three blades. The audience started to modestly applaud unsure if he was finished. "That's not the trick," he exclaimed. "I honestly need silence. The audience chuckled as he again began to twirl the blades. Despite his mock requests for silence, the crowd continued to speak in hushed tones. Again he stopped and this time placed his hands on his hips. Sarcastically he scolded the crowd, drawing out certain words and enunciating others for comedic effect. "Fine! Ignore me. Just keep on rambling *on and on*. My personal safety is of *no* concern to you. *That's fine*. Just keep *on* with what you're discussing. I can wait. I can wait." He started taping his foot in the dust and looking toward the heavens. A few people from the crowd urged him to continue, but he continued to ignore them. Finally they became silent. Sarcastically he looked back at them, "Oh ok? Are we all ready then? Can you all remain quiet?" The crowd agreed in unison. "I thought you were going to be quiet," mocked the juggler. The crowd laughed and he began to twirl the blades again.

"Ok, I need you to count back from three." The eager crowd obliged and began the count back. Three...two... "**WAIT**," the juggler shouted as he stopped juggling again! "Didn't you agree to be silent?" The confused crowd laughed. "Ok, ok, ok I'm just kidding then. Now remember that this is extremely difficult and I'm going to need your assistance. Ready? Ok." He began juggling again, "Ok, I need you to count back from three." The crowd again began to count back, "three, two." Again the juggler shouted, "**WAIT!** Didn't you hear me when I said that it's extremely difficult to do this? Here you are counting down to my doom! What kind of people are you?" his hands on his hips, blades in hand again. The crowd laughed its approval. "Ok, I guess it's time. No more of this silliness," as he started juggling again. "Everyone, back from five." They count back five, four, three, two, one! "Hey you folks are pretty bright. I did this on Cape Rendu and they didn't know what came after five," the juggler joked. This brings a big roar from crowd at the joke against a rival seaport.

"Ok, ok, ok. No more jokes. Here we go," as he started twirling the blades again. "And a one and a two and a, hey did I ever tell you about..." The crowd cut him off with a groan. "Ok, ok, ok. Seriously this time. No more jokes. Here we go," again he started twirling the blades. "This time, this is it! No nonsense and it's gonna be fantastic. I assure you! The kind of thing to write to lost loved ones about. Wow, what a spectacle it is going to be. It's just un-bloody-believable isn't it my good folks? I mean really, just amazing. Fantastic. Incredible!" Again the crowd started to grumble causing him to stop again putting his hands on his hips taking a now standard pose. "Well now, if you're just going to sit there and grumble maybe I just won't do me little trick." The crowd was split. Half groaned and half applauded. The juggler looked around in mock amazement, "Well that's just buttons! Maybe your half should just bugger off! I mean really! Here I go to all the time and trouble to twirl me little razor sharp blades. Almost certainly assuring you of seeing me, the modest juggler, come to some horrifically bloody misfortune; and all you can do is groan. Well I'll be!" He paused a moment then cracked a half smile, "Naw, I'm just funnin' you good folk. These things aren't even sharp. See." He tossed an orange in the air and sliced it clean through with one swift stroke. In mock amazement he stood wide-eyed, "Bloody hell! Who switched my blades? Bloke can get down right hurt with something like this! No-no-no, this won't do." He looked around a bit. "Anyone see the dull ones laying around?" No one spoke up only laughed. "Ok, I guess I really better be serious this time, eh?"

He started to twirl the razor sharp blades once again. "One more time everyone. Back from five all. Nice and loud then. Here we go." The anxious crowd, now knowing how deadly the blades really were eagerly obliged him. "Five, four, three, two, one." He kept juggling in the same way as he had been. "Wow, I told you that it'd be impressive eh!" This brings out a small laugh. "No? Ok, how about now?" He closes one eye. The crowd laughed more. "Huh? I told you it'd be great. Now, watch this." He alternated eyes; one open one closed, back and forth. A few people clapped their amusement. "And now for the next big trick." He exaggerated his facial features as he continued still switching his eyes, which brought out a bigger laugh. "No, ok? How about this?" He closed both of his eyes twirling the blades. This brought about his first real applause until he misjudged a catch as the blade came down and sliced into his hand. Screams of terror shot out as blood poured out of his clenched hand. "AAAAGH," he screamed dropping to his knees! The crowd watched in terror as he suddenly stopped, looked up and smiled. "Got 'cha," he giggled. The prop had been a fake that he rigged up with a red liquid inside the blade, designed to spurt open when hit in a certain spot. The juggler laughed as he got to his feet. "See, I'm ok. However, this is exactly why I need quiet." The relieved crowd exhaled a heavy breath and the tension left the air. They gathered around again as he grabbed the real blades and continued the show.

The juggler picked up where he left off. First he began with one eye closed at a time, followed by both. This time he went one step further, pulling out two more previously concealed blades and now juggled five razor sharp daggers as his eyes remain closed. "Impressed yet," he asked knowing the answer. The crowd roared its approval and applauded wildly. "Really? You sure," he asked in mock amazement. "Well then how about this," he sped up the pace and in rhythm grabbed something from his pocket? He quickly threw it into his mouth and then blew a gigantic fireball out of his mouth. This again gained ravenous applause. Faster and faster he twirled the blades and spun himself in circles in the process. One by one he caught them and tucked them under his right arm. Then with his left extended out, hand open, "TA-DA!" The crowd wildly cheered their approval. Bowing to the cheers, his hand still open palm side up, a blade fell from the sky and landed flat in his hand. This elicited a roar and more monstrous applause from the crowd. He stood tall, looking shocked as it was a cutlass he was holding; whereas he was only juggling daggers, "Now where in blazes did that come from?" The crowd continued their roar and dropped coins into his sack while continuing to applaud him. Still, the juggler pondered in earnest where the sixth blade came from.

The happy crowd began to disperse talking about what they just witnessed. The juggler still looked at the cutlass in his hand in amazement. His mind ran wild with wonderment. Suddenly a voice from what remained of the crowd jostled the juggler.

"The fire is a new bit eh mate?" He shook off his shock. "Why captain Payton! How long has it been," the juggler asked. "Just last night. Bar wench, why? And why in blazes do people keep asking me that," Payton wondered. "No captain. The last time we saw each other," he replied. "Oh! That. I don't quite remember," Payton responded. "But I'd wager a guess that it was about the last time we saw each other." "I thought you said you didn't know anyone in this place," Martin said flatly. "People move about don't they? I mean only yesterday you weren't here either, and now here you are," the captain returned. "Explain that!" "Got ya der senor," Pedro added. "How ju been Senor Bertrand," Pedro asked the juggler. The juggler, John Bertrand was also a former member of Payton's crew during Santiago's' tenure. "Well Pedro, as you can see I'm still alive and have all my fingers, so I guess that's something. Not too sure what, but something. Anyway, what you doing here sir," the still surprised juggler inquired. "Here to possibly pick you up old chap. Interested," the captain offered. Sarcastically Bertrand replied, "I've put on a little weight since the last we saw each other," the extremely thin man said. "I don't know if I'm in good enough shape. And besides, how do I leave all this behind? The life of an entertainer is *very profitable!* Why just last week I could actually afford to *pay* for me own food... well, once. 'Course I didn't... but I could have... had I been so inclined," he said with a smile. "Well then, if you're not interested…"

Bertrand cut Daniel off, "Course captain! Always excited about another adventure with you!" The two shook hands on their new agreement as smiles came all around. Martin suddenly interjected, "Aye Mr. Bertrand is it? Know of you anyone from *the Astonisher*" with an authoritative voice. "Aye, a few men who say they were crew are about," he offered cautiously sizing the stranger up. "Any ideas where then if you please," Martin interjected with more authority.

The juggler straightened up raising an eyebrow and very cautiously asked, "And who might be inquiring?" "Easy mate. This here is Mable Finnski. If you couldn't tell, he's new to the operation. However, he's ok," Payton interjected.

"Martin Finny," he corrected extending an open hand. "Sorry, I'm just very anxious to meet up with them. They're old mates of mine." "Well if the captain vouches for you then you're ok with me," Bertrand exclaimed shaking his hand. "Just outside the west side of the square. There's a lodging building with a boars head above the door. They stay there," he explained. Martin gratefully thanked him and turned to smile to Daniel, "I better be doing this on my own sir. I can probably get them easier than if they see all of us." "Godspeed William," the captain wished. Martin quickly exited the group on his way to recruit some old mates for the mission.

"Can he be trus'ed alone," Pedro asked with concern.

"No more so than anyone else," the captain relayed flatly. "E look li' a loofter ta me capt'n," was Pedro's response to that. "Aye, that's a popular thought," Daniel joked. "Dat Martin tis'int likin' dat comment ya know," Pedro injected. "A pirate needs to have a tough hyde," said the captain. "Like you Capt," the juggler asked with a smile. Mockingly Daniel replied, "No, more like Poncho here. I'm delicate. Like a daisy." This self-deprecation caused the guys to laugh and call him daisy. This was until Payton flashed them a horribly wicked scowl. Payton turned away and smiled again as the two stood motionless in fear. "Oh by the way Berti; can I have me cutlass back?" Bert look down and realized that he was still holding the phantom blade. "I shoulda known. Here ya go sir," he said handing it back with a smile. "That was a nice trick," he added. "Hell I'm just glad it didn't come down blade first," Payton replied. Suddenly realizing the damage that could have been done to his hand Bert chuckled nervously, "Aye." He had a newly found appreciation for just how special his hands were to him and how prophetic his little gag might have been.

Chance Meeting

Payton strolled through the marketplace observing the business being transacted and wondered why anyone would want to live life in this way. No matter he thought. He'd be back to doing what he lived to do soon enough. The thoughts continued until his concentration was suddenly shocked back into the moment.

"Oh no," a tiny voice yelled. "It can't be!" Daniel slowly turned, feeling deep down that he knew what was waiting for him. "How can it be," the voice asked. "Well, well, well. If it isn't my favorite munchkin, um, ah…," he paused racking his brain. "BARTHOLOMEW," the tiny voice interrupted Payton. "Why doesn't it surprise me that you wouldn't remember it," he spurned. "Well I wouldn't want to let you down. Fancy meeting you here." 'Yeah, great,' he thought to himself. 'Why of all places is he here? Oh yeah. The boat. Right. They're probably still looking for it. And me. Oh and,' he was suddenly cut off.

"Are you unconscious, or are you just ignoring me sir," Bart asked. "What," the suddenly puzzled captain wondered. "I asked if you were ready to go to my father or if you were going to put up a struggle," the little boy questioned, fists held high. "Ah," Daniel started. Patting him on the head, "Yeah, I think that I'll be heading off now. It was good to see you again young Bill." "Bart," he said. "And father whooped me quite severely after you took the boat again!" The pirate looked down at him, "How did he know you helped me? You didn't tell him did you?" "No sir, he was just angry and started hitting me. I lied and told him I knew nothing of it, but he didn't care. Later he said he was sorry and to make it up to me took me on this venture." The pirate smiled down at him, "Well, no sense in getting in even more trouble by talking to me now then eh? Off with you before he sees us."

Payton started to stroll off when he suddenly heard in a loud shrill voice. "FATHER! FATHER! COME QUICK! THE PIRATE!" "Oh bugger," Payton said and quickly slipped into the crowd concealing himself behind a merchant's stand. From his viewpoint he could see a guard coming to get Bartholomew and take him back to his father. Even though he protested as best a child could, he was quickly put into his place by his very proper English father who didn't even want to know what he was talking about. All of Bart's protests were squashed and he was taken away in silence. Payton wondered why the child was trying to turn him in. He thought that he must be trying to get into his father's good graces. Maybe then the unmerited punishments would end.

Once the governor had taken his son away, Payton found himself free to make his way out of his concealment. Suddenly he was overcome with the thought, "Hope that they don't see that piece of rubbish boat of his." He quickly increased his rate of travel. "Must find them or this is going to be difficult getting off this rock." He darted to and fro in the crowded bazaar trying to follow in the direction he believed they had traveled.

"That's him father," a high-pitched voice shouted. "Blast," the pirate thought, quickly ducking behind an extremely tall bystander. The bystander looked down upon him. "Pardon me sir! Might I be of assistance to you," he asked in protest. The hunched over pirate merely looked up, "Um no. I'm alright as is… just stretching. Thank you though," he tried to say as matter-of-factly as possible. This didn't appease the gangly man who started to back away. "Look here. I will not have you crouching down beside me like that!" The pirate captain remained in his crouch side stepping along with him. Whichever way the tall man went, Daniel followed with several mini shuffling steps. "Really, I'm not harming anyone. Just think of me as a shadow," Daniel tried to reason with him. "I will not," the lofty gent disapproved. "I'll have to alert the authorities if you refuse to cease your actions." Payton hoped that Bart had been taken away again so that he may not be arrested. "Fine," he said clearly as he stood up tall looking around for Bart. "I'll bid you good day sir," Payton said rather boldly as if he were the one bothered! After a few steps he quickly hunched down a bit making his way further in the crowd.

Payton finally happened upon a vantage point where he spied Bart and his father boarding their vessel. "Wonderful," Payton said to himself still filled with tension. Payton knew that he wasn't really safe until the boat was off. Too many times in his past he thought he was in the clear, only to find that at the last moment someone jumped off a departing ship. Things usually went from bad to worse for him whenever that happened. He remained as casual as possible watching the proceedings making certain that they were departing. Once the ship had made way he finally breathed a sigh of relief. "Good riddance. I haven't the time for these bloody distractions."

Why Not?

As Payton avoided the possible entanglement with Bartholomew's father, Martin busied himself at the Boar's Head Inn. After some pleasantries that old friends seeing each other for the first time in years would exchange, Martin got down to business.

"Gentlemen, I have a proposition for you. I have had the good fortune, well…" he paused to collect his thoughts. "Let's just say that for the time being, I have come to serve under a new captain. And although he cannot be trusted, nor do I quite know his full intentions. Nor do I know his full capabilities…" he wandered off in his own thoughts and sat silently for a bit. The group of men all peered in closer to draw his gaze. "Eh mate," one finally spoke up. "You all right sir," another chimed in. Martin shook off his blank stare. "Ah yes, I am truly sorry about that. I was just wondering why the hell I was doing this," Martin exclaimed. "What did you concur," the second man asked completely puzzled. Martin exhaled a heavy breath and spoke, "Well, even though a man claiming to be of sound mind, as I do, would hear my thoughts and say you've gone quite mad! No one could possibly be that foolish to do this, he'd say. And I agree. He'd be right. However, I still must do the opposite and ask you to consider joining us on our quest."

The men just sat in silence. Not a one could understand what Martin was talking about. So he clarified his thoughts, first in his own head, then he spoke with passion in hopes of inspiring the men to join him. He told the tale beginning with that dreadful day, days in solitude, and finally of how he came to be on the island and in the small rented out room with his former mates. Upon hearing the story they sat looking around at each other. Finally one man spoke up, "Uh sir? Are you feeling alright? You aren't making much sense." Martin again plead his case and promised them things he could not definitely ensure.

Slowly the men relented and agreed to his request, much to Martin's enjoyment. It was Martin's previous service with them that they remembered. He was a stout man, loyal to his captain, crew and king who would do anything for the men. It earned him the respect that convinced the men to join them. Upon hearing the news, Martin instructed them to meet at a later time to meet the rest of the men. Martin left them in good spirits to rendezvous with Payton and share the good news. Behind him the puzzled men sat in disbelief. They weren't sure of what to make of the story. Back and forth they conjectured everything from he had gone mad after the battle, to living in solitude and talking to parrots made him daft. Every now and then they came back to the possibility that he was telling the truth. "What if," was the thing that they said. "What if…" their former mates actually needed them? That was the only reason they agreed… "What if?" The very least they could do was to go have a look.

Pledging Revenge

In the evening the men had been instructed to gather at a predetermined spot where the meeting would take place. A few men had started a fire for light and it centered them all to the one spot. Already there were Martin and some of his former crewmates. None of which were of close relation to him, but all were still indebted to their former captain and crew. This zeal persuaded them to join the task even if they had previously pledged against piracy. A couple of other men had overheard Martin speaking with his former mates and volunteered their services. The island was a bustling seaport, but they were just poor sailors yearning for something more. Finding men to join a pirate ship in many ports wasn't that hard to do. It offered them possible quick wealth or the gallows. Either way, most reckoned that it was a better future than they currently faced.

Bertrand had also summoned the assistance of a few men he trusted to the meeting. A few had also previously sailed under Payton at various times. There were even a few escaped slaves that were welcomed as equals. The sly captain had been standing in the shadows watching the proceedings eying the men as they gathered. Each of them also kept a sharp eye on each other, as most of the men did not know one another. They weren't willing to freely mingle as it was not in their nature. When he was satisfied with what he witnessed, Payton strolled out of the shadows and climbed upon a stump. He looked around the group, put two fingers in his mouth and whistled so loud that everyone immediately was silenced.

"Aye gentlemen! I am Captain Daniel Payton. Some of you have previous experience under my direction and I welcome you back. Most of you have not. Rather, you've sailed under your royal majesty's flag. You sailed with honor and vigor, zest and zeal for your king and country. And for that you should be and are commended! What I am asking you to do this day is to disassociate yourself from that life in order to celebrate it. Only with your complete cooperation, assistance and *willful* participation can this mission meet a successful resolution. I ask you, can you, will you, under sound mind and *without* pain of duress sail under my command and follow my orders? Can you dismiss your previous allegiance to the crown, and gain your revenge on Admiral Brightside? Mind you, that this will require you to *go on account*, take up the Jolly Roger as your flag, accept being a member of the brethren of the coast; even if just temporarily, as well as take up all the codes of conduct and the consequences of the trade?" The men knew that if they went on account then they were liable for all consequences that befell pirates if they were captured. This was not an easily accepted concept for many whose entire life was lived in fear, honesty and respect for the crown. If they were captured and tried, they would most assuredly be convicted and sentenced to death. Shame would be brought to their families, those that still had them, and those family members would be made to suffer for their kin's transgressions.

"And what's in it for us," a random voice pushed. Coldly Payton shot back, "*Revenge!*" Most crew nodded their approval to that simple yet all-inclusive statement. "And what else," the man pressed on. "Your former captain and crew who fell that day may finally rest in peace. We shall sink *The Destroyer*, and," he paused for effect, "we commandeer *The Scavenger!* She's a fast ship, a relatively small ship, a perfect *pirate* ship! We can loot and plunder the entire Spanish Main and live like kings!"

This elicited a big roar from the crew, even those new to piracy, except for one lone voice. That same man again inquired, "So, we are just supposed to up and join then? Bloody well what for then? To follow the ramblings of a well known mad man? We're just supposed to up and follow a smelly, scurvy ridden, foul mouthed, indecent buffoon who…" His vocal lambasting was suddenly cut off as a dagger disguised as a lightening bolt pierced his throat dropping him stone dead. Blood poured from the wound and pooled around the man. The men standing next to the corpse were too afraid to move, so they stood fast in the crimson fluid.

"Oh, and there's one more thing," Payton began. "I do not tolerate being called indecent very well." The rest of the men stood completely still like statues, only allowing their eyes to move side to side. Instantly Payton returned to his previous state, "So have we an accord then?" The crew not wanting to possibly suffer the same fate quickly, loudly responded with an approving , "AYE!" As soon as the tension dissipated from their outburst, the men standing directly around the fallen one slowly, cautiously slinked a few yards away from his fallen body.

"Then gentlemen, let me introduce you to a couple of, *officers*. Yes, yes, yes I know that normally in piratical matters there would be a vote for all positions; however, as for now, as I've been commissioned to carry out this task by the spirit… I'll be commissioning the crew," he paused. Any dissenters," he inquired with a single raised eyebrow. His fingers strummed the handle of another dagger tucked into his belt. Not a one answered, nor dared to even blink. "No," he said standing erect. "Well then," Payton directed waving his hands slightly about in a lighthearted mood. "This is Mr. Pastro Consuelo, Quartermaster." "Pedro Santiago," he corrected. "Right! And this is Mickey Binney, 1st Mate," he continued. "Martin Finny," he corrected. "Right! And soon we hope to find Dr. Fitzgerald and persuade him to join us. Now are you ready to take the oath?" Daniel continued.

"AYE," the eager crew cheered. They were swept up in the excitement of Payton's charisma as it started to take its hold over them. "Then stand tall and take the oath," he directed. The crew stood as directed and Daniel suddenly realized that he was stuck for an oath. Ragging through his mind, this was the best he could create.

"Raise yer mugs," he commanded and they willingly obliged. "Repeat after me… I"
"I," they responded.
"Will,"
"Will,"
"Abide by and adhere to,"
"A bly by an a'here to,"
"The pirate code,"
"Da pirate code,"
"With, uh, plundering and debauchery for all," Payton concluded!
Unanimously, "Amen!"

With this the men raised their mugs and toasted their new vocation. The revelry was the beginning of the group merging together. Albeit it was a minute step, but a step nonetheless.

"Mr. Fanswella," the captain started. "Finny, sir," Martin corrected. "Right. Who was that man that I cut down. He seemed like one of yers." "Aye captain," he began. "That was Mr. Schoop. He was a small fiery chap who used to rant on and on even though he typically hadn't a clue as to what he was speaking of. The rest of the men used to make fun of him incessantly. Somehow he had gotten promoted, but made a mess of things on several occasions and demoted as his punishment. He was to be dealt with further, but then that fateful day befell us." "So it was no real loss to us," the captain asked hoping that he hadn't ruined any of the plans. "Not in the slightest. I'm certain that if you hadn't done that, then one of the crew would have before the mission was ever completed. In fact, that probably made the old man proud. Even if we don't finish our quest, he'll appreciate that. It probably gained you some respect from the new men too." "Interesting," the captain thought to himself. "Tis not like Martin's character to not care about a former mate being cut down. Very interesting indeed," he pondered.

Payton smiled and nodded his head and clapped his hands together, "Wonderful! Mr. Samtigo," Payton called. Santiago stepped up, "Si senor captain?" Payton kept his eyes transfixed on his new crew. "How many souls will be on board when we depart tomorrow?" Pedro did an impromptu head count as best he could. "Es seem ta be 'bout tirdy-four soul sir." This pleased the captain.

"Tirdy-four eh. Yes that's a good start; however, we'll be needing more if'n we're to do this right. Mr. Flimsy." Martin cut him off, "It's Finny sir." "Righty, Flippy. Mr. Flippy, record all the names for the ships log. I want all souls accounted for." Martin nodded his understanding and immediately went to work. "Ju tink man gonna stay true? Or do ya tink he'll start a mutiny," Pedro asked. Payton shrugged, "Don't know my friend. All I do know is that we'll need more of our former mates to balance out the crew." Pedro agreed and they watched as Martin tried to gather the men's names. Unfortunately for him, a few of the men of lesser mental ability didn't quite understand what he was asking. Due to the misunderstanding, conditions quickly deteriorated into an all-out battle of fists.

"Ju gonna stop dis senor," Pedro asked the captain. Daniel eyed the proceedings and since his men were more proficient and experienced at this sort of thing he decided against it. "No, let's see how this plays out. If our new friend was thinking of mutiny he should rethink it after this. Besides, this is rather fun… as long as no one pulls out any daggers," he half joked hoping for the best. He didn't want to have to find even more men for the crew if they started killing each other off.

The fight raged on and on and it was clear that the experienced pirates had the upper hand on the newbies. Sensing that they might take it beyond an acceptable limit, a pistol shot rang out. At the end of the pistol was the outstretched arm of Payton. "Alright, alright gents. Ye had yer fun for the night. Let's just hope that you have that much spirit when we find Brightside and his crew eh," he said with a raucous laugh. The old pirates cheered and laughed loudly, whereas the new ones were stuck in amazement. The men started to rub their aching bodies hoping to ward off the impending swelling. Some of the new men were still overcome with anger and couldn't understand why these veteran men weren't still fighting. One character, Meier let his emotions get the best of him and he struck a veteran pirate with a stick he found on the ground. The pirate fell to his knees bleeding. Not fond of this, Bertrand fired a dagger into the attackers hand from twenty paces. The dagger found its mark through the darkness and the man recoiled in fright and pain as blood poured out of the gash. "Damn Bert. You have gotten even better than I expected," Payton praised him. "Just trying to please me teacher," Bertrand reciprocated the compliment. Payton didn't want this to go any further though. "Let's not have any more of this. At the very least not until we find this doctor of yers. We can't afford to be offing each other. Now Bert retrieve the dagger, mate." Bert made his way toward the bleeding man. He held his hand at the wrist in pain. Bert expertly removed the dagger, took the poor mans shirt and used it to wipe the blade clean. "Thanks mate," was all he said then turned and strode away leaving the man in his agony. On his way he stooped and grabbed Payton's, still embedded in the previous dissenters' neck. The wounded man wrapped his bloody hand with his shirt and recoiled in pain.

Payton raised his voice to properly address his audience, "Gents that are new to this occupation listen up. Pirates need to blow off steam from time to time, eh. It's never done on board ship just like in your navy. Any true disputes are carried out on shore until a final solution is met. If that means that only one-man returns, then so be it. That is left up to those who are in dispute, no one else. However, for little incidents like these, they are meaningless. Keep in mind, *you* are the reason that yer together now and save the real fighting for later. Besides, I promise you that at some point ye'll all be in a tavern on some rock when ye'll both start fighting over some wench." This made the men chuckle. "Of course, while yer out beating the bloody hell out of each other," he looked side-to-side and stretched out his arms. "I'll be swooping in and taking her off her feet," he said as he impersonated a hawk screeching and swooping in on his prey. This brought out boisterous laughter from the men.

Returning to normal, "Ye'll need a tougher hyde if'n yer gonna make it with us boys. This was more of a 'feel out' skirmish. It's nothing personal blokes, just business as usual. See these men have all done things that ye'll never dare dream of. They all know what each can bring to the fight, and how it can save their, and yer, skin. They're just trying to see what yer made of. You'll have to get over it and learn that, just like in yer former navy days, ye'll be fighting fer each other. Ya got to stop thinking like yer an individual, or a royal navy man. Yer all now pirates. *So start acting like one!* Now give Mr. Matzo," he was cut off. "Martin sir," Finny's exhausted voice puffed as he corrected him from inside the former center of the melee. "Whatever," continued Payton, "give him yer name. I want a full account of all souls before ya board in the morning. Don't think that just because I'm a pirate that I'm not concerned with yer soul. You understand," Payton said in a stern voice. "Aye," the crew responded. With that they all willingly gave Martin their names, which he recorded in the makeshift log. "And someone help that man. Take him to the ocean and dip that hand in the salt water. It'll burn like hell, but it'll save yer hand," the captain ordered.

"Ju really believe wha' ju jus' said capt'n," Pedro inquired a safe distance out of earshot of the others. Payton shrugged, "I mostly just make it up as I go. Hell, even that one surprised me. It sure sounded good though, eh?" Pedro couldn't help but laugh. "Si senor. Ju never stop wit' da surprises eh?" "Well when I do… that's the day to start worrying, eh mate?"

Keys Crab Shack

The morning sun readied itself to rise and the crew, bruised and swollen, was at the boat getting ready to set sail. The boat was small and the men were very cramped. Making their way around on board proved difficult and tempers again began to rise. Sensing this, the astute captain headed it off before it became another problem.

"Gents. I understand that space is tight. Your full cooperation with each other is extremely appreciated. If this is going to be a problem just remember that for those making trouble ye will have the *Devil to pay*, or ye can sit *between the Devil and the deep*." These were more than mere stern threats. These were precarious positions that the men at sea did not want to be a part of, if possible. It involved them either squatting in the stifling hot bilge or hanging over the side of the ship, possibly by their feet. Bearing this in mind, the men quickly made the best of a bad situation.

"Where do you think that this doctor of yours is," the captain questioned Martin. "I had the privilege of speaking with Schmitty, our carpenter this morning, sir. He says that he's heard the doctor is now on Cayo Hueso," Finny informed him.

"Aah... good.... Very good," Payton uttered smiling to himself. He quickly resumed a normal conversational tone, "Well of course! Where else should a physician be but Bone Key? "Bone Key?" Martin interrupted. "I said it was Cayo Hueso." Payton looked on, "Aye, tis one and the same. It all depends on yer nationality, be it Spanish, English, or," he paused, "Conch." Martin looked puzzled, "I beg your pardon?" Payton ignored him, "Now any particular reason he chose *that* particular Key," Payton inquired. Martin responded, "I would assume that he's there because of its relative isolation; especially from the crown." Payton nodded his head. "Aye gentlemen! We make sail," the captain shouted.

Sarika sat on Martin's shoulder softly saying, "Conch, conch, conch, conch," swaying in time with the words. Martin looked up at him, "Got a new favorite word mate?" Sarika didn't answer, but just kept saying the word quietly to himself.

The crew jumped into action. Although they constantly bumped into one another, they readily went about their work, what with the captain's recent remarks. Wind filled the sails as they made their heading toward Bone

Key. Payton gazed off into the distance with a hazed look in his eyes. A faint smile crossed his lips and occasionally he would even let out a chuckle. Thoughts were obviously flooding through his brain like wind blowing in a hurricane. Finny kept an eye on him and wondered to himself what the captain was recalling. His naturally curious nature prodded at him until he could no longer keep his silence. "Sir?"

Payton didn't respond and again he tried to get his attention. "Sir?" This time he broke Daniel's gaze and he responded with a mild "um?" "Sir. You seem to have some kind of affinity for this Bone Key. Is there something you'd like to share?"

Smiling the captain responded, "Yes, yes. I have a special interest in that place. It's a place of adventure. A place of magical happenings. A place of birth." Martin was somewhat puzzled, "Sir? Your former ship was berthed from there?" "Well yes in a sense, yes," he started, "but, tis the place from whence I came." Getting clearer, "Really captain? You were given birth there?" "Aye. Haven't been back in a while either. Tis be a good feeling to be a heading home," Payton said still looking off into the distance." Martin mulled this over, "Sir, I didn't know that the island was settled with families." "Twasn't. Still isn't," Payton said mysteriously. "Actually, I was told that I was the first birth of European descent on the island." Martin continued to press the man as long as he was freely giving information. "What know you of the modern day island. I mean it has certainly changed since your birth." Payton continued to stare off to the horizon. "Well from what I hear, no one really stays long. They're there mostly to fish or gather sponge or conch. Then there are those who are shipwrecked. A few of them have stayed on and built some shelters. However, I'm certain that they won't stay too long. Will be good to step on old soil again." "What brought your parents to the island?" Payton suddenly stopped, snapping to attention, "Mr. Limmey? What speed do we sail at," Payton asked avoiding the question.

"Finny sir," he said getting used to having to correct Payton. He turned to a crewmember, "Mr. Ware, how many knots sir?" There was a brief pause as Mr. Ware tossed the line over the side, "I read seven knots sir." The ship was small enough that Mr. Ware's voice easily reached the captain. "Excellent," was all that Payton said.

Santiago had been busying himself organizing the lads so much so that he hadn't even had the time to ask, "Senor, where sail we?" "To the heart of the *Conch Republic* lad, Bone Key," Daniel said energetically. Pedro smiled a knowing smile, "Cayo Hueso! Tis been a while sin' in I set foot dere." "Aye," the captain smiled in return, "me'n as well." "Tis still a pirate friendly," Pedro joked knowing full well the answer he was about to get. "She'll always be matie. After all, I sprang from there. How could she be any other way," he mused.

Not much more was said for a while as Martin sensed that he was going somewhere that he was foreign to. Not only was he foreign to that land, but also to its history. Even though he had already been exposed to a new lifestyle, something told him that this place might be something special. He worried about asking the captain more of the place, but again his curiosity plagued him. Sarika didn't like the sound of the name and decided to quiet down and just take it all in.

"Sir," Martin cautiously asked to get Payton's attention. "Aye, Mr. F," Payton responded again without casting his gaze towards him. "This island of yours, Bone Key, that's a horribly frightening name. Why does it bear that name, Bone Key?" Martin asked. "Simple mate," he responded. "The island is riddled with the bones of men. Men long dead. The men who met their demise on the place were left to their rest. Unfortunately for them, many men have followed in their footsteps. They disturbed their remains and therefore their eternal rest." "Why have so many men met their end on the island," the nervous Englishman asked. "Fear not chap," Payton began still not looking at him. "They are bones of the natives of the land, not visitors. Well, maybe a few visitors by now. A long time ago the Calusas were the inhabitants of the island. At one point there was a mighty clash between them and another tribe. Countless horrors occurred during the skirmish. None like you or even I have ever seen… and I've been through quite a bit. All that remained of the war was a blood soaked island and the cold bodies from which that blood flowed. The bodies were left as they were and so now it's a burial ground. The ground is shallow and so burying them wasn't really a viable option, plus there were just so many of them. So with the passing of time they decomposed, leaving only their bones to bake and bleach in the blistering island sun. Even though the passage of time has not brought any more island wars, the bones just never seem to stop showing up. It's as if the ole natives are still fighting. This time they fight for dominance of the island as if to tell the living that they are still the rightful residents," Payton spoke. "So for the visitors who happen upon the place may be a bit surprised when they stumble upon someone's remains."

"Amazing," was all that Finny could say. "Oh, and one more thing," Payton started. "If'n ye come upon the ole bones of one of them dead natives on the island," he paused, "leave it be." Again he paused. He finally turned to look Finny in the eye, "*Trust me* on this one, eh mate?" Martin wasn't sure why, but he believed him and this time he knew better than to pursue it any further. Payton had an unbelievable ability to make himself look absolutely frightening when he wanted. He could almost transform his very facial features to intensify his desire to appear horrible. Then in the next moment he could change to an almost childlike innocence. It was this uncanny ability that caused much of his feared reputation. Many thought that he was the devil himself while others saw him as a kind and gentle, misunderstood man. Whatever the truth was, Martin felt that it was in his best interest to follow his directions.

Payton raised his voice to address the entire crew, "Aye gents, we sail to Bone Island. If'n ye come upon ANY bones on the island… leave them be! Anyone even joking with one of them will not only have the Devil to pay… but me as well!" The crew was unsure of why he so cared about this, but his passion and fury showed. They would all oblige his direct order as most looked upon him at this moment with sheer terror. Not a soul dared to question their captain.

Just as he finished, the winds picked up as a summer squall came upon them. These unannounced storms made their way upon the Caribbean and sailors knew these were daily hazards. Even though they were commonplace, they needed to be respected. The skies grew fiercely and almost instantly dark while the wind began to howl, bringing an unsaid uneasiness to the sailors. All except the captain that was. For he stood fast and strong at the helm, effortlessly guiding them to their destination. His steadfast presence was a reassurance to the crew. The formerly terrifying appearance was replaced with one of utter confidence and determination. The captain was extremely excited to be heading back to the island of his birth and nothing would stop him from arriving today. The skies were menacing and water began to fall near the ship. They managed to stay just out of reach of the rain. The waves began to come in series. There would be typically six large waves crashing about them followed by an equal amount of smaller calmer ones. The captain was well versed in this type of weather and made sure that he didn't let the waves come upon their stern. This small boat already had all that she could handle with the sheer weight on her. A few good waves could easily sink her. Payton changed his course to a zigzag pattern when the waves decided to try to push her away from their destination. The new pattern allowed the fragile ship to stay the course and not be pushed as much by the current. She was better able to control her own destiny and avoid the many coral heads that frequently claimed passing ships.

The smuggler made her way toward the island through gale force winds. All the while, men on the makeshift dock ran panicky amok preparing the tiny seaport for the incoming storm. The ship continued to make way toward the derelict pier. Sailors on board and on land both were showing signs of distress at the pending collision between boat and dock. The more the men worried the bigger the grin on Payton's face became. Closer they sailed. Closer and closer to the dock they came. Winds screamed and whitecaps crashed against the hull of the tiny ship and the waterfront. Sea spray filled the air and many of the men were now soaked with salt water. Closer and closer they came. The normally teal waters were churned by the angry waves. Back behind the helm the fearless captain gracefully glided the boat to the dock. On his command the mainsail was de-powered allowing the ship to be guided by the waves.

Miraculously, the ship came elegantly to rest at the dock with a dull thud. The crew jumped into action and tied the ship fast. The winds howled at the men on the land as they observed in amazement as the ship came to port safely. They had stayed ahead of the rain to the relief of the men. They knew that this ship could easily be swamped which would lead to her, and their demise. There was no harbormaster for Pedro to speak with here, as the island hadn't yet achieved the population, or status to require one. While Daniel and Martin made their way, Payton was stunned to see the high number of people currently ashore. Sarika was perched on Martin's shoulder eagerly taking in the sights. His nails were digging in for safety as the howling winds were tearing him near off his master's shoulder. The crew stayed in and near the ship as the storm grew. They huddled for safety in the shanty erected at the dockside amid the strange looks of the men who currently called this place home. The crew, new and Payton experienced, marveled in complete amazement at the captain's ease, calmness, focus and mastery in navigation to the dock. A newfound respect was growing in all the men.

The officers continued their walk through the winds. Finally, rain misted in as the precursor to a heavy downpour. "Where do ya think this doctor of yers might be," questioned Payton. Unsure of his answer, "He might have set up shop to help the victims of shipwreck sir," Finny answered. Squawking above the wind, "Ale, ale, I need an ale," Sarika sang. "You know, there are times where I think you should be my parrot the way ya think," joked the captain.

They made their way through the wilds and scattered ramshackle buildings and came across a rather bleak looking structure. Above the door a crudely carved sign read "Captains Quarters." It was a very small tavern, as it were, brimming with life even this early in the day. They entered a room filled with sailors and fishermen. It was a noisy active place, the few window openings were covered with shutters. The overcast skies were promising much more rain. A few lanterns tried in vain to cast a light upon the dark room. The pirate captain was immediately at home, while Martin wiped the mist from his face. Sarika spread his wings and shuddered the water off as best he could then folded them back. Pedro smiled as he viewed the proceedings as they made their way to the bar.

A bar wench spied the group and exclaimed, "Good lord look what the storm made the seas spit up." "Nice to see you again too fair maid Nikki," Payton gushed. Stunned, but not surprised Martin queried, "Do you know all the tavern wenches sir?" "Aye! I sure try to. They're a good lot," he exclaimed. "We're a *fun* lot anyway. We definitely have our moments eh," she smiled. Finny was stunned, "But surely this place was not in existence the last time you were here," he insisted. "True," Payton replied. "However, like us, she was not always here. Last I remember she was in Nice." "Now what can I get cha," she smiled.

A bolt of lightning filled the room full of light followed immediately with a clap of thunder. It was so strong the building shook causing mugs to fall, spilling their contents. The disgruntled men got up to refresh their glasses when suddenly in the distance a bell was rung, accompanied with a voice shouting, "*Wreck ashore! Wreck ashore!*" With that, a massive panic ensued and a rush came over the tavern. The men pushed and shoved each other on their way out the door. When all had made their exit, a sudden calm came over the darkened tavern. All that could be heard was the sound of rain hitting the roof, while the shouts of the men faded into the distance.

The barmaid exhaled a heavy sigh, "Well there goes the day's business then. It figures that on such a nasty day that ye'd blow into port. My dear captain Payton, what brings an old pirate like you back to the Isle of Bones?" In typical nonsensical Payton fashion replied, "Last I checked it was a trashy ship and a mighty wind, but I could be incorrect. I've discovered that half the time I've found that I'm always wrong. And only sometimes right. And even then that's usually correct. And besides, who's old? Regardless, it could have been a mighty ship and a trashy wind that brought me fourth. Then again maybe it was a mighty trashy wind filled ship. Or a shippy filled trashy wind. Or," Nikki knew that she had to stop this or it would continue possibly indefinitely. "Enough! Please," she paused taking in a deep breath. "You still can give me a headache in seconds flat! But I've strangely missed that," Nikki confessed with a smile. "And I retract the 'old'". Martin was standing back, again in utter amazement, "Unbelievable. Totally unbelievable! What is going on here," he wondered aloud, more to himself than to anyone else.

"Pay attention man," Payton cut into his self-dialogue. "I'm speaking with the barmaid, who's obviously overcome with me, as all good lasses are, and you're babbling on and on. So in other words, everything is status quo. So what's the problem?" Smacking himself in the head, Finny replied, "I meant *how* do you do it, *and* what was the mass exodus while we're at it?" Sarika squawked in agreement.

"Ah! Well first off, I am Captain Daniel Payton... need I say any more? And secondly, you are aware of the gale we came in upon?" "Frightfully well," Martin confessed remembering the tumultuous adventure they just executed. "And you remember how you were weeping like a little hand maiden, thinking we were going to take a pounding on the reef," Payton continued with a half smile. "I never," Finny protested stamping his foot! "*Right*," the maid replied sarcastically nodding her head. She knew that Payton was probably just having a bit of fun at his expense. "Well some poor ship that came in after us is now a permanent resident of the reef," Payton finished. "There are hundreds of wrecks out there." Nikki then picked up, "Aye, and those, ahem, *gentlemen*, are the island's fishermen. This island is home to fishermen, spongers and conchs. Course they can't fish in weather like this so they make it up hoping for situations just like this one."

"This one," Martin inquired. "Aye," she replied. "See, most of them blokes are wreck victims themselves, cast a way's, marooners, things like that. So, when there is a wreck, the men like to scavenge the ship for instant profits. They salvage the wreck and fight incessantly amongst themselves. Sometimes they spill each other's blood in the process. Should be given it all back to the rightful owners they should, but that's not how it happens in the modern world. The rightful owners may get part of it back. If they're lucky that is. And if they do, it may come at a price. Remember, the men need the money to get off this island. Many an owner who sailed along with their cargo did not get his items returned, but wound up at the bottom of the ocean with his throat slit."

Smiling Payton said, "Men after me own heart." "But they do save any sailors that survived the wreck," Nikki added contentiously. "So they're not all bad," Martin said half asking half mocking. "Absolutely not, they're somewhat good at heart. Mostly homesick," the wench replied. "But everything's a business these days laddie," said Payton flatly. "Seems that lately we've had us a run of wrecks. For those not lucky enough to wreck near a House of Refuge, there will be a ship along soon that will take the survivors with them… at a price," Nikki continued. "This way they'll have the fee for their passage."

"Now, what's being the real reason you're here today my good captain," Nikki interrupted. "We're looking for a doctor," Payton said, the mug to his lips and ale beginning to flow. Laughing heartedly she exclaimed, "Oh my word, what a surprise. Crabs," she joked. "Love some! I'm starving," Payton said lowering the mug. "Haven't had a bite in quite some time." "Haven't had a bite or the crabs in quiet some time," she continued to amuse herself. "Share, share, we need to share," Sarika finally chimed in. He sat with his wings extended fully to dry now that there was much more space in the empty room. Being the voice of reason and diplomacy Martin cut them off. "We're looking for Dr. Royden Fitzgerald. We've heard that he's been last seen on this island. Perhaps he's taken up residence. Perhaps he's even taken up practice," he inquired. Nikki smiled and began to nod her head "Aye, the good doctor is indeed on the island and staying in Hopper house… not too far from here," she answered.

This of course perked up all the men's heads. Martin could hardly contain his exuberance, "Are there any other of his old shipmates with him," he half demanded. "Yes, a few," she smiled. "However they don't speak much of their past and no one on this here island much cares. He helps out as much as possible. Actually, he's been quite a busy and well respected man since he arrived." "Tremendous," Martin shouted. "Which way to this Hopper house if you please?" "Tain't but a few strides up the path," she said. "FABULOUS," Payton interjected. "Now, how about those crabs?" "Right, right, I need a bite," Sarika followed!

Back to her joking, "Feeling a little itchy there boys?" Daniel was sitting back in wonderment, "Now that you mention it, yes. Why," he asked? His little feathered friend added "Scratch, scratch, I need a scratch." "C'mon captain. We should be heading out," Finny urged. "I love a good crustacean," Payton continued off in his own world. "Yum, yum, gotta get us some," Sarika injected also still in Payton's world. Shaking his head in embarrassed disbelief, "Great," Martin said.

Taking a moment after watching Payton and the bird, Nikki puzzled, "Shouldn't that parrot be on your shoulder, not his?" "Lately I'm beginning to agree," Finny said. The captain took her hand, slipped a few coins into her palm, turned it over and kissed the backside. He smiled and thanked her for the drink and information. "I'll see you soon my dear," he said before exiting. She raised her eyebrows, "Ya'd better if you know what's good for you! And from what I remember, you do." Payton smiled as he turned back toward her and took a mock bow.

Quickly they made their way out the door and down the road. The rain had momentarily stopped, yet the skies remained ominously overcast and windy. The island was barren as the wreck was the major news of the moment. Every available man was out to "earn" his share of the bounty.

The men strode up to the Hopper house and knocked on the door. Promptly it was opened and the doctor's face on the other side turned pale white. "GREAT GHOST," the doctor shouted. Turning around to the palms and tall island grasses behind him shocked, Payton expected the spirit. Payton professed quietly, "Melbourne," expecting to be joined again by his ghostly overseer! "Mr. Finny! My word! Is that you? Is that really you," Fitzgerald asked. "Aye good doctor," he replied nodding his head. "Tis me." The excited physician exclaimed, "I was certain that you'd met your unfortunate demise when no one heard from you after you disappeared during your voyage to England!"

They eagerly embraced and he welcomed them into the crude house. "I was recuperating and waiting for the right opportunity and time to rustle my sails again my friend," Finny began. "Found me, found me, at that time he found me," Sarika continued. Fitzgerald looked up, "Aye, and what would your name be good parrot," Fitzgerald asked the bird. "Sarika! Sarika! My name is Sarika." "Aye he's been a good friend and somewhat of a vision of the forthcoming winds," Finny exclaimed. "I'm not certain I understand," the puzzled physician replied. "Aye, by that he means me ole chap," a voice exclaimed from behind Martin. He was somewhat startled and taken aback suddenly realizing that the pirate was standing here before him. "Um, yes, and who might you be good sir," Fitzgerald diplomatically inquired.

"I am the kin spirit of that bird in that we both have a taste for the rum, and oddly enough, seafood" the pirate said. The doctor grew unsteady and unsure of the man, "Right..." Martin sensed the physician's uneasiness and hastily tried to put him at ease. "Please forgive my manners," Finny apologized. "This is the," Payton inserted himself, "Great." Half rolling his eyes Finny corrected himself, "Great pirate," Again he inserted himself, "No, maybe dread is preferable," Finny sighed and responded with a compromise, "This is the great, dread pirate," he paused waiting for approval raising an eyebrow. "Um, a bit long eh," Payton judged. Again exhaling, "The great pirate," and again he paused. "Ah yes," a satisfied Payton said smiling. "Daniel Payton," Finny said flatly. Rolling his eyes Payton exclaimed in a subdued tone through clenched teeth, "*Captain*." Correcting himself, "Captain, Daniel Payton," Finny introduced. Suddenly the doctor shrieked, "Good LORD NO!"

With that a pistol was placed at Daniel's head from behind. The unmistakable sound of the pistol being cocked accompanied it. Payton breathed a heavy sigh saying to himself, "You know this is getting quite repetitive. Perhaps there is a better way. Another pistol in a matter of days is getting rather annoying." "Silence blaggard," the man holding the pistol commanded. "You wouldn't be wanting to do that my good chap," Daniel said plainly. He didn't know whose hand was holding the weapon, nor did he care. Daniel had been in this exact same predicament so many times that he had the confidence to overcome any would-be assassin/ bounty hunter. "I be thinking I do pirate. I'm cer'ain that there's a bill on yer mangy head. Cou'd be the ticket I need ta get me off this blas'ed rock! And I believe that ta worl' wo'ld be a better place with one less shabby pirate upon her," the irritated man shot out.

"Last time I checked I wasn't a duck," Payton began, looking down at his mouth, fingers examining his face. "And furthermore this pirate be the only way for ye to extract yer bloody revenge." "Aye, the only revenge I seek is on," the angered man was cut off by Payton. "Admiral Brightside." The man holding the pistol was extremely shocked, "How ye know of him? You say somethin' Mr. Finny?" Sharply Martin commanded,

"Ian, put the pistol down. If it weren't for the captain we wouldn't be here right now." "Down, down, put it down," Sarika commanded.

"Mr. McMahon please lower your weapon," Fitzgerald pleaded. "But 'e's a filthy pirate then," Ian protested, regaining his composure. "You spend as much time at sea and see how April fresh you might be," Payton said. "Wha'," questioned Ian. "Lower your weapon before you get yourself hurt," Payton suggested rather calmly. "You sh'uldn't be talking so, as in I'm the one with the pistol at yer head eh. In this here situation I'm in control," Ian demanded. "Righty. Are you absolutely certain that you want to do this," Payton offered one more time. "What mean you," questioned Ian.

"I mean, do you really want a, what did you refer to me as, a mangy, no scruffy, it was scruffy, wasn't it, pirate? You know a lot of men's lives have ended before their time on this island. Luckily for you, today is not your day. However, do you want a scruffy pirate to take your pistol, force you with ease, mind you, to the ground, embarrass you in front of yer mates, and then have to accept the pirate's offered hand to help you up again?" Payton predicted. "I mean honestly, is that how you want it to be?"

Ian not certain he followed this train of thought quickly surmised, "Can't be ..." In a flash the captain had whirled around, his left arm wrapped around Ian's right; his right hand on Ian's throat. He kicked out the man's leg and Ian tumbled to the floor. Daniel stripped the weapon from his hand as he went down. Payton's knee was down on Ian's chest forcing the breath from his lungs. "I'm guessing that the word you didn't get to say was 'done' then," Payton questioned. "Now before I give you your pistol back, have a seat and listen to what we have to offer." Payton stood up and backed away. "If'n you decide that you want to decline said offer, then so be it. We'll be on our merry way and no further harm will befall you. Either way you'll be getting your piece returned at the completion," he said with a nod and a smile.

Ian and the doctor sat obediently as Martin and Daniel retold the entire story. The stunned doctor mumbled, "Remarkable! Simply remarkable!" Still embarrassed at being disarmed, "How do'n I know that yer telling tha truth? How do'n I know that yer not gonna slit our throats once'n we git tha ship," Ian asked. "That's the beautiful thing there laddie," Payton said with a smile. "You don't," he continued. "But, I don't know that you won't go and try somethin' stupid either then do I? Think of it this way. Tis a big ship from the sounds of her, and I can't rightly sail her by me self now can I? So I'll be needing an able, *willing* and completely voluntary crew then, eh mate? Wouldn't do me much good to be offing you then, would it?"

Ian turned to Martin, "Mr. Martin, I can't hardly believe that you've a gone an turn pirate! I mean of all tha men in the royal navy, you sir?" "I wouldn't have believed it either Ian," Martin began. "However, I want revenge more than I'd ever dreamed. And that bastard let all of our men, *real royal navy men*, get slaughtered! Plus," he paused, "I'd have never dreamed that I'd have more freedom and more of a say on a pirate ship than I ever had in all my years with his majesty's royal navy."

"Look, I'm still not sure about all this Martin," the doctor exclaimed. He went on, "I know that what that man has done was reprehensible, but he'll have God to reckon with for his sins." "Look, all we ask is that you accompany us on this mission. I'm certain that your dear Captain Melbourne would be most appreciative of any of his former crew that went an avenged his death. The more of his surviving men that help, the more certain his freedom will be. Then once the ship is ours and the blaggard Brightside is beneath the seas, we'll gladly drop you off wherever your heart so desires. Course, we won't be forcing you to join. Only asking," Payton directed. "We'll probably need your skills to repair any men who are injured in the process of revenging your former captain. And as far as God judging him for his sins… think of it this way. Yes he'll be the judge. Of that there is no doubt. We'll just get him there faster," he said with a smile.

"How we know that we won't be enslaved or marooned once tha ship be ours and you 'ave more pirate crew to outnumber us," Ian again questioned. Payton exhaled an exacerbated sigh, "Same old song with this bloke. Yeah, even though I be a lowly pirate my word is my bond. I live and I shall die by my word," Payton said. "I wouldn't be so eager to retain the services of a doctor if'n I hadn't a care about the safety of my crew."

Fitzgerald spoke up, "I have read many an account about you sir pirate. And from all accounts what you say is true. Every one who has had dealings with you has always held up that you were a man of your word. One chap, Master Winford Hamill, went so far as to say that you demanded that your word be treated like biblical truth. When one man in your service tried to bypass your word you had him flogged with the cat-o-nines. When the man was given one extra lash, breaking your word of honor, the whip was raked out of the bosun's hand and then he was keel hauled for the transgression."

"Aye," Payton said reflecting with a dour mood on his face. "He was William Wilson, Carpenter's mate. The man being flogged that is. He was a good lad. Just misguided and blinded by those around him. I hated to do it to him, but on a ship there are policies that must be maintained. As for the man who was keel hauled, well, his was another story. He was Maximilian Butler Simms, bosun. He was a man of pure evil who took excessive pleasure in punishing his own men, more so than he ever offered any enemy we had ever encountered. Many in the crew feared that he was possessed by the Devil himself. The keelhauling was as much for the morale of the boys as it was the extra lash. The extra lash was uncalled for and needed to be addressed. It violated my word."

"That's shockin' brutality eh mate," Ian spouted. "Aye, and in yer royal navy there were never any occasions of abuse of power and torture. I do know for sure that ye'd never purge yerselves of a devil for the moral and wellbeing of the crew. Right mate," the captain sarcastically shot back. Ian relented knowing that the pirate was correct. "But why is it so important that *my* services accompany you," the doctor asked.

"I may be a pirate, good man, however," Payton started, "when a crew is sailing under me I take every possible means to see that they are well cared for. If'n a man wish to serve as my crew, then I'll be seein' to it that if'n he gets hurt while in me service he'll not be cast aside. As you may have already read, I don't take well to my men being uncared for."

"That's not ta pirate way," Ian fought back. "With 'em it's all for one and none for all." "What know you of pirates? Have'n you ever been one? If'n not then I'd mind you to watch yerself. Tis the pirate way...," shouted Payton above him. "If'n the pirate wants to stay in business that is," he followed more calmly. "Business? Wha' say you of business! You cowardly steal and gouge from others," Ian continued the argument. "Tis nothing personal good man," Payton stated. "When I commandeer a ship, it's typically not from any personal affair or grudge. Granted this is an exception, however, typically it's just business. I can't be held responsible because our business plan is a bit more aggressive than the competitions." "Bu' it's still stealing," Ian returned. "From a certain point of view. And remember that history supports a winner lad," Daniel said. "How do you figure," Fitzgerald asked. Payton smiled, "Take for example Alexander the Great. His place in history is that he was great because he overran and controlled so much of the world. Didn't he then?" "Well yes. I guess," Fitzgerald stuttered. "Well the people who were overrun weren't so enchanted with the bloke then eh," Payton continued. "No, I guess not," Fitzgerald pondered.

"I'd venture to say that any survivors he left behind had many names for the bloke, and I'll wager that none of them was 'Great.' However, you never hear history being told from their point of view, eh. The only one you get is from the victors, eh matey," Payton said flatly. "You never hear the horrors placed upon his victims during and after his sieges. Yet he will forever have the moniker associated with his name." Stunned, Fitzgerald uttered, "I can't believe that I can actually see your thought process, even if I don't necessarily agree with all of your positions. However, you do make a valid point sir."

"I'm wit ole Doc an I'm still not certain Martin…" Ian offered. "What can it hurt Ian," Martin said. "If we go and get the ship, we're back on the seas. If we do and if Daniel…" "Captain Daniel," he interjected. "Doesn't keep his word," he continued, "we'll have enough of *our* men to *persuade* him otherwise." "Right, sounds like you've thought a lot about this then Marnie," Payton directed to Martin. "Who," asked Ian. "As you've said yourself, I'm on the way to becoming a pirate," Martin said slyly back to Payton. Smiling back Payton offered, "Aye jolly good times indeed Micki! But mutineers won't be tolerated." "What," a puzzled Ian uttered. "Aye," Finny spouted. "I have to admit it. I'm as confused as poor Ian then," Fitzgerald said. "Look Dr. Referral," Payton started. "All I need to know is are you, or are you not willing to avenge your poor captain's demise? His eternal soul, as well as those of your fallen comrades beg for your assistance. Our men will need a good doctor to help us achieve our goal." Payton turned and looked to Ian, "And can you, or can you not keep it together enough to assist us as well in our quest?" "If'n I do. Can I also be released upon ta completion of ta mission," Ian questioned. "Aye, so I have already said. Besides, that's part of our law," Payton nodded. "May I speak with Ian and Martin alone for a minute," the good doctor asked. "With whom," asked Payton? "Ian and Martin," Fitzgerald again said. "Um, he and I," Martin said pointing at himself. "Ah, aye," Payton said. A moment passed as he stood there patiently. "Um, well," Martin offered waiting for Payton to leave. "Done then," Payton questioned. "No we haven't yet started," Finny retorted. "Ah! Well you should then shouldn't you," asked Payton scratching at his beard. Martin looked at him plainly, "Yes." "Right! Well, don't let me hold you up," Payton said back, arms folded, looking around. "But you are," Ian said flatly. "How so," Payton pondered. "Well you're right there," the doctor said. "Aye! And you're right there and he's right there, and he's right there," he said pointing them out. "Gosh this is jolly good fun," Payton said with glee.

"But you can 'ear us," Ian said, his frustration growing again. "Yes! That's what these are for," Daniel said now pointing to his ears. "Wonderful things these ears. They're great for hearing with; holding your burial rings handy; wonderful for storing your quill while you have yourself a good scratch. If you know how to write that is. The only bad thing is this wax they ooze. Then again it's good for the candles," Payton trailed off. "Good Lord, I think I'm gonna be sick eh," Ian muttered. "Right! And that's why we need a good doctor to join us," Payton shot in. "No I mean…," Ian interjected. "Never-the-matter! Can we please get on with it then," Martin interjected. "Righty! Have a go then," Payton said.

There was a pause accompanied by silence in the room that hung heavy. Martin leaned to the other two and spoke in hushed tones, "He just doesn't get it." "Actually I did! Just the other night. And hopefully again later tonight," Payton said amused raising his eyebrows a couple of times quickly. "No," Martin said slapping his hand over his face. "Actually I'm quite certain I did. I believe I was there," answered Payton. "Jolly good time… jolly good indeed! And tonight," he said clasping his hands together. He started to growl like an excited animal, eyebrows bouncing up and down again, "Nikki-Nikki likei my..." he was cut off. "Alright, we get it," shaking his head in disbelief Martin commanded, "We'll adjourn out back for a moment." "Delightful," Payton stated.

Sarika jumped off Martin's shoulder and landed on the floor. "Cherry, cherry, I've found a cherry!" Payton looked at the parrot, "Looks rather pleasant, that island cherry there." "S'mine, s'mine, all's s'mine," Sarika said. "Why don't we have a debate over who the rightful owner of the fruit be," Payton queried.

Sarika stood wings stretched out, "S'mine, S'mine, I said s'mine!" Payton mimicked the bird stretching out his arms, "Not yet, not yet, not bloody well yet!"

The three other men quietly made their way out the back door in disbelief over what they just witnessed; a man arguing with a bird over a small piece of indigenous fruit.

The sky remained dark as the winds continued their assault. The wind carried their voices away from the house so they didn't have far to move to remain unheard. "The good news is, that should keep him busy for a few minutes," Martin said. Ian was the first to speak freely, "Martin, you can't be serious! Tha man's a blitherin' idiot!" "Yes Martin, I concur with Ian," conferred the doctor, "How indeed could such a buffoon possibly commandeer the ship from Brightside? I mean this could not be the same man I have read so much about. Could it? By the way, when was the last time he bathed? I've never smelt such a stench!"

"Look, I've been with him now for a few scant days and yes, I'll give you that the man is a handful; a complete moron. That being said, he's also a pirate genius. He's navigated channels I never dare dream. He's out talked men smarter than he. Ok, yes I'll give you that isn't saying too much, but never-the-less. He's charmed near ever bar wench from here to Calcutta. And as far as his combat skills go, I think we've seen just the beginning. As for the accounts you've read, I believe that they were not glorified at all. I mean if anything they downplayed his ability as to not have scoundrels up and join him," Martin said. "But..." interjected Ian. "Yes I know," Martin said cutting him off, "that he can't even remember mine or your names, but that seems to work for him. I think the day he gets them properly is the day he hangs from the gallows.

"Aye and we'n alon' sidea him," Ian said. "Absolutely," the doctor agreed. "So then we shouldn't be letting that happen shall we," Martin said. "But...," Fitzgerald started. "Look," Martin said again cutting the other man off, "I've had a lot of time on that wretched island to ponder things. And never in my wildest dreams could I ever dream up a way to truly get revenge and not swing from the gallows. This is our perfect situation. If we need to mutiny we will have enough support to at least get off the ship ourselves, if not him. Or if seized, we'll all agree that you were brought under duress of pain of death. I also want you to remember that on a pirate ship all men have an equal voice and vote. Once the mission is accomplished, if he turns out to be an awful captain we can merely vote him out of his captaincy. He's a man of his word right? Well his laws state that all men have an equal vote. All we need to know is how many more of our crew can we find and how quickly?" "Well I'd venture to say we have twenty and three out on the wreck right now," Fitzgerald said. "Wonderful," Martin replied. "How many would be willing to join us?" "I'm not certain. For the revenge factor, probably all. For a pirate… of that I'm not certain," Fitzgerald replied.

After a short pause and much internal debate they agreed to the terms and reentered the house. Daniel and the parrot were still debating over who the rightful owner of the cherry actually was. As they continued their argument a rodent ran through, grabbed it and made off.

"Rat! Rat! That bloody rat," Sarika shouted. "I guess we know whose that actually was then. Well I see that we're all returned then. What have we decided? Have we an accord," Payton said standing up, brushing dirt off his pants. "Aye we have an accord, if you agree to a stipulation," Martin said. "That bein'," a leery Payton replied. "If we fail in our mission or are seized at any time, we allow them, and only them, the right to say that they were brought on under duress of pain of death," Martin laid out flatly. "That'd be a fib then, wouldn't it" Payton said raising his nose up slightly. "Please hear me out…," the doctor pleaded. "Look good chap, I'm just funnin' ya. I love a good fib time to time," Payton said. "I am in full agreement with yer terms of service." He offered his hand to Fitzgerald who hesitated, then exhaled deeply and shook it. "See, it's not so bad eh mate," Payton said with a dirty smile.

"We sail in two days. Make certain that all your affairs be in place and be ready to go. We have a crew meeting tonight on the shore nearin' sunset. Be punctual. Tis a beautiful sight," Payton informed them. "One that you won't want to miss, and one that you'll never forget."

With that Payton bowed a half bow clicking his heels together. He turned and exited, Martin followed suit and they headed back to the ship. The dark skies remained, but they held their watery contents. Upon reaching the vessel the captain shouted out his orders. "Avast ye scallywags! Now hear this! There's a crew meeting set for tonight on the southern shore justin' before sunset. Anyone tardy will be docked one ration of rum and will miss one hellova good time," Payton commanded. His words were followed with a hearty cheer from the crew.

Conch Republic Sunset

The crew convened on the beach before sunset as directed. An obvious division between pirates and former royal navy men was present as the two groups stood in separate huddles. The men were in good spirits yet they couldn't help but size each other up as two rival armies might before a fight. A fire was already raging where some men were cooking fresh fish, chicken, conch and shrimp. The rum and ale were flowing freely as the captain made his way to the gathering. Off the path he strolled on the island of his birth when he came upon a sun-bleached skull resting on a sand hill surrounded by beach grass. He knelt down and gathered it up. Eyeing it side to side he spoke. "Fear not ole chap, I won't make the same mistake again. Me crew had better not as well. For I have given them yer warning. If they don't heed it," he looked directly into the empty eye sockets and drew it closer, "take it out on them, eh. Not me… please." He smiled a little smile and moved it away from his face, "I wonder what my final moments will be," he pondered. "Hope that it won't come anytime soon, though. I can wait to find out." He paused a moment, "Rest in peace friend. Rest in peace," he repeated. Replacing the skull where he had found it, Payton stood up and nodded his head and touching the brim of his hat to the skull. It was a sign of respect for the dead, then he made his way.

Upon arriving unheralded at the gathering, he strolled through the crowd. He wasn't surprised by what he saw with the two groups eyeing each other. He was happy that they weren't at each other's throats… yet. His seemingly never-ending hunger overtook his interest and he helped himself to a tasty dinner feast.

After quickly finishing his meal, he stepped up high on a stump to be above the rest when he called for order. The crowd fell silent and all eyes turned toward him. "Gents! End your conversations and gather round if you please." He stood with a fire in his eyes, an overflowing stein in his hand, and all his moves were performed very animatedly, and with specific purpose. "Gents! We convene here tonight for a momentous occasion. Tis the day that His Majesty's Royal Navy and the Pirate Order join together to alter history!" The men indicated their approval, nodding their heads. A few even knocked their mugs together. "Tis the day that we all agree upon the demise of the scalawag scoundrel that has brought us to this day! The death of Admiral Brightside!" This proclamation elicited even louder cheering from the former navy men and more toasting of mugs. The navy men were desperate for revenge, whereas the pirates were just excited about the mission… and to rejoin their old captain. Most of the pirates found enormous satisfaction in the fact that the naval men were not only turning to pirates to aid them, but also that they would be committing acts of piracy. It validated many of their miserable lives. "Tis the day we become *the* force that will commandeer a great ship," he paused, "and make her a *legend!* Besides what else should a ship be doin' other than pirating with a name like *Scavenger!*" This elicits a laugh from even the staunchest of royal navy men.

"Now, some of you were with us the past few days before we sailed here and we went through this. If you were, I ask that you please oblige me and take your oath yet again," Payton began. "As stated in our previous meeting, normally there would be a vote for all positions. However for now, as I've been commissioned to carry out this task, therefore, I'll be commissioning the crew," Payton directed. "Dissention will not be tolerated, nor will there be any voting fer a new captain till the mission be done, eh! Every man has a voice and every voice a vote. Gentlemen, let me introduce you to our officers and leaders."

He began, "This is Mr. Pasqualie Cohanran; Quartermaster." "Pedro Santiago," he again corrected.

"Right! And this is Manuel Blastronao, 1st Mate," he

continued. "Martin Finny," he also corrected.

"Right! Dr. Fitzgerald our ship's physician. Startled that he got his name correct, "Yes, thank you."

"And that is, oddly enough, Doc Neilsen; our ship's cook," Payton said rather puzzled himself pointing to a heavy set man in the front row of the crewmen. "Aye," the cook nodded in reply. "Don't let the name fool ya," Payton started, "He be called Doc and when yer done with his grog ye'll be needin' a good one," he joked nodding his head towards Fitzgerald.

"This is James Fall, Bosun." Payton introduced. "Um, Hall," he corrected.

"'Coop' Dalsh, yer cooper," Payton continued. "That's Walsh," the man slurred as the corrections continued.

"Gent's this is your master gunner, Bearded Clem," he continued the introduction. "Gdy blkes," Clem uttered tipping his hat.

"Now as for the rest of you, you will be assigned positions based upon skill and experience... and in some cases, appearance," he said looking at a very dirty man. "For instance," he said still looking at the dirty one who now grinned a toothy smile, "you'll have absolutely *nothing* to do with meal preparation. At least mine anyway." He turned away after making a non-approving face and continued his discourse. "All hands will assist the others, even if you typically aren't in said position to do so. We are a unit and therefore must think and act as one. Any man trying to act outside of the best interest of the ship, her crew's safety, or in detriment to our mission will be dealt with harshly. It's not that I want any harm to befall you. But remember, yer actions have serious consequences fer yer fellow mate. Am I understood," Payton asked.

The crew agreed, "Aye!" "Good," the captain replied. "Except," he turned back at the filthy man, "for what I said about the food thingy. Keep yer fingers off me grub," he said, bringing a laugh to the group.

"Our quartermaster will read our laws," Payton commanded. "Now as for *the laws*, I want you to listen, understand and abide by them. I was in service under *the Great Pirate Bartholomew Roberts* when he created these very rules. They worked for ole Black Bart; they have worked for me… they'll work for us. Verstehen?"

Pedro stood before them and read the list. He was bold and he was loud. He flowed through the rules with ease at having served under them previously. When he was finished most of the crew stood in silence looking upon one another. Confusion rampant on their faces, as most couldn't understand what was just said. Payton scanned the audience and sighed, "Fantastic read Manuso. And now for the English version, please follow along," he said taking the sheet from a smiling Pedro.

Payton stood tall before them. His eyes scanned the group and fell upon Pedro, still smiling his apologetic fake smile. Payton smirked to himself, lightly shook his head and began. "Firstly, every man shall have an equal vote in our affairs dealing with the mission. He shall also have an equal portion of fresh provisions and liquors that we seize.

Secondly, every man will have an equal share of the plundering. However, if you defraud the crew ye shall be marooned with one pistol and one shot. If ye shall rob another of us ye shall have year nose and ears slit; one eye put out and then marooned, without pistol and shot.

Thirdly, cards and dice shall only be played when so allowed by myself.

Fourthly, lights out will be promptly at eight at night unless advised by myself.

Fifthly, each man shall always keep his pistol clean and ready, blades sharpened and ready for action. *No exceptions!*

Sixthly, if any one should carry a woman on board in disguise he shall be immediately keel hauled until dead. They are frightful bad luck, which we absolutely do not need.

Seventhly, anyone who deserts in time of battle shall be marooned.

Eighthly, any quarrel shall be done and ended on shore. If done on board each shall be shackled on deck until such time as we can reach shore where the argument may be finished in whatever means necessary.

Ninethly, none shall speak of breaking their way of living until we have completed our current mission. If'n ye decide to stay on post that, then none shall leave until he has a share of 1,000 pounds. Nor may he leave while under a current mission. If anyone shall become a cripple or lose a limb in the service, he shall have 800 pieces of eight. Whether or not ye decide to remain in service.

Tenthly, the captain and quartermaster shall receive two shares of any prize. The 1st mate, bosun and master gunner shall receive one and a half share. Other officers receive one quarter. All the rest of you private gentlemen of fortune shall receive one share each."

He lowered the sheet, "So, ifin ye shall be able to live under these simple ten rules and abide by them ye can and will become my latest and greatest crew. If not, ye are free to walk right now. No questions will be asked. No offences will befall you. The choice is yers and yers alone. Now ya scurvy ridden lads, what say you?"

A moment passed and the men looked around without saying a word. The captain looked at the array of men, raised an eyebrow and asked slyly, *"Well?"*

At once the crew stood up and in unison, "AYE!" "Excellent! Gentlemen enjoy the night and debauch till satisfied! Now are you ready to take your oath," Daniel continued. "AYE," the crew again responded.

"Gentlemen, I know that this may come easy for you who have sailed under me previously. I also know that it may be difficult for others to swallow their pride and take up under the pirate flag and join the brethren of the coast. Please know that you are doing it for your former captain and mates. Also remember, anyone of you will be free to leave, when upon completion of the mission, we are free and clear. Also, special provision has been made for Doctor Fitzgerald and Mr. McMallon." "Ahem, McMahon sir," he corrected. "Right," Payton continued. "If'n there be a reason that we are captured, not that that'll happen of course, but if in the unlikeliest of circumstances that be so, they are to be treated as if they were brought on under duress of pain of death. There shall be no dissenters to this. Agreed?" The men all nod their agreement, though some of the veteran pirates thought them weak because of it.

"Now then stand tall, take the oath, and when finished sign the round robin," Payton directed. The crew did as instructed and Daniel again suddenly realized that he was stuck for yet another oath. "Blimey, again? What did I say last time,' he thought to himself.

"Raise your mugs," he commanded. They willingly do.

"Repeat after me... I"
"I," they responded.

"Agree,,"
"Agree,"

"To,"
"To,"

"Abide by and adhere to,"
"A bly by an a'here to,"
'Nitwits,' Payton thought to himself, but continued.

"The pirate code,"
"Da pirate code,"

"To the completion of the mission,"
"To the completion of the mission,"

"And to comply with,"
"And to compile with,"
'Morons,' Payton thought.

"The laws placed upon us,"
"The laws placed upon us,"

"Without failure,"
"Without failure,"

"Unto pain of death,"
"Unto pain of death,"

"With, uh, plundering and debauchery for all," Payton concluded!
Unanimously, "Amen!"

"Now raise yer hands and toast to our good luck on our mission." Obediently, the men all raised their mugs. "We toast ye mother ocean. We toast ye stars, God's little lanterns, up above in the heavens and be asking ya that ye keep a watchful eye oer'n us that we may complete our mission! We toast to your fallen comrades, though we may have been one time enemies we are linked this day and ask that you guide us that we may avenge your deaths. To the last," he turned his gaze from the men towards the sun as the rain had long since ended. "We drink to you sweet sun and ta this beautiful sunset that you have blessed us with."

The crew joined him in raising their mugs in tribute to the sunset, "AYE!"

As many started drinking, they all signed the round robin. It was a plain sheet of parchment paper where all names were signed in various directions to not have anyone's name be listed as first. As Martin oversaw the signing, Payton watched intently as the sun set along the horizon. Near the sea, it was brightly colored and gradually grew darker as one would look higher into the heavens. The sky was dotted with various flowing and swirling clouds, catching the rays of the sun displaying a vivid tapestry of color, shapes and texture. It was a picture that only the master painter, the good Lord, could create. Lower and lower the sun dipped in the sky as Payton looked on. Vibrant colors swirled around the ever descending sun. Without a word one by one the men began to take notice of Payton and cast their gaze along with him toward the sky. Within a matter of moments all the men, pirate and navy stood side by side staring at the sunset as if seeing it for the first time. Each stood in awe of the vision cast before them, as if this picture was displayed just for them. Just as the sun slipped away below the horizon, the inspired captain lowered his stein and began to applaud the sight. Without command from their leader the crew followed suit, all began applauding the heavenly vision. "Gents, that's a vision of beauty that harkens our future success," Payton said.

Part 5: Elbow Room

Tight Fit

Two days gradually passed and the men began to slowly accept their new mates. It would be a slow process, but a necessary one in order to ensure success. However, as to be expected, the former royal navy men were suspect of the pirates as were the pirates of them. Neither could be certain of the loyalty of the other group of men; yet, they made due best they could. The pirates especially enjoyed playing little pranks on the naval men to see what type of rise they could generate from them. Generally the men took it all in good stride, but that was not always the case as some of them were still steeped in tradition. This resulted in the occasional exchange of words and even a few fists. The quarrels were always broken up quickly by the other men and none were subjected to the bosun's cat-o-nine tails.

A regular watch was established to ensure that no one not of the necessary crew got anywhere near their boat. Many of the new men hadn't even seen her yet. Even though she was odd, she still was sea-worthy. A trait that any stranded man would find irresistible. She had many gawkers and comments abounded, but no one came too close. Anyone who tried was met with an uneasy response from several unsavory individuals.

It was just before sunrise when the dock slowly began coming to life. The local inhabitants continued their work on the ship that crashed the other day, working in shifts and stripping her remains bare. This, like most wrecks was not fit to be resurrected and repaired. The sharp coral heads and the changing currents made swift work of her hull. She was shredded and embedded in the living rock. Over time she would become part of the very reef until all her wood rotted away. Carefully the men would bring all the pilfered goods to the shore for drying and cleaning.

At their camp Payton and his officers had conversed among themselves as to the direction they must take. Payton thought to himself that the men needed an incident to hopefully draw them together. If they could get into a skirmish that would definitely help gel the men together… or end the mission quickly. Either way he thought, it would show him what they were made of. The first call of business just might fit the bill. It was to be commandeering a larger ship as theirs was unfit for such a large crew. Sadly, it was all that they had and they would have to make do; until such time as fate smiled upon them laying a gift at their feet.

"Gents, I realize that the boat we'll be sailing today is a piece of rubbish. She is not fit to carry our load and so we must address this," Payton spoke. "I feel confident that she's going to take us to our first destination, due south," he said, "Havana. From there I have a few connections that will aid us in acquiring a larger, more accommodating vessel. If I am correct, and I usually am, except for the times I am not, we should be in a phase where the seas will be calmer. We'll just have to keep an eye on our freeboard and our confidence in our little, ahem, boat will carry us safely," he said confidently. Then quietly to himself, "And pray that no storm befalls us."

"Captain," Mr. Hall spoke up. "Will we even all *fit* on that thing?" Payton scratched his face in wonderment over that question. He looked over his shoulder down the road towards the dock. Even though he couldn't see the ship he peered as if he could, then back towards the men. He looked back to the water and again to the men. He repeated this a third time when Mr. Hall spoke again, "Sir?" Payton replied, "I'm thinking, I'm thinking…" he answered, "and I'm thinking…*yes*," he said questioningly. He then shook himself as if to shake the cobwebs out of his head, turned and boomed, "TO THE SHIP!" The men looked around at each other and a few shrugged their shoulders and began to follow. "You sure about this," Doc asked Bertrand. "Well, I've got nothing better to do today… so why the hell not? Besides what's the worst that could happen? We go for a swim? You could use a bath you bloody little bugger you," he said with a smile as he began to follow the few who started their walk. There was a group of men who upon hearing this were suddenly disbelievers who shook their heads, yet still followed the rest. Making their way to the dock those who hadn't been on a watch couldn't believe the boat that sat before them. "What the bloody hell is that," Langley asked with a laugh. The crew couldn't believe that they had to board the most embarrassing vessel that ever floated the Caribbean. "I'm certainly glad that me father isn't alive to see this day," Johnson spoke up.

"Mr. Masserson, Make way to sail," Payton directed. Masterson guided the men aboard and packed them in like sardines in a barrel to be shipped home.

"Captain, begging your pardon," Langley interrupted the pirate. "Aye helmsman," Payton answered. "Sir, haven't we too many men aboard to sail? I mean our waterline surely must be too high to make safe passage," Langley asked with concern. "Should we make two trips?" "Normally I'd agree with you mate. However, today we sail under the watchful eye of the spirits. They will guide us and keep us safe," Payton assured him, while squeezed in tight. He turned and looked up to the heavens, "You are watching us right mate," he asked quietly.

Unfortunately the crew didn't necessarily concur with Payton's assessment of the situation. Granted they kept their disbelief to themselves, but the feeling was surely palpable. The spirits may have been there to guide them, however, they weren't there to cease the jeers of the men on the shore.

"Aye mates! Tis won't be but a few minutes till we be'n a seein' ye again," one joked at the overcrowded boat. Another called to his mates, "Come one, come all! Cast yer bets at how far they'n be a gittin' a till the first of us gits our hands on her!" "Shut yer bloody gobs," Chips flared back at the mob. "I'll sever any one of ya's hands before that'll ever happen!" "Alls I'm sayin' is that tis been nice fishin' ana wreckin' wit somea ya. Tis a pity we'd be a meeting 'gan under such conditions," they joked back. "Coop, ya outta jump off now and save them several stone in tonnage!" "Ha-ha," the robust cooper snidely shouted back. "Yer lady she always liked me belly," he said rubbing it. "She said it brung her good luck, 'cept fer you!" This of course drew many men into the laugh. "Aye good lads," Payton began, "if'n we be a needin' ya, at least we know where'n ya be. Till then, I tip me hat ta ya. Tell ya what. Ye can have this piece of rubbish once'n we be done with her."

One man shouted from the crowd, "I wouldn't touch that thing even if'n she were loaded with all the gold of this new world." "Well then old mate, remember that when ye finds this ole lump not to stumble over her just to pick up a single piece of eight. She's got a lot more to her than meets the eye," Payton returned. "Make way," he commanded. The crew jumped to life untying the ship and raised the sails. A full wind was blowing yet the boat refused to budge. There were so many men that some sat upon the gunwales, while others hung in the stationary lines and ladders as there was nowhere else to be.

A few moments passed without a budge, "How goes it," asked one of the fishermen. "Splendid," Payton returned. "I can almost make out Havana now." Still the boat lay heavy in the water. This elicited a big laugh from all the men, crew and bystanders alike.

"Looks like ya mighta run aground mate," a random sponger shouted. "Ye certain that ya wouldn't be wantin' us ta ring da bell," another asked. "Would ya care for a push? Perhaps a tug," another random voice from the shore questioned. "Naw, tis been tugged enough lately. Besides, I haven't the time seeing that I believe that we'll be making way momentarily," Payton replied as the boat sat under its weight.

One of the islanders started, "Ahoy captain, I hear that you are in the brethren of the coast." "Perhaps," Payton replied still looking out over the seas. "Who be asking?"

"My name is Leon Blumberg sir," he replied. "What can I do for you Mr. Blumberg," Payton said looking forward as the boat continued to sit, men sprawling over every inch, others hanging over the sides. "Well sir," he started, "perhaps you be needin' some men fer whatever it is that yer up to," he joked. "Seems like yer yea shy of a full crew," he continued to joke. "Are you inquiring if we're hiring," Martin injected. "Well sir, perhaps. It seems as if you may need an extra hand eh. I mean if you're a pirate, where be yer buccaneers?" "My dear Mr. Blumberg, they're under my buckin' hat. Where're yers," Payton shot back. This elicited a huge laugh from Payton's men. As if having waited for an exit punch-line cue, albeit a weak one, the sails suddenly filled with air and the ship bolted to life commencing their journey. "Auf wiedersehen gents," Payton called as he waved his hat back to the onlookers.

Cuban Crime

The winds blew them in a southerly direction towards their destination in Havana. Being on the windward side aided the overloaded ship along. Fortunately for them the seas were very calm, yet many feared for their existence as they clung precariously to the riggings. Many said little prayers begging for a safe passage and in return they'd give up something they knew to be wrong, knowing full well that they'd break their promises. A passing ship didn't help their morale as they all jeered and hurled insult after insult at the overloaded boat.

"Aye, let 'em laugh," Pedro said. "Some day 'dey all be a headin' down to Havana like dis." Payton eyed him, "You certain about that?" " 'Course, why wouldn' ju wan ta go ta Habana," Pedro asked in earnest. Payton merely shrugged not having a verbal reply. One of the men was overheard by Payton grumbling, "Why don't we bloody well take her then! She's a proper ship at least and we have the 'so-called' pirates eh?" Payton shot back, "Well my good man, while we have the men and the means, they have the upper hand. We have no maneuverability. No speed. No grappling hooks. We'd be fish in a barrel eh. We're too tightly packed in here and don't think that those cannons aren't loaded. One good shot will take this overloaded pile of useless timbers to the bottom of the sea faster that you can pee your britches." He paused a moment, "Are there any further questions?" Not a sound was heard, except for the creak of the heavy timbers and the waves lapping at the hull.

"Gentlemen," Payton said drawing in everyone's attention. "When we arrive in Havana go about your business as if you were just regular passengers or sailors looking to find work in a new port. We will seek out a new ship and decide the best means to acquire her."

The crew was eager for better accommodations, even the royal navy men who used to chase after men who did just this type of deed. "Bet this is all part of his plan then, eh Sails," Blackie whispered to Ian. "Wha' 'chu mean then," Ian inquired in a normal volume. "Sssh," Blackie fired back. "I mean the pirate mate," again he whispered. "I think that he'd done and got this piece of rubbish just to drive us all batty. Then we go'n steal us a bigger ship and suddenly we're all a feeling better about our lot in life, and so we take to pirating more eagerly."

"I don' know," Ian whispered in reply. "I mean I've talked to that bloke eh. He's not that clever. I don' think he coulda' though' it that far through." "I don' know mate. I still don' trus' him completely," Blackie said back. "Oh Blackie, neither do I mate," Ian replied. "Then again, prob'ly most blokes on this mess don' either," he continued.

The boat sailed on in a steady wind as they made their way south. Time slipped by and soon the day had passed. The hungry crew already grew mutinous as they pondered their fate. Yet closer and closer they drew to the island till Jute shouted, "Land ho!"

"I told ye that we'd make it, eh lads," the captain bellowed. The overjoyed crew roared their approval, more so at the sight of land than at the captain's words. "Langley," Payton shouted, unnecessarily in his ear, "Aye, captain," Langley responded, his finger in his ear. "Make way best ye can towards the port. Gents, they had some pirate trouble in the past so we'll have to be watching our step. Should be good now, but tis better to be safe than dead," Payton spoke. Well come close to shore, west of the port. We'll unload a bunch of you blokes there just so as not to draw any more attention to us."

That said, the tiny ship made her tattered way to shore. A few hundred yards west of the port they off loaded as many crew as possible. Many were just happy to have the room to move freely. Once, enough were safely on shore they continued their trek to the port.

Again the sight of them brought out mixed reactions from the workers and sailors on the docks. They stood from bug eyed, to doubled over in laughter and everything in between. Of course this only bolstered Payton's reserve as he stood tall like a conquering hero coming home to port. .

"Dock here Langley," he ordered. "Aye-aye captain," he replied.

The boys began jumping off the rigging onto the dock. Quickly they tied up and made their way to sturdy land. Santiago paid the small fee to dock and of course, listed the incorrect names and number of souls for the ledger. They could not help but draw a crowd of on-lookers jeers and comments. The boys huddled one last time and quickly dispersed into the surroundings. Each made their way into the fort and quickly found their way to food and libation. It took a little longer for the men who went to shore earlier to catch up, but eventually they all arrived. Meanwhile the captain and his officers had different plans.

"Ok gentlemen," Payton began. Let's stay focused and find out what we can about who is here and who may be heading here in the next few days. We need a crafty ship to take us to our destiny. Finny agreed, "Aye captain. Perhaps the local bar wench will tell you what we need to know." Smiling, "I knew that there was a reason why I like you so much Limmey," Payton chuckled. With that they were off to the tavern. As usual Payton's muscle memory knew the way as he led them there, even side stepping an exposed root that typically grabbed visitor's feet. "Beware," was all he said as he did so without looking down. "Wha…" Finny said as his foot stuck directly under it pulling him to the ground. Sarika jumped off his shoulder as his master toppled. "Told you Mildred," Payton started, "We, Mr. Pepper, we might need an interpreter so don't enjoy the ale too much too quickly." There was a pause, "Si captain," he responded.

The group strolled casually into the tavern. A few of Payton's men were already inside enjoying the local talent. "Aye captain this is," Coop started to introduce the bar maid, but as usual, was instantly cut off by Payton. "Margarita so nice ta be seeing yer pretty vision yet again," Payton said to the maid. "Si senor Payton," she gushed in return. Finny just rolled his eyes. "This is honestly getting ridiculous," he uttered to himself. "Good, good, da captain's good," Sarika softly spoke in his master's ear. Martin nodded his agreement. "True, but one day he'll come across one who isn't happy to see him. I hope I'm there to see that day," he said in response. Coop and Doc just sat back in amazement as the scene unfolded before them.

"My dear lady might I have a word," Payton asked softly. "For you senor, anyting," she replied. Payton drew her in looking around the crowded room. His eyes darted the room as he spoke, "We be needing a bigger ship than the one we came in on. Is there anything that might be suitable for a crew of sixty three souls?" "That's a nice size senor," she whispered back taking his hand. "Gracias," Payton replied, "Now how about a ship?" Margarita at first just smiled in return then spoke, "Tis a bit dead right now. What are you sailing right now?" Looking deep into her eyes, "Well my dear, imagine the most wonderful ship that ever sailed the mighty seas. Her bow strong, her sails unfurled, her hold large, her lines long. Can ya see her in yer head," he asked. "Si! She's beautiful," she smiled as she slightly nodded her agreement. "Fabulous," Payton said coyly. "Now look to her immediate right. No, no, to the right. No my right, stage right. Yes. Now ya see the biggest lump of junk that ever had a ratty sail strung upon her half hearted mast sitting right next to her? It looks like the mast was plunged through her long dead heart" "Aye," she giggled. "Dat be'n our so called ship fer the time bein'," Payton joked. "Ok," Margarita started, "There's a small vessel, not heavily guarded or crewed that might be ok fer now. She is at the far end of pier Six." "Six. Aye me little senorita," Payton smiled. "I'll be right back." Payton winked and kissed her forehead.

With that he was off alone to spy the ship in question. Payton made his way out of the bar and slipped unnoticed through the crowd. Quickly he darted through the square trying to go unnoticed keeping his face concealed with his hat tipped low. "Wonder what this ship may be," Payton thought to himself. His train of thought was cut off by a disturbance in the crowd. A scuffle had broken out. "Fabulous," Payton thought. "A much welcomed diversion."

Havana had been sacked by pirates in the past and therefore a fort was erected to protect her people. Once this was finished, the Spanish military presence quickly diminished. Fortunately for Payton, the remaining guard had been recently detached. A Dutch smuggler, the Spanish king placed a bounty on, had recently been spotted in the area. Havana being a poor port, the local governor sent his men out to gain him a quick prize, and in return, some desperately needed funds. Payton finished making his way until he came across the boathouse. Quickly he slipped behind a pile of barrels and bundles, finding his way down to a secure place to spy the ship. He scanned down the docks. The first dock held his boat and he chuckled to himself, "No. No. No," he said as his eyes scanned down the row of ships in waiting. "Not that one, no, um…" he pondered to himself. "That won't do… ah yes. Well it's not the best ship I've ever commandeered, however, tis better than the lump-o-junk we came in on," he thought as he sized up the ship. From his vantage point he could see both ends of the dock. Whereas from either end, the opposite edge of the dock was hidden by its oddly shaped curve. "Well this explains why I couldn't see her when we arrived," he thought.

Next to the prize he had come to scout out, the ship builders were nearing the end of their construction of a new sloop. "Too bad they're not further along," the captain thought to himself; "She has the makings of a fine pirate sloop," he pondered, eyeing the ship. His thoughts were again disturbed by the scuffle now making its way to the dock. The fight was no longer going on, but tempers still flared. Shouts were exchanged, but Payton couldn't make out the language until he heard, "Blimey!" He knew that voice. It sent a chill down his spine as only one person was able to do to him. How? How could it be? Here in Havana? "You stinky vagabond pirate," the voice squeaked. Taking a deep breath and rolling his eyes up into his head he knew that it could only be one person. Exhaling, he slowly turned to see the little boy he loathed to see. "Why Petie, how good to see you yet again," he exclaimed clapping his hands together. It wasn't that he didn't like the boy. Actually he was becoming rather fond of him. He had spirit. That was for certain. It was his father whom he didn't want to see. "BARTHOLOMEW! I knew that you wouldn't remember it again," he shouted. "Ssh. We mustn't disrupt the proceedings," Payton whispered taking a knee still watching the group.

"I'd wager a pound that you're spying on father's ship," he exclaimed. "Wagering now eh boy? I'm starting to like you more and more. Wait, let me guess. That pretty new sloop is father's ship, eh," he asked motioning towards the ship under construction. "Wrong you stinky man," the little boy gleefully remarked at his error. "Ah, then you mean *that* sloop," he said motioning at dock six. "Correct. And you'll never have her," he demanded. Again Payton sighed and shook his head. "And why *shouldn't* it be his," he thought to himself. "Where might yer father be young…" he was cut off. "Right behind you, you scallywag," Governor Blankenslip said. Payton raised an eyebrow and turned his head over his shoulder. "Why it's good to see you again governor," he said with a half smile. "On your feet you slimy pirate," he demanded. "Why is it always hygiene issues with you," he puzzled. He scanned the group that was accompanying the governor. "This time we'll take no chances with you. I'm placing you under arrest pirate. Men, clap him in irons," Blankenslip commanded.

"Bloody hell," Payton thought. With that Payton drew his cutlass. "Sorry gents, however, I have something else that's really pressing on me time right now. So, I'll have to pass on the shackles. Well for now that is. Nice and shiny as they may be. They really are quite nice. Where did you get them?" "Silence," Blankenslip commanded. "GUARDS!"

The guards drew their swords and then Payton engaged the closest man while still trying to retreat. The two men's blades clanked in the battle as another guard circled around to cut off Payton's escape. Trading his cutlass from his right hand to his left while still engaged, he grabbed a dagger hidden beneath his coat. Without even glancing over his shoulder, Payton flipped the dagger in his hand so as to hold it by the blade. As quickly as he caught it between two fingers, he snapped it backward under his arm. The dagger quickly found its intended target, the center of the chest of the second guard, who fell to the ground dropping his own sword. Clutching at the imbedded dagger he fell to his back. His hands grabbed for the handle as blood rushed out around it. In a moment, he was dead. Payton continued his gradual egress, now engaged by two men from the front. Without looking down, he stepped over the now dead guard. Reaching down with his still open right hand, he removed the dagger and again snapped it off. This time he didn't throw it behind him, but rather off to the side where another guard was making his way around the bundles to cut off his retreat. The dagger struck the man in the side of the neck, killing him instantly. Still the duel remained in front of him and from what he could see, there were the two he was engaged with, one more guard, Governor Blankenslip, and not much dock left. Although he was trading slashes with the two guards, his attention was more so on the other guard who was foolishly following in his predecessor's footsteps. As he made his way around the bales Payton didn't throw a dagger, oddly he just let him pass. The duel continued until the voice from the right of Payton said, "Halt! We have you now pirate!" The gleeful guard said. "Certainly," Payton replied. With that the other two guards ceased their attack and stood in shock. They kept their blades raised and ready though. "HA! You are good, I'll give you your due pirate," Blankenslip said from well behind a bale. "However, you're not good enough."

"Perhaps, however, you must admit that it isn't a fair fight. What with you being so outnumbered," Payton said, guard's swords drawn around him. "Um perhaps you've had a bit too much of the rum pirate. You misspoke when you said that 'we're' outnumbered. Yes you made fast work of two of my good men, but from where I stand it's still our four to your one," the governor boldly spoke. "Well, those weren't good men for starters. They were target practice," Payton smugly replied. "As for you numbers, it seems you're a bit off." "How so," inquired the intrigued governor.

Payton who was still hunched over in a defensive stance grabbed one of the pistols that hung around his neck under his coat. He fired on the wide open single guard who fell dead backwards into the water with a big splash. "It's your *three* to my one." Promptly he released the single-fire shot pistol and drew another sword.

Battling with two swords he pressed ahead and started to overtake his enemies. Seeing this and fearing for his own survival the governor fled towards the main square.

Payton's experience and expertise quickly led him to victory over his remaining oppressor. He cleaned his weapons and retrieved his dagger. He stood a moment knowing that soon there may be more men coming after him and he fought back and forth in his mind. "Should I, shouldn't I? Should I, shouldn't I," he debated in his head. Then finally he exclaimed out loud, "Why not?" Quickly he searched the men for anything worth his while. He found some money and a rather intriguing map that he'd investigate later. As he finished, Payton climbed the barrels and made his way onto the roof of the boathouse. Crawling up and over he spied on the square below. Blankenslip was nowhere to be seen, nor was his son. "If we are to take this ship, we'd better do it now," Payton said to himself. He quickly made his way down off the building and took concealed passage ways back to the tavern. Bursting through the door as best he could, Payton found his entire crew in the building. Along with them were more of Payton's former crews and still more who needed employment and had volunteered their services.

"Well, I guess that makes it easier than having to search for them," he said aloud. Climbing onto the nearest table Payton addressed his men. "Gentlemen," he shouted. The room fell silent. Blood of the guards was upon his shirt. "I have found us a ship." Cheers went up from the crew. "She's not the greatest, but she's better than what we arrived on." Again, more cheers followed. "The funny thing about it is, is that the same bloke whom we acquired the first ship from owns this one as well. So as I see it, we're just going to trade him his sloop for the tattered remains of his smuggler." Laughs and toasts rang out. "Course, that means that we need to make sail right now," he said. The men all continued their revelry. Rolling his eyes Payton sighs, "No really, we need to go. I'm not joking about this." Sensing his urgency Mr. Finny speaks out of turn in his militaristic fashion, "WE SHALL BEAT TO QUARTERS!" The men who all served in the royal navy begin to look around and a few even began to scramble not knowing where they should be going causing a minor havoc. No drum sounded as would have occurred on a naval ship. All this did was to lead to a confused mess. Payton still stood above the crowd looking down, he slapped his hand over his face and shook his head. "Mr. Royal Navy, would ye please cease and desist. Yer starting a bloody football hooligan training session in here."

"A what," a befuddled Finny asked. "Never mind. Perrdo, a little help here," he replied. With that Pedro put two fingers in his mouth and whistled so loud that a glass shattered. The confusion came to an abrupt stop. "Grazie," Payton nods to Pedro. "Si senor," he replied with glee. "Men, we make our way now to dock six," the captain commanded.

Obediently, the crew made their way out, led by their captain who a few feet out the door suddenly realized he forgot something. He turned and rushed back into the tavern and headed straight for Margarita. "Senor, I thought you forgot me," she mocked shyly. "I could never forget my favorite tropical Margarita." With that he grabbed her, pulling her on the bar kissing her passionately. "For that I'd had better be your *only f***ing* Margarita," she said staring him straight in the eyes. "Well you're definitely my saltiest Margarita," he replied. With that she laughed and he stole another deep kiss before making his way off. "When should I expect your return," she asked as he was walking to the door. "When the mess I left on the dock is finally forgotten," was his response. As quickly as he had arrived, Payton was out the door and back with his men.

Margarita stood there alone in the *Manana* tavern. She surveyed the damage left behind and sighed. "They probably forget that about the same time I finally get this mess cleaned up," she chuckled to herself in Spanish.

The men made their way to dock six and a crowd stood on the dock talking about the dead guards that lay before them. If Payton had forgotten to take something off the men it was too late, as they were stripped bare causing the pirate to make a nauseated face. Payton walked in the center of his men to conceal himself from any possible attack, not wanting any further disruption, only to board and be off. The men started to board the ship, their hands on their holstered weapons in case of emergency. As they boarded the dock master approached the boat.

"Senor," was the only word Payton could understand. Quickly Santiago spoke up and had a conversation with him. "Capt'n, he say dat we can not board dis ship as is not ors," Pedro said. "Ah," Payton said. "Well tell the good man that we have acquired this sloop in trade." "Trade senor," Pedro asked. Payton just nodded. Pedro exchanged the message to the disbelieving master.

"He I believe 'e capt'n," Pedro said. "He asks what we traded fer her." "Tell him it's on dock one," he said. Pedro looked at him straight-faced. Payton urged him on.

"Go on, tell him. Tell him," Payton said. Pedro still looked at him with the same expression. Payton continued to urge him on, nodding his head towards the master. Pedro rolled his eyes back and took in a deep breath, biting his upper lip trying to control his swelling laughter. He turned to the master, then back to Payton still urging him on with a smile, then back to the master and told him. The dock master also looked at him straight faced, then looked over Pedro's shoulder at Payton, then back to Pedro. He simply burst out laughing and shaking his head. The master knew that this was a fib, but the man they were stealing from was an Englishman. A sworn enemy, and a rude one at that. He didn't care. Feeling that his guards were all dead the repercussions didn't seem very large.

Payton pulled out the map he recently acquired from the dead guard and flashed it around, "See, this is the note saying it's all legal. It's even notarized," he added. The dock master just continued to laugh and said something to Pedro, threw up one hand, turned and walked off.

"What was that that he said," inquired Payton. "He jus sad dat he can't wait ta see da man's face when he a-come back far his ship," Pedro said. "Wish I could as well. Men, we…" he was cut off. "Ahoy there," a man dressed in uniform called to the captain.

"Blast," Payton thought to himself. There was something familiar about this bloke. "Aye sir, what can I do fer ye," Payton asked him. The man looked at the captain, "You are the pirate captain Payton, are you not?" Payton eyed the familiar face with a discerning eye. "Why do you ask?" The man looked from the dock as he spoke. "You don't remember me do you then? My name is Reginald Holden and this is Samuel Fry. We were on the guard for Governor Blankenslip when you commandeered his ship. The one over in slip one." Many of the pirates slyly went for their weapons. "We thought that we'd taken you back to the island. However, when we reached the dock, you somehow had escaped. The governor wasn't pleased with our efforts. This was nothing new for him though. He is an evil, overbearing man. He is as ruthless as he is stupid. His punishments toward his men were no different than the torture he gave his enemies. It is for this reason that I renounce my affiliation to him and wish to join you and your men."

Payton nodded his head as he listened. "If'n you're telling the truth, we have room for you blokes. If'n you be a lying… it won't take long to discover and punish you. And believe me what we come up with will make the governor look like a missionary." The two men nodded their agreement and pledged themselves to the pirate captain. They were welcomed on board by their new mates, stripped of their military coats and quickly put to work.

"Gents we sail," Payton commanded.

Part 6: Not Always As It Seems

A Sign of Things to Come

The men made their way out of the harbor aboard their new ship. The sloop was a smaller one than the captain would have desired, yet for now she'd do. "Captain, what heading make we," Langley inquired. As Payton looked around, he spotted the binnacle. He strolled to it, yet no compass sat upon it. Suddenly he was want of an answer himself. "That's a fair question lad," he spoke. "Mr. Mallory, come forth." "Martin sir," he said as he stepped forward. "What make you of that then," he motioned towards the empty binnacle. "Um, not certain sir," Finny replied. "Well I gather that it'll be a fabulous place to hold my chips and dip then," Payton remarked. "However, we need a heading." A puzzled Finny responded, "Chips and what sir?" "Any ideas on what our heading should be," he asked quietly leaning in to him. "Um, no sir. I thought you'd know where we needed to go," Finny said. "Swell," Payton said. "Mr. Lankow, make our heading west then south around the island." "Yes sir," Langly replied.

Payton looked around the ship backing up to the binnacle. Without a hesitation he hopped up hoping to find it a comfortable seat. Instead once he made contact, the dry rotted binnacle gave way under the full weight of the captain. He went down to the deck with a mighty crash. "Bloody hell," said Payton reclining on his backside, resting on his forearms. "I'd say that this ole tub has a bit of dry rot eh?"

Langley offered him his hand, which the captain accepted and was helped back to his feet. Dusting himself off Payton spoke, "Have that removed." "Aye-aye captain," Langley answered. "Sir," Finny approached him speaking softly, "Are you alright?" Not looking at him, "Never better. Why?" "Well sir you took a frightful fall then," Finny stated. "Did I? No. Never," he said trying to sound serious. Payton leaned in and spoke very softly, "Hurts like a bugger. However, ya can't let it show. Bad for the crew to see the captain hurt." The captain stood back, "Perhaps that's why they removed the compass." "Why's that then," Finny asked perplexed. "Well I'm light as a feather aren't I? Some heavy ole compass would shatter that flimsy thing," he joked. Payton thought to himself, "Well who got the better of this deal? That idiot governor is probably laughing to himself. It figures that we went from that rubbish heap to this one. Can't the man have a decent ship?"

The ship had made its way to the western edge and changed her course for south. Payton walked to the stern rail and looked out at the island growing smaller the further they went. "Captain," a voice said from behind him. "Who approaches," the captain asked not turning around nor being familiar with the voice. "My name is Hillberg sir," the voice said. "What can I do for you Mr. Hillenburger," Payton asked. "Well sir below deck I found," he was cut off. "Me, captain," the voice said. Payton closed his eyes and thought to himself, "Oh you have just got to be kidding me. No, no, no." He turned to see young Bartholomew standing next to Hillberg. Payton slightly shook his head. "Young Bill, what are you doing here?" Heaving a sigh, "Bart sir,"

Martin leaned over to Pedro and whispered in his ear, "I know that sigh. I know it well." Pedro contained a laugh. "I ran aboard when father and his men came upon us on the dock. I thought I'd be safe here," Bart said. "Well, what are we to do with you," Payton questioned. "With some training you could make a good lieutenant some day," Martin chimed in. Payton just rolled his eyes at Martin then back. "But I'm not a pirate sir," the young boy said. "For the time being my good boy, you are," Payton said back. "Mr. Blannenslah, or whatever your name is, there are no stowaway's allowed aboard my ship." "Your ship? You mean my father's ship," the boy darted back. "Mind your tongue in front of the captain," James Hall shot back.

"It's alright Mr. Dollyland. This boy and I go a ways back," he said smiling to Hall. "I know that you wish this to still be yer father's sloop. However, you have to come to grips with the fact that this is now *my* ship and that he can have her back when we acquire our *next* ship. Just like we exchanged his other ship for this one. I'm certain that he's excited to have it returned."

"You mean, *steal* your next ship," Bart said arms folded. "*You mean, steal your next ship,*" Payton sarcastically shot back. "It's always the same ole same with you ain't it boy? Now, unfold those little arms of yers and get to work." "Work," the little voice stammered out. "Aye, work," he said with a smile. "A little work will be good for you. A man must earn his keep aboard the… the… what is the name of this vessel," Payton asked. "*The Dreamers Delight,*" Bart answered back with glee. Payton closed his eyes, lowered his head as he shook it and exhaled a heavy sigh. "Figures. What a stupid name.

Couldn't be *The Revenge; Treasure Seeker; Captains Lady; Malicious Intent*; no I get the bloody *Dreamers Delight*," he said to himself. "Mr. Hilgenburger, what is your occupation sir?" "Blacksmiths mate sir," Hillberg replied. "Tremendous," Payton replied. "Meet your new apprentice." "Sir," Hillberg questioned. "I know, I know, I know, just humor me eh," Payton replied. "A little hard work will do you wonders me boy. Enjoy!" "Aye-aye sir," Hillberg replied taking the boy by the hand leading him away. Bart looked shocked and scared as he was ushered off.

"Mr. Lantonsboogie," Payton said turning to Langley. "Aye captain," he responded. "Is it me or is she a bit sluggish," Payton asked. "Aye sir, she is," Langley answered. Payton turned to Finny, "She probably needs a good cleaning. We'll have to do that if she's going to be of any use to us." "Aye sir," Finny responded. "We should be able to find a place to careen if we head west toward mainland." "Lumpy, make your heading south by southwest," Payton instructed. "Aye captain," Langly said, "South by southwest."

Payton made his way off the quarterdeck towards the fore mast. "Mr. Rikardo," Payton called up the mast. "Aye, Captain," Richards called down. "Might I have a word," Payton inquired. "Certainly sir," Richards replied. With that Payton shimmied up the mast like a monkey. "SIR," Richards exclaimed eyes wide! "Ricky me boy, this isn't the first ship I've been on," Payton said with a smile. "I didn't mean anything by it sir," Richards said apologetically. "Don't fret it boy. I need you to keep yer eyes open for a good spot to careen ourselves. We're very sluggish and the keel needs a good cleaning. Even if we find another ship to commandeer, we'll never be able to catch her, eh. If we don't find anywhere good on your watch, advise yer follow-up of our intended goal, eh" Payton instructed. "Aye-aye captain," Richards replied.

With that the captain surveyed the horizon. "There's nothing quiet like it eh," he asked. Richards just nodded his head in agreement. "Even though the seas may be rolling, there's something so peaceful about her. A great place to clear yer head eh," he paused. "There's just nothing quite like her. Well, keep a weather eye open lad. You are our eyes now." Richards nodded his head and watched as the captain descended the mast as easily as he had climbed. "What the devil was that all about," Richards thought to himself. The boat continued on her way seeking safe haven. Unfortunately for the pirates, no such place was found.

Midsummer Nightmare

The Dreamers Delight sailed through the night. Most of the crew was fast asleep while the night watch was on deck. The men remained mostly silent as they went about their work. It was the first night aboard their bigger ship and they were still familiarizing themselves with her. The crew was still cramped below in the foredeck and the ship was not what they needed, however, she was better than what they had. She'd do.

From the crow's nest a voice called down, "Aye, Eric!"
"What is it Rammer," Eric 'Jute' Johns called back.
"We've got bloody trouble mate," James Ram replied.
Suddenly shocked, Jute called out in return, "What?"
"Storm is blowing in quick," Rammer returned! As quickly as he could, Eric blew the whistle that alarmed the rest of the crew. Just as the crew jumped to life, the first wind gusts blew and the storm ripped in. The crew was getting tossed around and waves began crashing into the hull. Salt water spewed across the deck and knocked several men off their feet. Payton strolled unfazed upon the quarterdeck. Seemingly calm he took over the wheel. "Gentlemen we've got ourselves a bit of a blow! Drop the sails except the main and jib!"

"Drop the sails, except main and jib," Mr. Hall shouted out. From the crew a voice returned, "Dropping it sir!"

Payton began to sense more trouble was afoot. "Grab the gunwales or something that's nailed down boys unless you're part fish." With that command, a wave crashed over top of the ship. Payton continued to shout commands, "Mr. Martin have the bilge checked and begin pumping immediately." Martin holding onto a gunwale for dear life, completely missed the fact that Payton actually called him by his real name. He attempted to scream over the wind, "Mr. Walker check the hold and pump her if necessary!" Sliding from side to side Jake Walker yelled, "Uh, ok sir! Bert! Come with!" Jake and John Bertrand dove down the stairs. While all hell was breaking loose around him, Payton stated in a loud voice, "Ah boys! What a lovely night for a bath! We needed this. Many of you were *really* beginning to stink!"

Holding onto the main boom Santiago apologized, "Aye sir! Sorry 'bout dat!" A moment later the men heard a loud sizzle followed by a bolt of lightning striking the fore mast. The wooden mast exploded under the sheer energy of the lightning bolt. The remaining mast tumbled to the deck and into the ocean. James Ram fell hard to the deck. His head smashed into the wood rendering him unconscious. His leg became tangled in a sheet that was still connected to the fore topsail. The fore top mast to which it was connected tumbled into the ocean. Quickly the sheet became taut and pulled at his leg dragging the unconscious man overboard. The rigging was still attached to the bowsprit and threatened to tip the ship.

Not seeing Rammer dragged overboard, "Well that's a bit of a pisser," Payton exclaimed. "Dat be da worst," Pedro chimed in. "Cut the rigging! Save the sails," Payton ordered.

Men dove across the ship as she raised along with the thirty-five to forty foot waves then quickly fell. Waves continued to crash across the deck as the men tried to carry out the latest orders. Axes in hand, they savagely hacked at the riggings in an attempt to free themselves from capsizing. "Quickly men, quickly men," Hall commanded. One by one the ropes were cut when suddenly Hall saw something odd. "What's that by that sail? Wait MAN OVERBOARD! HEAVE THAT LINE," he shouted! Hall and Walsh frantically pulled the rope that encircled Rams leg. "Keep cutting the rest," Hall ordered. "The sea wants him, the sea should have him," a superstitious crewman shouted. "Shut yer gob," Hall shouted back. The rain continued to pelt the men as the accompanying wind howled. Not giving up the crewman shouted back, "If the sea gods aren't appeased they take us all! LET HIM GO!" Hall spun around and struck him with a closed fist dropping him to the deck. "One more word and we'll appease the water gods by throwing YOU in!"

"We've got em," Walsh tipped in. The two men pulled the still unconscious Ram back on deck and Walsh dragged him below deck to Doctor Fitzgerald. The mast dangled deep into the water and the current opened the fore sail in the water. A sudden jerk of the sail pulled at the ship like an anchor suddenly tossed overboard. A few more men were tossed overboard as the ship began to tip to her side.

"I told you! I told you," the frightened crewman shouted. "We're all going to drown!" This time it was Payton who addressed the man. Taking the blunt end of the hatchet he struck the man in the jaw, shattering it. "NEVER SAY THE 'D' WORD ABOARD SHIP!" The captain quickly returned to his work as the man again sat on the deck in shock and pain.

"Keep ackin'! Ders still some dere," Pedro commanded. Schmitty cried, "MEN OVERBOARD!"

Finally, the last of the rigging was chopped by Payton and the mast and sails freely broke away. The ship righted herself immediately and the crew quickly focused on the men in the sea. Schmitty grabbed a loose line and tied it to himself. Grabbing some loose lumber he threw it to the men, then dove in. "Secure that line," Payton commanded. Schmitty swam to the nearest man and grabbed hold. "AVAST! HEAVE YE CURSED DOGS,

HEAVE" Payton shouted.

Payton and several men hauled the man back to the ship and pulled him below deck. Dr. Fitzgerald was up to the task and quickly worked to resuscitate him. Richards was holding for dear life to one of the planks Schmitty threw. As quickly as Schmitty was pulled aboard and released the man, he turned and dove right back in. The waves and pounding rain impaired his visibility markedly. The ship was unable to turn due to the size of the waves and the limited maneuverability. Fortunately for them the current carried them toward the men in the sea.

Blackie shouted from the ship as rain pounded his face, "KEEP GOING! KEEP GOING! HE'S DIRECTLY AHEAD OF YOU!" A wave suddenly took him off course. "NO! TO YOUR PORT SIDE! YOUR PORT SIDE!" Schmitty turned left and the next wave carried him towards his mate. "RRRREEAAACCHH! RRREEEAAACCHHH," Schmitty called out! "Come closer Chips! CLOSER," Richards cried out!

The two men struggled against the wind and the waves. They finally came within inches of each other. "GRAB ME," Schmitty screamed. A wave crashed over Richards causing him to swallow a mouthful of saltwater. Immediately he began to vomit.

"GRAB ME RICHIE," Schmitty demanded. Richards continued to vomit as he reached out his hand again. "I CAN'T COME ANY CLOSER! I'M AT THE END OF THE LINE," Schmitty shouted.

Trying to maneuver the plank towards Schmitty and still

vomiting Richards replied, "I'M, uuuuuhhhh, I'M, uuuuuhhhhhh, I'm trying uuuuuhhhh."

From behind, the churning waters caused a wave to suddenly push Richards directly at Schmitty. The plank slammed into the side of Schmitty's head knocking him unconscious and bleeding heavily. Richards grabbed hold of him and tilted his head above water. Water kept rolling over their heads submerging them then freeing them. "Dang it Chips, hang on," Richards thought. The pull was felt aboard the ship where the men were almost pulled overboard themselves.

"PUL...PULL...PU...," Richards was trying to call. He barely could get the word out before the next wave covered them. Again salt water went in Richards' mouth causing more vomit to gush out. "HEAVE YOU BASTARDS LIKE YOU'VE NEVER HEAVED BEFORE," demanded Payton.

Payton and the men pulled with even greater force then before. Finally they pulled the men back on deck. Again Dr. Fitzgerald followed his calling as the survivors were brought below deck and began to work on them. Being tossed side to side made the work extremely difficult, but he managed to revive both men in due time. Even with these amazing victories there was one unfortunate crew member who was lost to the sea.

As quickly as the storm had arrived it passed. Rain still fell but much lighter than before. They had weathered the storm and come out a tattered mess.

"Ahoy Pedro," the captain called out. "Aye capt'n," was

his typical response. "Head count sir. I want all men accounted for," Payton demanded. "Aye-aye," Pedro called. With that Pedro quickly began to scramble and take a head count of the men.

"Dr. Fitz," Payton bellowed calling below deck. A voice resonated in return. "Yes sir?" "Status report of the men please," Payton asked. "All are alive. With the exception of Ram, all will be fine.," Fitzgerald returned still dressing wounds. "And as for Ram," Payton inquired. "Too early to say sir," the doctor replied. "Tremendous work Dr. Tremendous work. Is Chips available to work," Daniel wondered not knowing that he was previously unconscious. "I wouldn't recommend it," was the doctor's advice. "Understood," Payton replied, then turning "Sails!" "Sir," Ian replied. "Check the status of our sails and note what repairs need to be attended to," Payton ordered. "Aye-aye sir," Ian returned. A weaker voice calls up from below deck. "Aye captain," the voice said. "Chips," Payton wondered as he called back. "Aye sir! I'm available," Schmitty said. He ambled up the stairs holding on as he was still woozy from the head trauma. Payton eyed the man ambling up the stairs, his head wrapped in a white dressing. "Are you certain you can work?" "What do you require sir," he inquired. "We need to assess if we can assemble a jury mast or if we can make it ashore under our current power," Payton offered. "Aye sir. Can I have assistance," a woozy Chips asked. "Certainly. You can have your carpenter's mate." Pausing he looked around the deck until, "Pid," he bellowed. "Aye," Pid called back rushing over. "Assist Chips and do as he instructs," Payton ordered. "Aye sir," Pid replied. Pid assisted the woozy Chips as they made their way off to assess the damage.

Daniel went below to the hold, which had several feet of water in it. He jumped in creating a large splash. Looking around, he assessed the damage, "Well, this is a bit unsettling, eh Walks," Payton said flatly. Running down the stairs with buckets in hand, "Aye captain. She's got a bit of water in her sir," Jake replied. Also running by with a full buckets in hand, "But we're doing well sir," Bertrand chimed in.

Payton watched in amusement waiting for one of them to return. Jake was the first one back, "Um pardon me Jasen. Pump not working then," Payton inquired. "Clogged at the exit port," he responded. "Please, continue your work," Payton injected. He did just that and ran out to empty the bucket. Bert had come down and Payton only smiled at him. "Ah, Jerome wonderful. Um trouble with the bilge pump then," he asked. "Not working sir," was his response as he made his way up the stairs. "Ah yes," he said. "And why isn't that a surprise eh," he said to himself. "Are there more buckets," Payton inquired. Running back up with full buckets, "Not sure captain," Bert puffed. "Walts," Payton said. "Sir," Jake replied. "Jape, When you're done, note the ballast stone and fix them if necessary," Payton asked politely. "Will do sir," Jake replied happily. "Well done lads. Two extra rations of grog in the morning," Payton rewarded. In unison, the two men reply, "AYE! Thank you captain!"

Payton walked the hold speaking softly to himself, "Well they'll be weary in the morning." He paused and surveyed the items in the hold, some floating others not. His attention turned to a rat balancing on a floating plank. "Hello Purvis!" The rat looked at this strange man and squeaked. "Yes, I understand you're a bit wet, but frankly you too needed a bath eh," Payton said with a smile. The rat still eyed him up and stuck his tongue out at him. "Right! I'm off," Payton replied to his gesture. The captain headed back up the stairs as Jake and Bert continued to run frantically past. "Good work chaps!" Calling back to him, "Thank you sir," Jake said.

Back on deck, Payton looked around suddenly puzzled, "Now what was I going to do?" "Is dere a lot ta water in da hold," Pedro inquired. "No, I just went," Payton responded. Completely baffled, "Sir," Pedro mumbled? Standing tall adjusting his jacket, "Status report please," Payton demanded. "All head but one accounted for," Pedro said. "Whose," Payton asked not wanting to hear the news. "Ware," he said. "What," Payton asked. "Not what, Ware," Pedro said. "There," Payton inquired. "No Ware," Pedro returned. "Nowhere," the confused captain asked. "No, dats his name," Pedro returned. "Whom," Payton requested. "Ware, Jeffrey Ware," Pedro said. "Ah," Daniel said frowning and nodding his head. "Right. I'm certain that you double checked that?" "Si."

He surveyed the scene aboard the deck while the men frantically worked to get her back into shape. Sails returned to Payton. "Capt'n," Ian addressed him. "Sails what's the damage report," he countered. "Our main an top main are fine. We've gone an lost 'ar fore an fore top sails then. Fore stay's tattered, but can be mended. Jib's salvaged but damaged. She'll be able ta be mended. Flying jib was lost," Ian reported. "Excellent work Sails. Repair what you can, we'll address the rest when we get ashore," Payton said. "Aye-aye sir," McMahon replied saluting and returning to his work.

Payton made his way below deck to visit with the wounded. He strolled upon the sawdust strewn floor absorbing the blood of the injured and looked upon them with concern. The concern was both as a captain and as a friend. He wanted them healthy for self preservation's sake as they were sitting ducks; as well as, he was beginning to admire the lot of them. The men who were awake saluted and appreciated his interest in their status. Payton made sure that they were fed first that night and the next morning. Upon approaching Ram, he saw a figure and not the actual man. His head was wrapped, save for his nose and mouth allowing him to breathe. His torso and arms also were wrapped in the white cloth with crimson spots giving away his laceration sites. His legs were also heavily bandaged, the right splinted between two planks. In plain English, he was a mess.

The captain looked around and also saw the cowardly crewman nursing his broken jaw. Seeing the captain's gaze, he righted himself and stood up to show his respect. Payton strolled over to him, his hands clasped behind him they stood face to face. Only Payton spoke. "Sir, your actions today were reprehensible. Your eagerness to let fellow shipmates perish is deplorable. Your insolence is reprehensible. I do believe in your heart you truly believe what you said. And in so, you were looking for the safety of the ship first and foremost. I commend you for that. However, on *my* ship we look out for one-another. Understood?" The man simply nodded yes. "Good," the captain replied. "Good." He turned to walk away but quickly spun back. In a brief moment the crewman's relief turned back to terror as the captain spun back towards him. Again, he looked the man straight in the eye, "I wouldn't complain much if'n I were you. And ye'd better hope and pray that the rest of the men don't know what you said. Could be trouble, eh mate?" Payton turned and walked over to Ram. Surveying the mess in front of him he shook his head in disbelief and leaned over and spoke quietly in his ear. The supine man didn't move or make a sound as the captain whispered to him, and with that Payton left.

The nervous crewman took a moment and let his words settle in. Taking his advice, he approached Fitzgerald and mumbled, "I want to be your assistant." Fitzgerald looked stunned at him. "I'm sorry? Did you say you wanted to assist me?" The man nodded. "But I already have a mate. OH!" He quickly realized that the man was looking for penance and agreed. Promptly he put the man to work.

Last Rites

The men worked till the early morning hours, and the sun began to rise. "All hands on deck," Payton bellowed. The men all gathered on deck. Bleary eyed, the ragged men gathered around the captain.

"Gents, you are all to be commended for the wonderful work you valiantly performed last night. We are not out of danger yet. We are severely crippled. We need to find a new mast and sails. But more pressing matters are at hand." The lightly misting rain finally ceased. The winds calmed and the boat drifted lazily in the current.

"Sadly one of us did not survive the storm. He was claimed to the deep last night by mother ocean. Gentlemen, remove your hats," Payton continued. He turned to Fitzgerald, "Dr." Fitzgerald made his way before the men where he opened his Bible and read to them a passage he felt fit the situation. The men stood in silence in respect for their fallen comrade. Even though they were criminals most still had a respect for the reading of biblical passages. Additionally, they had a tremendous respect for any among them who fell in defense of their ship. Their ship was their home, their country their very being no matter what it looked like. When the good doctor finished, the men just stood amidst the wreckage that once was their sloop.

"Thank you doctor," Payton offered. "Mother ocean, you have claimed one of your faithful servants to the deep. Watch over his soul and give him peace," Payton continued. The men bowed their heads over their lost mate. Payton finished, "Gentlemen, we sail for the nearest land to make our repairs. Normal shifts will return to work. Get some food and everyone not on shift, get some sleep. Again men, excellent work. Excellent work indeed all."

Then men eagerly did as instructed… especially those who were off to get some much-needed sleep.

What's In A Name?

The ship limped her way as best she could to a tiny isle that didn't appear on their charts. It had been a couple of days since the storm interfered with their plans and most of the wounded were fine again. Ram was even out of his mummification and ambling about. Miraculously all he had were several cuts and a sprained ankle that was hobbling him a bit. He would use a makeshift cane for the next few days as he continued his healing process.

Waiting for the peak of high tide, they sailed as close to the island as possible till she hit bottom of the shoal. They knew that when the tide went out she'd be totally aground making cleaning the barnacles off her hull easier. It would also make it as easy as possible to drag their new mast to the ship. Payton organized the crew into groups. 1st unit was placed on hull duty to scrape the hulls clean. 2nd unit was placed on mast duty. They were sent off to the island to find a tree that would do to replace their destroyed one. 3rd unit was placed on interior and exterior hull duty to check her for cracks, areas that needed tarring, rot or anything that stood as a potential hazard. The rest of the men went about their specialized areas.

Ian sat on deck with the monumental task of repairing the sails alone. "Coop," he said. "Yeah, Sails," he returned. "Ya got a lot 'o barrels to repair," Ian questioned. "Naw, got em all done already. Twasn't that many to begin with," he replied. "You need a hand?" "Ya ever do any sail work in ta pas'," Ian wondered. "Nope, but I'm good'n wit my hands. I'll do the smaller mends and leave the important ones," Walsh offered. "Thanks mate," Ian said. "We got a deck load a work ta do. That storm really shredded 'em."

Ashore, Roger "Blackie" Smyth and Steven Hillberg had already made a fire pit and readied the area to begin their blacksmith duties. Onboard, carpenter's mate Pid made repairs as best he could to the various damaged areas of the deck. All the while, injured yet determined, master carpenter Schmitty was in the expedition for a suitable mast.

"Anyone seen anything on this god forsaken spit that'll do? Hell I'd even settle for a jury mast. Anything till we can get a proper mast somewhere," Hall said. "I ain't seen nothin' worth nothin'," Jackson said. "What say you to that one over there," Williams said motioning towards a tree that might be suitable. "Possible," Richards returned. "She's more'n possible there mate," Hall started. "She's our new mast. Well done Richards, well done." "Thank God," Williams stuttered. "These bloody hatchets is a gettin' heavy." "Think that's heavy eh," Blase said, "wait'l we have to carry that bloody log!" Bertrand spoke up, "Let's just fell her and be done with this as sharp as possible mates." Arriving at the tree the bosun took charge. "Get to work gents," Hall ordered.

***

"Coop, you havin' any difficul'ies then," Ian asked. "I keep prickin' me self with this damn thing Sails," Walsh replied. Ian looked over at Walsh's work. Indeed he was bleeding all over the Jib. "Well, yo've defini'ely made her a pirate jib. What with all that blood all o'r her," Sails joked. "Yeah, I'm sure she'll strike fear in the hearts of all who see her," Walsh returned. "Too bad I won't be round to see it." "Why's that then," Ian wondered still laughing. "Well, I'll surely be dead. All me blood is soaked up in this stupid cloth! I'm startin' ta get a little lightheaded," he continued to joke. "Ligh' headed. Blast Coop, you daft drunk git. Yer always ligh' headed from all ta grog," Sails shot back with a laugh. Smirking, "If I just had the energy left in me body I'd come right up and throttle you a good one," Walsh shot back.

***

"Hillie, you got that caster ready," Smyth asked. "Aye Blackie," Hillberg replied as he finished the molds for the blacksmiths. The new mast would require new mast hoops, partners and tangs to hold the mast and riggings in place. They had taken the old ones off what remained of the former mast and were stoking the fire getting ready to melt them down. This was a time consuming task, so they attended to this first. They would need measurements off the new mast quickly, before new ones could be made. "Hopefully we can pour em soon as they start stripping the bark. Which means we'll need ta measure it up fast. The captain ain't gonna take kindly to any loafing I feel," Roger said. "Aye. You think that this captain can get us *the Scavenger* back," Hillberg questioned. "He'd better. Or it'll be our heads," was all Smyth could muster.

***

The tree fell and the men attacked the limbs with the hatchets. Quickly the tree was scaled down to just the trunk. They were allowed rest to drink what little fresh water they had with them. The men sprawled in the shade of the humid day trying to regain their much needed strength. When it was time, under the direction of their bosun, they labored to lift the tree. Thus began the arduous journey as they lugged the heavy tree back to base camp on the beach. Seeing this, the captain made his way from the ship to inspect the new timber.

"Mr. Pips. Is this sufficient for a replacement," Payton asked. "She'll have to do sir. She's the best we could find," Chips replied. "Tree-mendous," Payton joked. Looking around for a reaction and getting none he tried again. "Tree-mendous," still nothing. Disgusted, he shook his head. "Well I trust that you'll make the best of her then. Time is of the essence men. I'll leave you to your work." "You heard the captain men," Hall spoke with authority. "Start strippin' that bark!" The men quickly took to the arduous task. "Blackie, get your measuring tools at the ready. We'll need you to work fast as well." "Aye- aye," Smyth returned. As Payton strode away a thought flashed across his mind. "Blimey!" He turned back and approached Blackie. Hall spoke up, "Captain approaching!" All the men stopped and stood to face the captain. "No need boys, you're too busy. Blackie, a moment?" "Ay- ay sir," he said approaching him. "Blackie, we need all the luck we can get eh." Smyth nodded his agreement. "Can you fashion a horseshoe and have her nailed on the new mast?" "Course sir!" "Excellent," he said patting him on the shoulder. "Excellent."

Under the mid day heat of the blazing Caribbean sun the men labored. While the crew cleaned the hull they had to fend off angry crabs and the occasional water snake looking for a shadowy place to hide. Inside the ship it was no easier. The jack-tar crew had the most despised job off all. Squatting in the stifling hot bilge, the air lay heavy and stagnant. There they lay the pitch along the longest seam, otherwise known as 'the devil.'

"This bloody ship hasn't been serviced in I'd wager five years! Hell, she may never even had any work done at her at bloody all," Jake huffed. "She's more a burden than she's bleedin' worth!" "Walks, I'm surprised she held through the storm last night," Dooley said. "Look at this ballast stone. Barely enough to keep her steady," Walker replied. "We should just burn her down an start over. Probably be easier," Dooley joked. "Pid, how's the mast step comin'," Walker asked. "Finished. I don't know how you fellas do this. I need some air," Pid replied. "You certain yer finished," Dooley inquired? "Why," Pid asked. "You put a mast stamp in that," the veteran Dooley inquired. "It's bad luck if'n ye didn't put in a mast stamp." "Bloody right," exclaimed Pid. "One of you gents got a coin?" "If'n it'll give us better luck, blast, you can have mine," Walker offered. Digging into his pocket he extracted a small coin and flipped it to Pid. "Most obliged," Pid returned. Upon reaching the base where the mast would sit, he quickly knelt down. Inspecting the base, he could see that at one time a coin had been set, but now was gone. A myriad of thoughts raced through his head, ranging from someone stole it, to other mystical explanations for its disappearance. After carefully placing the coin, he dripped hot candle wax over it to seal it into place. "There we go," he thought. "We can use the luck!"

"I noticed that you gave him the smallest one you had," Dooley joked quietly. "It's a small ship," Walker fired back. "That's in then. Many thanks again Mr. Dooley," Pid said. "What 'chu got next," inquired Dooley. "Gotta put in a new bowsprit. Vaughn was supposed ta git a good piece a wood ashore. Hope he got one already," Pid remarked. "Right, well off with you. No dallying," Walker joked. "Yeah the captain will have us tar you if'n he catches you slackin' off," Dooley teased. Pid's face went ghostly white. "You fellas serious 'bout that," he asked. "Boy, the captain once had me cover a bloke in the pitch and dangle him off the bowsprit when'n our figurehead fell off," Dooley started. "The figurehead was more than just good luck for our ship. She was carved in the image off his beloved Linda who perished the year before from typhoid. The loss of that figure head set him off and he grabbed the carpenter who had carved her. Feeling like he'd lost his beloved for a second time he made me cover that poor bloke in tar to protect him from the water. He then strung him up himself and made him serve out his punishment as the replacement figurehead." Pid just stood there in shock. "How long did he keep him there?" Dooley raised his eyebrows and turned his head towards Walker. He flashed him a half smile, then turned back to Pid. "Don't right know. See we just kinda forgot about him an after a while, an well, we just stopped noticing that he was there. Then one day when we was in our jolly boat heading back to the ship when one of me mates just said, 'wha evr happen'd ta the figurehead?' We just shrugged, laughed a bit and went bout our business laddie." He paused and repeated himself, "Just shrugged an wen' 'bout our business. I guess the moral of the story is, don't piss off the captain!"

"Blimey," was all Pid could muster, straight faced and flushed of any pigment. With that he tore off topside. Walker looked at Dooley, "Was there any truth in that?" Dooley just turned to Walker, "Naw, made it all up mate. You think that the captain would ever marry?" "That kid crapped his trousers but good," Walker laughed. "What good is it having these royal navy guys round if'n we can't have some fun wit 'em? Besides, his name isn't Pid by accident, eh mate," Dooley said. "I've been wondering 'bout that mate. That bloke's real name is what," Walker said searching his mind for the name. "Phillips. That's it. How does that become Pid?" "It doesn't," Dooley said. Walker looked dumbfounded, "Huh?" Dooley continued to go about his work, "What I hear is he isn't the brightest chap to ever sail the seas." "Right," Walker agreed. "But Pid?" "Eh. His first name just so happens to be Stewart," Dooley continued. "Stewart Phillips," Walker questioned. "So what?"

Dooley sighed stopping his work and turned to face the wondering mate. "He's not bright. His name is Stewart. Pid. Stew. Pid. Stupid; Stew-Pid. Get it?" Breathing a sigh of relief, "Oh," exclaimed Walker! "Pid! Right, very funny indeed!" "It's not funny if'n ye have to explain it," Dooley said. He paused, then thought a moment, "No. It *is* still funny."

***

"Damn Sails, you do good work," Coop exclaimed. Receiving the compliment with a sly smile, " Just doin' me craft Coop. Just doin' me craft." "Sure, but that sail was in tatters and by god I swear, that thing'll not only fly; she'll catch a mighty blow for a long time to come," Coop declared. "Ya know, I could use a hand," Sails said not taking his eyes off his work, fingers still mending canvas. "What 'cha need," Coop asked intently. "I need ya ta bleed all ov'r this one and make her look like her coun'erpart," he joked. "Cap'ain won't be happy if'n we don't have a matched set," the joke continued. "Oh, ha-ha Sails. Perhaps you should give her a try. Really, it doesn't hurt after a while," Coop retaliated. "Once you don't have any more blood ta give, ya git numb to it. C'mon, giver 'er a try," he continued.

Suddenly a voice shouted from shore, "Coop, we found a water supply!" "Aye, be right there," he returned. "Well, I'm off." With that Coop went to the hold and started getting the empty water barrels together to take to shore and refill. He organized some help and expedited the welcome surprise mission.

***

Pid made his way to the island to find the crew designated to find a suitable bowsprit. The fear of the fable stuck in his mind. His heart raced as he made his way to the group. There he found them stripping the bark off a limb. "Good work gents," Pid congratulated them. "Aye, this bloody stump goo' n'uff fer yer highness," a disgruntled Richards asked sarcastically. "Look Ritchie, I know that it's bleeding hot out, but get yer ass in the stifling bilge fer a couple of hours an tell me how happy ye'd be'n then," Pid snapped back. "Everyone just calm yerselves," Schmitty shouted over. "If ya can't keep it together I'll have ta step in," Hall commanded. With that, the men all shut up, even Schmitty.

Pid surveyed the crew then suddenly realized that he forgot his swag bag of tools. "Damn!" He screamed in his head then quickly took off for the ship. "Where in blazes is that idiot off to," whispered Richards. "Got me," Jackson replied then suddenly realizing. "Bet 'cha that he fergot his gear." "Damn Pid, c'mon," Richards huffed in hushed tones. Pid raced his way aboard the ship to where his bag should be. Unfortunately for him it was nowhere to be found. His pounding heart nearly burst out of his chest at the realization that his tools weren't there. Thoughts of torture and marooning flooded his head. Nervous sweat now poured out of his head blinding his vision till he wiped the salty fluid out. It stung his eyes badly as he began to tear the hold apart. Throwing miscellaneous items haphazardly he frantically searched. Still the sweat flowed impairing his vision even worse. The nervous energy distracted his thoughts as he began to recheck places he had already searched. In all the excitement he had forgotten to remember the predicament that brought them to here in the first place. The storm. The storm had knocked the ship about and during which the contents of the hold slid about. His tools lay hidden under the debris. Feverishly Pid widened his search. Not caring now what he did, finding the tools was his only mission. That and finding them fast. Pid's energy raised the suspicions of the men working below. They came up and welcomed the temperature change.

"What goes on here," Dooley shouted. "ME BLOODY

TOOLS ARE MISSING," Pid screamed. Holding back a laugh as best as possible, "No kidding," Walker said. "DAMN IT WALKS! HELP ME LOOK! IT'LL BE MY BLOODY HEAD," Pid continued to scream. "It'll make a fabulous figurehead ya know," Dooley joked. "DAMN YOU BOTH! HELP ME!"

Walker and Dooley knew that he was accurate in his assessment and came to help in Pid's search. "It's a right mess in here," Walker said. "Very astute assessment," Dooley replied rather sarcastically. The three men spread out rifling through equipment, personal belongings, swag, and hammocks. Then in a moment, "This it," Dooley asked holding up a rather heavy bag. "GOD BE PRAISED," Pid screamed grabbing the bag out of his hand, tearing off topside. The two men just stood there looking at each other in the stillness. "God," Dooley questioned. "Wha' 'bout me? I'm the one who found it." Walker looked around at the mess, "Ya know, we'd better get outta here 'for someone thinks we be pilferin.'" Dooley agreed and they returned to their work in the blistering heat.

Pid arrived back as the sun was setting. Fires roared and the men continued the arduous tasks that befell the various crews. No one really noticed that he returned and that was just fine with him.

***

"Gentlemen," Payton began, "finish your tasks for the day. 'Doc' has fixed yer meals and will be serving till every last one of ya is full. Doc, what is the meal?" "Turtle soup captain, along with a variety of fish," Doc

Nielsen replied. "Terrific," Payton said sarcastically, "that's totally different than oh, every other day. Thanks. Nevertheless, then we'll have lights out, fires out, and everyone, sparing the watch must be asleep by the end of the last dog watch. No exceptions," the captain ordered. "Wha if we can't sleep der captain," Dooley inquired. Payton shifted his gaze to the questioning man, "I'll just have Blackie clunk you in the noggin if ya wish," he said with a smile. Scratching his chin, "Naw, I think I can do it alone," Dooley replied. The men laughed with what energy they could muster. "Sure," Payton asked. "Probably a good decision. Last bloke Blackie clunked didn't wake up the next day. But on the positive side, we did use his head for a lovely football." Payton paused a moment, But then it started to stink and we had to leave it behind." Then men got another chuckle.

"We could always use Pid's head," Blase said. "He isn't using it much." "You should talk Blase. Yer head can't even stop shaking," Ram joked, pointing out Blase's odd habit of bobbing his head as he spoke. "Yeah Blase, we woun't even need ta play. Yer head would do all the work," Richards chimed in. "Hell even Bert couldn't juggle with that thing," Hall exclaimed. The men roared their approval and started to sing. Even though their day was miserable their morale stayed high as they drank and sang into the night.

Part 7: Sea Legs
Making Way

A few days had passed since they came ashore. The crew endured several passing storms and a few miscommunications, yet they triumphed. Even Ram was barely using the cane at this point. The new mast was finally in place and the hull was cleaned and patched. Ballast stone was added and arranged under the direction of Payton himself to aid the handling of the ship. Even though the ship was still sub par and had many flaws by Payton's standards, she was finally good enough to set sail and continue the mission. As the sails unfurled and the ship began to make way, cheers from the men rang out at the successful accomplishment they undertook. The crew's morale was at an all time high.

A few hours at sea, the captain and Finny sat in the captain's quarters. Payton raised his mug and toasted, "Here's to a successful task." "Aye captain. It seems that the men have really gelled under the circumstances," Finny replied. "Good, good, we're all good," Sarika offered. "That storm was exactly what we needed. It very easily could have ended the mission and all of us dead on the shore," Payton said. This shocked Finny, "How so? Drowning? Starvation?" Payton sat and shook his head, "Nay, not starvation my good man. Well, not at first anyway. The men would have reverted back to their old allegiances. Separated into two camps, pirate and former Royal Navy, the two would have eventually continued to separate until they could take no more. Eventually all hell would have broken out and they would have fought till the death. Then the remaining ones would eventually starve."

"You're joking right," a young voice cracked. This startled Payton and Finny. "What in blazes are you doing here Richmond," Payton asked. "Bartholomew," he corrected. "I'm just wondering what's to become of me?" "Well, if Doc can't find anything other than turtles, you might be the main ingredient in the next pot of stew," Payton said straight faced yet jokingly. "SIR," Bart squealed. Payton just sat straight faced, eyes beaming directly into the young boy's. Payton slowly began to show his horrible face raising the terror level in the child for the amusement of the pirate. Bart began squirming at the thought that the captain could be telling the truth.

"Now, what do you wish Lester? Hum," Payton said breaking the tension. "I wish to return home," the young boy trembled. "Can't do it," Payton said. "Pirate, pirate, the boy's a pirate," Sarika squawked. "See, even the bird knows," Payton said continuing in his frightening way to make the boy more uncomfortable. "Why," pleaded the boy. "The mission, boy, the mission," Payton said. "What is the mission sir," Bart asked. "You know for a properly trained and mannered young lad you certainly pry into matters that mind you no heed," Finny responded. Bartholomew lowered his head in shame knowing that Mr. Finny was correct in his assessment. Payton smiled and nodded his head at Finny's comment. "Perhaps you need to relearn your manners," Finny continued. The boy really began to squirm uncomfortably. "Cat-o-nines, cat-o-nines, the boy needs the cat-o-nines," Sarika commanded. "Viscous little bird ya got there Flappy," Payton pointed out. It seemed that everyone in the room, except for Bartholomew, was in on the fun. The fun was at the expense of the little boy who now was physically trembling.

Payton changed his disposition back to his jovial side. "Alright, alright calm yer britches," Payton said. "We not gonna harm you boy," calming the lad down. "We were just funning ya. If'n yer to be with us yer gonna have to toughen yer hyde, eh boy." He paused, "the mission is to take back something that doesn't rightfully belong to someone." The boy scrunched his face, "You mean you're going to steal from a pirate," he asked inquisitively. Payton sighed and rubbed his eyes with his fingers, "How many times must I explain this? I acquire items. I commandeer things. I borrow objects. I make use of substances. I scrounge, ahem, uh, stuff." "In other words you steal things," Finny chimed in with a smile. Not breaking his stare at the boy, "You're not helping, mate," Payton exclaimed. "Captain," the boy began, "why isn't it possible to drop me off at home? I'm begging you sir. Please take me home." "Son first of all I haven't the faintest idea where your island home was and secondly, we are on a mission," Payton began before being cut off by Finny.

"Tell him who recruited you for the mission," Finny edged. Now breaking his glare, Payton turned to Finny, "What'd be the point of that mate?" Finny shrugged a shoulder, "Could be fun." "I really don't see a purpose in it," Payton said. Finny continued to push, "C'mon captain. Tell the boy." Finny was obviously feeling more at ease with the captain as this was the first time he pushed him in such a manner. Payton didn't like the way

Finny pressed, but he remained calm. It was nice to see his real personality begin to come out. Finny again pushed, "C'mon sir, I believe the boy would be fascinated with it." Finny had begun to fall back into old thought patterns without realizing. Suddenly there speaking with the boy he realized just how absurd the entire story indeed was. Within a matter of a second his thoughts raced from, how did he ever get involved in this, to how did he recruit all these men under such conditions? He questioned the legitimacy of the entire mission and decided to push the captain to prove himself. He continued to nod his head, "Tell the good boy."

Payton's eyes scanned about as he waited. Then with a sigh Payton relented, "A ghost," he said. The boy tried to fight off a smile and a laugh as he repeated, "A ghost?" "Yes boy, a ghost," Finny said trying not to sound sarcastic. The boy's demeanor changed in that instant, "A ghost you say? Was he ashen or was he translucent," the boy chided. Finny tried to contain his smile. "Ooh, perhaps he was one of those scary monster ghosts," the boy continued. "Was he? Was he scary," the boy kidded. Sarika sensed something and began to shriek. The frightened bird waved his feathers and let out shrieks and caws. He jumped from his shoulder to a chair and paced its high back. As if on cue from the bird a thunderclap rang out. The vibration shook the ship and Payton's mug fell to the floor spilling out the contents. The sound of a raging storm could be heard outside the ship. She rocked and creaked. Thunder again rang out so loud it would seem the lightning had struck the ship. "Not again," Finny cried out thinking another storm was upon them! A booming voice filled and shook the cabin some more,

"You tell me *boy*. Am I *scary* enough for you?" Bartholomew and Finny turned ghastly white and trembled at the sound.

"Right, I was wondering when you'd speak up already," Payton said plainly. "How did you know I was here," the disembodied voice questioned sounding dejected that he didn't scare the captain. "Well my dear fellow, when the voices from above ceased to be heard and the breezeway between me windows fell stale I knew you had returned. Or rather that we'd returned to your territory," Payton explained. "Besides, when there's a storm raging outside and yet no rain blows through the open portholes, it's fairly obvious. Don't ya think?" "You *are* good, pirate," the voice said.

"Captain Melbourne," Finny said stunned as the words trailed out of his mouth. "I, I can't believe it." "Well then why did you ever agree to join him," the ghost asked. "Well, I did," Finny stuttered. "It's just, just…" Payton cut him off, "You needed to be certain." "Aye captain," Finny said again filled with all the belief and disposition he had previously carried. Yet his heart felt heavy with shame of momentary disbelief.

Bart cowered in the corner as the conversation unfolded. He could hardly believe that this buffoon of a man could so easily speak with the dead. He marveled at the captain's courage in the midst of a spirit. He saw the difference in how Finny cautiously handled himself and compared it to Payton's relative calm.

"Thanks mate, but you could have knocked over his mug and not mine," Payton told the spirit. "Yes, sorry about that. I got a bit excited. I'll fix that." With that, the ghost knocked over the other mug just as Payton's hand went for the handle. "Well now, thanks again," Payton said sarcastically. "You're determined that I won't get a drink today, eh spirit," Payton kidded. "Again. Sorry about that. I didn't know that you were going to go for it. Sorry, sorry" the voice said. Looking down at the two now empty mugs, a sarcastic "Fabulous," was all Payton could muster.

"So captain, how are you," Finny asked uneasiness still in his voice. "I'm parched," Payton said. "I'm dead," Melbourne said. "Gotta one up me eh mate," Payton joked. Finny looked about the room, "Captain, why is it that I can't see you?" "Because you've got your back to me," Payton explained thinking he was being addressed. "Because, you haven't finished your mission yet," Melbourne explained. "But why does that matter," Finny questioned. "Well unless you are like that iguana whose eyes can look behind him, you won't be able to see me, as previously stated, you have your back to me," Payton continued on in his own conversation. Finny shook his head. "You see Payton was to have told you that I and our crew can not return to our form and rest until Brightside is done in as I was," the voice stated. "Yes, and if you'd listen to me from time to time you'd already know that Ricardo," Payton mock scolded. "Yes sir. Sorry sir," Finny said without correcting him. "I guess I didn't quite understand that bit."

"Now, young man. Why is it that you question the captain so? A young Lieutenant has no right to question the captain," the voice said. "I'm not a Lieutenant sir," the boy said still cowering in the corner. "What rank are you lad," the voice asked. "Stowaway," Payton said. "That's entirely unacceptable," the agitated voice stated, again booming and shaking the cabin.

"Hold up, matie," Payton started. "He's the son of that Blankenslip bloke." "You didn't kidnap that boy," the voice asked coyly. "Course not. He just happened to be round when he shouldn't," Payton stated. "He'll get home when we're finished. Course, by then he may not want to go home." "What mean you pirate," the boy pushed. "Mind your tone boy," the spirit commanded. "Stop speaking out of turn!" Payton just smiled, "I'm just saying that you could make a fine addition to the crew. If'n ya'd like. But we still do need to do something about those tiny hands of yers." Bart looked again at his hands and just smiled nervously not wanting another scolding from the spirit.

"Now good spirit can you give us a heading so that we can be on our way," Payton queried. "Aye, Mr. Finny listen up. Gather your charts and I'll give you the safest and fastest path to your destination," commanded the ghost. Finny took off with a flash to gather his things. Quickly he made it to his shared quarters. "Mh. Finah," Bearded Clem said standing in the doorway blocking Finny's path. "Ah, um. Pardon," Finny returned. "Wa ga ya ere," Clem mumbled in curiosity. "Ah-ha. Yes, um. Ok. Will that be all then Mr. Clem," Finny tried his hardest to get past. "'El, us a wonern' wz d ash," Clem uttered. "Oh, ok then. I really need to get on…" Finny tried in vain to pass. "Oh, ait, ait, ait. Wz gotn s a unnin' ule an 'e wazzn ollowin' zzt a all. Den a ya gonna git er ina rublea," Clem expressed.

Finny stood there dumbfounded not knowing just what to say or what was said. All he could do was stand still scratching his head. "Ana oer 'ng. Waz a ort we'n onna git?" Finny agitated, shook his head, "Step aside Mr. Clem. I have work to do." Undaunted by Finny's urgency Clem persisted in his ramblings. "Buaz a wen eed a rackus r aza nna e ropy." "Look Mr. Clem. I haven't the time nor the translation for whatever it is that you are trying, helplessly in vain to convey. Now, one side with you. Well, I said one side," Finny commanded. Clem merely tilted his head to one side and smiled a mostly toothless smile, but he didn't budge. Clearly agitated and knowing that time was of the essence, "LOOK! For the LAST TIME! ONE SIDE WITH YOU!" Clem knew he had had his fun and tipped his hat. Stepping aside Clem watched as Finny pushed past. "Eh-eh-eh. Upd it," Clem chuckled.

In a haste Martin flew into the room. Captain Payton sat upon a chair, his feet resting upon a table top. His eyes focused on his diligent attempt at cleaning the dirt from under his fingernails with the tip of his dagger. Bart sat on the floor, legs crossed, picking at a loose thread in his pants. "I'm back! I'm back! Sorry all, but I have re…" he paused looking around the room, "turned," he finished his thought rather flatly. "Um Captain Melbourne? Sir? You there?" "Hold yer breath there matie," Payton said. "The ole chap has buggered off," he continued still not averting his gaze from his nails. "I know that it is a huge ship and all, however, you'd think that a man in such fine health as you are, could have retrieved the tools of his trade in a much more rapid fashion." "But captain it's not my fault sir! It was that chap Clem. He had engaged me…" Finny spouted but was cut off. "Well, there's your second mistake bloke. When the spirit of yer former captain gives you an order, you carry it out man. You don't take up with a random bloke on the ship," Payton scolded. "But sir, I tried, but he was persistent," he was stuttering. "Oh well. He was persistent was he? Last I checked I made you an officer. An officer of higher rank I do believe. Just give him orders. Besides, ole Clem? Chaps got no choppers! You have to have a bit of experience to understand just what the hell old Bearded is saying. I mean honestly, how long did it take you to realize that the man was speaking in a gibberish language that only a select few can understand?" "Sir it wasn't like that," Finny pleaded. "If'n ya want to learn to converse with him, and he is a fine chap when you get to know him, I'll give you that, that's splendid. However, I'll be asking that ye do it on yer own time. Thank you very much," Payton ordered. "I am truly sorry captain. I don't know what else to say sir," a dejected Finny said, eyes looking downward. His heart sank. "Yes well, that isn't going to help us out now that your old captain has written us off. You let him down old man. He said that if he couldn't trust you to make haste in a non important moment, then how in blazes was he to trust you in the heat of battle," Payton reported.

Finny looked distraught and dejected as the chart in his hand slipped from his fingers, falling to the floor. The air hung heavy and Payton still kept his annoyed gaze from him. Bart sat motionless and emotionless, staring directly at the floor in front of his still folded legs. Moments seemed like hours to Finny who felt like the repercussions for his failure ended the entire mission.

What would be his punishment? Thoughts blew like a hurricane through his brain. Would he be flogged? Keel-hauled? Tarred and feathered? The tension was building in him. Sweat began to flow from his brow like a waterfall he once gazed upon in a southern continent. Tension ravaged his body and it tensed under the pressure. He slumped down into an empty chair like an old suit. What would this madman do? He had heard of stories of pirate revenge and torture. Would he be gutted? Drawn and quartered? WHAT! The silence was maddening him. "WHY WON'T HE SPEAK," Finny screamed in his head. "WHAT IS THIS DEVIL CONCIEVING? THE BLAGGARD MUST BE BUILDING HIS HATRED!" His eyes darted around the floor as the thoughts continued to swell in his brain. "SPEAK! SAY SOMETHING! THIS IS KILLING ME!" His tension grew till he could hold it no more, when...

"Got 'cha!" The voice was of Captain Melbourne! Finny spun around getting out of the chair, yet no one was standing there. "WHAT," Finny screamed as he shot up? Payton and Bartholomew burst out laughing. "WHAT," he screamed again? "Got 'cha," he repeated. "Is this a joke," Finny demanded. Three voices filled the room with heavy laughter. "I can't... this is... why the... a joke," the confused man sputtered. "Lighten up me boy," Payton offered. "You really need to loosen up." Melbourne's voice filled the room, "He is correct ole chap. You always were a bit high strung, even for me. You needed that." "I thought I was going to be bloody well KEEL-HAULED," Finny shouted.

More laughter filled the air. An exacerbated Finny

slumped over again. The bag of swag fell to the floor joining the chart. "I can't believe it. You, I'd expect it from," he said looking at Payton, "but you Captain. And you young Bart!" "Beggin' you pardon sir. They made me," Bart defended himself, still smiling. "Can we please just get on with it then," Finny requested. "You certain you're ready," asked Payton. Exhausted Finny looked up, "Yes certainly, why?" "You don't need to change yourself," the voice asked. "Change myself sir? What mean you by that," an intrigued Finny inquired. "Really, you don't need to go to the head," Payton asked. Finny sighed and scrunched his face as he said flatly, "Why?" "You looked like you had just filled yer britches boy," Payton joked. With that all the laughter returned. "I just wish I'd thought of this gag me self," laughed Melbourne. "Alright, alright then. You've all had your laugh. Can we please get on with it then," Finny urged trying to get the subject changed. "Did you see the sweat pouring out? I thought that he was gonna sink us. Bloody near filled the bilge again," Payton continued. "Good thing the lads just fixed the pump!" "You almost had the same fate as I," Melbourne added.

Finny exhaled a heavy sigh and looked up toward the ceiling as if to the skies above and shook his head. When the men had finished their chiding the spirit gave them their direction to their objective, the Port of Elizabeth.

Clem or Clam?

They headed back top side. "Young Ball, you need to be heading back to yer master, Mr. Hilltopper." "But sir," Bart protested, "I wish to stay with you." "That is a pity boy, but off with you. A young man needs skills. All hands must work for their ration of grog. Besides, the ladies like a man with skills. Now go," Payton commanded. The boy grudgingly obliged and went back to Hillberg.

Finny quickly grabbed Payton's arm, then realized he laid hands upon him, "Uh, begging your pardon sir," he said letting go. "What are we going to tell the men about what just happened?" "Nothing," Payton said with a smile, "Why?" "Well, won't there be questions about the thunder? The thunder shook the whole bloody ship! The laughter," he questioned. "It doesn't work like that," Payton said. "Ghosts only make themselves known to those who need to know. Yes he was once half this crew's captain; however, as of this moment they need to be in service to me. Hence they have no recollection of the events that just unfolded down below."

Finny was surprised by this, not sure if he should believe him or not. Perched back on his shoulder, Sarika squawked "Gone, gone, spirits are gone." "Yes, thanks for the update Murrow," Payton muttered. As they made their way to the quarterdeck Finny noticed the sun was shining and only a mild wind filled the sails. "Amazing," he thought to himself. "Simply amazing this life is." "Mr. Langleton," called Payton. "Aye sir," Langley responded. "One side please, I'll be taking over for a bit," Payton informed the helmsman. "Aye-aye captain," he concurred. Finny took out his compass and sextant and read their bearings. Quickly he pointed them in the direction they needed to sail. The coordinates fresh in their heads, the ship turned with a heading towards Port Elizabeth.

"Captain. Might I have a moment of your time," Finny questioned. The captain kept his eyes directly forward, his hands on the wheel. "You might, but then I'd have to fain interest in what it is that you have to ponder." Martin paid no heed to what was just said and pressed him anyway. "Mr. Clem…" he was cut off. "*Bearded*. He prefers when most blokes call him Bearded Clem," Payton corrected him. "Right. Mr. Bearded Clem. What's his story then," asked Martin. "Why ask me then? Ask him if you're so interested in the chap. He is a gifted story teller after all," the pirate said. "*Gifted story teller*," his voice went up three octaves. "You can't understand a bleeding word the man says," Finny remarked. "If it weren't for him…"

Again he was cut off, "If'n weren't fer him we wouldn't a had such a good laugh. You really need to understand that ole man. You need more good laughs in yer days." "Ok, ok sir. But how did he come about," Finny questioned. Payton stood back. "Well chap. You see when a man and woman meet and fall in love they wed. On their wedding night they…" Now it was Finny's turn to cut him off. "That's not what I meant sir." "Ah! Good then. That's a relief. That was getting a right bit uncomfortable. What is it that you wanted to know then," Payton pondered. "How is it that he came about to be adorned with the moniker *Bearded* when he has no beard? Nor does a single follicle even grow upon his face. Not even an eyebrow or single lash! How is it that a master gunner, who by definition commands the entire gunnery, has no teeth and can not communicate," Finny pried.

"Well firstly, be fair," Payton began. "He does have a *few* teeth left. Or at least he used to. He may have lost them by now, I'm not certain I haven't ever checked him. So you may be correct there. If so, then I apologize. Nevertheless, he can communicate. Have you not met Mr. Jallson?" "Jallson sir," questioned Martin. "Are you certain that is the bloke's name?" Payton thought for a moment. Looking up to the heavens, "Hum, no, that's incorrect. What is it? Jerrson, Jillson, Jowson, Jabson, Jickson, Jerrson, " he continued to ponder? Martin took a stab in the dark, "Johnson?" "Ah yes," Payton declared with glee. "That's not it," he followed up flatly. "Joeson, Jibson, Jifson he continued on and on.

"Those aren't even real names," Finny thought to himself. "Where the devil is he going with this. Think, THINK MAN THINK! What could this man's name be," he continued. Racking his brain Finny took another shot, "Jackson?" Elated Payton exclaimed, "Ah yes! That's the chap! Jazzson!" Martin shook his head. "Yes Jackson. What does he do sir?" "He's Bearded's interpreter," exclaimed Payton. "Wonderful," Finny said. "Now how is this related to the story?" "Story? What story? I love a good story," Payton exclaimed. Finny's patience level was beginning to fall again. Holding a deep breath he calmed himself then proceeded. "The story of Bearded Clem."

"Ah yes," Payton recalled. "Well, he had been my master gunner for many years. At the time he had a long beard that was to be rivaled by only ole Blackbeard himself. He loved that ole thing. I warned him that working with blast powder and having a long beard wasn't a good idea; however, he felt that he knew better. 'The ladies loved the beard,' he said. 'Couldn't get enough of it,' he'd go on. He used to sing in the taverns as well as on deck with the boys. Wonderful voice he had. Truly wonderful. Anyhow, we were making way towards Nice, when we had come upon the Spanish captain Bolibar. He had been a pirate hunter for many years then when we had happened upon him. He had been on the trail of the pirate Captain Rogers at the time. Mr. Bolibar was a terrible pirate hunter and had the misguided thought that he was a great and feared man. He thought that I was Rogers; even though we look nothing alike, and we were flying a neutral flag of a merchant ship. Without warning he opened fire upon us still thinking we were Rogers' ship and took us off guard. We were young and not well experienced. Well a melee took place and we rose to the challenge. Cannon fire was exchanged between the two ships and each side took losses. Ole Clem took a blast right in the face during the fight. His beard and hair caught fire and a plank took out most of his teeth. When he had made his recovery and his scars had healed, his beard was never to return. Neither would his teeth for that matter. So since he had been a man in good standing and fought valiantly I couldn't take away his position. The men had voted to retain him in the position; therefore he went on as our gunnery master. Granted, he wasn't easily understood and we didn't fare too well in battle immediately following, but then we miraculously came upon a beleaguered merchant ship one day. She had been done in by a Dutchman, the name fails me. Some of the crew had taken up with the bloke and the rest were left to die. He had left the ship with no sails and the remaining crew with no food. So when we happened upon them, they were so grateful that they took their allegiance to me. Amazingly, one man in their crew was able to understand old Bearded right away. Bloody remarkable he was. Naturally, I named him the gunnery mate."

"Ah, and that man is Jackson," Finny exclaimed. "No, actually he went by the name of Robbins or something like it. He died of scurvy a few months later. Pity it was. However, Jackson was a good friend of Robbins and he learned from him what Bearded was saying." Finny shook his head. "Nothing's easy with you is it captain?" "Easy isn't always the best route mate," Payton said with a smile. "I'm beginning to learn that," Martin returned. "Bout bloody well time," Payton said under his breath, still with the smile. "Anyway," the captain went on. "Clem has never erred in his allegiance to me and therefore will always have a job as long as he may wish. You'll see when it comes to action, there is no one better at being a gunnery master than he."

Martin nodded his head. "Well, I guess that I'll just have to wait and see for myself," he thought. He smiled at Payton, "It's hard to believe that he used to have a singing voice." Payton smiled as he reminisced to the days before Clem's accident. "Yes it was *truly* remarkable. A choir boy in his youth. Now... well now he's just one hell of a funny guy, eh." "He is?" Martin asked. "Of course he is. The only thing about it is, is that you just gotta be able to understand him."

Best Laid Plans?

It was a five day sail from their current position to the location of their next conquest. While the crew went about their tasks topside, the officers gathered to devise their plan of attack. Mr. Finny unfurled his maps, charts and laid out topography of the region.

"Alright Mr. Marzipan, give us the lay of the land," Payton commanded.

"There are two neighboring islands alongside the main isle where Port Elizabeth sits," Finny reported. "The northern one lay as a rocky outcropping. She's crescent shaped, small in comparison, with a little cove on the far side. Not much there by way of use as anything. The southerly one is larger with a much larger cove, thickly vegetated, and a wonderful outcropping whereby to spy upon the Port. She has been used in the past by the Navy as a tactical safety watch place for the Port. When the tide is low there is a naturally occurring rocky pathway that extends from the southerly isle to the Port isle. The only unfortunate thing is that the pathway is well known, and therefore a watch is always placed with duty of monitoring it."

Payton sat back stroking his beard listening extremely attentive to the proceedings. His eyes darted across the map as he ran through all the possibilities he could engage. Finally he spoke up, "Interesting. Very interesting. How many men are typically stationed there?" "Anywhere from twenty to well near two hundred. It all depends, if their flag ship is in or any other war ships are in port," Martin reported. "How big of a port be this place," Payton inquired. "It's actually not that large at all. It's only a military outpost, no civilians. We had run a few missions out of there and at times we had soldiers quartered on land and on the ships. The largest number we ever had there in my station was just over eight hundred," Finny boasted.

"Eight-bloody-hundred," Payton said stunned. "Effie, waz we gonna do if'n dere's dat many caballeros," Santiago asked Payton? "We're gonna cut bait and run, Pizano," Payton joked. "No bloody way ... eight hundred men," he said with a chuckle. "Wem ot ta go ot nuff ta lat em wy atin," Clem added. The room fell silent as the three other men just stood looking blank-faced at Clem. The awkward pause seemed to last hours, until simultaneously they all started nodding their heads in agreement. "Right," they all said.

Snapping back into the present moment by shaking his head quickly back and forth, "Uh, but sir, I did say that that was just the one time. Typically it was nowhere near that number," Finny corrected. "Yes, but still, we may be severely outnumbered. Therefore it'll take some shrewd planning" Payton said. "Es! Ewd lannin ineed! Heh-heh-heh," Clem chimed in. Once again the other three men stopped and looked at Clem, blank-faced, not knowing what he said. And again in unison, the three men started nodding their heads in agreement, "Right." This time it was Payton who shook his head to snap himself back to reality, "Uh, righty then. Ok, gents leave me be for a *momentitia* while I review the information." The three men agreed and exited. As Clem closed the door, the hinges gave way due to dry rot, and the door came off in his hand. "Oody l," Clem exclaimed! "What the devil," Payton trashed out. "Rry atin! Ont ow e wn eth," Clem mumbled in apology! "Righty then," Payton said walking over to the door, the handle still in Clem's hand. "Let's just try and place her bac…" Payton was cut off. WHAM! Payton spun around in shock, "BLOODY HELL," he screamed! A plank from the quarterdeck gave way and collapsed onto the table where they had just been planning. The crewman's leg that broke the plank dangled through the ceiling, all-the-while his shouts could be heard below. "This shoddy thing is falling to pieces," Payton professed. "She'll be lucky to even get there. Didn't anyone check the bucket for dry rot?" "Uh, capt'n," Pedro answered, "Jou never said dat we was ta do dat. Dey jus check da hull and fix dat." "Terrific," Payton muttered.

Finny stood on the other side of the doorway, still obstructed by the unhinged door that lay across the entrance, handle in Clem's hand. "Really, Mr. Cl.." he caught himself just as Clem shot him a dirty look. "Bearded. Mr. Bearded. Sorry. You can release the handle now." Clem did as advised and the door slid to the floor with yet another loud thud! Payton looked over his shoulder, "Now wha…" he cut himself off seeing the door now splayed out upon the floor. "Really, it'll be a miracle if'n we even make it to this stupid Port."

"Well, the good news is that it's only about five more

days away," Finny uncharacteristically joked. Payton just glared at him. Finny recoiled in fright, but offered, "Sorry sir. But ye did say that I needed a better sense of humor." He lowered his eyes to the floor. "Payton just smiled, "I thought it was funny mate. I just wanted to see if you had any backbone to stand up for your joke, but you caved like a sumo at an all you can eat buffet." Finny was befuddled, "A who at a what?" "Never mind," Payton replied. "Ahoy! You up there," Payton said tugging on the man's pant leg. Who be you?" From up above a muffled voice could be heard, "Me sir." Payton closed his eyes and shook his head, "No kidding." Then he thought to himself, 'What a bunch of imbeciles.' "Who is me sir," the captain inquired in a nicer tone than he truly felt. "Oh, sorry sir. Me, Jenkins sir," he responded, erring for formality as he didn't recognize Payton's muffled voice. "I should have known," Payton said softly. "Ahoy, Jenkins!" "Yes sir," he responded. "You think that you could get your leg out of the hole in my ceiling," Payton inquired. "Uh, yes sir. I'll give it me best sir." With that the leg started jiggling and gyrating. Muffled gasps and grunts were audible, yet no progress was made. Payton stood by watching the proceedings with a smile on his face, arms folded, "Ahoy Jenkins!" "Yes sir?" "How you making out," Payton asked with sarcasm in his intent, yet voiced with concern. "Not too well. It seems me leg is rather stuck," he responded innocently. "Excuse me gents," Payton said to the men, "I have to go have some fun with this. Oh, try not breaking anything while I'm gone, eh?" Payton passed them and headed topside.

He walked to the quarterdeck where a group of men

stood gathered around Jenkins who was still in the hole. "What are we looking at here," Payton inquired in a curious tone. "Seems that ole Jenkins fell through the deck," Vaughn said not looking at whom he was addressing. "Anyone try and help," Payton continued. "Naw, it's Jenkins. It's funnier this way," Vaughn replied. "Yes it is indeed," Payton answered. "Yet, maybe someone should lend a hand?" "Perhaps," Vaughn said leaning his head back towards the unknown person whom he was conversing with, eyes fixed upon Jenkins. "But we haven't had a good laugh in a while. Why end it so quick?" "True, very true," Payton answered. "Pardon me," he said passing by. "Oh crap," Vaughn thought as he saw it was the captain whom he was speaking with. Payton calmly pushed past the crowd, "'Ello Jenkins. How goes it then?" "Not too well captain," he said as he saluted him. "It seems that I got me leg stuck in this here hole." "You don't say," Payton said doing his best to sound like he was unaware of the situation. "And here I thought you were laying down on the job." "Sir! Never! I would never do such a thing," he replied. He wouldn't either. Although he was rather dim, he was definitely loyal and had sailed and fought along side Payton in the past. Payton ventured up to him and knelt down. Scratching his beard he pretended to be surveying the scene. "Hum, any thoughts then?" "Um, anything sir. This is getting a tad uncomfortable," his leg still dangling through the deck boards. Payton stood up and walked several circles around the trapped man. "Well, as I sees it, we've got ourselves one of two options." Jenkins got excited, "Yes sir! Uh, what are they sir?" "Well," he began, "either we can just leave you there and you can receive a new title." "New title sir?

What title is that?" "Well," Payton said scratching his head under his hat, "I'm not certain. We could call you the 'Jack-all." "Jackal sir," Jenkins asked. "No, not jackal," he corrected. "Jack-all. As in Jack of all trades." "Oh," exclaimed Jenkins. Then he paused and thought a moment. "Beggin' yer pardon sir. I don't follow." "Well as I sees it, since you aren't going to be going anywhere, anytime soon, you'll sort of do whatever ye can staying right there." "That doesn't sound half bad captain," Jenkins replied. "What kind of things can you see me doing?" "Interesting question Jenkins," Payton congratulated. "Thank you sir," he replied. "Jenkins, I see you doing many important tasks that we were never able to have done before." Jenkins eyes widened. "You Jenkins, you will be able to do things to assist the rest of the crew. Your proximity to the wheel will make you invaluable to the helmsman." Jenkins' chest started to swell with pride. "For example, you can ... you can hold the helmsman's drink. You can fan him down on hot days." Jenkins' chest started deflating and his new found pride was quickly turning to dismay. "You can keep the dog watch awake with tales of the sea. Course, if'n ye don't know any, ya better learn some and fast. We can rig a sheet to a pole that you can hold to shield the helmsman from the beating rays of the midday sun. Seeing as we have no binnacle, you can hold the compass for the navigator. You can," Jenkins cut him off. "Beggin' yer pardon captain," he said. Payton tried to look stern at being cut off mid sentence. Jenkins worry escalated and he turned his gaze downward. "Sir, what was the other option you spoke of, sir," he said sheepishly. "Oh yes," Payton said righting himself. "The other option is that we simply have Dr. Fitz cut yer leg off. I'm certain that Chips or Pid could fashion you a nice new one." Payton kept a straight face while many around him could not. His unchanging gaze terrified Jenkins to his very core. Jenkins eyes darted wildly, terror grabbed his heart.. "Um," he cleared his throat. "Sir? Can we stick with the first option please?"

Payton crossed his arms, "Um," he paused. "You know, now that I think about it. I'd *like* to do that. However, that doesn't change the fact that I'll have a leg, your leg, dangling in me quarters. This ship isn't that big to begin with and I'm not certain that I want a gent's leg hanging in my quarters like a chandelier." "But sir," Jenkins sheepishly pried, "it could be useful for something." "Hum," Payton said scratching his beard yet again. "I don't know." "Please sir," Jenkins pleaded. "Besides," Payton began, "what do we do with you when we acquire our new ship? Leave you to die here? That'd be a pity what with your long history of devotion and loyalty." Jenkins fright began to overtake him and he started to tremble. "Tell you what," Payton started. "If you can come up with one good use for your lone leg in me ceiling, you can keep it. If not," he paused, "we'll start calling you Tippy."

Jenkins mind went haywire. Try as he might he couldn't come up with anything that would save his leg. Tears began welling up in his eyes at the thought of his leg being severed from his body. "Captain, please! I beg of you! Please don't cut off me leg!" Payton looked down and simply shook his head. "Sorry bloke, I can't see any other way." Jenkins began to weep openly until Payton could no longer take it. "BLIMEY!" Payton shouted. I've got it!" Jenkins heart began to pound, "WHAT SIR!"

"Here, give me yer hands," commanded Payton and Jenkins did so. With a mighty heave Payton pulled Jenkins from the trap, freeing him and saving his leg. "I can't thank you enough sir," exclaimed the jubilant Jenkins. "Ah, don't mention it me boy. Just watch yerself around that hole eh," Payton replied. Pid was in his line of sight, "Pid, fix that hole," Payton commanded. He paused to think about what he just said. "Wait. Chips, fix that hole mate." "Yes sir," Chips replied. Payton returned to his cabin thinking to himself, "God that's fun."

Sea Friends

It was late in the night when the wind died and the ship lay in doldrums. The captain had allowed the men extra rum and allowed cards and dice this night to stave off boredom. The wise old seadog had been in these circumstances many times before. If he had acquired any knowledge in all his years, it was when he could allow suspension of certain rules for the good of the ship as a whole. This was one of those nights. There had not been any grumblings, yet he could sense when something dangerous could grow.

The crew began to entertain themselves with music and gamboling while the officers just drank and sang their songs. Payton strolled topside and scanned the flat seas. A pod of dolphin came close to the ship, a crewman new to Payton's command had wanted to harpoon one. The veteran sailors knew better as Payton was to have none of it. "Aye gents, those are the watchers. The angels of the sea they are. They are good luck. Not a one will be harmed on my watch. I owe a debt of me very life to one and pledged that they should never be harmed! So any one that shall try to harm one will fall dead to me bare hands," he said coldly. "That also goes for the sea cows," he added. Quickly the men returned to their goings on.

"Aye Pedro. What did he mean by that," Martin inquired. Sadly, Pedro had been in the rum, which caused his already broken English to fall apart even more. Stumbling over and slapping Martin on the shoulder, "Aye, da aptn' ife honce sabbed ey da phins," he slurred. "Ano'r ime by a seeee cow, eh," he chuckled. Martin rolled his eyes, "Great. Thank you for the clarification."

"Paolo," Payton shouted. "Si," he replied as he stumbled over to him along the gunwale. "Paronto, didn't we see a dolphin the day we caught the bounty of fish a few days back," Payton asked. "Si." Martin wondered aloud, "Why? Is that important?" "No, I'm just curious. The little fellers could be following us," Payton replied. "That could be more good luck you know. So how many were there," Payton asked Pedro again. "Juan," Pedro replied. "Ah yes, sorry about that Juan. How many was it," he pressed him. Pedro swayed and stumbled even though the seas were dead calm. "Juan," he said plainly. "Yes, you Juan, me Daniel," he said plainly. "Jou wanna oew da, na(burp)ber eh? 'L I tell jou ana ... ana," he began to trail off losing his train of thought. "Anna, iz JUAN! Daz right," he said stomping his foot. Pedro tried in vain to stand tall with his mug in hand. Yet he was still stumbling as he grabbed for a climbing line. His hand missed his target as his weight shifted causing him to topple face first to the wooden deck. Payton winced at the thought of the pain a sober man would be feeling. "Well, good thing yer nice an numb eh Juan?" Payton leaned his body weight over to grab the same line that Pedro missed. His hand found its target, yet it didn't help. The old woven rope was full of sea spray and weakened from years under the strong Caribbean sun. Payton's hand went through the line like sand slipping through his fingers under water. There was nothing solid there and he too toppled to the wooden deck with a thud! This time he winced from knowing the pain a sober man would feel. "Bloody hell," he spat. "Mr. Mosby." "Finny sir." "Right! Remember to have the men check all rope on the ship in the morning. We'll need to replace any more disintegrating lines eh!" "Yes sir," he replied obediently.

Trying To Reason...

The day had passed without further incident. The following morning was ushered in with the ship still in doldrums.

"Captain," Langley said. "Aye Langer," he replied. "We've got a bit of bad luck sir." "I see that," Payton replied looking around, the sheets lay dead. "Dis is a gonna be a bad..." Pedro had started to say as he sat down on the gunwale. With a crack the gunwale gave way and Pedro fell backwards into the water. Payton just shook his head. "Cripes! What the hell is going to happen next?" "MAN OVER BOARD," screamed Masterson.

Payton recoiled at the man screaming in his ear. "Masterman," Payton said calmly. "We're standing still. Just relax and throw the bloke a rope eh?" "Oh yes! Brilliant idea sir," he replied as he rushed to get the nearest coil. With a flash he tossed the coil over the edge, holding a loose end. Instead of a splash a voice responded. "HEY! Watch wha yer doin' dere Effie! Ye beaned me in da melon," Pedro called.

Payton leaned over the edge placing his hands on the remaining gunwale. "How goes…" he was cut off as the next section of gunwale cracked and fell off; Payton tumbled in after it. Splash went the pirate! Coming up for air and treading water next to Pedro he spit out the salty water and finished his thought, "it down there. Here." "Is not so bad eh? Da water's warm and refreshing. Plus I hada pee anyway," Pedro answered. Sarcastically, "*Fantastic*, that's why it's so warm over here," Payton replied. "Well, what do ya think? Should we go topside?" Pedro thought a moment, "Ja. I tink so." He looked up, "Eh, anyone wanna pull me up?" A voice called down, "Sorry! Hang on." Effortlessly he was pulled back up. A moment later the rope came back down and quickly Payton was also hoisted up. Getting back topside, "Well that was a refreshing bath," Payton said. Might I suggest that everyone give it a try?" Oddly no one took him up on his idea.

Payton looked around the deck and addressed the crew. "Gents. Let's be honest here. This ship is a Greek tragedy waiting to happen. Someday a folk singer will no doubt get a top ten hit, in regaling our tale. All I can suggest is that ya watch yerselves mates. Beware of where ye tread on this floating deathtrap and be at the ready for any trou..." Payton was cut off as the wind suddenly whipped up filling the sheets. The skies remained clear, but the swirling winds quickly grew in intensity. All heads turned as the main mast started to creak under the pressure and seemed as if it were about to break. "...ble," Payton finished his thought. The men stood paralyzed in fright as the ship began moving forward. Many of the superstitious men began saying good luck prayers and phrases. "Just hang in there boys. Hang in there," Payton reassured them. "Everything's gonna be al..."

"CAPTAIN," a voice screamed from the crows nest! "WATER SPOUT!" "Blast," Payton called! "All hands to your stations! We must not get hit by that thing!" Payton rushed to the wheel. "Langley, we must avoid that thing at all costs. She'll tear this tinderbox to shreds." "Aye-aye sir," Langley replied. The men scattered to their respective stations and tried valiantly to avoid the water spout. "CAPTAIN," the voice returned. "TWO MORE SPOUTS CAPTAIN!" The wind and water had suddenly formed spouts that swirled around the waters. "Damn," was all that Payton remarked. One spout quickly went upon shore of a close island and almost immediately died away. "Well that just leaves those two," Finny pointed out. Not looking away from the swirling air, "Aye, but all it takes is one Jasper," Payton returned.

The twisters had now grown nearly two hundred feet in height. Danced they did; twisting, crisscrossing their paths and circling in the waters. Round and round they circled until almost simultaneously they turned and marked their bearing directly at the sloop. "Oh bloody hell," Payton said. The crew began a mass panic. Wildly they scattered across the deck. "CALM YERSLEVES," Hall screamed! This order had no effect. "EH DER! SHUT DE HELL UP," screamed Pedro. Again this had no effect, until, "GENTLEMEN!" Payton spoke up and his words froze all the men in their places, yet all eyes turned still towards the incoming spouts. "Martin, quick what is our EXACT location?" Finny was too caught up in the moment to notice that the captain again called the correct name in time of danger. Finny gave him a response to his question, "Northerly Pass sir." "Your absolutely certain about that," he questioned. "Yes sir," he replied. "LANGLY! HARD TO PORT," Payton shouted.

Langley obliged and spun the wheel turning the rudder as fast as he possibly could. Caught in a puff, the sheets filled with air and accelerated. This only turned the ship broadside to the incoming winds. "They're coming right at us," Walsh said rather calmly. "Easy boys," Payton reiterated, his eyes darting back and forth trying to ascertain his exact point. He ran to the bow and looked at the water below. The ship continued on its path, accelerating moment by moment. Still, the spouts seemingly continued to be aiming directly for the center of the sloop. "GET READY FOR FULL SHEETS," the captain commanded.

"But SIR," Finny replied. The spinning winds full of seawater continued their assault towards the tiny ship. "I SAID READY THE FULL SHEETS," he spouted. The men did as commanded and waited for the command when all the sails would drop catching even more air. A sudden jolt hit the wooden ship and many men lost their footing, tumbling to the deck. A visibly nervous and shaken Finny, white knuckled was holding the gunwale making his way to the bow, "Captain, what's your plan," he asked, voice quaking. "Look," Payton commanded. One spout had gone at the other and the two conjoined to form one. "See, we're down to just one," Payton said with a half smile. Oddly this didn't do anything to calm Finny's nerves. "Aye, but all it takes is one, Jasper," Finny recalled Payton's earlier words. "Aye, so all we need to do is out-maneuver it," Payton continued without missing a beat.

The winds had suddenly changed direction and the ship began to decelerate. Payton eyed the sea and then to the various directions the top waters swirled. He gave a quick smile, looked at the telltales and then returned cold faced, turning to the men. The spout began picking up speed.

"Mr. Langley," Payton shouted. "Aye captain," Langley replied. The spout was about fifty yards off the starboard rail. "At my command hard to starboard," Payton commanded. Thirty yards and closing in fast! "SIR," Langley replied; asking a question with only one word. Twenty yards and Payton again glanced at his bearings. The islands around him, the churning waters below, the water spout bearing down upon him. "CAPTAIN," Finny said nervously. "I know, I know," Payton responded. "We'll be heading straight for it. You have to trust," Payton cut himself off doing a lightning quick recheck of his bearings, "NOW! NOW! DO IT NOW!"

Langley panicked but quickly jumped upon the wheel and spun it so hard that the base cracked when the rudder could turn no more. The ship turned quickly and sea spray blanketed the crew. About fifteen yards of saltwater was all that separated the bow of the ship from the spout. "HOLD STRONG LANGLEY! HOLD STRONG!" All eyes stayed fixed upon the swirling water-filled wind just a mere stones throw away as it stalled out. The winds were blowing loose objects across the deck and hats began to be ripped off the heads of the owners. The sails flapped endlessly in the wind. Bow to spout they remained deadlocked to see which would move first. All hands grasped objects they felt were strong enough to hold them from being sucked off the ship and into the spiraling winds or to the sea below. The rudder continued to fight the current; the sails continued to grasp hopelessly at the ever changing air. All the pirates' breath collectively was held in suspense at what would happen next. The spout continued to spin yet she failed to regain her deadly approach. No eyes blinked, hearts seemingly stood still, yet no one perished. All men stood frozen in the moment, until. THUMP! The rudder could no longer fight the current. "HOLD STRONG LANGLEY! HOLD STRONG! READY THE SHEETS, ON MY COMMAND" the captain shouted. Langley valiantly grabbed the wheel returned her to her hard point. In the split second the rudder caught the current Payton shouted, "FULL SHEETS NOW!" "The sheets filled with puffs of air. "NOW LANGLEY. LET LOOSE THE WHEEL," Payton screamed! The rudder shifted breaking the ship out of a hold pattern, sheets full of air and the sloop jolted to life. Like a shot she took off, again throwing men to the deck. Equaling the moment, the spout also regained its traveling velocity and charged the port rail. Ten yards off port rail, the ship and the spout were passing side by side. Then without warning, spout quickly changed directions and bore down on a tiny island, similar to the one where the first spout perished. The crew cheered wildly as they watched the water spout swoop upon the island and disintegrate into an innocent summer shower. Those that weren't celebrating their good luck were breathing huge sighs of relief as their hearts thumped strong in their exhausted chests. They marveled that their lives were just sparred.

"But how," questioned a stunned Finny, "how?" Fitzgerald, still visibly shaken as well also inquired, "Yes. Captain how did you know that would happen?" "Easy mate," the pirate began. "Just like you like to read yer books, I like to read the oceans. They tell you wonderful things. Plus, remember where you said we were Maldin?" "Martin sir, and yes. We're in Northerly Pass." "Well, why do you think that someone decided to call it that? Because the currents suddenly shift to the east? South? Hum? Think boy, think," he said with a smile. "Chips! Check the main. Make certain that she doesn't topple over. Mr. Hall, assign someone to check the rudder chain eh." Again the men began to cheer as Payton retired below deck. Martin and Fitzgerald still didn't fully comprehend how Payton knew that the spout would act the way it did. Perhaps he didn't and was extremely fortunate. Then again, he may be as cunning as his legend would belie. "Well," Payton began, "the current changed rather sharply at that point, Right? If you noticed that I kept checking the island too right? Well, just so happens that there's a divide in the rocky hills that lines up with the cut where the current changes. The winds have blown it away over the years and I knew that if we could just hold on long enough that the spout would hit that wind tunnel and carry off there. We just needed to hold strong and catch the wind to take us the opposite direction. Really quite simple, eh," he asked. Indeed, the doctor thought, this was one shrewd sailor. His natural curiosity was growing and desperately wished to be able to sit down and engage this man's experienced mind. The secrets he must know! The places he must have seen. What knowledge could possibly be gained from this man. Fitzgerald's view now was a far cry from the day they met.

Payton ambled below deck and a few moments later Santiago knocked on the door frame, the door now missing and asked entrance to the captain's quarters. "Aye then, enter," Payton replied. "Scuse me capt'n." he started. "But I taught you said dat dat senor Flinney chap were some sora master navigator?" "Right," was Payton's reply. "How come he wasa screaming li a lil' sissy den," Pedro responded. Payton scrunched his face then answered, "Bad day perhaps," he said with a smile. "Or, ya lied 'gan," Pedro said with a laugh. "I am but a humble pirate, mate. If I told you the truth at that time, ye'd have never have jumped in with the likes of us," Payton said leaning in. "Si. Dat's a possible. Or p'haps I'd 've. I'm not but a pirate me self Effie," Pedro returned with another smile. "So other dan he's part of da ole crew of dat ship, has he got anyting special bout him?" "Just the tools of his trade mate and his average skills as a navigator. Well, that and one incredibly difficult name to remember."

Another Distraction

Holden and Fry were given the task of checking the rudder chain. They descended via the hand lines that the crew handled. Reaching the rudder they could see that the mechanism was still intact. That was the good news. The bad news was the rudder itself was cracked and just about to separate.

"Ay, Holdie. This thing's in terrible shape," Fry stated the obvious. "Right," Holden responded as his eye darted about the rudder. "We'll have to replace her before we leave."

They relayed the message back up to the deck. "Blast," Martin huffed at what he perceived as bad luck. "Easy mate," Payton responded. If that's all we came out with, I'm calling it a great day. This tinderbox coulda exploded under that breeze and we'd all be acting like fish right now making for one of them islands." "Fly, fly couldn't I just fly," Sarika questioned. "Why not," Payton shrugged him off. "Da capt'n. ave a point eh," Pedro injected. "Yes. Yes, I guess I see your point then," Martin replied. "Yet…" "No yet," Payton inserted himself. "It's just great to be alive and in one piece. Just let it be then." Payton gave the orders for a crew to be sent ashore to search for the proper wood to replace the rudder as none was aboard. If they had planned to maintain this vessel they would have gathered a larger supply of lumber for future repairs when they acquired the mast. However, as this wasn't the future they sought, they were able to stay relatively focused and grab only a few extra necessities. The crew consisted of Chips, Holden, Fry, Dooley, and

Pid. Quickly they rowed to the nearest isle where they disembarked and took to their mission.

They arrived upon the place near where the spout made landfall. Wet sand and dirt welcomed them. Look though they did, there wasn't anything that would be easy to convert. Chips was going to have to work some magic to assemble a new one. Finally after a half hour had passed the men took their hatchets and made quick work of a tree suitable to their needs. The wood would have to be returned to the ship first as Chips didn't have the necessary tools with him. Quickly the men carried the lumber to the jolly boat. Carefully the cargo was loaded and the men were back to rowing. Upon reaching the ship, the lumber was bundled and hoisted along with the boat. As the master carpenter worked with his apprentice at his side, the rest of the crew went about their daily duties.

"Fantastic," Chips said. "Let the captain know that it's just about ready." Pid fled in a hurry to relay the message. Seeing a man in a rush, Clem decided to have more fun.

"Blky, 're ya afta," Clem asked standing in Pid's way. "Um, sorry then Mr. Bearded. However, I mus…" Clem cut him off, "kiky ate. All'e eared fa siks ake. Oh's a's nna o toning on 'er, eh?" Pid stood looking blankly at him. He blinked a few times with a blank stare on his face. "Smattar? Oww ot omein' attin'lin' ond in at rain o' ers?" Pid remained completely motionless, staring blank faced at the gunner. "'L, ah ottoa mit at's a 'igty ine ay!" Pid could only stare until he simply blurted out, "I'm sorry sir. I just don't understand a single word that you're trying to say. I don't mean anything by it mate. Yet I have very imp…" "At's arite oke. A nodda ay ohka." Pid again just stood looking blankly up at him. "Righty. So I'll just be off then," he said hoping that Clem would move. "I… see then… um. I," he stammered pointing at himself and then around Clem. Yet Clem stood his ground with a large smiling face. "Well then… I'll just be…um. Please move," he suddenly said. Though he was meek, it was a bold move for him. Yet it was to no avail, as Clem continued to block his path. "I have to get to the captain. I have to… I have… I…" the flustered mate stammered. He suddenly looked up pointing above Clem's head, "What the devil?" As Clem looked up, Pid dropped to the floor. Crawling like an infant, he scurried his way through Clem's legs and off to the captain. Clem was impressed and chuckled to himself and thought, "Aye, that's a new one. Got to give him credit for that!"

"Sir," he said puffing out of breath. "The rudder is finished." "Marvelous. Get it to Holden and Fry to assemble," Payton ordered. "Aye, aye sir."

Pid was off with a flash to find the men and upon discovering them, he relayed the message. It wasn't long before they were being lowered again and back at work. "Well that just about does it eh mate," Holden exclaimed. "Aye, will be good to be finished," Fry answered. "C'mon mate. It's not that hard. Don't be afraid to get your hands a little dirty from time to time," he said with a laugh. "Naw," Fry replied with a smile. "Tis not for me. I'd rather just supervise. So… back to work," he jokingly commanded. Holden played the straight man, "Ya'd better start helping or it'll be you that's strapped to this bloody thing! How are you at guiding a ship from under the bloody water line?" The two smiled and finished their work quickly.

Now What?

The officers ate their supper in the galley enjoying a few bottles of rum as the crew sang and danced topside. Dooley blew his harmonica as Richards and Walsh strummed their guitars. Neilson plucked a fiddle along with Pid's melodies on the accordion. Walker led the men in song after song while Ram danced to the delight of the men. Alcohol flowed freely that night and lights out was suspended for the evening under direction of the captain.

"Capt'n, you tink dat dis ship'll git us to da Port den," a partially intoxicated Pedro inquired. "I'll be surprised if she'll hold up manana," Payton joked. "Maybe the men can hold the bloody planks together if need be. Could use the sails as rafts," Hall chided along. "We'll probably just float the masts and crossbars in as the rest will have been blown away," Finny added. "Ride the masts, ride the masts, sail upon the long logs at last," Sarika offered. "Well this Jonah of a ship will have to do her part; and we'll do ours," Payton exclaimed raising his mug. The others responded by doing equally and drank to better fortune. "The deep will not commandeer any more of our souls until we sack Port Elizabeth" Payton exclaimed. The men all cheered and drank some more.

Topside the men continued to revel well into the night.

Many passed out where they sat, only to remain till the morning sun would awaken them to bleary eyes and parched throats. A select few passed out and awoke a short time later and resumed their tawdry pace without ever realizing that they had passed out.

Until the morning sun would eventually rise, they continued singing, even creating a few new songs along the way.

> Away we sailed, through wind and rain
> to fight the men who'd steal our souls
> and trade for them, with the Devil
> those he already owns

Back below deck Payton addressed the men. "Gents, I believe that I have a plan that will ensure our victory." The intoxicated men cheered, laughed and raised their mugs. "What is this plan," Fitzgerald inquired. The men all stopped cold and looked at Fitzgerald. Uncomfortable at having all the eyes fixed upon him in dead silence, he squirmed, "I'm just curious." His discomfort made him stammer a bit, "From a medical point of view that is. I need to wonder what I may be up against." He continued to squirm at the uncomfortable tension he had created, only making it worse as he spoke on. "I , I just, well, where shall I set up..." He stopped speaking while his eyes darted the room.

"My dear Doctor," Payton stated, "you have proven your skills after the storm. Your mind is sharp and your hand is steady. Skillfully you repaired the men and have done your deed in full conscious. I'm wagering that you will have not a soul to save come that day. I can feel it in me bones mate. However, if'n ye do, I'll personally see to it that ye have the absolute finest area to practice yer craft." Payton's cocksure attitude was greedily accepted by the men. "I'll personally see to it that you have anything you need to perform yer duties." Fitzgerald smiled a relaxed grin. Payton winked back as if reading his thoughts, "Don't mention it." "Thank you sir," he said anyway. "I said to not mention it bloke. Follow directions," he said jokingly. "Rest assured, I'll explain the plan when we are on dry land. However; I'll tell you this." Payton started walking around the galley looking intently at the wood work. He ran his hand along a futtock. "This ole ship has got some life left in her. She'll be integral to our success. So mind your steps. We can't afford for her to come apart... before she needs to."

> "Today, today we sail that sea
> To fight, to pillage
> To claim the treasures we all believe,
> That befall the chosen ones
> That take and give not
> Without heed
>
> But who shall stop us,
> Not a one can see
> If it be not the king's navy
> Then none could be,
> For it be Captain Payton
> Who shall lead us to certain victory!

The revelry continued long into the night. At the conclusion of the morning watch the whistle sounded and most of the men still lay unconscious on the deck. The morning watch was sounded by the ringing of the ship's bell.

Payton welcomed the day walking out topside. He looked about the ship and the men who decorated her deck with their sprawled out bodies. "Morning gents." "ALL HANDS RISE," Hall announced. The panicked men quickly awoke one another, rose to attention and toed the line. Each of them saluted, as the captain again greeted the day. "Morning gents, I am very happy that you all had a great time in the evening past. Today is a bold new adventure and this old tub is likely to fall apart if'n we don't keep a wat...," he was cut off as his foot hit a dry rotted plank with a loud *crack!* He stopped dead to not put any more pressure on the plank. "Okay," he said sarcastically. "Jenkins," he shouted loudly. Jenkins rushed to him, "Sir?" Payton then speaking plainly to him, "Avoid this spot," he said pointing down. "Back to your place." "Yes sir," Jenkins replied. "Alright men," Payton spoke, "just keep yer eyes and ears open." He looked around the ship and saw the damage of the dry rot. "This thing's a splinter passing as a boat." He turned and nodded to Hall. Hall cracked his whip in the air and the hung-over men scurried to their posts. "Swab that deck, you mangy mongrels. Watch for splinters," Hall commanded with a joking tone. "And have a good time while yer at it. No sense in being miserable lads. Oh and Jenkins," he said quietly only to him, "mark off that spot eh," his eyes darting around.

The ship headed out of the channel and made way back

on her mark. The winds were mild and the men began to worry that perhaps the doldrums would yet again return.

"This could be a long day captain," Finny remarked as the soft winds blew. The cloudless sky seemed to hang heavy as the air was already thick with humidity. "It's early lad," was his response. As the ship made her way the captain spotted not one, but several eagle rays jumping. This brought a big smile to his face. "It's not going to be so bad after all. See that gents," he asked merrily. "What sir? The fish," Finny inquired. "Was dat wha I tink sir," Pedro asked. Fitzgerald looked on with growing interest. Payton shrugged, "Well it all depends on what you're *tinking*, then, eh mate? I mean if you're *tinking* that I'd like a bite to eat, well you'd be correct! Hum, a bite to eat, "he trailed off. "Ah yes," snapping back, "if ya'd *tink* that I'd be liking fish fer lunch; again, ye'd be correct." Once again he drifted away, "Um, fish fer lunch." Regaining his train of thought, "If ya'd be *tinkin'* that I'd like to see Margarita again... um Margarita... ye'd be right. If ya'd be *tinkin'* that all's well that ends well, well that's yet to be determined, isn't it? And it'd end well with a fine breakfast. Doc! What's to eat then? I'm famished!" Payton said strolling across to the entrance to the stairs. He turned and walked back to where Pedro and Finny stood waiting for a response. "Mr. Fabulous," he was corrected, "Finny sir."

"Fanny then. Doctor, you seem interested in this," he motioned him over. "Those *fish* as ye'd have em weren't fish at all. Um-um, fish... tasty... Uh, sorry. Those my lad, were eagle rays. Me grandfather told me when I was but a lad no taller then his knee; 'Daniel' he said. 'Daniel when ya see the eagle rays jumping yer in for a bit of good fortune. Well good fortune if'n ye be in need of a good wind. Bad if'n yer making a house of cards.' Ole grandfather was a bit off," Payton said. He went on, "'He continued to say that there'll be a strong northerly wind blowing in about five minutes." Fitzgerald procured a small sand glass timer from his pocket and turned it over to check the accuracy.

Langly was within earshot of their conversation and disagreed with the captain's excitement. "Sea devils," he thought to himself. His superstition almost got the better of him, but he bit his tongue. "That's all we need is more bad luck. I'd like to run 'em through. Filthy fish," he thought to himself. He feared going against the captain even in matters such as this.

Doc ambled up the stairs, "Captain, grub is ready for you sir." "Fantastic, roll me another of those burritos then, eh mate." "Sir?" the cook questioned. Payton looked back at him, "Well, go on. Go on. Make haste," he commanded. The cook looked flustered and ran below deck.

Payton took over command of the helm and checked his markers. It took just four turns of Fitzgerald's glass when Payton saw the ripples coming upon the surface of the water. An all too familiar smirk came over his face and he turned to Finny who was oblivious to the incoming winds. He turned to Fitzgerald, "Five, four, three, two and one," he counted and pointed up to the sails without looking at them. The northern winds reached the ship, filling the sheets and powering the sloop on her way with a jolt. "God I love sailing!" "You are remarkable. I'll give you that," Fitzgerald responded. Finny agreed.

"Only a few days journey left till our… what the devil," Payton uttered. He spied a tall ship sailing in the distance. He pulled out his spyglass and investigated. "Yes, perhaps our fortune has changed indeed," he said quietly to himself. "Captain, ship at…" Jute was cut off by Payton. "Yes," he said flatly. "Thanks for the update. Couldn't get by without you boy. You're the best. Remind me at Christmas to get you something nice." "Langley, back at the helm if you please. New heading. We're going after that ship," Payton commanded. "Aye-aye captain," Langley replied changing their course. "Capt'n. Ja tink dat we can overtake dat ship," Santiago inquired. "Just as long as we can catch her," Payton remarked. The bosun ordered the men to their stations and everyone excitedly readied themselves for the chase.

The ship cracked and creaked as all the sails were opened and filled with the salty breeze. As the ship increased speed she started to shake even more than previously. She hadn't had this much action in years and wasn't maintained well enough to sustain the sudden activity level changes.

"If we can…" Payton was cut off by a dull thud emanating from the bowels of the ship. He looked around, but continued. "If we can…" Payton was again interrupted by another thud followed by a soft scraping sound. "Damn… shoals," he muttered. Before orders could be given, the ship hit aground, tossing the men to the deck. Payton just sighed, rolling his eyes shaking his head. "Never mind."

"Sir. I think we hit bottom," Pid called. "Really? What was your first inclination of that," a sarcastic Payton inquired. "Well I think that it was that bump we just hit," an innocent Pid answered. He waited a moment then looked around, "Oh, and it seems that we've stopped moving sir." Payton just looked over at him with a blank stare, "I can't seem to find a time when a name was ever more fitting than yours." "Thank you sir," Pid responded in earnest not fully understanding why he was just told that.

No Leg To Stand On

"Mr. Hall. Damage report if you please," Payton ordered. Hall shouted below deck, "Mr. Walker, Damage report if you please!" "Mr. Maudlin. I want to know why we weren't aware of these shoals!" Martin scrambled for his charts, "Yes sir. I'll check." Whirling around, "Where the devil is that burrito already?" A few moments lapsed when Walker shouted back up, "Shockingly sir, we seem to be alright. "Sir, reports seem to be all clear," Hall reported to the captain.

Payton looked around, "You're joking right?" "No sir. It would seem that structurally we're fine," Hall replied. "Positive," Payton questioned his good luck. "Absolutely sir," Hall reported. "Tremendous work," Payton exclaimed. "Well, my compliments to the crew who worked the hull when we were careened. Excellent work. Yes, excellent work indeed! An extra ration of grog to all who worked the hull," Payton exclaimed. "Thank you sir," Dooley replied without thinking. "You've very welcome," Payton said sarcastically. "Now, to the lines.

Lower a few men overboard to assess the situation."

Pid whispered to Jenkins, "Hope they don't pick me. I can't swim!" Jenkins agreed, "I won't even bathe in the ocean. Tis bad luck it is!" Richards was standing behind them sniffing the air, "By the stench of you, I don't think you bathe at all Jenkins." "Never-you-mind-that! One taste of you and the sea will come back to claim you later," Jenkins continued. "Ave you two got chowder for brains," Dooly asked. "We're on a sand bar. You won't drown, you won't have to bathe… and if'n we're all lucky you won't have to come back topside," he joked.

A group of less-superstitious men were chosen to be lowered to the sand bar. Quickly they were dispatched and went to their business. Doc emerged from the darkness with a metal tray upon which sat what he thought a burrito might be. Payton looked blank faced at him, to the tray and back at the nervously smiling cook. Doc nodded, "Yer food sir," he stammered. Hunger overtook the captain ignoring the fact that the tray held something indiscernible and tore into it. Quickly he finished the meal and was back at the task at hand.

"Mr. Maltese, where are you in *discovering* our mystery shoals?" Martin scanned the maps under glass, "Sir, nothing appears on my charts." "Wonderful;" he said sarcastically, "that helps. Well either you can jot that down, or you can get yerself a new map, eh?" "Yes sir," Martin stuttered, feverishly marking his map. "Mr. Hillberg!" "Aye sir," Hillberg shouted. "Might I borrow your apprentice," Martin inquired. "Gladly sir. Bart! On yer feet and assist Mr. Finny," Hillberg ordered. "Yes sir," Bart replied as he rushed to Martin. "Young Mr.

Bartholomew, take my spyglass and view the surrounding waters. Look for the reflection of bright vs. darker colors reflecting. Note the brighter colors on the chart as corresponding shoals. I'm taking a big risk in trusting you Mr. Bartholomew. Do not let me down. Do not fail your captain either boy." "Help, help, be of help to the captain," Sarika inserted. "Yes sir. I won't sir," the excited boy said with pure confidence and joy at being assigned such a task. Quickly he ran to the bow and started his task. Payton leaned in to Martin, "Grooming the little buggar for officer eh?" "Some things you just can't wash out of your system sir," he replied.

The men lowered Bertrand, Masterson and Williams. Their feet repelled down the hull till they came to rest below the surface of the water on a sandbar. "We're on a sand bar captain," Williams shouted. In the time it took for the ship to become lodged and safety checked, the winds had died down, the seas calmed to nearly flat conditions. Sarika flew off Martin's shoulder to take a closer look. He sailed down and came to rest on Bert's shoulder. "Ello bird," he said. "Bad. Bad. Is it bad," he inquired. "Naw, shouldn't be a problem." With that the bird took off and flew back to Martin.

Payton put his hands toward the gunwale, then suddenly remembering the previous one breaking away he stopped, hands open only an inch away from the rail. Making a face, he thought the better of placing his hands on the rail. Wiggling his fingers, his eyes darted side to side, "Ah yes," he said. He placed his hands deep in his coat pockets, leaned over without touching anything, "Just how bad is the situation down there then?"

Bertrand was the first to speak up, "Not to bad sir. We should be able to break free with enough help." "What do you propose," Finny questioned as his hands came upon the gunwale. Payton looked at him, "Isn't that my line?" Finny looked surprised at what he just did, "Uh, sorry sir. Didn't mean to overstep my bounds." "No problemo," Payton responded. "Um," he thought, "carry on," he said with a hint of glee. "Please… carry on." Finny looked over the rail and Sarika looked around unsure of the situation. Payton looked on in anticipation. Finny continued, "Again, what is it that you propose Mr. Bertrand?" Payton's eyes widened in more anticipation. A smile broke upon his face.

"Well sir," Bert started, "if we could just get a few more men down here, we should be able to push her off the bar." Finny leaned his body weight on the rail bringing an even bigger smile to Payton's face. The bird grew ever more uncomfortable as well. "Where is it best to push from?" Payton began moving about as excitement began to well in him.

"Sir, if we had a few men at this location," he said pointing, "and all heaved, perhaps we could set free." "Perhaps," Finny shouted. "Perhaps is not good enough," leaning his full weight on the rail, arms waving. Sarika could take no more and flew off to perch upon the mast. Payton's anticipation began to overflow and showed in his childlike mannerisms.

Bert took another look, "Yes sir. This spot is where she's the worst sir. We definitely can dislodge her with enough hands. Shouldn't be too difficult." "And line," Masterson piped up, Bertrand ignoring him. "I repeat, you're positive gentlemen," Finny stated as he lay his full weight on the rail trying to see the exact spot Bertrand was pointing to. Moments passed and Payton's smile began to flatten out and was replaced by surprise, "How the blazes is that thing holding that chubby little man," Payton thought to himself. "I have fallen through and off this blasted ship yet he's on the damn rail and nothing happens."

"Mr. Finny. If we were tied together on a safety line, we could use extra logs from below deck that we recently brought on to help dislodge her hull," Masterson volunteered. "Where mean you to use the log," Martin wondered. Payton's smile completely vanished only to be replaced by outright disgust. He pulled his hands out of his pockets, crossed his arms tapping his foot.

Williams spoke up first, "Sir, we can pry her off the bar in this spot," he said pointing further up the hull, "as the men heave right there," pointing to the spot previously pointed out. Martin nodded his head, "Sounds reasonable gentlemen. How many do you suppose?" "Maybe ten sir," Masterson responded. "Sixteen," Williams said confidently. "Sixteen," Masterson corrected himself. Payton's disgust level escalated, "BLAST," he screamed in his head. He began to pace back and fourth.

"Great then." Martin turned around, "Well then we need thirteen to volunteer. Who will stand forth?" Payton lowered his head and shook it in disappointment as thirteen men volunteered. Martin turned back around leaning over the rail, "We have our thirteen and they'll be down soon."

Payton raised his eyes, stepped over to Martin and caused what he had hoped all along would have happened naturally. He hip checked Martin over the edge, causing him to splash in the shallow water. The men on deck who witnessed the event let out a hearty laugh. "Mr. Mellon, don't you realize that thirteen is an unlucky number," Payton joked. Martin looked up at him in disgust, "Captain!" "Yes Mr. Morton," Payton said coyly with a little smile. "That thirteen is *in addition* to the three who were *already down here*," Martin huffed! "Ah," Payton proclaimed, the tips of his fingers tapping it's matching one on the other hand. His eyes darting back and forth, "My mistake," he exclaimed his eyes widening as he spoke. "Mr. Milton, as long as yer down there cleaning yerself, and you've been doing such a spectacular job thus far. Please finish coordinating the task to free us." Payton spun around and as he walked away, "Lads! Someone toss the crew a couple of safety lines," the smile returning to his face. It felt good, but not as fulfilling as if it had happened naturally.

Once the logs had been jettisoned for use on the bar, Martin quickly organized the men into two teams. Five men were stationed on the logs to gain some leverage for the other team to heave. Each team had been tied together, the long end of the lines rested in the hands of the crew still aboard *the Dreamers Delight*. The log crew placed one log perpendicular to the hull with just enough room to wedge the other log in between. "Are you dogs ready," Martin barked. "Aye-aye sir," they responded. "Then *HEAVE!*"

The crew threw all their weight onto the log again and again, trying to help free her from the sandbar. The hands crew pushed with all their might with every heave of the log. On deck Payton ordered the lines tied to secure posts and the men to the far side of the ship, to help with the weight distribution.

Martin shouted again and again, "C'mon you dogs! HEAVE, HEAVE!" Despite the uncharacteristic hard surface of the sandbar, the base log began to push into the bar. The men grunted and yelled as they thrust the fullness of their weight and strength into the log. The ship began to rock, yet couldn't get free. The hands crew pushed and pushed, their footing unsteady. "IT'S STARTING TO WORK," Martin shouted. "WE NEED MORE! KEEP HEAVING! KEEP HEAVING!" They did as instructed and the ship began to rock more and more.

"Al-mo-st th-ere," Williams said between breaths as the ship and the log rocked up and down. "Need-a-lit-tle-mo-re," he continued. Then to everyone's dismay, the log gave off an ominous "crack"! The men's eyes flashed among each others. "Keep going," an exhausted Masterson ordered. The log crew kept working, shouts rang out between the two teams. Still the ship rocked and she started to slip backwards foot by foot off the bar. "C'mon, you stupid ship! Get-off-the-damn-bar," Williams yelled at the boat as she continued to back off. His tone was more excitement than real anger as she slipped into the deeper waters. The anticipation of nearly being free caused Williams to continue his verbal assault on the ship. "Get-off-this-fu…" he was suddenly cut off, "whoa!" The pry log snapped in half as the men plunged into the water, the log half under some of them. The ship had slipped far enough off the bar that she was able to slide the rest of the way off, suddenly yanking the two crews off the bar and into the ocean. Topside the men all started to cheer and they ran to the lines. With haste, they hauled up the lines, bringing the men to the ship like lobster traps full of their catch. A great deal of shouting could be heard from the men still in the water.

"Pull them up you scurvy dogs," Payton ordered. "Keep pulling. Your mates depend upon it!" The crew had a constant tension on the first line pulling the hands team up. One by one they made it to the ship, walking up the hull as the rope pulled them higher. Yet the log crew continued their distraught shouts. Wiles, well known as the quietest of the crew, shouted as if he were alight with fire. His weight had been atop the log when it broke. The resulting lurch of the ship off the sand bar yanked the lines and all the men attached. Most of them only shot under the water momentarily. Wiles' was not so fortunate. The jerk of the rope tied around his waist hauled him into the wedged section of the broken log. The jagged wood pierced through his thigh, shattering his leg. Blood streamed out of him as the salt water burned his gaping wound. The agony was shown in his wretched face and heard in his screams. Bertrand, next to him on the line, got his bearings and tried to make his way back to Wiles. The second lurch of the ship was to be Wiles' undoing. The force created from the jolt pulled Bertrand away while tearing Wiles from his leg. The bloody appendage remained impaled upon the log. Wiles in his agony, kept his eyes fixed upon his leg as he was being pulled further and further from it. He was in shock and disbelief as the severed appendage grew smaller and smaller in the distance. It would be quite a while for this meek man to come to grips with what just befell him. As for now, tears streamed down his face as the pain overwhelmed him. As the crew pulled him up the side and on deck, Fitzgerald had already spread out the sand on the deck to soak up the blood. Quickly he went to work as he desperately tired to save his life. The men crowded around as they watched as the doctor and his assistant Blase performed their work. Bart peered through the crowd to see what was the matter. The vision of the man's agony would haunt him for years to come. Jute looked down and saw the young boy and put his arm around him. "Pray for his soul today lad. Pray for his soul." Bart nodded as the tears streamed down his face before burying into Jute's belly.

The wound was managed expertly, but the remaining part of his leg was bitterly mangled. The grisly remains of his once proud leg was now reduced to a stump with a gaping cavity from where the crimson life giving fluid rushed. As the blood-soaked man slipped into unconsciousness, his last vision was of Fitzgerald holding him still as Blase pulled out the amputating saw and went to work cleaning the jagged remains.

Part 8: Missionary Help
Just In Time

The next few days were spent with the men on constant watch so that no more accidents would befall them. Wiles' condition improved dramatically, yet he remained in convalescence in his hammock. Slowly they made their way along their route when they happened to spy a tiny island. A church bell rang quietly in the distance.

Payton called to his bosun with a sense of urgency in his voice, "Mr. Hall!" "Aye sir," he replied. "MUSIC! STOMP! ANYTHING! Make noise till we reach that island!" The very confused bosun didn't question the captain, he knew better by now. He obliged the order and commanded the men to make as much noise as possible. Thinking that they were possibly going into battle the men eagerly obliged.

"Mr. Maryweather," Payton called still concerned. "Martin sir," Finny corrected wondering what the confusion was all about. "Whatever. Is that a monastery that you are aware of?" "Yes sir. It's an English settlement." "Langley, take us to that monastery," Payton commanded. "Ay, sir," he replied. Finney still followed the captain, uncertain of what was happening among all the commotion, "I believe that Father Osborne is still there. Why do you ask? Have a change of heart? Want to make a career change," Finny joked. "In a manner of speaking, yes," he replied. This stunned him and he pressed for more. "Begging you pardon sir?" "Si, wat, chu talkin' 'bout capt'n," Pedro inquired.

Payton didn't respond but walked off below deck. The sound of the men on deck was still apparent, if not louder with the echoing. His journey took him to the bunk hammock where Wiles was recuperating. He came upon him and Wiles gave him a groggy salute. "How goes it Mr. Wiles," Payton inquired softly with concern in his voice. "Good sir. I should be up and around in no time," Wiles replied. Payton smiled a compulsory smile. "Tell me about yerself. You had served under Captain Melbourne eh?" "Yes sir," he responded. "I had just gotten on with him when the evil deed happened." "How well did you know the man," Payton inquired. "Not at all sir. I had just gotten on and he didn't mingle with us. Not like you sir." He paused, "I like the sea. I like my work. It will afford a good life for us... my wife and I that is, when we return home again." Payton jumped in, "You're a married man are you?" "Aye," he replied. "Been five years now. Haven't seen her in about two now though."

Payton nodded then spoke, "You tend to be a quiet one, eh?" Wiles nodded in agreement, "I don't enjoy speaking very much sir. Not that I'm opposed, but I like to listen. You can learn quite a bit you know." He was silent a moment and looked toward the empty space where his leg should be. "Plus, if you speak a lot people tend to ask you things that you don't wish to speak of." "I've noticed that," Payton muttered. "The crew has noticed that about you as well." "I've always been that way though," Wiles interrupted. "Why is that," Payton asked of him. "Well sir. I'm not certain. I've always kept to myself. Even as a child I preferred to be alone, playing with myself as opposed to others," he spoke. "Playing with yourself eh,"

Payton repeated softly, yet puzzled in his head. "Yes sir. I would always play with myself as I fantasized myself into all sort of fantastic situations," Wiles professed. Payton smirked and nodded his head. "Are you a religious man?" "Yes sir. I was baptized and took my confirmation," Wiles answered. "How does it feel to be aboard a pirate ship, on a revenge mission, being a man of God," Payton inquired. "Well sir. I try to not think about that portion of it sir. Actually, you seem to believe as well. You know I've heard all sort of tales about you, but none of them mesh up with the man you have portrayed thus far. I just wanted to get off that awful place and hopefully find my way out of service once the mission was accomplished. No offence at all to you sir. That is still valid, isn't it," he wondered. "Course it is chap. That's the rule of the ship and I stick by it," Payton returned. "I mean, I just want to get home to my beloved wife," Wiles spoke softly, distantly. "Well then I just might have some good news for you," Payton said jarring Wiles back to reality. "Actually, I have an offer for you that you may truly enjoy," Payton stated. "Offer sir," Wiles inquired. "Did you happen to hear any bells ring?"

Wiles stopped and listened yet heard nothing other than the ruckus that the men were creating. "No sir." He grabbed the sides of the hammock and sat up, intently focusing on trying to hear a bell. "But it's rather difficult, what with all the commotion going on, on deck." His eyes rolled around the hold as he strained to hear. Payton closed his eyes and shook his head, "No, it's not ringing at this moment." "Oh sorry sir," he said sitting back, his eyes fixed upon the captain. "So you didn't hear any bells then," he paused, "before...at all?"

Wiles shook his head, "No sir. Sorry." Payton breathed a sigh of relief, "Nothing to be sorry for old chap!" Indeed he had nothing to be sorry for at all. Superstition held that church bells heard at sea were bad luck. In fact it meant that someone would soon perish. Payton didn't want anyone to possibly hear them, hence all the uproar on deck.

"Mr. Pinnicle has told me that a Father Osborne runs the monastery on this here island. What I propose is that you are a fine upstanding sailor and not at all a pirate. If you please, we will take you ashore to stay with the father as you heal from your wounds. And as long as you tell no one, I will pay you in advance not only for your services rendered, but also for your loss as agreed upon in the laws. Plus, a little extra just because… well, because you're a good man. And I'm in a rather good mood right now. What do you think about that," he asked tossing a small bag of coins into Wiles' hands. Wiles' eyes widened, "You mean that sir," he exclaimed with excitement! "Course," was his reply. The sudden relief swept over the man as he was being freed to live among quiet God-fearing folk. "Oh yes, thank you sir! Thank you very much! I would be most appreciative!" "Good. Then I'll have the jolly boat readied and have you taken ashore. Now, hide yer payment." "Yes sir," the shocked man stuttered. The excitement began to well in the man and showed upon his face. Payton turned and began walking from him then turned back, "Oh, and one more thing." "Yes sir?" "Don't let the father catch you playing with yourself. They tend to frown on that."

Ungrateful Freeloaders

The jolly boat was lowered and a landing crew was placed aboard. Captain Payton was among them as the crew rowed their way ashore. It was the first time in days that Wiles had fresh air in his face and lungs. It was apparent that the new adventure and the sunshine was already doing the man good as the color returned to his face, along with an ever present smile.

Once having learned that they were in fact not going into battle, the men's mood diminished a bit. But once the reason was made clear, they appreciated the lengths the captain went to protect one of their own.

The boat glided its way ashore where the father was there to greet them. "Ah, Mr. Finny isn't it? Yes, it's so nice to see you again my son," the father said kindly. Payton looked at the father, then to Finny, "Son… well I'll be. I can completely see the family resemblance." Finny turned to Payton, "That's not what he meant sir." "Ah yes. You sure… the resemblance is uncanny," the pirate said. Everyone looked at the rather small, chubby, tanned Finny, then to the tall, lanky, pale father, "Right," most of them said in unison.

"Yes father Osborne. It is me Martin Finny. How have you been father?" "Well. Very well thank you. Are you still with the royal navy," he inquired. Martin shook his head, "No father. Those days are beyond me. I am now but a humble merchant sailor." "Good for you sir. Honest work is the Lord's good doing. What is it that brings you here though?" "One of our crew was injured during our travel," Martin was abruptly halted as several men carried Wiles from the boat. "My goodness! Son are you alright," he asked of the injured man. "I'm feeling much better now father," Wiles responded. "Still to weak to walk though as you can clearly see." "Is it possible that Mr. Wiles remain in your care as he continues to regain his health father," Finny asked. "Certainly! Why certainly! I would never leave anyone in need at my doorstep," the kind man stated. "Wonderful," Payton interrupted. "Also, my good padre, is it possible that I might have a word with you? Alone? Er, ah, a confession of sorts, eh" "Why of course my good man. This way," he said motioning with his hand. "Yes, terrific," the pirate scurried past. Making their way to a more secluded place, Osborne pondered what this man may be thinking. He had a frightful appearance and thought him to be a pirate more than merchant. "Uh padre, you see this man we're leaving here is a bit of a dreamer." "I don't understand," Osborne replied.

"You see before the accident, he was a quiet man who stayed to himself. Often fantasizing himself into all sorts of adventures. Then after the accident he just started retelling his stories as if they were fact," the pirate continued. "Ah, dementia. The poor man." "Not surprising for what he went through," Payton added. "Well this will be a wonderful place for him to rehabilitate," the sympathetic preacher stated. "Ah, yes. Dementia! He tells tales so fantastic that you can't believe a one of them!" Payton's mind was swirling, "Then again, he might not say anything at all! So I guess it's best to not press him… or believe a word he says," he ended with a big smile, trying desperately to look innocent. "Absolutely, absolutely. I won't push him," the father said. "Good then," Payton began. "So he'll be well cared for then." "Absolutely my good man. Thank you for your kindness towards this man. It is obvious that you are a fine man of God to look after your crew as such," the preacher continued. "Great then," the men turned back to the group and suddenly the pirate spun him around again, "Oh wait good padre." "Yes my son," he inquired. "Um, might you have a bite to eat to spare," the pirate asked. "Yes of course! Come in, come in all of you," the father insisted. Payton turned around, "Wonderful news gents! We're all going to have a quick bite then we're off!"

The crew cheered and followed for their free, albeit, bland meal. Not forgetting that they were pirates, the crew crowded in the small room pushing Wiles to the back of the line. The bowls were filled and handed out. Natural distrust overcame them as man after man looked at each other and their bowls, unsure if they were about to eat a possibly poisoned meal. Cheerily the preacher dolled out ladle after ladle of grog to the uncertain men. Some of the men considered rampaging the place and looting whatever there was to be had, yet Payton fearing retribution from the spirit world squashed the uprising.

"Are you certain we should be eating this," Vaughn whispered. "I don' know," Walsh said shrugging his shoulders. "Eeh, wha' the hell," he said before putting the bowl to his mouth and downing the concoction. The gruel was bland and without texture and slid down his throat in an almost snail-like fashion. All eyes turned to him. Father Osborne looked on seeing who would scold him for his uncouth actions, whereas the men were waiting to see if he fell dead. After a few moments with no one speaking or moving, Walsh began to rub his belly.

"Oh," he uttered as he began wobbling and looking as if he were about to vomit. Several men suddenly dropped their bowls and put their hands on their weapons, eyes still on Walsh. He continued to grasp his belly and look more and more nauseous. Cutlasses and daggers were slowly becoming unsheathed. Pistols around their necks hung at the ready. Walsh groaned again looking down, one hand on his belly, the other reaching for the wall for support.

"You alright Coop," Jute asked his mate. "Uh," was all he could mutter as he continued to clutch himself. The men began to slowly move around to position themselves to attack the man who dispensed the food in case Walsh fell dead. Walsh looked up, "This is it boys, watch out." Cutlasses were almost fully drawn when… an awful sound cracked and was trailed very quickly by an even worse aroma filling the room. The men in unison showed their dismay, "Awe Coop!" "What? I've had the trots lately," he exclaimed. The men quickly sheathed their weapons and picked up their bowls again, quickly exiting the room. "I'm so very sorry father," an embarrassed Finny exclaimed. "They are but sailors." Osborne nodded his disapproval, "I know lad. These aren't the first seafaring men to ever grace this abode." "Yes still, I am so very sorry father," Finny apologized. Payton unfazed by the complete proceedings strolled up to the father, "Um, 'scuse me padre. Is there any more of this? This is fabulous," he exclaimed looking into his empty bowl. Surprised by this request the preacher stumbled, "Um, yes... certainly. Have all you wish."

"Wonderful. Simply smashing," he professed digging into the caldron and feeding himself. He spoke with his mouth half full, "Can you share your secrets with our cook?" He continued to stuff his mouth, "This is fantastic!"

Making The Best With The Hand You're Dealt

After an interesting meal the men all gathered back at the shore and were readying themselves for departure. Payton came ambling down and raised his left foot to place it in the boat. "Whoa, that could have been bad." The superstitious captain knew that stepping on a boat, no matter what size, with his left foot first was bad luck. Quickly he corrected himself and placed his right in, but stopped as he straddled the side. "What is it sir," Martin asked. Payton's eyes darted about, "Anyone know the day?" The men looked around at one another all suddenly realizing that it was Friday. No one had to speak up as Payton took his foot carefully out of the boat. "We'll put it to a vote. Gentlemen," he started. "Today is Friday. Shall we take our chances on the tinderbox or shall we stay the night?" He looked around, "All in favor of staying say Aye." All in unison shouted "Aye!" Although they all agreed Payton still had to ask, "Opposed?" No one spoke up. "Then it's agreed, we stay the night. Oh, but let's make sure that no one sees the padre on the way to the ship in the morning, or we'll have to stay another night." That too was deemed bad luck, which they didn't need any more of.

The men found their way back up and made themselves at home for the night, lighting fires, singing songs and getting into the rum. "Cripes man, of all the places to be holed up for a night... a blasted monastery," Langley spat. "Why couldn't it be a port?" "Right, one with *lots* of ladies," Pid added. "Pid, you wouldn't even know what to do with a lady even if one sat on yer lap, bosom in yer face," Walker said. "And a map to her *buried treasure* tattooed upon her face," Hillberg quickly added. The men roared as Pid disputed their taunts in vain.

Bartholomew hid himself next to a tree and watched the proceedings not sure what to think of what he saw. Coop brought them back together, "Eh fella's, don't forget that soon we'll have a new ship, a new home, and many, many nights out fighting, drinking and pillaging!" Again this made the men cheer. The men began increasing in intoxication and commenced to sing the songs they sung nightly.

<blockquote>
Away we sailed, through wind and rain
To fight the men who'd steal our souls
And trade for them, with the Devil
Those he already owns.
</blockquote>

On we shall sail
Not a whaler
Nor a merchant ship
Not a naval brigand
Nor a governor's sloop

We are but humble pirates now
Come to take all we can
While we give nothing back
We're sixty three strong souls now
Hell bent on deep seas mastery

Today, today we sail that sea
To fight, to pillage
To claim the treasures we all believe,
That befall the chosen ones
That take and give not
Without heed

But who shall stop us,
Not a one can see
If be it not the kings navy
Then none can be,
Four cheers to Captain Payton
Who shall lead us
To certain victory!

Captain Payton sat upon a window ledge as the words washed over him. The officers sat in the room enjoying all that they could of each others company, also accompanied by their favorite beverage. "Captain, we should be less than a day's sail to our destination," Martin addressed the room. The captain's gaze continued upon the reveling crew a short distance away below them. "Si, Senor capt'n. Dis feel like we's a soon ta be slashin' and a stabbin'," a rather intoxicated Pedro slurred. As always, his speech grew more difficult to understand the more intoxicated he grew. "I'll second that," Hall said not knowing at all what Pedro said! "I'm all for getting this done with and getting on to the next port and those women that the lads have been singing about me self," he chuckled raising his mug to the appreciation of the group.

Still Payton sat and watched the crew, listening to the men on both parties. A silence fell upon the room as Payton spoke up. "Ya know gents, only a short time ago we had two distinct groups out there. It took a storm, a waterspout and a grounding to bring em together as a crew." The silent men looked around and nodded their agreement to this statement. "Now the real test will be shortly upon us. They came together, but how well do they stay together in all out battle? Mother nature and ocean's tricks are one thing, the sting of a cutlass and the burning of yer spilling blood be another. Not to mention the hangman's noose. Aye," he said standing up and began to walk around his captive audience, "the next two days will be the real test to see if this was all predestined … or total failure," he said ominously. "All hands need to be at full alert. Good Dr. Fitzgerald, your skills may be put to their ultimate test. Regardless, our agreement still stands."

"Thank you sir," Fitzgerald acknowledged, yet puzzled by his seemingly change of heart on the certain victory.

The captain previously said that he was so confident that he probably wouldn't have anyone to mend. Now he seemed not so sure. What the doctor didn't realize was that Payton was still certain of their impending victory. What he didn't want was for them to feel the same and grow in complacency. That would be their downfall.

Payton simply nodded and continued, "Mr. Hall. Mr. Santiago. All hands should have sharp blades, but personally make certain that all men's blades are so. All guns are loaded, all locks loaded with fresh flints. Bearded, all cannon the same. Mr. Marauder, your charts better be accurate this time." Finny wondered to himself, "Why only my name?" "It'll be a test for certain," Payton continued. "However, I am also certain that we will persevere and come out with a glorious new ship. Lights out will be in one hour… but, till then," his eyes scanned the group and he cracked a smile, "drink it up!" The men cheered their approval.

One Last Detail

Payton slipped out unnoticed and made his way to the father's room. Knocking upon his door a gentle voice called out, "Come in my son." "Padre, I hope I'm not waking you sir," the pirate spoke softly. "Be not worried my son. Your men have done a wonderful job of that," he said with a smile. Payton bowed, "My most sincere apologies my good sir." "Be not worried my good lad. While I do not approve of their consumption of those beverages, nor of the content of their songs, it is truly wonderful to hear some jovial voices filling the air," he replied. "Besides, it's only one night," he said testing the pirate. Payton ignored the question and pressed on. "Father, I have among my crew a stowaway. A young lad... William, Walter, Wadsworth, Milton... I forget his name. That's beside the point though. Would it be too much to ask, too much of a burden to ask to leave him in your charge as well," the pirate captain inquired. "Heavens no good sir! To tell the truth I was hoping that you would ask that," the father replied. "No offence sir, but I have always felt that a ship like yours was no proper place for a boy to get his education. I will see to it that he gets passage to his home."

"Fabulous! You're correct, our ship is no place for him. What with the men as they act and all. I know that you could do more for this lad than I ever could," Payton said playing on the father's good nature. "However, I'm not certain that home is the best place for him." The man of faith inquired, "That's odd. Why not?" "Well, it seems that his father isn't the most level-headed of men. The boy has received many beatings for things he had not done. Please, keep him here in your charge and see to it that he receives the proper treatment." "Certainly! I would enjoy raising this boy in *His* name while he is here," he said merrily. Payton's confused gaze gave away his befuddlement. "*His*," he asked inquisitively. "Yes, *His*," the father continued. "*His* work is what I do after all." "Whose," the pirate wondered aloud. "*His*," the priest said nodding skyward. "Ah," the pirate said suddenly understanding, "*His*... yes. Anyway, thank you good sir father. Where can I have him bed down for the night?"

"There's an empty room down the hall to the right that he may have," the preacher offered. Payton again sat rather puzzled, eyes rolled up in thought. He raised one eyebrow, then lowered it and raised the other. Then he changed back again. "Yes, that one," the preacher interrupted, "Your starboard brow is the one on the *right*." Payton's face lit up, "Ah yes," he said, "I forget from time to time. Dankeschon!" The bewildered man of God could only nod and smile a confused smile. "Uh, begging your pardon a moment sir," the preacher stopped the pirate. Payton turned back to Osborne as he spoke, "You know, I have a bit of a confession to make." "How's that," Payton questioned. "Well, I have to admit that I rather judged you before speaking to you. See I thought you to be a pirate, what with your, pardon the expression, horrific appearance and all. I have come to learn that you truly have a compassionate attitude in taking care of your men. A trait not often seen in men of the sea." Payton smiled, "You know," he started, "one can rule by the whip, but that only goes so far. When I was a lad I sailed under such a man and all that did was fill the crew with contempt. Fear is a motivator certainly; however, for him all it led to was mutiny and marooning. One day he had gone too far in his abuse of his first mate. Next thing I saw was that ole captain being left behind on a tiny isle pleading like a child for forgiveness. Forgiveness never came from that crew." "Whatever became of the man," the padre inquired. "Not sure. Never saw him again. Probably became food for the gulls, crabs and vultures," Payton replied. A shocked Osborne could only reply, "Mercy!" "Aye, mercy comes to those who seek it father," Payton quipped. "You say you were but a lad at the time. How old were you," the father asked. "Couldn't have been much older than that boy you're now sheltering. Perhaps a bit younger in fact." Payton's eyes drifted away trying to recall that period of his life. "Is that why you seek help now? That he might lead a different life than yours," asked Osborne. "Aye," he said winking back at him before turning away. "Captain," the father stopped him again. "Are you a pirate," he asked sheepishly. Payton looked over his shoulder and grinned, "You tell me mate." With that he turned back forward and took a few steps out the door. He paused, befuddled again which direction he needed to travel. "Starboard," was all that the padre said. "Right! Correct. Thank you," Payton responded as he strode off.

Payton exited the preacher's room and made his way out to the crew where they reveled. Richards was the first to see the captain, "ATTENTION," he shouted. "At ease boys," the captain said calmly. Bart climbed up the trunk of the palm a bit so he could see above the crowd and hear the proceedings. "Gents, tis warms me little heart ta see ya'll a gettin' along so bloody well," the crew laughed. "However the night is upon us and the morning sun will bring us that much closer to our destination. Lights out will be in thirty for all men. There will be no after hours revelry. Watch duty will remain as usual. Yer gonna need yer wits and we're gonna push yer mangy backsides hard. So have one more for yer dear ole captain. WE SAIL AT DAWN!" The men all cheered and continued their songs. Payton slipped around the crowd and snuck up behind Bart who had climbed back down. "Good evening young Billy."

"It's Bartholomew," he growled. "It's fanny face for you my young stowaway for all I care. Come with me," he said holding out his hand. "Where are you taking me," the nervous youngster inquired? "To get you to bed my boy. It's well past your time when you should be awake," the captain said. "A bed? A proper bed," the excited boy asked. "Absolutely me boy. I spoke with the padre myself to ensure that you had a good nights rest," Payton said. "Why thank you sir," the boy said. "Perhaps I have judged this man incorrectly," he wondered to himself. The sleepy boy followed him willingly to the room and quickly made his way to the bed. "Captain?" "Yes," Payton replied midway through closing the door? "I just wanted to thank you for this accommodation sir. I need to be fully rested if I'm going to be of assistance in your big mission," he said eagerly. Payton just smiled and spoke softly as he closed the door, "Sleep well young Bart. And Godspeed."

Part 9: Falling Into Place?

Stakeout

The early morning sun was climbing high in the Caribbean sky as the ship glided down to a chain of isles. Captain Daniel and his officers readied their plan of assault.

"We'll base ourselves at that island. These are low waters, but there's a small cove on the windward side. When the tide will go down we can leave the boat hidden there and she won't be totally aground. The far side of the isle has a small rocky hill where we can safely spy on Port Elizabeth," Martin spoke. "Are you certain of that Manuel," the captain inquired. "Martin. And yes, I've been on this isle many a time and know her quite well sir." "What was your purpose on the isle Millie," Payton butchered his name again.

"Martin. I was in the historic "Battle of the Port" many years ago when we took her from Spain. Ah, it was an amazing time. We overtook the fort in a matter of hours and lost not a single hand. We quickly imprisoned the survivors, rounded up the Spanish loyalists and sailed them off. Knowing full well that this wouldn't sit well with the King of Spain, he'd quickly send more troops. Therefore, we had to reinforce the port and her surroundings. More regiments were sent and all prepared for battle. I had been commanded to take a battalion of men to scout that isle. The mission was to set up a lookout and a strike site. We were stationed there and waited for a month until we finally saw the Spanish flag on the mainsail of their man-o-war. She had underestimated our might and came in unabashed and rather arrogant. We had surprised her from both sides and blew the ship back to the bottom of hells pass. After we defeated the retaliation and knew that the port was ours, the overlook site was eventually abandoned. I'm certain that it hasn't been put back in use. You might be asking yourself right about now why I feel so?" There was a slight pause. "Correct?" Again a pause as no one says anything. "Correct?" Yet again he paused, "Sir?"

"Ah! What," the startled captain said. "I said, you might be asking yourself right about now why I feel so," Martin stated. "So. So what. Um, no. Actually I had drifted off several minutes ago as you had gotten deeper into your tale," Payton mumbled. "My but you are long winded eh?" "Fine," the perturbed Finny spat. "Then I leave you to your fate." "Oh c'mon now Billy. Don't be sore. We're just funning you. So what were you saying," Payton mock apologized. Martin sighed, "I said you might be asking yourself right about now why I feel so." "Feel so what? Bloated? Hungry? Cold," the pirate mused. "I knew that you weren't taking me seriously," Martin said rather sullenly. "That's exactly what we've been telling you. You take everything too seriously," the pirate captain countered. "Better serious than dead," Finny said. "Aye. I'm always serious when it comes to that lad. It's just the getting there that's more fun for me," Payton instructed with a smile. "Mr. Samson, ready the ship for anchor." "Si Capt," Pedro replied.

"So you don't even want to know why," Martin interrupted getting back to the previous conversation. "Is it because you think that the Admiral is too arrogant to think that anyone would be bold enough to attack his island," Payton interjected. Startled, "Why yes. So you were paying attention," Martin sputtered. "Hum? What's that," a disinterested Payton mumbled. "Aye helmsman," he bellowed. "Aye Captain," Langley answered.

"Luff her," Payton commanded. "Head for that cove and ready her for the low tide." "Aye-aye captain," Langley said obediently. The sails were loosened as the ship was turned causing the air to come about as they made their way in and dropped anchor in the deepest part of the cove. "This ought to do just fine! What say you Peppy," Payton asked Pedro. "Si mon. Dis look good ta me sir!"

They lowered the jolly boat to the water while others chose to jump in and swim to the sandy shore. There they followed Martin up through a thicket where the hard-to-follow path led to an overhang full of wild vegetation. The path had mostly grown over with disuse, which pleased the men greatly. Machetes hacked down some of the overgrowth, clearing the way for the followers. At the summit, the remnants of the makeshift English stronghold lay in shambles. The pirates pulled out their brass telescopes and spied on the port for the first time.

"Mr. Martin," Jute inquired. "Aye Jute," Martin responded. "Look just two degrees north of your current view. There's the blaggard Brightside himself," Jute said. With that discovery, the crew grumbled and spat their revenge. "Easy boys, easy. He'll be reckoned with soon enough," Martin reassured them. "Aye gentlemen. Remember this," Payton paused. "We must avenge him in the exact same way he took Captain Melbourne's life;

or *The Scavenger* will always be cursed and not worth the trouble." Payton's words fell on some of the men for the first time. They wondered what he meant but knew not to ask as the plan would soon become apparent.

"*The Scavenger* is in port sir," Blackie excitedly shouted. "No sight of *The Destroyer* though," Ram stated. "They might be out on patrol," Martin offered. "So finally capt'n. Wha's ta big plan Senor," Pedro inquired?

Payton looked intently into his spyglass. "The plan. The plan. Well, Mr. Matty says that at low tide there is a path only two feet deep from isle to isle. That's where we shall cross." "But da low tide be at mid day! We be picked off fore we e'er get cross," Pedro countered. "Right! That's why four of us will crew our lump of junk boat to that forested isle on the far side of them. Bearded Clem and Jack's son will you volunteer," Payton asked of them. In unison they nodded, "Aye." "Who else then," Payton asked of his crew. Phillips and Williams eagerly raised their hands. "Four, four now there's four," Sarika pointed out the obvious. "Wondrous you can count too," the captain sarcastically rolled off. "Pid, are you certain?" "YES SIR," Pid said eagerly. Payton breathed a heavy breath, "Ok then. Phillips, Williams, Bearded Clem and Jacks' son you four will be integral to our plan." "And that plan is sir," Martin prodded. "Plan, plan what's the plan," Sarika followed his masters line of questioning.

"First, get that bird a muzzle. Then after sunset you four will take the ship out around at a safe distance around the Port and lay at anchor round the far side of the island that is neighboring the Port. Make no fire or torch that the enemy could spy and give away your position on land or on the ship. Stay on board till the early morning hours of manana when you shall disembark and make your way to the southernmost tip of the isle. Stay hidden in the grass and await our signal. Mr. Smithers," Payton shouted. "Milton, er, I mean Martin. Wait, Finny." "Captain?" Payton's eyes crossed from confusion until he shook it off. "Is there a place where we can signal that isle from here," Payton inquired. "Aye captain, there is a banyan tree a couple of hundred meters from here that is perfect to signal that island. It's far enough back so as to not be obvious to Port Elizabeth unless they're intentionally looking for it," Finny retorted.

"Excellent. We'll send a signal light to you as the tide is returning. Use your mirror to catch the sun to signal in return. We'll then use our timepieces to… to…" He paused his commands as he saw Bearded Clem getting antsy. "Uh, it's below deck and to the bow. Anyway, as I was saying we'll use our time pieces to, to…" Again he sighed, "Oh, that's right. We're on land. Just use some bushes." "At's otit apn," Bearded mumbled. The captain's blank face told of his uncertainty as to what he just said. Payton raised an eyebrow as he looked to Jackson for clarification. "Uh sir," Jackson said rather meekly, "He said that that's not it captain." Enlightened, Payton's gaze returned to Clem, "Ah! What is it then?" "Era apn. Wa'f 'n e don av a imease," Bearded garbled. Payton's head started to hurt from trying to comprehend his incoherent ramblings. So again, he turned to Jackson without saying a word. "He said, what if he doesn't have a timepiece. Sir," Jackson stated. Nodding his understanding, "Ah! Well, use someone else's. Fantastic.

Now then back to the plan. Where was I? Ah yes the timepieces. We'll, we'll…" The four men destined to go on the journey all started looking uncomfortable. "Gent's, you can all just use the bushes if need be when I'm finished. Honestly, is this your first time on a deserted island?"

Jackson spoke up for the group. "Ah sir. It seems that none of us has, in terms of is in possession, that is to say is in ownership, at this current moment in time, at this time and place, being that this is where we currently *are* in relation to where we *were* at the moments of previous possession to, and of them at different occurrences before having bartered them for other said items and/or so called said services…" Payton abruptly cut him off, "GET TO THE POINT!" "We haven't got any sir… timepieces that is… in relation to the previous point that I was alluding to… to assist us in the said mission… therefore previously mentioned. Sir." "My bloody head hurts," Payton said flatly. So what you're telling me is that none among us happens to have a timepiece other than myself." His eyes scanned the crew as they all held their heads down as if in shame. "No one? Not a one?"

"I had one sir," Jenkins said proudly. "*Had*," Payton questioned. Jenkins proudly bolstered himself, "Yes sir!" Again the captain asked, "*Had?*" Smiling ear to ear, "Yes sir!" The pirate sighed and repeated himself once again as he closed his eyes, "*Had?*" Suddenly Jenkins discovered the folly of his statement. "Oh! Wait… I guess that won't assist us now sir. My apologies." Payton shook his head, "Pid, looks like you've got some competition. Ok, so scratch that idea. We'll do this the easy way then. We'll do everything the same, then when they signal back, both parties will have to count back from one hundred. You will have to hustle, for just as you reach zero you should be at the ship.

Clem again sheepishly raised his hand to get Daniels attention. "Er, apn?" "When we reach zero we'll...," Daniel was cut off. "apn," Clem persisted. Payton tried to ignore him, "We'll..." "apn," Clem said bouncing up and down. He sighed again, "Yes Bearded? I take it that you do not need to use the head, nor do you in possession of a timepiece. So what is it this time?" "Er, wa if'n we'n own 'ow a umers ack rum a unred," Clem sputtered. "Mr. Jack's son? Repeat please," the captain commanded. "He said, Er, wa if'n we'n don 'ow a numers ack rum a hunred?" "Ah yes, that clarifies it then. Thank you. Nitwit," Payton scolded him sarcastically. "Me pleasure captain," Jackson stated. "Swell, now can I have a translation for your retelling of that ponderous statement please," Payton inquired, hitting Jackson on the head with his hat. "Oh, beggin' me pardon sir. Old bloke Bearded said, what if'n we don't know how to count our numbers backin' from a hundred," Jackson corrected.

Payton paused, nodding his head, He looked at the four men, "Can any of you count back from one hundred?" One man excitedly raised his hand. "Anyone from the *advance group*," Payton clarified. The man slowly lowered his hand again. Breathing a sigh, "Yes, quite. Why would anyone in your party? Alrighty then. What say you to this? Take an hourglass an flip it when you see us flash you a signal. When it completely empties, be aboard the ship, anchor up and ready to sail. Is that simple enough for everyone?" "Yes sir," Jackson said eagerly. "You do have access to an hour glass correct,"

Payton stated. Jackson's eyes roamed the deck... "AH YES! YES WE DO! YES WE DO, he said excitedly!" Payton clapped his hands together, "Tremendous!" "Da agodn' iea ir," Clem said. Daniel looked to Jackson for interpretation. "He said, dat's a good idea sir," Jackson said. Daniel cracked a smile and nodded at Jackson who then turned to Clem and did the same. "Uh captain," Williams spoke up, "What do we need the hour glass for?" Payton turned to him, "Simple, we need to go at the exact same time eh. If we flash our mirrors and you take off, cannon blazing, an we're just heading down to the water, you'll be fightin' em all alone then. This way, we all go at the same time." Williams looked at him, "Huh, guess a time piece really woulda come in handy after all." Payton tried to ignore him as his frustration welled.

"Righty then! Back to the plan already in progress. So, now that we have sixty minutes instead of what, two," he started sarcastically. "We'll have more time to wait. Nonetheless, when our hourglass reaches empty, we'll begin our crossing. To aid in the safety of our crossing, the ship will fly the flag and fire the cannons. Yes, both of them, it'll be very impressive indeed," more sarcastic. "You two are the best gunners we have," he paused taking a deep breath at that statement, "and so your speed and accuracy is vital to the plan. Philly and Willy you will act as powder monkeys. Therefore you must make haste in your assistance to the gunners. You must draw their attention and fire. Just be certain not to hit *the Scavenger* while blocking her from leaving port! According to Mr. Swit... "Martin, sir," he corrected. "Right, the channel is at times too shallow during the low tide to even sail out. So *the Scavenger* may not even be able to help them. Their cannon fire should make our crossing go unnoticed. The only snafu in the plan is if we mistimed our crossing. Reason Mr. Watson:" "Martin sir. The reason is that once the current returns the tide, the surrounding corals stir up the waters and it makes them very treacherous. At times there can even be mighty waves that crash their way through.

"Correct! So it is imperative that once the plan is set in motion that not a one dawdles! And ye'll have ta mind yer steps out there as it'll get rather treacherous in some places. Back on board you boys will have to reload the cannons as quickly as possible, and if possible, stay afloat. Watch for the long cannons from the fort. Since the boat is small she should be hard to hit. We'll make our way into the fort and overrun them from behind. No quarter shall be given to any man as they will show you none as well. Remember, *I* must be the one to take the Admiral's life, and we *will* be victorious!" "Das ar rate ran apn!" "Jack's son? If you please," Payton asked. "Dat's a great plan captain," he responded. "Ah, jolly good. Thanks for your support then," Payton replied.

"Er, begging your pardon captain," Martin interrupted. "Yes Mishke?" "Martin sir. What if *The Destroyer* should come in?" "Well, if *The Destroyer* should come in, our old boat will be the sacrificial lamb," Payton said. This shocked Clem, "APN! APN!" "Yes Bearded," Payton said bluntly. "At's ot a ood an! at's a oorble an! Oorble," he sputtered! Daniel just looked at Jackson. "He said that's a not a good plan sir. That's a horrible plan." Daniel raised his eyebrows and glared at him. Sheepishly, fumbling his hat in his hands, nodding his head towards Bearded, Jackson said, "His words sir, not mine." "Look, you four gentlemen are far too valuable to lose. Are you not," Payton inquired. "I inko," Clem said "I think so too sir," Jackson agreed. "As do I," Payton confirmed. "If *The Destroyer* should come in you'll be set. We'll fill the hold with powder and if need be, run a long fuse line, light it and run her at full speed into or in front of *The Destroyer*. She should be occupied with that so we can either make haste or sink her. Just make sure that there isn't *too* much powder on her, aye gents?" "Aye. That could be a mistake," Schmitty said. "Rough for you boys," Blase confirmed. "An aht aut us," Clem asked. "And what about us, Sir," Jackson automatically interpreted.

Exhaling, "Use yer noggins gentlemen. We'll lay cover fire from either the long nines of the Port or from *The Scavenger*. After you ignite the fuse, run like hell and jump off the ship. Just make sure that she's in the way of *The Destroyer*." "iht," Clem shouted. "Right? Light? Fright? Might? Bite? Kite? Flight," Payton quizzed trying to answer for himself. "Alright," Jackson corrected! "Ah, yes. Alright. Anyway, Jute...," Payton changed gears. "Yes sir," Jute responded. "Jute, you and Richards stand watch and let us know if anything changes," Payton commanded. "Aye-aye sir," he replied obediently.

The group made it's way back down the overgrown path to the temporary base of operations. "It's getting dark. We'll have to make the ship ready. Jack's son, Bearded Clem, Willy and Pid, go and make the ship ready. When night is upon us and the moon is high, make your way to the designated spot. Gentlemen, make certain that your blades are sharp and that your pistols are loaded. And as always, go an have some fun," Payton said cheerfully!

Four Offshore

As the moon rose high their ship made her way out of the tiny inlet. The scant crew sailed her out and round the corner, no lights in or on her. "There they go eh Coop?" "Aye Chips." "Think those four idiots will find their way," Coop asked. "I think there's a better chance of Blacky joining the French navy," Chips said. "Aye, you've always been a bit of a fancy lad eh Blackie," Coop chided. "Bugger off the two of you! The day I'm a fancy lad is the day that Doc weighs less than me," the agitated blacksmith shot back. "I beg your pardon? I'm not overweight," a confused Dr. Fitzgerald retorted! "Relax doc. He meant Doc Nielsen the cook," Coop responded. "I'm confused," Fitzgerald mumbled. "Shocking," Payton chimed in. "Relax mate," Nielsen started. "I'm not after yer job. I just 'doctor' the grub remember? I'll stick to the dead stuff and you keep to the live ones. I can't fancy putting me hands in those bloody holes like ya do." Dr. Fitzgerald breathed a sigh of relief. "Wonderful. Well I'm certain that this won't ever get too confusing." "Gents," Payton corralled them back! "Are you all prepared?" In unison, "Aye," they responded.

"Then Pero here will divide you into your watch. Then it is lights out and time for sleep. Morgen will be here quickly," Payton was cut off. "Captain Morgan will be here," Schmitty asked. "No, that's Germanic for morning," Payton said flustered. "Sleep well gents,"

Payton commanded. "Tomorrow's gonna be *a hell of a lot of fun!*" Pedro set up the men for their night watch duties as the crew readied itself for sleep.

Morning Signs

The morning watch sounded its morning call quietly and awakened the crew. As the sun broke the horizon its rays created a colorful tapestry across the sky. The excitement in the pirates roused their spirits and they quickly got ready. "Aye Captain, da word from Jute an Richards is dat da Port Elizabeth is just as we left her," Santiago reported. "Wonderful," Payton said devilishly. "Then there's no sight of *The Destroyer* then?" "Daz correct sir. And da morning tide shou' be a-goin' out soon," Pedro said. Even more devilishly, "Splendid. Gents first everyone have a good bite and then we shall set our plan into action," Payton commanded with an evil look in his eyes! The men cheered as Payton, Finny and Santiago made their way back up to the lookout.

"Captain. Morning finds the Port ready to be taken," Jute proclaimed. "That's the best news I've heard all day. Actually," correcting himself, "it's the *only* news I've heard all day. Good thing that was this news that I heard first today." "Sir," Jute said confused. "Yes Mute," Payton replied. "Mute," an even more puzzled Jute asked. "Flute," Payton struggled for his name. "Huh," Jute replied. "Scoot," Payton ventured a guess yet again at his name.

Martin leaned to Pedro, "Finally, it's someone else's turn." Pedro just smiled. Sensing Sarika was about to squawk out a reply, Martin quickly grabbed his beak and whispered, "Shhh!"

"Um, Sir. Should we signal Bearded yet," a puzzled Jute tried to gather himself. "No. It's too early. Go grab a bite to eat first. Jute looked at him not wanting to go. His nervous energy was welling up inside him. Payton recalled the words the old woman had imparted upon them earlier, *"Eeat, eeat!"* Jute knew better than to ignore a direct order and was off. When the men had finished and all weapons were rechecked they made their way to a shady spot to await further orders.

When the tide had gone out enough Jute returned to the captain, "Now sir?" "No Shoot," Payton began, "you can do the honors." "Shoot," Jute asked himself. Martin whispered to Sarika, "I'm liking him more and more." Quietly Sarika replied, "Aye, aye, no more for thy." "I'd wouldn count on dat senor," Pedro countered. Martin sighed his understanding, "Yes, but it is nice to dream."

Jute took out the mirror and carefully flashed it into the sun's rays aiming the beam down to the others. A few moments passed with no response. Payton leaned into the tall grasses as he peered looking for a response, "Flash them again." Jute did as commanded, but still no response came. Watching the proceedings Martin offered, "Perhaps they were discovered last night?" "Perhaps," Payton agreed. "Or perhaps they're just a couple of morons who can shoot the hell out of ship but can't maneuver a simple mirror."

The Plan Begins

"C'mon Pid," Jackson shouted. "That's the second time they flashed us! "It's not me fault," Pid cried. "Blasted thing doesn't work!" "How can it not work? It's a mirror! Just catch the light and flash them back," Jackson responded! "Right! I've got that. However, it doesn't seem to shine," Pid nervously sputtered still trying to catch the sun's rays. Williams looked at the mirror, "Hey Michelangelo." "Who," Pid replied. "Never mind. Try flipping the mirror over," Williams corrected. "Ooooh. Righty. AAGH," Pid cried. "Now what," Williams spat. "Bloody thing just blinded me," Pid screamed. Jackson yanked the small mirror out of his hand, "Gimme that!" He aimed the mirror correctly and flashed the light back at the crew signaling that the port is ready to be attacked. "Quick, flip the hourglass! Let's go," Williams commanded. They hurriedly made their way back to the ship where Clem was already aboard.

"is out ime is!" "Yes, yes we know. Bea…" Pid was cut off. "ls o ave ome un," Clem smiled a toothless smile. "Aye, lets have some fun indeed," Jackson agreed. The four did quick work and made the ship ready to sail.

And Now, We Wait

"Finally! Flip the hourglass and let's make haste," Payton commanded. "To the beach," Martin cried. "AYE," the crew gleefully responded and cheered wildly, yet trying not to make excessive commotion while hustling down the hillside. "Dis way gents," Pedro led them. More excitement began welling in the crew. Finally, after all they have been through they were going to do a full act of piracy. For the old pirates this was simply picking up where they'd left off. For the new pirates in the crew, it was sheer nervous anxiety taking over as they were stepping into a life of crime. The fear of criminal action was offset by their burning desire to bring their hated rival to justice.

"Finally we get to have some fun lads," Bertrand said juggling three daggers. He quickly threw the twirling razor sharp blades one at a time into the bark of a narrow palm. Loudly the crew responded to his skill and words, "Aye!" They made their way down the path to the beachfront. "Alright boys here we are," Payton said stopping the group as they looked across the water, sheltered by the vegetation. "Are ye certain that you want to partake? If not, this is yer last chance?" "Aye," the crew responded. "Mr. Sample." "Finny. Yes sir?" "Mr. Pimple how much time is left?" "Martin sir. Um, I'm not certain sir." "Well gestimate man," Payton scolded. "Um, ok. I'd say we have roughly," he paused looking at the hour glass, "fifty-five minutes or so to go." Daniel raised an eyebrow, crooked his head to one side then to the other. "Oookayyy."

"Captain," Langley inquired. "Aye?" "So, what do we do now," he continued. Payton stood tall in his reserve, "This," he said trying to maintain the excitement. "What exactly is this sir," Bertrand continued. "This is us waiting for the sands to go through the hour glass because no one owns a stupid time piece," Payton said trying to end the line of questioning. The pirates stood still looking around and at each other. Various men shrugged their shoulders as if to say, 'I don't know what to do... do you?"

"Um cap'ain," Ian questioned. "Ah, yes Sails," Payton asked not wanting to hear his question. "Cap'ain, wha' else can we do rig't now eh?" "Um, you can mill about," he replied for lack of a better answer. "Mill about sir," he pried further. "Yes that's right. Just don't make yourself known to them," Payton continued trying to look official. No one moved which caused irritation to the captain. "Well go on! Start milling!" The pirates again shrugged their shoulders and began to mill about. "Hey," Payton injected, "stay out of sight!"

"Blackie?" "Aye Coop?" "Not exactly what I had expected," Coop stated the obvious. "No it ain't. I thought that the pirate life was more exciting than this," Blackie replied. "You don't find sitting on a beach waiting for an hourglass to empty exciting," Coop said sarcastically. "Not particularly," Sails chimed in. Overhearing the hushed conversation Payton strolled over, "Starting to change your mind toward the pirate life matie," he asked mildly perturbed "Well cap'ain," Ian began, "I must admit, I figure dat there'd be more debauchery, violence al'on wit tha cons'ant struggles." "You've changed yer tune since we first met, eh," the captain said to Ian who just nodded modestly. "It's not all fun and laughs chap. Sometimes we wait. Sometimes we fish. Sometimes we throw dice. Sometimes we sing. Sometimes we take random women. Sometimes we read," Payton said running out of items. "We read sir," the befuddled sail-maker said. "Well no," Payton said correcting himself. "I was just checking if you were paying attention. Mr. Fipps," he quickly said to bring an end to that conversation. "Finny. Yes sir?" "How much time now?" "Oh, I'd guess… fifty-two minutes or so, sir." He could no longer hold his reserve as he deflated himself, "Blast. Should've sent a bloke who could count backwards." "What's that captain," Martin inquired. Payton snapped back, "Um, nothing! Nothing." He spoke louder, "Keep milling gents," trying to regain the confidence, then he repeated himself softly, "Keep milling."

Random Thoughts

"Well boys, what say we start," Jackson inquired. "We can't," Williams scolded. "ill ot rand eft," Clem babbled. "Yes Bearded," Jackson said. "I see that we have sand left. A lot of sand left. I'm just bored." Pid exhaled and paused, "You guys think it'd be funny if we just went ahead and got started without them?" "uh," Clem said. "You know," Pid began, "we just sail out there and shoot the hell out of the place. Then on the other side the boys just start freaking out and have to run through the water in disarray." "rd ta ay," Clem sputtered. "Huh," Pid asked. Jackson interpreted, "He said it's hard to say."

"You're telling me," Pid replied. "uh," Clem puzzled. "Does anyone else get the funny image in their head of the captain and the guys sloshing through the water? They're cursing us out, tripping over themselves trying to get here in time," Pid continued.

"Um, at this point I have to ask a question," Williams interrupted. "What's that," Pid asked. "Are you totally, or just partially insane," Williams prodded. "How so," a curious Pid replied. "How so," Williams shot back. "You're suggesting we go out there and get the hell blown out of us with no surprise backup. I mean the entire purpose of us even being here is to create an ambush to get the rest of our crew safely across so they can wipe em out. Did you not understand that part of the plan? That's what that whole thing about the timing was about. Remember?" Pid looked down and shrugged his shoulders, "Well, I was just going for the funny thought of it."

"Yeah, well we'll just see how funny it is when we're all swinging from the gallows because you wanted to jump the gun," Williams said. "As we're all standing there with the nooses around our necks I can see you just standing there going, "Don't you think it'd be funny if none of our necks broke and we're all just swinging there, writhing in agony. Wouldn't it be funny? I'm just saying is all." Pid looked up inspired by this thought, "Now that you mention it, that would be kind of funny too." Williams could only shake his head. "Idiot."

And Wait...

Back on the island the sun continued to beat down. The terrain and vegetation was blocking all airflow causing the pirates to sit in a virtual oven. Sweat was draining out of them as they fought off heat fatigue. "Mr. Dithers," a rather confused Payton sputtered. "Finny. And I guess about forty-five minutes or so." "BLAST!"

"Aw c'mon capt., can't we just get a going," Langley stated growing disgruntled. Payton shook his head and sighed dejectedly saying, "No. Just keep milling." The men just looked at him causing him to speak bolder and nodding his head, "Well, go on. Keep milling!"

You're a Pid

Back on the boat the men were also just hanging around waiting on departure time. "Willy," Phillips said. "Yes Pid." "Do you think that I need new a nickname?" Williams couldn't believe that he just heard that question. He's not in the middle of a battle, but rather entertaining this most ridiculous question. He dropped his head down, "What?" "A nickname." Rolling his eyes and head up and back to the sky, "Why," Williams asked. "Well if I'm going to be a pirate now, I think I need a new nickname. Blackbeard has one. Ian has "Sails;" Roger has "Blackie;" Schmitty has "Chips;" Eric has "Jute;" Walsh has "Coop." "Bearded Clem" even has one.

"Well Blackbeard has a *black beard*. Ian is a *sail maker*. Blackie is a *blacksmith,* Chips is a *carpenter* and coop is a *cooper*. And if you couldn't guess, Bearded has a ... a ...," Williams stopped hoping that Pid was catching on. "Beard," Pid said finishing his thought. "Congratulations... except that he no longer has a beard. Yet he did and so the name remains. See, the name comes from a physical trait or an occupation. What makes you unique? What makes you special? What makes you different? What is it that we should call you?"

"Pid!" This was the first thing Clem said that everyone could clearly understand. Everyone looked shocked as Clem just smiled his toothless smile. "Me thinks that that's a fitting name," Jackson agreed. "But I'm already called Pid!" "Well that's because it's so fitting," Williams said cheerfully. Pid disputed this, "But I'm not! I'm sick of this stupid nickname!" He turned quickly tripping over a coiled rope sitting on the deck. Falling face down on the deck, he just laid there, blood trickling ever so gently out of his nose. "Don't say it," he said plainly. Williams turned to Clem nodding his head in approval, "Right on. 'Pid' it is! And Pid it shall remain!" "No! No! No! No Pid. I'm not Pid," he shrieked pounding his fists and feet onto the deck. "Quiet Pid," the men said in unison!

And Wait ...

Back on the isle, the men grew ever more weary. Daniel mumbled, "Mr. Moby," his head bobbing around. Martin sat listlessly on a rock, chin resting on a closed fist, answered matter-of-factly, "Martin. Maybe thirty minutes. Maybe more, maybe less… whatever." "Ugh," Payton replied, head hanging low. "Keep moping men." "Milling," Langley corrected him. "Ah yes, milling." He paused a short pause, "Oh bloody hell… Mope if ye want."

Who Has The Time?

On the ship, "ow uch aggin me," a sun-baked Clem babbled. "Huh," Pid replied. "How much flagging time," Jackson stated. "Good question," Williams said. "What's a good question," Pid inquired. Williams traveled off, "Why are we here? What's our purpose? Can anyone else smell that?" "Yeah, how much time till we bleeding go already," Jackson said.

"at's ut im skin," Clem said. "You're asking," Jackson replied. "Who's asking," Williams inquired. "Asking what," Pid wanted to know? This irritated Clem, "OW UCH IGGIN IME! Williams couldn't understand him, "What?" Jackson replied, "Huh?" Clem shot out, "R A AST IGGIN IME OW UH CKIN IME ILL WE O?" Jackson understood and asked, "Yes, how much time?" Williams looked around and tension suddenly overtook him in his belly, "Whom has the hourglass?" Jackson perked up, "Yes whom?" "Not to nitpick, but it's 'who,'" Williams corrected. "What," Jackson countered. "Are you certain?" "Where is the hourglass," Pid asked. "Aye," Williams answered, ignoring Pid. "In this case the correct form of the word is who," he said with a smile. Jackson countered, "I don't know. I feel that it's," he was cut off as Clem shouted out, "AAAMMITTTT!"

Suddenly panicked they sprang to their feet and began to tear apart the entire ship.

And Wait,

Ram sat perched and watched intently as the soldiers went about their daily tasks completely oblivious that their time could be running out. Hunger began to grumble in his stomach and he had to decide to sit tight and maintain his watch or to investigate his area for a bite to eat. Ram was unsure if Payton sensed this or just good timing on his part, but the captain shot him a glance that answered his dilemma. He sat tight.

"How much time then," Payton babbled. "Probably ten minutes," Martin answered. It seemed more like ten hours to the men.

LET'S GO!

The four men continued to tear their ship apart searching in vain for the hourglass that was left behind at the signal site. They looked and looked around when they finally, sadly came to the conclusion that no one had taken the hourglass after all. "Wa… What should we do? Should we go back to the spot? Stay here? Go," Jackson blurted out. Williams took charge, "We need to just go," he said trying hard to gather his resolve. "What if we're early," Pid inquired. "Shut up Pid," Williams shot back. "It's only a matter of moments. We'll be fine! Dang it! We may be late! Oh and if we're early then you get your stupid joke... idiot." Jackson shouted, "GO! GO! GO!" "AAAAARRRRR," Clem shouted!

The men scurried to get the sails taught to catch the wind. Finally the airflow came across and the sails filled. The ship began to move as a silence fell on the men; suddenly focused on the important task at hand. They all hoped that they were right on time. If not, this was going to be a horrible failure. As the ship sailed along the silence was finally broken.

"After all this wouldn't it be funny if we were late," Pid asked. "Shut up Pid," they shouted.

MAKE HASTE!!!

Back on the isle the men sat baking in the sweltering Caribbean sun. "Mr... Mr... Mr... What's your bloody name again," Payton babbled. "Marbin. Markin. Martin!" He rolled his head casually over to the hourglass then suddenly realized they had missed their mark. **"DAMN! GET UP, GET UP, GET UP! THE GLASS IS OUT!"**

Payton shot up to his feet. *"AHOY! AVAST YE SCALLIWAGS! ON YER FEET YOU MANGY DOGS AND FALL IN! THE TIME IS NOW! WE FIGHT!"*

The men sprang to life and quickly formed into a single file following their captain. The men dipped their hats, scarves and other materials into the cool waters and doused their heads as they refocused their minds. All the forlorn dismay had suddenly vanished as a razor like focus had taken over the group. As the men made their way, they began to hear the sounds of cannon fire as their ship began the attack. Captain Payton raised his sword while saying, "Aye men there be the cover fire! Make haste and watch yer footin'. There are some rips coming through the current!" He couldn't believe that of the two groups, the one that Pid was on, was actually the side that was on time. Swords and pistols were drawn as Captain Payton lead the silent brigade along the rocky water covered pathway. The passage ranged anywhere from only four inches wide in some places to over four feet in others, marked with deep sharp coral laden drop-offs on either side. Cautiously and meticulously they filed on as quickly, but silently, as they could through the swift moving current that was rapidly bringing the tide back in.

Surprise!

Back on board, Jackson was partnered with Williams as Clem had partnered with Phillips. They worked in tandem to load the cannons with powder and shot then quickly aimed and fired. "Keep going Willy! Keep going," Jackson shouted. "'on strd! 'on strd," Clem shouted as well.

Sweat sheeted like rain off the men as they quickly

labored under the backbreaking conditions. Return cannon fire ripped through the air, but as predicted the ship being so small made her a very difficult target indeed. The port being much larger and stationary was easily hit repeatedly by the cannon fire of the pirates.

In the fort the British soldiers taken by surprise scrambled to get to their posts. "Admiral! Admiral!" "What is it Johnson," the admiral responded. "Admiral. We can't seem to hit that ship. She's just too small," the nervous man stammered worried for his career. "So what are you telling me," the angered commander shot back? "I'm saying that we're having unexpected difficulty with such a small vessel, sir!" "MR. JOHNSON," Brightside shouted his disgust. "Are you trying to tell me that we could repel the entire Spanish horde, but a small handful of moronic, scurvy-ridden pirates, on a tiny boat, with what, only two cannon per side are going to wipe us out?" "Um, no sir. It's just that she's more difficult..." Brightside grabbed him by his lapels, "I should think not! Get *the Scavenger* on her then!" Sweat began draining out of his forehead, "But sir, the water level is too low. The tide hasn't yet fully returned and..." "Stop right there," Brightside spat in his face! "I want every available man on this wall immediately! Fire at them with cannon and pistol or anything else available. I will NOT be embarrassed by a couple of dimwitted buccaneers! Do you understand me!" Johnson replied, "Actually a couple is only two sir. There are clearly four men on board that ship." The admiral peered through his tightly squeezed eyes and penetrated through Johnson as his face reddened from anger. He grabbed Johnson by his lapels and drew him in close. "You are only heartbeats away from demotion and a meeting with solitary confinement," the admiral grunted through clenched teeth. His reddened eyes protruded from his skull and deep veins throbbed on his forehead. Johnson cleared his throat, his lapels still in his Brightside's hands, "I'll be getting the men sir!"

With that he tore from his grasp and sounded the alarm and all hands ran to the aid of the useless cannons.

Redemption in Blood

Meanwhile the pirate crew finished their treacherous journey across the straight as the waves started to intensify. Payton lead them up the hill to the fort wall. There the men deployed the grappling hooks and scaled the wall with ease. Once over, the pirates fell into formation and quickly came up behind the British soldiers. The diversion from the ship was working better than they could have ever hoped for. With all the confusion the soldiers didn't even notice the pirates as they came up behind them. Even though the pirates were clearly undermanned, the sheer will for revenge for their fallen commander and comrades fired up the troupes. The pirates ran roughshod over the thoroughly surprised Brits. Shots rang out, the smell of gunpowder already filled the air as smoke quickly began to hang heavy, impairing their vision. The sting of the smoke didn't bother the well-seasoned pirates whereas it made the Brits eyes begin to water and to cough.

Scabbards and daggers slipped effortlessly from their sheaths, only to quickly find new places to temporarily rest. Those places being deep inside the soldiers' chests and bellies. Screams of anguish filled the air to the accompaniment of the clink, clank of metal upon metal as swords clashed upon each other. The bodies began to pile up and crimson blood flowed freely from the gaping wounds and began to pool in puddles on the hard stone surface. Bertrand saw Ian about to be stabbed in the back and threw a flash of a dagger into the soldier. Jute and Walsh ran roughshod while Hall made easy work of the beleaguered British. Hillberg easily ran over anyone who stood in his way while Ram had a more difficult time being a bit more inexperienced. Dooley laughed at the apparent ease at which they were succeeding.

Captain Payton fought his way through redcoats over to a terrified Admiral Brightside. Seeing this horrible man Brightside turned and ran through a door into a room from which there was no escape. Realizing his mistake he quickly turned and cowered in fright. Payton kicked the door open with sword in his right hand. His dirty tattered coat semi-concealed more weaponry strapped to his sides. His eyes seemed to glow as a cloud of smoke surrounded him. His heart was beating through his chest as he gasped for fresh air. A maniacal smile graced his dirty face.

"Mercy pirate! Mercy please," Brightside pleaded falling to his knees, hands clasped together! "Mercy good man? The same mercy as you had shown for yer ole mate, Captain Melbourne?" Thoroughly stunned, he stuttered, "Ma, Ma, Melbourne? What do you mean?" "DON"T LIE TO ME," Payton shouted! "How, how, how did...

how do... how is it possible," Brightside asked?

"How is it possible indeed, that a man like you, a man of the British Royal Navy could watch a fellow seaman be slaughtered just to take over his command," he asked as he walked about. "How is it possible that a man like *you*," he said pointing his sword at him, "could take credit for saving that ship and the few men that survived, as you cowered in the shadows? Only then to be promoted? And people call me scum! You are more of a villain than I."

"But, but, but, how? How pirate? How know you?"

"I was visited by the ghost of Captain Melbourne. It was *he* who beckoned me to take his revenge, after showing me the vision of his demise and the events that led up to it. It was *he* who then guided me on the path to finding the remnants of his old crew. The same crew that is currently wiping out your pitiful battalion," he said motioning to the door. "It was *he* that said he'd rather see his beloved old ship in the hands of a pirate like me than in the hands of a traitor. And so, to fulfill my half of the accord upon which you now find me I must finish you off and claim," he slowed his words and smiled menacingly, "my new ship."

"Mercy! Mercy! Please have mercy," again he begged. "Melbourne did tell me you were somewhat of a sissy. However, he may have underestimated just how much," Payton chided. Brightside continued his pleading, "Please, I'll pay you anything! Anything you wish! You can have the ship! I'll, I'll even join your crew!"

"Sorry chap. I can't trust you. I can't trust any of them either, but I *really* can't ever trust you. Besides, that wouldn't be in keeping with our pact. It's nothing personal mate. Well, not between us anyway. Any last words," the captain inquired. His mind raced, what could he offer the man to save his life. "Jewels, riches, I, I could make you a very wealthy man," he whimpered. "Those are some odd last words, but," Payton was cut off. "No, no, no," he said, tears still rolling down his cheeks. The pirate shook his head. "How do you know that I'm not already a rich man," Payton inquired. "Because, you are still a pirate. I could make you a respectable man. A very wealthy, respectable man. And you could still have that ship," he said getting on his feet. Payton raised an eyebrow looking intrigued. Suddenly the beleaguered admiral was sensing that he could possibly buy off this man. He was a pirate after all. Why wouldn't he go for easy riches? That was after all the profession he was in. He continued his lies, "Just think of it mate, you, a privateer with an official note from the King of England that would allow you to legally plunder any ship in the Spanish Main." The man spoke deviously and tried to sidle up to the pirate. "What do you say? Easy plundering. Respectability. Wealth. Land. Fine women," he spun lie after lie while coyly sliding his hand to a concealed dagger. Closer he slinked to Payton, lost in the vision that the admiral was painting. Softly he spoke, "What say you pirate? I can give you all that you can possibly want… and more!" Payton still lost in the vision cracked a devilish smile, "Aye."

As he spoke that single word, the admiral pulled a dagger to do him in. But even swifter than he, the pirate took his sword and finished him off. The admiral fell to the floor and breathed his last. With that, he was done in the same manner that Captain Melbourne had been previously. Melbourne wasn't scheming for his life, but he had lost his sword and had pulled a dagger in his final moments. The dagger in a one on one situation was good enough to validate the retribution. A sudden thunderclap blasted out that shook the entire island.

"Captain Daniel Payton." Payton spun around to see materializing before his very eyes the translucent figure of Captain Jonathon Melbourne. "Captain Jonathon Melbourne I presume." "The very." "It's a pleasure to make your acquaintance," the pirate stated. "The pleasure is honestly all mine. I'd like to shake your hand except..." "Except," Payton inquired. "Well, I am a ghost and all." "Ah yes. I guess that that would be difficult." "I would like to thank you for keeping your end of the accord. Although, I was beginning to wonder," Melbourne said. Payton replied, "but you had to be avenged in the exact same way that you were done in. I had to sidle up to him on his left and slash him across his chest. I feared that he wouldn't take the bait and continue to prattle on, on his knees."

Melbourne smiled, "Thank you. Thank you for allowing me and my crew to now find our rest. Now I would like to help you," the ghost said. "How so?" "Follow me outside," the ghostly figure motioned.

The two men walked out the door to the remnants of the melee. The stone floor ran red with the blood from the bodies of the fallen soldiers. Around them the pirates stood in stunned silence staring at the ghosts of all of

Captain Melbourne's men mingling around them, smiling and nodding. They were joined by the few remaining survivors of the scout crew who were released from their cells. The free men were elated at being reunited with their former mates and confused at the entire situation.

"Gentlemen," the ghost said, "most of you know me. For those who do not know, I am Captain Jonathon Melbourne of His Majesty's Royal Navy. The men you see before you are the honorable men who perished with me on that fateful day so long ago. To some of you, they are familiar faces and former mates. To the others they are your former enemies. Today they are all your brothers. With your act, you have given us our spiritual forms back and the ability to rest at sea in peace. To you I hereby lift my curse on *The Scavenger* and bequeath her unto you. She was once a pirate ship. Then she became the most feared ship of the entire Royal Navy. Now she returns to her former life, forever will she be the most feared pirate ship these waters have ever seen!" The ghostly crew shouted their approval, "Huzzah! Huzzah! Huzzah!"

"Also, to my trusted and loyal former crew who undertook this event under the direction of a pirate, I implore you to stay on under his direction. He will treat you well," Melbourne said. "Thank you Captain Melbourne," Payton said with an honest heart. The pirate crew cheered as the ghosts slowly began to vanish.

Payton turned to his crew, "Well boys, your term of service has come to its end. As previously stated you are all free to go. I will see to it that you all receive what you have earned and wish you the best. I leave it up to you each and individually to decide what your course may be. If you choose to stay on, once we finish plundering this place and divide our take we leave toward our next prize. If you choose otherwise, you can stay here, which I whole-heartedly do not recommend. Or you can venture on with us till we can make port at the nearest island. However, let me say this. You all have proven beyond a shadow of a doubt that you are truly the greatest crew I've ever the good fortune to sail with."

With that Daniel stepped down and looked upon the men as they slowly started to look within themselves. It was clear that each was weighing the decision with great reverence as to continue or be finished as a pirate. The men took a few moments and slowly began to come out of their thoughts and focus upon the captain that stood before them.

"Well," Payton sheepishly asked. "What decision have you made?" The men looked around at each other and slowly a smile cracked upon their faces. "I choose… to stay," the first man said. "I stay," joined another. "I stay as well," added another. More and more they all came to the same conclusion causing a smile to grow on Payton's face. Payton turned to Ian and Dr. Fitzgerald the lone two that had the freedom to plead their innocence if captured. Fitzgerald smiled, "I have too much to see, too much to learn that I can never gain holed up in an office somewhere. I choose to stay." Payton smiled intently and gazed upon Ian. "I'm in!"

Payton grinned ear to ear and instructed, "Gents, lets loot this Port then on to *our ship!*"

Déjà vu

A mighty cheer rang out as the pirates quickly began to loot the contents held within the port and load it on their ship. While the men were plundering in haste, Payton took a bottle and walked the dock, his finger sliding across the smooth hull. A smile was clear on his face. Finding a good spot, he said a few words quietly and smashed the bottle on her for good luck.

As the joyous men worked at finishing their tasks, Payton heard shouting. He quickly turned to see Bearded Clem still on their sloop shouting something inaudible. He ran back on board to the furthest point where he could see the commotion. "Jack's son! What's the report," Payton shouted to the boat. The faint voice returned, "It's *the Destroyer* sir! She's coming in quick!" *The Destroyer* was entering the channel the pirates crossed earlier which now was a swirling torrent. Waves broke on the underlying remnants of the coral reef. Unfortunately for the pirates, the only cannon on that side of the Port was destroyed by a lucky shot from their ship. Jackson had intended to hit another cannon, but it flew above the intended target and hit the other by mistake.

"Ahoy men," Payton shouted. "All hands on board! We sail for *the Destroyer* is approaching!" The men suddenly become frenzied as they ran aboard with whatever plunder they could manage. "Langley," Payton commanded. "Sir," he replied.

"Steer us out behind the blockade ship, Payton commanded. He leaned over the rail and yelled

"Bearded!"

Yelling in response, "r?" "Lay out some fire. Then ignite her and set her course for *the Destroyer!*" "Aye-aye captain," Jackson replied.

Jackson guided the boat out of the harbor to block the path of the incoming vessel. Carefully they aimed their cannons towards the incoming ship and fired the first round. The cannon shot ripped into the hull of the wooden ship.

"RELOAD! RELOAD," Jackson shouted. In a frenzy the pirates reloaded as the men on *the Scavenger* scrambled to ready their cannons. The British, completely unaware of the impending attack were caught completely off guard. They were in preparation for docking, not battle.

"IRE," Clem shouted. Again the cannon fire ripped into the ship. "UN ORE AN 'ITE DA IP!" With that command they knew that there was enough time to reload and fire one more time before igniting the entire ship. Their third shot, aimed at the foremast, hit its intended target splintering the pole. Williams ran below deck and ignited the fuse to the powder kegs. Above deck Jackson steered the ship pointing her head on to *the Destroyer*; tied the wheel locking her rudder in place as Clem de-powered the sails. *The Destroyer* was stuck. Her deep draft forced her to stay in the deeper part of the coral laden channel. She dropped her sails, but would never be able to stop in time. Phillips ignited a small flash pot on the deck starting a large smoky fire, which quickly took over the mast. With that the four men dove off the stern rail amongst rifle fire and swam to *the

Scavenger. *The Destroyer* valiantly tried to stop, as they dropped their anchor, but they were too late. The strong current slammed her port side into the fiery ship. The incoming current continued to rake *the Destroyer* along her side into *the Dreamers Delight*. The powder kegs had been moved to the fore section below her deck. As the fuse came to the first keg it ignited causing a chain reaction into all the others. The blast ripped a hole into the hull of *the Destroyer*, killing some of the soldiers while other British sailors fell into the ocean as she shook. Payton grinned and thought to himself, "'Bout time that thing hurt someone else."

The captain grabbed the wheel and turned hard to starboard trying to right the ship. The ship had been taken out of the narrow deeper channel by the collision and current. The rudder was taken to far and the anchor jerked the ship running her onto a jagged remnant of the shallow reef. The incoming tide was now blasting in heavy waves into the starboard side of *The Destroyer* pushing her almost onto her port side. She was stuck on a forty-five degree angle and sailors continued to slide off the deck into the water. The remnants of *The Dreamers Delight* continued to burn as they slowly sank next to the immobile *Destroyer*, causing more fire damage to spread across her deck and sails.

The rising tide would eventually free her given the chance. However, time would not allow it. Aboard *The Scavenger*, Payton and his crew exited the harbor and made their way to the far side of the mess. The men had dropped a jolly boat down where the four gunners climbed in and were raised to safety. *The Destroyer* lay sideways in the canal with her deck facing the only remaining part of the old destroyed sloop. The still burning section billowed plumes of thick, black smoke into the air. On the opposite side of their sloop, *The Scavenger* now lay her assault.

"Mr. Langley," Payton shouted. "Aye Captain!" "Turn hard to starboard!" "Turning to starboard sir," the ship turned hard. Payton called, "Gunners, ready yer cannons!" "ediyg da anns ir!" Jackson repeated, "Readying the cannons sir!" "Gunners take yer marks," Payton shouted, "FIRE!"

The cannons fired just above the burning sloop, through the smoke and pummeled the deck of *The Destroyer*. Brits terrified at what was happening tried, some in vain, to flee the doomed ship. "Gunners reload," Payton commanded. "Gunners take yer marks!"

We'll Be Right Back

"Uh, captain, captain, captain," Martin interrupted. Suddenly stunned, Payton turned, "Yes Mel?" The two men were back to the island where they were still in the planning stages of the attack as they spied on Port Elizabeth. "Martin," he corrected. "And it'll never work!" "How's that," the perplexed pirate inquired. "I said it'll never work," Martin said confidently. Payton cocked his head and scratched his beard. "You sure?" "Positive," Martin confirmed his resolve. "Absolutely positively sure," Payton pressed. Martin stood his ground, "Absolutely, positively, 100% certain!" Payton looked at him, "Why not?" "Its just too ludicrous! I mean how will they not see us? How will we ever overrun them without a single loss? How..." Payton cut him off, "My dear Maggie, you ask entirely too many questions." "MARTIN," he shouted. "And they're all good questions!" "How come I'll still be called Pid," Phillips asked. "Well they *are* good questions; however they've all been answered," Payton said plainly. "How," Martin inquired. "Why would they forget the hourglass? Why would we miss our time mark? Huh, answer me that," he huffed. The captain smiled, "Well, it's a group with Pid after all." Martin shrugged and nodded his head. "Well look at it this way bloke. If all that couldn't happen, how did we get here?" "What do you mean," Martin inquired.

Back To The Battle, Already In Progress

They are suddenly back on the ship and still in the fight, "FIRE!" The cannon balls ripped the damaged ship in half while the incoming tide began to claim its newest prize. Martin still stood next to the captain, "I still think it's bloody impossible!"

Payton stood tall and smiled, "Mr. Langley!" "Aye Sir!" "Sail *our* ship away from here," he commanded. A huge cheer came from the victorious pirates. "Oh and Mickey." "Yes sir," Martin said sheepishly. "You're absolutely correct. It is a horrible plan. *Horrible!* It'll never work." A huge cheer rang out again from the crew, while Martin simply stood in disbelief. Payton eyed his men, "Get to work you dogs," he said with a touch of glee in his voice. The men obediently obliged and began carrying out their duties.

After the initial duties had been undertaken and they were underway Coop spoke up. "So when do we do this voting thing then?" Hall turned to him, "Anytime now. Captain, we had us an inquiry to an officer vote." "Did we then," Payton replied. He didn't want to be voted out of his position, especially because most captains that were voted out were either marooned or worse. Coop also became nervous thinking that there might be retribution for bringing this up. Sarika leaned into Martin for safety and spoke quietly, "Oh no, oh no, here we go." Martin nodded his agreement.

The bosun called the men together as Payton stood before them. Uncharacteristically, he didn't put on a show, nor did he make his appearance terrifying. He spoke with humble integrity. "Gentlemen, it's been offered that we put up our officers to the vote. Every man has an equal voice in the matter." He paused looking around the deck, "Now then... Who wants to push for a new position?" The men all looked around yet no one spoke up. "Well," Payton asked with sincerity. "C'mon boys, now is yer time. Anyone can step up for any position... even my own," he said with a lump in his throat. His scanned the crowd when finally one man spoke up. "Uh sir..." Jute started, "Why don't we just leave well enough alone eh?" The men started to nod their agreement. "Is this your vote then? We remain the same for now," Payton asked. "Aye," the crew voted. Payton smiled, "Thank you gents. Carry on then."

The crew went back to doing their duties. Coop breathed a sigh of relief as did Payton as he ambled up the stairs. Reaching the stern, he looked upon the open water making sure not to look at the port, not wanting to start the journey with bad luck. As his eyes scanned the water seagulls flew by; he as many sailors believed, they were carrying the souls of dead sailors to their resting place. He tipped his hat to them as one pooped on Martin in the distance. Smiling Payton chuckled and winked to the bird, "Nice shot lad." When the birds had departed his head had cleared and he enjoyed the moment. Wondering to himself, "Wonderful... now where shall we make our heading?" He began looking about as he watched his men going about their business. He hadn't been the captain of such a fine vessel in quite some time and it was rather overwhelming if not for a moment when a thought struck him. "That cloth... where in blazes had I put that cloth." Feverishly he began patting himself down searching for the cloth he had procured from one of Blankenslip's personal guards after the dock skirmish. His actions aroused Martins interest. "Sir?" Payton's gaze darted to him, "Um, yes?" "Sir, what's going on," Martin quizzed. "Never mind. Back to what you were doing then," Payton said obviously covering up his current compulsion. He darted his hands into his pockets until, "AH-HA," he thought to himself. His eyes shifted side to side. When he saw that no one, not even Martin was observing him, he slipped his hand into his inside coat pocket. His hand quickly found its destination from which he procured the cloth. Cautiously he pulled it out and unfolded it. He spied his cloth and within moments he was satisfied with the information gained from it. Slowly his right eyebrow and left edge of his lip crooked in concert as his eyes rose above the top of the cloth. He thought a moment then darted his hand deep into another pocket. Feeling around he came upon another desired item. He slowly pulled out the small map he acquired from Albright's ship. He held them side-by-side and it didn't take him long to realize that the two maps clarified each other. The devilish smile returned to his face as he quickly folded the cloth and the parchment and slyly replaced them from where he had procured them.

Payton stood tall and could be heard shouting commands in the distance. The men worked feverishly as the ship suddenly changed direction, heading towards their next grand adventure.

Made in the USA
Charleston, SC
24 September 2010